STRAWBERRY FIELDS

Map of Mexico, Texas, and the Midwest, and presumed location of
the mythical town of San Felípe.

STRAWBERRY FIELDS

A Book of Short Stories

Chuy Ramirez

FIRST TEXAS PUBLISHERS
San Juan, TX

9/13
gift

Ram

ISBN: 978-0-615-32672-6

Jacket and text composition: Bellerophon Productions
Jacket illustration: "IT'S STILL ME!" by Judee Koester Soendker

Printed in the United States of America by Publishers' Graphics

FIRST TEXAS PUBLISHERS
SAN JUAN, TEXAS

TABLE OF CONTENTS

Part I

Part II

Part III

Part IV

Part V

PART I

1

Nostalgia

"**WE HAD SOME GREAT TIMES** in Michigan, didn't we?" Joaquín's face
lit up as he said it, losing the deep furrow that lined his forehead.
Bennie put on an I'm-confused sort of frown but nodded in response,
and Joaquín returned him a slight frown as well.

"Not a single good memory?"

"Well, yeah, some," Bennie agreed, feigning an animated excitement.

"You're laughing at me?" Joaquín was disappointed.

"No. I don't mean to make fun of you. I agree. Occasionally, we
did have fun in Michigan, but that's hardly any reason to go back to
visit — particularly the places that we went to," Bennie said. He
turned away as if something had jogged his memory and he did not
want to lose the fleeting thought. Both of his elbows were on the
table, and he grasped his hands as if he was about to pray.

Joaquín attempted a whirlwind recollection back to a time when
the two had been in their middle teens. He counted the years: *the last
trip to Decatur . . . that summer before my high school senior year, 1967.* He
shoved his sandwich to the side, took a gulp of the orange drink (his
eyes dancing), and nodded as if it were all unbelievable, and put on
a contented smile. Joaquín had just turned fifty and had celebrated
his twenty-fifth year as an attorney. Bennie was a public school principal, beginning his fourth career. His longest stint had been in the
U.S. Army where he'd served during the Cold War. Before that,
he'd strung electrical wire for a living. Since his retirement from the
service, he'd taught public school and then piled on more schooling
until his recent promotion to principal of a middle school.

"You know what I'll never forget?" Joaquín asked, entreating
Bennie to join in his enthusiasm and beginning to undo the knot of a
striped navy blue and gray tie as he swung back in the chair.

"What's that?"

"Endless fields of flowers." He looked up as he said it, as if imagining the scene. "I mean . . . it's just fixed in my mind." He laced the

fingers of his hands over his belly, an image which projected a thoroughly contented soul. He squinted for effect. "I remember being in the back seat of someone's car. We're drinking really cold Stroh's beer and listening to Motown music. To my left (I think you're sitting to my left) through the car window, I see these endless fields of flowers. Row upon row of flowers. Thousands of flowers. Man! We had some fun times in Michigan."

"We did have fun in Michigan." Bennie finally smiled a sincere, suppressed smile. "I actually remember that early Sunday drive to Silver Beach. The flowers you remember were either in Holland or Benton Harbor."

On that day, Joaquín and Bennie had tagged along with Blue and Junior. Joaquín and Bennie had been in their mid-teens. Blue was in his late twenties, and Junior in his early thirties. Blue had on his cheap felt gray fedora, which he hung onto like a security blanket. Junior and Joaquín, in spite of a huge age difference, had become close pals during that summer.

"We kept the Stroh's beer in a small cooler at my feet in the back seat of the Rambler — what was it, a late fifties model? — and Blue kept asking that I get a beer for him every fifteen minutes. That was fun."

"Fun?" Joaquín challenged Bennie's reluctance to share in his enthusiasm. "Those were probably the best times ever!" He frowned again as if Bennie was just missing the point.

Best times ever! What's he talking about? Bennie's thoughts were painted on his face, but he nodded in agreement nevertheless.

When Joaquín called earlier in the week, he told Bennie he needed to pick his brain. He admitted (and of course Bennie knew) that Joaquín had never been one for detail. On the other hand, being the youngest of the three siblings (Sis was the oldest), Bennie had always been the silent, observant one. He would memorize street names, the distances between towns they traveled, and the names of the friends he made. Decades later, he could still pull out names of exactly who had been where and when, and he could always remember faces and connect them with names.

"This is my problem." Joaquín put on an embarrassed face and crossed his arms. Bennie frowned as if he had anticipated that whatever was coming next included being imposed upon.

"What?" he complained.

"I need to figure out where I'm going."

Bennie cracked up. "Ay, ay, ay, ay, ay! What? You need me to help you figure out where you're going to start on your trip? Heck, take me with you," Bennie chuckled. "I need a vacation too."

"Not only where to start. In fact, I don't recall much. I don't know where to go."

Bennie relaxed. "How much time have you set aside for this trip?"

"Two, maybe three days."

"Two or three days? You're driving from Chicago to Michigan and back to Chicago and wanna visit Michigan and Indiana, and all in three days? Are you serious?"

"Well, maybe just Michigan . . ." His eyes searched around as if he was pondering the thought. "Or maybe just Indiana. Or heck, maybe I'll change my mind and take a whole week off. Where would you go, if it were you?" he pressed, placing both elbows on the table as if settling in to listen.

"Well, let me think. Do you recall a place called New Frankfort, Indiana? That's where I would start. Now, that place was a small town, and there were things to do. You probably wanna swing by there."

"No. I don't recall that town. What was it like?"

"Well," Bennie started, and he closed his eyes for a moment as if he were pulling a picture out from his memory.

Joaquín's experiences the past two days had not been as pleasant as his lunch with Bennie. In fact, the results from the lunch with Bennie had been more than Joaquín could have ever expected. He was certain that now, he at least had some sort of a plan. As his excitement over the anticipated trip began to wear off, Joaquín was again reminded of the embarrassing incident the previous day. Not only had he long ago promised himself never again to represent a criminal defendant, he had gone some twenty years without even as much as a simple arraignment. The results of his court appearance had been devastating, but not because he was ill-prepared. In fact, no one could have been prepared for what happened. It had all begun as a simple court announcement at the federal court, and he had intended to be out of there within fifteen minutes.

"Short little squirt, isn't he?" muttered the young defense attorney, standing at attention at the defense counsel table next to Joaquín. *Cocky little bastard, aren't you?* Joaquín thought to himself as he surveyed the attorney's navy blue pin stripes and horizontally striped, bold blue and red power tie. Joaquín blinked an eye at the attorney, acknowledging the remark. He avoided indicating any agreement with the statement. *Judge Gonzalez is indeed short, especially next to the U.S. Marshal (who towers at about six-foot-two),* Joaquín admitted to himself and wondered why he had never noticed this before.

"Please take your seats, ladies and gentlemen," instructed the judge as he settled into his bench and opened his docket. Joaquín sat at the defense counsel table and gave the court's bench his full attention. To the right of the judge's bench was a witness stand; to the left, a clerk's counter. Directly in front of the bench, but at a lower level, somewhat like a Spanish fortress wall and moat, was yet another counter where a small army of clerks normally sat receiving and stamping legal documents. Minutes before the judge walked in, lawyers were walking up to the counter, picking up single sheets of paper from the clerks and signing them. They then took the paperwork over to the jury box motioning for the marshal's permission to approach a whole host of bad-looking characters who appeared somewhat dazed and at the mercy of their lawyers, and often "shushed" if they attempted any inquiry. Once they had these reluctantly obedient signatures, they returned the paperwork to one of the clerks. In the public seats at the back of the courtroom, the usual array of loyal indigent wives and fidgety young children of the defendants had turned out in force.

The ceiling lured Joaquín's attention. Deeply vaulted, the high ceiling of the courtroom mimicked the style of the Italian Renaissance. But the selection of the wood stain on the false ceiling beams was too light. The ceiling thus came through as too plain and unadorned. Long, narrow windows facing Elizabeth Street below were laden with heavy, full-length, bold burgundy velvet drapes. The drapes had lost their brilliance thirty years ago. Around the drapes lingered a permeating musty, moldy scent.

Judge Sam Gonzalez peered down at the gallery of attorneys and uttered, "I see that we have some attorneys in the courtroom who may have not appeared here before." He raised his eyebrows and continued, "Please take note, ladies and gentlemen, that the microphones in front of you record everything you say." The judge paused and then looked over his reading glasses at the young attorney standing next to Joaquín, as if confirming that his remark sank in.

The young advocate's face began to melt. On the conference table, he noticed for the first time the microphones which he had previously overlooked. He was powerless to remove the worried look that formed on his face. The young visiting attorney took a nervous gulp and shot a quick, hurtful glance over at Joaquín as if asking, *Why didn't you warn me about this?* Joaquín refused to acknowledge the novice's gaze, and thought to himself, *Ándale pendéjo* (Serves you right).

The judge continued, "During the docket call this morning, no one may leave the well until we have finished calling all the cases and finished the arraignments, which I suspect will take no more than thirty minutes. I do this because it saves everyone time. First, I will take care of those cases that are not going forward today. If anyone absolutely needs to leave during the docket call, please indicate so now." The judge surveyed the attorneys in the well. A few lawyers made disappointed faces or dissimulated by appearing to search for some elusive object on the floor, but no one would dare indicate that there was anything more important in their lives this morning than appearing before His Honor.

"Thank you," continued the judge.

Just to his left, by the drapes, a female interpreter began to speak into her recorder. "The first case this morning is United States versus Francisco Mejía Mata, Case No. M-00-03033." The judge pronounced the name in perfect Spanish. He trilled the "R" into the flat A, which sounds like the O in con man — "FRRR an cisco." Through the corner of his eye, Joaquín noticed that a marshal motioned one of the defendants in the jury box behind the assistant United States attorney to stand up. The interpreter approached the defendant and handed him some earphones.

On the second-floor holding cells, attorneys can consult with their clients through steel wire-mesh reinforced windows, but they can't see each other's faces. Joaquín had introduced himself to Mejía Mata through the opaque window and gone over the counts of the indictment to make sure the defendant understood the charges against him. Mejía Mata's previous attorney had withdrawn for nonpayment of his fees.

A young woman in a navy blue suit stood up from the assistant attorney general's table. There was confidence in her well-rehearsed baritone. "Your honor, subject to the defense counsel's review of the file and pre-trial motions, the government is ready to proceed to trial with this case." The judge turned to Joaquín, but before he could continue, the young woman complained, "In fact, your honor, the government has been ready for quite some time."

The judge began to roll his eyes but caught himself and granted the assistant attorney general a diplomatic smile and turned back to Joaquín. "I have appointed new counsel in this case?" he asked.

"Yes, your honor," Joaquín responded.

Feigning surprise, Judge Gonzalez turned to the government table and inquired, "Motion for withdrawal of counsel granted two weeks ago. Does the government dispute that?" Then, turning to Joaquín, he asked, "Have you even had the opportunity to meet with your client?"

"Just briefly, sir. I just got called on this case just late yesterday."

The judge shot a quick stare at the assistant attorney general. "Counsel, let's give you a new schedule on this case," he said to Joaquín. "Why don't we do this," the judge began and then turned to the jury box to address the defendant. A slender, dark man, noticeably in his sixties, giving every appearance that he had been hastily awakened and delivered before the court, unfamiliar with the goings-on in these proceedings and therefore at the mercy of the powers that be, stood in the midst of about fifteen other men sitting in the jury box. His hair was choppy, short, and quite disheveled. Thin, sparse white hair was noticeable around his mouth, which displayed a pronounced under-bite. In the cleft of the man's chin, there appeared to be a blue tattoo. Mejía Mata fiddled with a black gadget the size of a television remote with wires running up to earphones.

For the first time, Joaquín saw his client's face, and he imagined, *How so much like a mire cat's this fellow's eyes are . . . how so perpetually burdened they appear.*

In the next instant, Joaquín felt an irrepressible sensation from that puke register somewhere between the throat and the gut. He knew how his brain reacts to fear, pain, and offensive odors. *It will sidestep fear altogether; postpone pain by inducing a faint. It's the brain's survival instinct that associates certain odors or sensations as portents of ominous consequences. The brain can trigger that warning device that calls out an irrepressible heave, giving me just enough time to pick a spot to eject. There's nothing I can do about it. It's the brain's call. But what is happening to me?*

What is threatening me that is inducing my brain to produce this reaction? His eyes shut to deter a perceived sway that in the next moment became a wide swirl buzzing in his brain.

Dismay formed on Judge Gonzalez's face as he watched Joaquín. But no one in the courtroom noticed the judge's reaction because all eyes, including those of spectators in the courtroom, had turned and trained on the lawyer in the middle of the courtroom who was searching out safe harbor with his outstretched arm. Joaquín's head was splitting with pain—a pain that now reminded him of a *tequila* hangover his first year of college. He had promised then never to take another drink. He struggled to get off his feet knowing that he was about to collapse. He then slouched into the closest chair. His colleagues around the table began to remove themselves from the table and edged backwards, figuring they could distance themselves from an eruption. The jingle then invaded his brain: *"Grandfather tree, Grandfather tree, please show me what I can't see . . . Grandfather tree, Grandfather tree . . ."*

Joaquín placed his elbows on the defense counsel's table and held his head to keep it from swirling. He did not puke. And when it was all over, Judge Gonzalez excused him. One of the marshals escorted him to the lawyers' lounge. As the judge called the court back to order, the lawyer with the power tie turned one last time in Joaquín's direction. As the door in the back of the courtroom closed after Joaquín, the young lawyer shook his head in mock disbelief.

———

Where had the weird jingle come from? Joaquín wondered. It had sounded like a rhyme from some children's book. He could still not begin to explain why his body had reacted so. But one thing he was certain of: it had felt to him like a strange déjà vu moment that had not quite developed in his brain for him to recall its significance, but which had possessed him—something horrid and sickening. *So what is going on?*

———

Joaquín sat on the doctor's examination table with a blood pressure gauge on his left arm, flipping through the pages of *Golf Digest* while his brain kept repeating the jingle . . . *Grandfather tree, grandfather tree, why don't you tell your secrets to me* . . . His reading glasses clung to his nose, which was slim and a bit long. It was his mother Manda's nose. He had not bothered to remove his tie, but instead just flung it over his shoulder and rolled up the sleeves of his white dress shirt. Below, a man of about Joaquín's age swiveled on a metal stool peering up at him, the bottoms of his untidy aquamarine scrubs dragging on the floor over his sneakers. Clipped to the pocket of the man's scrubs was a Formica tag which read "Dr. Ramshort."

"Jake, these palpitations came suddenly, you say?"

Joaquín was slow to react. He ran his open hand up from the forehead to the top of his head and revealed the thick, silky gray forming above both temples.

"Yes," Joaquín answered in a mood which couldn't hide his disengagement. "I felt the palpitations at the federal court house, in the courtroom, in fact."

"Well, apparently you're okay on the treadmill, my friend." The doctor didn't look up from the medical record he was reviewing. "But, your pressure is up a bit. Maybe you're just excited, or you could have borderline blood pressure." Dr. Ramshort scribbled some notations on the patient card. "I don't need to tell you, Jake, that you do need to lose some weight."

"Ahh . . . I know." Sounding almost apologetic, Joaquín volunteered, "I'm taking a trip next week, Doc. I'll get on the program after I come back."

The doctor replaced the pen to its holder, and a slight furrow formed on his forehead. "Well, good for you. Where you headed?" Doctor Ramshort drew some sample Monopril packages from a drawer and handed them to Joaquín.

The inquiry sounded to Joaquín more or less like a mechanical exercise and meaningless — a routine he felt the doctor had grown accustomed to. Sucking in his midsection, he rearranged his shirt. "It's a combined business and pleasure trip," he said. "I travel to Chicago every fall — it's my continuing education requirement — only I never get around to seeing much beyond the hotel. This time, though, I plan to rent a car and visit the countryside. If time permits, I'd like to make it out to Michigan and Indiana. I attended high school for a few weeks up in that area."

"In Chicago?" Dr. Ramshort inquired over his glasses, appearing quite interested.

"No, it was in Indiana."

"Indiana? Well, of all things."

"But just for a few weeks," Joaquín clarified. "But you know, I'd like to stop by if I have a chance. A place called Newton . . . Newton, Indiana. I don't remember a thing about it, but we're having a high school reunion next spring, and I may want to go there."

"Good luck. Here . . . take one of these pills every day. Check back with me when you come back from your trip." As Dr. Ramshort took his leave, he said to himself, *Newton, Indiana, huh? Catchy!*

2

Hot Catsup

ON JOAQUÍN'S FIRST DAY on the job in New Frankfort, when he was only about sixteen, the supervisor pulled him into the cavernous concrete and stainless-steel steam room.

On the street side, high Chicago red brick walls rose up to a height of about twenty feet. Light filtered in through small, dusty windows about fifteen feet off the floor, on which pigeons roosted. Through a rectangular opening in the wall on the rail track side, partly covered with rubber flaps, appeared a line of empty catsup bottles standing upright next to each other, clinking as they traveled on conveyer belts much like miniature train tracks. Steam escaped from behind the flaps each time a new line of bottles passed through. At the end of the conveyer belt, the empties converged and dropped into round slots formed into a wheel, which rotated under a circular robot. In one motion, the stainless-steel robot sucked up ten bottles at a time and elevated them to injectors at the ends of black pneumatic tentacles. The pneumatic rubber hoses — the heart and lifeblood of the robot — pumped the blood-red catsup into the sterile bottles, hissing as they forced air out and created a sterile vacuum.

Joaquín had just gotten hired minutes earlier at the front office, and the supervisor handed him the only tools he needed for the job — a pair of black rubber boots.

"You sit right here on this stool," the supervisor shouted over the sound of the equipment. And Joaquín sat. The supervisor pointed out, "The full catsup bottles come down along that railing up across there on the other side and will come right in front of you."

Once the bottles were juiced up with the steaming catsup, the robot capped them and sent them off on another miniature train ride in a stainless-steel channel half full of water. A woman dressed in white scrubs and a hair net went around the conveyer belt picking up broken shards of glass from the concrete floor. A man followed, rinsing the floor with a high-pressure hose, forcing the waste catsup and glass shards into numerous drain inlets.

"Across from you, the women put the labels on the bottles. One group puts on the bottom label, and the other, the top. The labels have sticky on the back and will attach to the moist bottle."

Every time the women placed a label on a bottle, they made painful face and hand gestures as if they were scorching their hands. They would then occasionally dip their fingers in the water on the conveyer track ostensibly to cool them off.

"Your job is to straighten out the labels as the bottles pass here in front of you. Top and bottom." The glass bottles had two labels — a small one on the neck, and a larger one on the lower part.

But Joaquín couldn't recall any of that.

"Are you serious?" Bennie asked Joaquín. "You don't remember any of what I just told you?"

Joaquín admitted that he did recall something about a catsup factory.

"Well, maybe that's why you were fired just a few days after you were hired. You also lied on the application and said you were seventeen. Once they found out you weren't, they fired you."

"Were Mama and Sis with us at New Frankfort?"

"Yeah, but they didn't stay in the barracks. They stayed somewhere else — a huge two-story gloomy place that looked like an abandoned witch's house where all the women were required to stay separately," Bennie told him. "It was company policy for some reason."

"Really?" His surprise seemed genuine.

"Yep."

"Strange!" Joaquín frowned, ironically detached from it all, as if it were strangers they were talking about.

"That's right," Bennie agreed, "and I was too young to work at the plant, so while you worked, I hung around the pool halls in New Frankfort all day."

Their stay in New Frankfort had been in 1966. New Frankfort was just off Highway 121 in Indiana, a small town of poor and middle-class folks who during the week did their shopping around the red brick courthouse at the town square, but on the weekends might have traveled to Lafayette or Kokomo. Back before the second war, a sprinkling of folks who had started off from Kentucky and Mississippi who were intent on getting to Chicago, Gary, or Detroit hadn't made it all the way, so New Frankfort had become their new home. Indiana was close enough to the South, so they could still feel like they could return home should things not quite work out. And, there had been just enough good-paying jobs in New Frankfort to allow folks to settle in. Joaquín had never seen so many poor white folks in one setting as he'd seen in New Frankfort. While he had never said it, he had often felt sorry for them. He had not known that there were white people as poor as Mexicans.

"How about New Lothrop?" Bennie asked.

"Sounds familiar," Joaquín answered with an ambivalent shrug. He smiled, almost embarrassed, biting on the nail of his middle finger.

Bennie insisted, "Remember the pickle plant?"

"God, where do you get your memory? What pickle plant?"

"Well, it wasn't a plant, exactly—more like a packing shed. They kept the small cucumbers in a salt and vinegar solution in large, round, wooden vats. For the first couple of days, you were barfing all over the place because of the stench. New Lothrop was near Saginaw. There was a creek. There were small crayfish in the creek. We would walk across the creek up to the little village on the other side. The little village was called New Lothrop."

"Yeah, I remember Saginaw . . . I think." But Joaquín didn't remember much of Saginaw either.

"Decatur?"

"Yes, Decatur I do remember . . ." Had Decatur finally jolted his slumbering brain cells?

"We used to walk up from camp to the drive-in grocery store on the highway. Remember that?"

"Yeah. There were a lot of squirrels and mosquitoes in Decatur, weren't there? Haa!"

"And strawberries," Bennie added, having finally prodded enough to get him to recall something.

"And bees . . ." Joaquín let the sentence trail off, and then asked again, a cautious faint smile forming on his face, "That was fun, wasn't it?"

"Yes, it was fun . . . at times."

"I remember the strawberry fields, the strawberry jelly. In fact, I even remember someone making strawberry ice cream." Joaquín kept it at that and gazed out of the sandwich shop window. Bennie chuckled at his brother's demeanor. Nodding his head thoughtfully, as if light was finally coming in through the cracks, Joaquín whispered, "Strawberry fields."

"I remember Papa," Bennie started and caught himself, wondering, *Is it time? After all these years, can two grown men—two brothers—talk about our taboo? Can Joaquín really expect to revisit our past without revisiting our lives with Benáncio?* Joaquín kept chewing and looking down at his plate, and when he looked up, he didn't turn to Bennie.

Bennie took the risk. "I remember that time Papa caught us swimming over at the canal." He paused for some acknowledgment but got none. "And he gave you a good whipping." Bennie mocked a laugh to engage him.

"Heh!" was Joaquín's reaction. Bennie couldn't tell whether it was an acknowledgment, but at least Joaquín had not said that he didn't want to talk about it.

Bennie grinned and mimed checking his watch. Joaquín caught on, and they got up to pay the cashier.

3

Black Rosary

A BLACK ROSARY HUNG from one of the iron bedposts. The walls of the bedroom were plain, drab, and lifeless. A single bulb in the center of the ceiling barely lit the room, the cheap light fixture having been long ago discarded. Dahlia Garza kneeled at her bedside. White strands streaked the once jet-black hair which covered her face. She closed her eyes and whispered a prayer. In the distance, she could hear the blast of a commercial jet as it circled to the east against the prevailing wind and then headed north. Dahlia disregarded the sound. She feathered her hair and then helped herself up by leveraging her elbows on the sagging mattress. With her foot, she slid the old pillow she had kneeled on under the bed. She pulled the hair back and tied it in the back with a rubber band. She slipped large, black bobby pins on either side of her temples to tug the shorter hair away from her face, revealing her high cheekbones and spacious forehead. Around her eyes, the few wrinkles belied her age.

From the small kitchen next to the bedroom came the sound of stirring as Dahlia's mother prepared the coffee pot.

The width of a door separated the two beds on which Dahlia and her mother slept. On one end of the small bedroom, a door opened to the front porch of the house. From there, a few steps led to the front gate of the chain-link fence and the street. Another door from the bedroom led to a wide, offset hallway, which led to the small, backyard made barren by the relentless South Texas sun.

There was enough room in the offset hallway for a small cot. Dahlia stared at the cot. She considered, as she often had through the years, getting rid of the three dolls which made their home on the cot. She nodded and smiled, recalling how in a fit of anger, Belínda had pulled the hair off the dolls' heads and thrown them in the trash, only to raise such a stink the following morning that Dahlia and her mother had begged the trash man to help them recover the discarded dolls from the garbage truck. Belínda had been erratic like that all through school. God knew Belínda tried, but there had been something so wrong with her. Dahlia knew this, and that was why she had never trusted the doctors. Their diagnoses had always been same: "She'll grow out of it." Dahlia recalled that even as a baby Belínda would sit in her crib and bang her head against the wooden wall of the crib. Sometimes the slamming seemed to go on for hours at night. The doctors had said all that would go away. Dahlia's thoughts drifted. Belínda had not really paid attention to her dolls until after she made them bald and Grandma sewed some raggedy dresses for them. It had been astonishing how attracted Belínda had become to those dolls after that. Even late into her adolescent years, she would still play make-believe with the dolls. Dahlia glanced over to the space by the refrigerator and caught a glimpse of the fading color photograph of a teenage girl. A comfortable smile grew on her face. She whispered, "She had her father's features . . . his blonde hair and those ice-blue eyes."

Sighing, Dahlia stared contemplatively at the ceiling and then at the corners where the plain walls of the room intersected. *How spacious this house appeared all those years ago,* she thought, *when my father returned from military service. How modern it seemed then, with its flush toilet and shower set out in a small shed detached from the house and its new sleek, white Frigidaire and black-and-white television set . . . and now how indigent it feels, trapped in some era that disappeared some thirty years ago.* She snorted as she thought about it.

"Blessed," her grandparents had often said of Dahlia, because compared to the other Mexican girls of the neighborhood, she was so light in color. Her grandma used to say to anyone who would listen, *"No es por nada, pero es un angelito"* (she looks like an angel). Someone even once said, "She might even pass for an *Americana.*"

Dahlia's father had invested all his military savings repairing the old homestead and building the detached, modern water toilet and overhead shower. Such a huge expense had concerned Dahlia's mother, but the young veteran had been undeterred when it came to his princess. "I don't want my little princess to have to use the same privy I've used all my life," he snorted to his wife, who dared question the investment. When the shower stall was complete, the young veteran set fire to the old outhouse in the back by the alley. But the fire got out of control, and the Fire Department had to be called.

"Dios lo va a castigar" (God will punish him) had been the prophecy from the wise women of the neighborhood, who charged that Garza

had burned his pit privy just to spite his neighbors. It would be another twenty years before any other home in the neighborhood would even have the luxury of a water toilet and shower.

As Dahlia walked the few steps to the kitchen, her father's voice echoed in her memory, *We need to get away from this neighborhood for our sake and Belinda's sake . . . we need to get away . . .* A frown grew on her face, and she swallowed. Dahlia had not been consulted about the trip to Michigan, and as usual, she had offered no resistance or opinion on the subject.

Dahlia walked toward the kitchen. "It's been thirty-three years today, hasn't it?" her mother asked as she pulled two cups from the cupboard. Her mother's voice was of a very elderly and frail woman.

"Yes, Mama. Thirty-three long years," Dahlia sighed.

4

First Communion

OH, HOW GOD LOVED HIM, Joaquín imagined. He was seven. He was not unconscious of his frown. In fact, his face showed a particular delight in it, animated as he was, like some impatient maître d' at a ritzy restaurant who has just reprehended one of his waiters. He tugged back the starched cuffs of his white cotton shirt, which reached out almost to the tips of his fingers, and eased them under the jacket sleeves. But the sleeves were far too long, and this seemed to unnerve him even more.

Manda went over to him between poses and handed him a comb, which he took and combed his wavy hair without acknowledging her. Joaquín had just finished his First Communion at the San Felípe Shrine. Sis and Bennie remained on the front row of pews next to the prayer rail while Sis cuddled cousin Nina's baby. Sis was a third-grader. Bennie was five and wouldn't start first grade for another year.

Adjusting Joaquín's collar and simple clip-on black tie, Manda put on a pursed-lip smile and posed next to him. Joaquín, however, refused to smile.

"Aunt Manda, your hair!" Nina called out before taking a picture.

Barely taller than Joaquín, Manda brushed aside the strands of hair from her face, straightened her shoulders, and took in a deep breath through her mouth. She looked down at her hands and tried straightening her calloused fingers. She tried hiding them, first behind her back, then one hand within the other. She finally gripped her left thumb with her right hand and cupped her left hand over her right hand. The black-and-white glossy would show Manda and Joaquín staring into the camera, somber looks on their faces.

Aunt Queta made it to the shrine just before the Eucharist. She was late, as usual, but she had on her powdered-pale, roundish face and embellished cheeks. Of all his relatives, Joaquín preferred Aunt Queta. Queta's plump body always gave him great comfort. "Hips as wide as a Frigidaire," his father Benáncio would joke about Queta's rump, but that never fazed Joaquín. Queta was a hugger, and he liked that. He liked her drawing his small frame into her warm bosom with her comforting, beefy hugs. Nina, Queta's only daughter, had shown up, too, with her firstborn, a girl only nine months old, and a Holiday Flash camera. Nina was eighteen at the time.

Joaquín took another pose, this time with Queta.

Behind Bennie and Sis sat Joaquín's *padrinos*, Francisco and María Concepcion Gutierrez. Francisco and María Concepcion were in their forties, just like Manda. Francisco was the shorter and stockier of the two, and a butcher by trade. His eyes were light brown, and his skin was the color of a walnut. He had a sparsely peppered flat-top and a large, round, cheerful face. The yellow short-sleeve shirt Francisco wore was two sizes too small, and it showed — especially on his neck, around which he had attempted to tie a checkered tie that was so short it came down to just below his sternum. María Concepcion was dark, and so were her long dresses and her veils. There may have been occasions when María Concepcion didn't frown, but Joaquín was certain he had never been around when that occurred.

"What kind of father would miss a son's First Communion?" María Concepcion whispered to Francisco. Bennie turned and stared at her. She disregarded the boy entirely, as if to say, *I don't care if you tell your mother what I just said. It's all true.*

Just then, Aunt Rebecca asked to be included in one of the photographs. She towered over her younger sisters, Queta and Manda. All three had natural wavy black hair like the starlets of the 1950s. Manda's nose was perfect and long. Rebecca's nose was like Manda's. Aunt Rebecca could have been mistaken for Eleanor Roosevelt. The lasting image Joaquín would have of his aunt would be her stride — slow and tall as she deliberately balanced each step on her thin, fragile frame. In his distant memory, her long back was arched from decades of stooping over a cash register at the family store. Her body and head seemed fused stiff at the neck. Her face was a tubercular, powdery-white. And her thick, wire-rimmed glasses inched ever closer to the white receipt being spit out by the noisy monster called a cash register.

A constant stream of pilgrims comes to the Catholic shrine at San Felípe. By the tens of thousands they come, especially during Catholic celebrations.

A diabetic had been wheeled in the Friday before Joaquín's Communion Mass. A somber entourage of women covered in black from head to toe — a suffering, desperately bleak kind of black — accompanied him, lamenting in dissonant suffering. Children followed in stride, as if marching to the silent, somber beat of a drum. From one of the two chapels on either side of the nave, Joaquín and Bennie watched as the entourage made its way up the long aisle to the altar where the lit candles were, their long shadows crawling up the Gothic limestone walls.

"They'll cut off pieces of his leg until they can cut no more. Then, he dies," Joaquín whispered confidently to Bennie.

"Why do they do that?" Bennie swallowed.

"Mucho pan dulce" (Too much sweet bread). Joaquín cringed as if he felt the pain. "Too much sugar. The sugar gets in your legs, and they rot, and then they gotta cut the rot out."

Bennie grabbed on to Joaquín's arm and looked up at him with a marveled admiration in his eyes.

On one occasion, a young mother (she couldn't have been more than twenty) made her way up the aisle on her bare knees. St. Paul and St. Peter observed from their distant perches on the nave's high, cut limestone walls. Behind her, an older woman (maybe her mother or her mother-in-law) kept pace, holding an infant, so swaddled that only his small pink face was visible. The young mother's pretty jaw trembled as she took each painful knee-step, and the granite floor ripped her knees. Every time she rested, she drew in loud gobs of air through a wide-open mouth. Pausing, she would rest on her rump and occasionally glance back up at her companion, who, closing her eyes and nodding her head, seemed to urge the woman on.

At the prayer rails, which protected the Virgin's small realm, the wrappings around the child were removed, and the child was offered up to the Virgin. Revealed, the child's small limbs showed that the child was Thalidomide's progeny. Above, the Virgin remained emotionless. Bennie looked back at Joaquín as if some explanation were due. Joaquín shrugged his right shoulder and brought his ear toward it as if it were all too irrational. Bennie sobbed uncontrollably.

Just the week before his First Communion, Joaquín and Bennie had insinuated themselves into a prayer group for the distraught mother of the quadriplegic boy. Rumor had it that the boy had been pushed from atop a cotton trailer. He had a broken neck and damage to his brain. The ambulance drove up to the front steps of the church. Joaquín and Bennie gave chase to catch a glimpse. The driver and his assistant wrestled up the steps with the boy tied to a gurney and wheeled him all the way to the front, near the altar. Dressed in black, several women and young girls huddled around the statute of the Virgin and begged and pleaded with her and made promises and offered their covenants. Joaquín and Bennie joined in, huddling with the women around the statue of the Virgin, putting their hands together and whispering their own prayers.

From the gurney, the boy peered first at Joaquín and then at Bennie. The terror his eyes conveyed was shriller than any cry Joaquín could ever imagine. The boy gawked, his face contorting in desperation. Guttural sounds followed, choking out from deep inside his throat. Joaquín imagined the boy's constrained soul, writhing within the imprisoning living tomb that his body had become. Bennie huddled behind Joaquín to avoid the boy's eyes. The women choked on their tears.

When he ventured back there, in his memory, Joaquín recalled the poignant scenes and was embarrassed by his own arrogance. He recalled crossing himself as he sat next to Bennie at a church pew. He recited a prayer without pause or error. Bennie forgot a word or a line in the prayer, and Joaquín motioned Bennie away, banishing him to a different pew as punishment for his iniquities. "I just can't remember it," Bennie begged him with tears in his eyes.

"Ten Hail Marys then," Joaquín charged Bennie, while he himself headed confidently to the confessional.

And of the hundreds of infirmed pilgrims whom they had observed all those years ago, Joaquín was now amazed at their faith. In spite of all their agony, they came. But the Virgin did not remove their undeserved ills. Perhaps their pilgrimage had been due not to the expectations of miracles, as he had once believed. Perhaps the pilgrims had sought to confirm that like Job, they did not seek to understand God, but to show him that their faith remained unshaken. And so, too, that the infirmed might find solace in knowing that they would never be alone.

During that First Communion, as the Mass proceeded in Latin, Joaquín felt the smooth, glossy beads of the black rosary in his pocket. Manda had delivered the rosary that morning in a zinc-plated jewelry box in the form of a miniature treasure chest. He had

clutched his miniature prayer book, a gift from his *padrinos* (godparents); then mentally repeated the "Prayers and Instructions for Children" by the Rev. Alphonse Sausen, S.B. *Will the angels ever visit me,* Joaquín wondered, *if I keep repeating the prayers and instructions that the good Father Alphonse has collected for good little children like me?* He continued with the "Acts of Faith, Hope and Charity" beginning on page 17.

"How many thousands and thousands of children have never heard of God? Some of these children live in fine houses, have many nice clothes to wear and much spending money; but, how poor they are because they know nothing about God? You may have none of the fine things they have, but you are a thousand times richer than they, because you have the great God to believe in, to love, and to enjoy in heaven. Often, therefore, say the following prayer . . . 'I believe everything that Thou hast made known to me about Thyself through my teachers and the priests of the Catholic Church."

How blessed we were, thought Joaquín, *to have so little on this earth, but yet to have everything in Heaven. And how soon thereafter I saw through all of that, saw it as one giant make-believe. I would have preferred then to be a thousand times richer and also to have the great God to believe in. They were not mutually excusive, were they?*

But at the time, the church ritual had overwhelmed Joaquín, and he had truly felt the spirit within him. He had made the solemn promise then to always follow Father Alphonse's admonitions . . .

I believe everything that Thou hast made known to me about Thyself through my teachers and the priests of the Catholic Church.

I firmly believe . . . I believe everything the Holy Catholic Church teaches. Please, God, I will believe it all to the end of my life.

Then the bread and the wine were miraculously turned into Jesus' living Body and Blood as they did at every Mass. Father Alphonse had prepared Joaquín well. He had instructed, "It still looks like wine, but it is not wine anymore — it is really and truly Jesus himself, who is in the golden cup now."

The year had been 1958. Cameras had flashed as other children posed with their families for photographs. At the end of the ceremony, Joaquín searched anxiously about in his white shirt and clip-on tie, as Aunt Rebecca reclaimed her spray of flowers at the altar. He prayed to the great God for one small miracle: that his father attend his First Communion — that on this day, Benáncio would appear and come up to him, unabashedly, in front of everyone in the church, and lift him up off the floor with one big hug, and show everyone, *This is my son, and I am proud of him.* But Benáncio had not shown up. Where was the great God?

Manda had smiled uneasily at the sight of Joaquín searching around the church. Instinctively, he had turned to her and found her licking the corners of her lips and then pressing them, a sure sign that she could lose her composure right there and then. How many times had Joaquín seen her gripped by that terrific agony that seized her when she imagined that that would be the particular day on which Benáncio would walk out and never come back.

5

The Tricycle

ONCE, BENÁNCIO BROUGHT HOME a tricycle. Abandoned at the garbage dump, the tricycle was rusty-brown and brittle from the rain and sun. While it still had attached the large front wheel and the right back wheel, neither had any rubber left on them. On the left side, there was no wheel at all. The metal axle rod where the wheel was supposed to be attached dug into the ground. Still, Joaquín and Bennie would sit on it. Joaquín imagined himself riding down a shady, tree-lined, suburban street on his shiny red bike with the neat and shiny white wheels and black rubber tires, streamers, reflectors, mud flaps, and all.

Daily, Joaquín and Bennie fought over whose turn it was to ride it.

Güero/Whitey

Things had come rather effortlessly for "Güero." He was lighter than most, and although his eyes were brown, it was common for the old men of the neighborhood to refer to him as "Güero," and he knew from a very young age that "Güero" was good. As a babe, he attracted all the mamas who wanted to experience cuddling him; "Güero" was better than dark; people preferred "Güeros"; he was a good-looking "Güero" kid; and "Güeros" were more intelligent than dark kids. People seemed to offer more to "Güeros." He had always been special because of that. Regardless of how well you dressed a dark kid, he would never look as good as a "Güero." You could color coordinate with "Güeros," and "Güeros" were always always picked first.

6

I'd Just As Soon Not Have Been Born

SIS SIGNALED ONE OF THE WAITRESSES to warm their coffee. Bennie nodded that he would take another cup, and when his cup was full, they returned to the conversation. Sis' neighborhood bakery and coffee shop was doing well and generating impressive sales at wholesale, in addition to the steady stream of winter tourists who spent five months out of the year in San Felípe. Sis was a retired teacher. When Bennie visited her shop the two would typically visit at a table away from the public. Joaquín had yet to make it to the coffee shop.

"Are you building a nest egg with this thing or just blowing all the profits?" Bennie teased her. She smiled at him as if he did not deserve an answer. "So," she asked, "what's Joaquín's sudden, new-found interest in the past? You think he'll find anything worthwhile in the boonies of Michigan?"

Bennie appeared perplexed. "I have no idea," he said and repeated the expression with his face. "Going back to Michigan would have been the furthest thing from my mind. He's turned those years completely on their head. What's so good about Michigan? I don't recall us being welcomed guests there," he complained. "With few exceptions, you know, we always kept our distance from the locals, and the locals from us. It wasn't anybody's formal policy. 'You're not welcome here' and 'you're never to go there' were not necessarily instructions we were given, but there always seemed to be a tacit understanding that as long as we did follow those unspoken rules, no one was going to mind us."

"I don't think he's going back to visit the people," Sis reminded Bennie. "There's something else afoot."

"Yeah, you're right. I just think it's a waste of time."

"He called me the other day." Sis squirmed in her chair as she said it, favoring her ailing hip. "He wanted Nina's number, and I complied, of course. I asked him, 'Why Nina? You've never been to any of her kids' weddings.' He told me there were questions that he thought if anyone had answers to, it would be Nina. I told him he was probably right but tempted him to tell me what it was all about. I said, 'You'll be surprised how much family history I know.' He didn't bite, though. I could have told him an interesting thing or two."

"So, he's really going back further than I thought?" Bennie chewed on his lip and paused. "I thought he was only interested in Michigan. I didn't know he was considering revisiting *our* past as well. But if he is looking to visit with Nina, then he must be on to something."

Sis rolled her eyes. "You think he wants to go there? I wouldn't."

"I don't know. It is quite coincidental, isn't it? Joaquín is the same age as Papa was." Bennie shrugged as he said it.

Sis frowned. "Same age as what? Same age as when he left? What's so wrong with saying it?"

Bennie retreated.

Sis poured herself more coffee, became outwardly thoughtful, and smiled at Bennie. "Joaquín was a mean kid." She nodded and chewed her bottom lip. "He could be heartless," she assured herself. "He was sharp; always sharp, but hurtful." Bennie sipped on his coffee and the affect he showed was of wanting to learn more.

"Times were very tough during the fifties. You don't remember any of that. Of course. But on numerous occasions, Dad was gone for weeks or even months. So much fear and apprehension would grow on Mom's face. In his absence she would always wonder aloud, 'What am I going to do?' You probably don't remember. You were too young. But we'd all sit around her as confused pups. Then, she'd start to bawl and we'd stare at each other until every one of us joined her in her misery. What a sight to see."

Bennie interrupted. "You started saying something about Joaquín."

"Oh, yeah . . . I got off track. Well, I don't have to tell you how tough times were. But once Joaquín got to go to school, boy did he learn just how bad off we were. He began to compare himself with other kids." She chuckled. "Now, he knew that we weren't only poor, but pretty close to the bottom. And it was constant complaining by him. He demanded things from Mom which she could not afford. Anyway, on one occasion, when he was about seven or eight, he came home from school and waited in the kitchen, staring out of the kitchen screen door toward the alley waiting for Mom to come home from work. He seemed to have worked out a script for that very moment.

"When Mom got home, he was in a fit. 'I'd just as soon have not been born,' he screamed at Mama as soon as she walked in through the kitchen screen door. She must've had a smile on her face when

she walked in, or at least I remember her that way because she was
always so glad to get home at the end of the day and spend time with
each of us before she started dinner.

"'Why did you have us!' Joaquín challenged, staring her down,
his tears flowing and nose running. He spit out, 'We have nothing!'
Mind you, this kid is in the second or third grade."

Manda had not answered. She held her apron with both hands as
if grabbing for a handhold. She bowed her head, and her tears flowed.
And then she looked back up at Joaquín with a wounded look. She
swallowed, but not without great difficulty. Without bending her
thumb, she formed a gentle fist and beat her breast twice, softly.

Through her tears, she apologized, "I had you because I wanted
you. I needed you. That is all I can say."

"Look at us!" Joaquín taunted, while Sis and Bennie looked on,
"We're so poor! I hate my life! I hate it."

Manda would be a very old forty-eight-year-old woman on the occasion of Joaquín's discontent. Joaquín and Manda faced each other,
and both were sobbing. Sis and Bennie looked on with pained confu-
sion painted on their faces. Manda often reminded Sis and the boys
that their father was working in Arizona and would soon be back,
but he had not written or sent money. At the corner grocery store,
Don Magín had apologetically instructed Joaquín to tell Manda that
he could no longer provide her credit. It was not his fault, he said,
but he had "a business to run." Each school day, Manda would hand
Joaquín three nickels for three slices of baloney, one for each of the
kids' school sandwiches. Don Magín's new, electric white deli-slicer
seemed to carve thinner slices of baloney after that.

"*M'ijo,* I had you because I wanted you. More than anything in
the world, I wanted children."

"I'd just as soon have not been born," he screamed at her, "not if
life is going to be like this." Joaquín stormed out through the screen
door of the kitchen, and the door spring pulled it back in with a loud
pop. As Bennie turned to Sis for some reaction, an ominous fear settled on her face, replacing her usual confidence.

Manda was again apologetic as she tried to explain to Sis, "I got
a letter from his teacher that Joaquín had been selected the emcee
for the school program, so I asked Mrs. Robertson for two hours off
to see him."

Halloween was just around the corner. Manda had made her way
to the school under the black and orange streamers tacked on all the

telephone poles that lined Main Street. In the school hallways, post-ers announced the annual Halloween school fundraiser. Mrs. Hub-bard's third-grade music class could be heard through the barred windows of the old music hall:

"Way down upon the Suwannee River, far, far away, that's where my heart is turning ever, that's where the old folks stay . . ."

"Well, what happened, Mama?" Sis inquired, trepidation in her voice.

"Joaquín must have seen me from the classroom. He came out to the sidewalk, running to me and . . ." Manda could not contain the tears, "I was going to hug him, I was so proud . . . but he screamed at me to go away."

Manda paused and took a breath. "You are embarrassing me," he shouted.

Sis hugged Manda and Bennie in a protective hold, and Manda let out a painful wail interrupted only by her need to breathe. "Ma-ma," Sis told her, "don't worry. Joaquín is just so selfish. That's all. It's not your fault. Please don't think it's your fault."

Joaquín had indeed seen Manda coming. All morning, as the teacher coordinated the dress rehearsal in the small auditorium that also served as the cafeteria, Joaquín had dreaded the possibility of Manda's visit and had been on the lookout. *What will my teacher and classmates think of mama? And more importantly, what will they think of me!* Manda had been wearing the same blue dress that she wore for all important occasions. She had not bought a new dress since shortly before the day she eloped with Benáncio. A self-taught seamstress, she had sewn that blue dress, along with most of the shirts the boy's wore. Manda knew only a few choice words in English. *What if the teacher asks her where she works? How embarrassing!* Joaquín dreaded her response. She would have to answer that she worked as a maid and washed and ironed clothes for the kids across the tracks who at-tended schools Joaquín couldn't attend.

Manda held onto Sis and Bennie in her arms as she melted to the floor and her strength seemed to slip away, and a frail and confused look formed on her face. A short distance away, in the shade of the *huisáche* tree, Joaquín could hear Manda's desperate sobs. She was not consolable.

Icarus Canal/*La Santa Chinguiza*

BENÁNCIO WAS OUT OF THEIR SIGHT when they heard him cut his usual goat and cattle-calling whistle . . . *fffriüüüst . . . ffriüist* . . . to summon them. They ran around the house and found him filing a carpenter chisel and stood before him at attention, bare except for their cutoffs.

Something must have set him off. It would not take much. He had a long memory. His admonishment was that of a judge. "If I ever catch you swimming in the canal . . ." Benáncio's dark eyes pierced Joaquín as if to say, *I know you're doing it. I'm just telling you that sooner or later I'm going to find out . . .* "Or even if I should hear a rumor that you went swimming in the canal," he turned his head slightly sideways for emphasis, "I will visit a massive beating upon you." The canal had once been owned and operated by the Icarus Water Company but was now the property of the local water district. Still, the locals called it the Icarus Canal. Joaquín's eyes fixed on his father's, unblinking and unmoving, for he knew that any slight movement might be interpreted as guilt.

Benáncio spoke with such rehearsed eloquence when it came to punishments. Bennie stood behind Joaquín, utterly intimidated, looking down as if counting and recounting the toes on his feet, sucking in air through his mouth.

Actually, what Benáncio had threatened was to *"suministrár una santa chinguiza,"* which meant to "administer a massive and saintly beating."

For Joaquín, the "saintly" only added to the exponential effect of the threat, as if his father's threat of a mere, run-of-the-mill, "massive beating" would fail to sufficiently convey the gravity of his potential punishment. These times apparently called for punishment of biblical proportions. His father's warnings to "administer" punishment always implied to him a cold detachment, as if the punishment was not meant to have any redeeming value, and they never quite conveyed the heartfelt, soulful misgivings which Manda was so adept at. Manda was not beyond giving the boys a good whipping as well, but she did it "for their own good," and she always sentimentally told them that their whipping was always more painful for her than for them — clearly not the case for their father.

Joaquín came to believe that his papa simply refused to allow the boys to have fun. That was it, plain and simple. Joaquín couldn't help feeling that for his father, the boys' childish indiscretions, regardless of their gravity, were always massive sins of disobedience. No atonement seemed to ever make up for those sins. He knew that "I'm sorry" and "I promise not to do it again" were looked upon by his father as empty and insincere gestures advanced by the boys solely to avoid the punishment that was due them.

And so it was that in spite of their father's worst, vile warnings, Joaquín and Bennie eventually disregarded Benáncio's threats of fire and brimstone and took the plunge in the canal on a regular basis.

One warm summer afternoon, the boys were enjoying their spot at the canal when Bennie noticed the shock on Joaquín's face. Years later, he would swear to Joaquín that Joaquín's face had turned pale right before his eyes as he struggled against the strong current, groping for the thick overhand to pull himself up to the sloping bank.

"It's Papa," Joaquín whispered, a terrified look on his face.

In the distance, the lone, tall figure, clad in khakis and a hat, walked atop the canal bank in their direction. They crouched, cat-like, through the tall grass and the banana trees, praying that Benáncio had not seen them, and rushed to where their bike was. They pedaled in tandem, Joaquín on the seat and Bennie forked over the frame between Joaquín and the handlebars, taking the shortest route home — the alley.

Not one more word was said between them as they made their escape. When they reached the house, they ran in, dried themselves, and hid under the kitchen sink. From down there, they had a view of the alley through the unflashed plumbing hole in the kitchen.

Bennie broke the silence, "Do you think he saw us?"

"I hope not," Joaquín answered, still spooked.

Benáncio was a tall man. Punishments were dramas in which everyone played a role. In acting out a *chinguiza*, Benáncio's preferred mode was to swing the belt like a whip. There was none of this "bend over" business that Joaquín was subjected to at the Mexican school. With his father, he got to see the entire swing of the belt coming at him. So, he would not only feel the pain when the leather welted the skin, but he also suffered the anguish of visualizing the backswing of his father's muscular shoulder, the threatening long leather belt listless in his father's hand as he measured the striking distance, and then the final swing, the belt snapping into a whip action. He could even anticipate where on his body the next belt-slap would land and the degree of pain it was going to inflict. The unwritten rule between the boys was that being older, Joaquín should take the first shot. During his *chinguiza,* Joaquín cheated. He would dodge blows and try to hold his father's hand a little like boxers do to reduce the other fighter's pummeling. Joaquín wouldn't cry; he would whimper. The more holding Joaquín engaged in, the longer his turn took. It frustrated Benáncio that Joaquín would cheat on a *santa chinguiza.* That would tire Benáncio out, and it worked to Bennie's advantage. The longer Benáncio worked on Joaquín and divested his anger, the less time, energy, and fury he would have for Bennie.

It must have taken Benáncio ten minutes to walk from the canal to the alley where the outhouse stood.

"Do you think he saw us?" Bennie nervously, hopelessly nudged Joaquín. But before Joaquín could answer, they saw their father pull out a knife from his pocket, and he bent down, grabbed an old piece of discarded rubber water hose, and cut a measured piece from it.

Joaquín's face turned ashen, conveying a fear in him Bennie had never seen before. "He . . . he's gonna kill us this time," Joaquín stammered.

Bennie ran to the bedroom, blaring out a wail that was meant to embarrass Benáncio. If there was one thing Benáncio hated, it was for the neighbors to hear the boys' wailing. Joaquín waited stoically in the kitchen for his *santa chinguiza.*

Swish, swish! The hose was missing Joaquín, and he saw that this only enraged Benáncio further.

"Suelta la pinche mangéra" (Don't grab the damn hose)! Joaquín obeyed his father and let go of the hose. Clearly, the water hose routine was not going to work, so it was time to resort to Old Faithful. Joaquín's father thrust the hose to the side and in one fell swoop swung his belt from his pants. Finally came the fine sound of leather slapping a juicy watermelon, the belt finding its mark.

"Y tú, cabrón, donde estás" (And you, son of gun, where are you)?

Bennie shuffled from the hallway to the kitchen, his eyes forced shut, his arms straight on either side, and fists on either hand.

"No, no, no, no, Papa, please! No, no, no . . . please, don't hit me! Please . . . ," he said, heaving. And then came the well-rehearsed and oft-heard contrition, breathing heavily, pleading, promising—a reverberating plea from the deep bottom of Bennie's throat. "I promise, Papa. I promise, I really promise, Papa, really, really, really promise . . . this time I mean it. I mean it. For real. Oh, oh, oh . . . I'll never . . . oh no, no, I'll never do it again. Promise. Joaquín is two years older than me, Papa. He's older. He took me out there."

"*Cállate ya. Te va oír toda la vencidáð*" (Shut up now. The whole neighborhood is going to hear you).

Bennie was able to get away with a few welts on the arms and legs. By week's end, Joaquín and Bennie had just plain forgotten about the *santa chinguiza.*

8

Where Do We Bury Papa?

"THERE HE IS, LARGER THAN LIFE itself, handsome, always the trim moustache, confident, authoritative! I imagine him, returning some-day—if that makes any sense to you."

Sis, sipping on her coffee, forced a cough and frowned in response, something akin to *Here we go again.* She ironed the left collar of her oyster-white silk blouse with her two fingers and then tucked it under the lapel of her smoke-gray business suit. Bennie gave Joaquín a sympathetic look and did not turn to Sis. For a minute, silence reigned. Joaquín stared into the whiskey glass and, finding nothing, excused himself to get a refill. The three had buried their mother Manda that afternoon.

Bennie turned to Sis. "Unlike Joaquín, there's was never a question in my mind that Papa would never return. Papa was a man of his word. By the time he decided to leave, he would have considered every option. When he left, I knew he had left for good."

On an early summer evening, after the picking crews had returned from the cotton fields and after the Ford and Chevy trucks had distributed the pickers to their homes (along with their heavy, bulky, gray denim cotton-picking sacks), stopping briefly on the narrow strips of paved roads, letting off a man and his wife here, an entire family there, and a group of boys over there, and after the sweltering heat had finally yielded for that day, Joaquín found his way to his papa's lap under the wide corrugated tin porch of Don Magín's corner grocery store as his papa engaged someone in conversation.

Joaquín breathed in the fragrant talcum scent. Benáncio always powdered himself with scented talcum after a bath. Joaquín played with his papa's chest, pulling at the few sparse hairs. Then with his small, closed fist, he tapped his papa's chest. This distracted Benáncio, who gave him a hug around the neck, and Benáncio's day-old scruffy stubble tickled Joaquín's peachy cheek.

How Joaquín longed for that hug—just a hug, just once more.

At Manda's funeral, Joaquín had searched among the crowd, first
during the Mass, and then at the cemetery, for the tall man in his
crisp felt Stetson. He even scanned the distant trees along the fence
line along the small rise for the chance that his father may have
watched from a distance. But his papa had not come.

"He would have stood out," Bennie acknowledged in delayed reaction to Joaquín's comments and turned back to the corner of the
living room to the small bar adjacent to the kitchen, which served as
Sis' gathering place. At the bar, Joaquín fiddled with the dimmer
switch on the bar lamp, dimming the light and then lighting it up
again.

"Wouldn't he?" Joaquín stared at Bennie wryly. "The tall, handsome man with the trim moustache and the proud felt Stetson?"

Bennie pinched his lips.

"I would have forgiven him for everything else—everything—if
he had only shown up—this once." Joaquín didn't hold back the
tears. He craned his neck in that habit he had, as if he was aloof
from it all.

"But Papa was immune to mere mortal sensibilities, wasn't he?"
Joaquín insisted, smiling ironically, his eyes dancing mockingly. "He
was beyond all ritual," he nodded, and then, staring at Bennie defiantly, issued his own covenant, "I'll never dignify Papa's own funeral." Sis raised an eyebrow as she took a sip from her wineglass.

Many years later, at his office, Joaquín picked up the telephone.
The receptionist had rung him. "Sir, there's a call from Mexico."

"A client?"

"No, sir. Says he's your cousin."

Why would I be getting a call from Mexico? Over the years, the relatives on Benáncio's side had drifted away. Benáncio had been the
only connection to that world. Memories had faded.

"Cousin! It's been a long time, hasn't it?"

"Yes, it has. It's good to hear from you."

"Joaquín, I just wanted to call you and let you know that my uncle, Benáncio, your papa, passed away last night. I'm so sorry."

Joaquín fought back the tears, and he hated it. *How can I cry over
this?*

"Well, you know, his wife will probably be making arrangements
for his funeral."

"Yes, that's probably true. Thank you so much for letting me know."
Joaquín hung up the phone, and his mind drifted into questioning

thoughts. *We didn't ask for much, so that's exactly what you gave us — not much. How did you do that, Papa? Why was it always so easy for you?*

Joaquín got on the phone to Bennie. He struggled initially. "Why do you think Papa stuck around until you turned fourteen?" He paused momentarily. "Perhaps he could leave with a clear conscience? Was that it? Or, did Mama and Papa have some covenant between them, and perhaps Papa fulfilled his end of the bargain to her? Is that the explanation? That he committed, but only for a term?"

"Why is it that Joaquín can't let it go?" Bennie had complained to Sis the last time the three of them had been together, at their mother's funeral. "We've let it go."

"No one will ever know," Bennie told Joaquín. "That was Papa . . . and Mama has taken that knowledge with her as well."

The three of them visited later in the evening after Joaquín got the call from Mexico. Throughout the evening, Sis avoided any eye contact with Joaquín but on occasion glared at Bennie with a conspiratorial eye.

Joaquín renewed his complaint, "I always naïvely imagined Papa would grow old with us. He would hold our kids on his lap and let them feel his chest and scruffy beard."

Bennie nodded in response agreeably, but as he did, an awkward smile formed on his face. "He doesn't even have kids," Bennie would later jest with Sis. "When will he get over it?"

Joaquín wasn't finished. "And he would make funny noises on their bellies with his puckered lips." He sniffed a dry sniff. "Maybe tell 'em tales of a faraway land in which he had raised goats; and like Solomon, he would cite his proverbs to his grandchildren. And on birthdays, the grandchildren would send Papa birthday cards, at first with chicken scratches and as they got older, they would craft beautiful letters with cute rhymes, and include their 'School Days' pictures so that Papa could see his grandchildren change as they grew. And Papa would say it once and again — 'your mama was a wonderful wife, an extraordinary human being. I so terribly miss her.'"

There was a second call to Joaquín the following day.

"He loved you very much, you know." *She sounds as if she's my age,* Joaquín thought.

"He did?"

"Yes, he spoke very highly of you. Often, actually."

Joaquín held back the tears. *How could this woman know that Papa loved me very much?*

"We were wondering where you wanted to bury him, sir?"

He found a book by the telephone, *Famous Quotations for All Occasions,* and opened it to page 49. He scanned the paragraph under the caption "Burying our Fathers."

> *Burials are ceremonies, rituals that bind father to son, and generation to generation. They are a time for spiritual reflection by those who remain of how definite and finite is our existence, of how infinite is the cosmos. They are a cleansing of the soul, a time to rationalize away all futility, to make amends and to reconcile. They call for a spontaneous overflow, for an inheritance of cultural cues, for thanksgiving and a communal confirmation and celebration of faith. A life worth living has to be celebrated at death.*

"I don't care where you bury him. Good day." Joaquín hung up.

9

Morning Serenade

JOAQUÍN WALKED SHEEPISHLY from the dark hallway into the kitchen, rubbing his eyes. The coffee pot was boiling and sputtering.

"*Ay m'ijo* [oh, son], go back to sleep. Did the coffee pot wake you?" Manda's wooden rolling pin rhythmically flattened out a flour tortílla, *cluck, cluck, cluck, cluck*. Her forward roll extended the flattened tortílla dough, *cluck*. She rolled the pin back toward her, *cluck*.

Joaquín did not answer. He glanced at his father sitting at the table and tried to blink away the sleepiness.

"Mama, what was all the singing and shouting about last night?"

Benáncio almost spit out his coffee as he rushed to answer Joaquín. "It reminded me of the village band we had back in *Lináres*, Nuevo León, *m'ijo*. Every musician played his own melody, *por anca la chingáda* (way off key). *Ha, ha, hah*," he laughed.

Manda stood by the stove turning the *tortíllas de harína* [flour tortíllas], maintaining a steady supply for Papa. "Don't pay attention to your father, *mi'jo, le trajiéron serenáta a Juaníta y a su Mamá* [Juaníta and her mother were serenaded last night]. And don't repeat your father's profanities either, *estos Nortéños* [these Northerners, referring to Northern Mexico] always distinguish themselves through their profanity."

Benáncio reacted with a grunt.

Cluck, cluck.

"What's a serenade?" Joaquín asked, half-interested and half-asleep as he sat by Benáncio and dropped his head on his arms, which he had placed on the vinyl red and white checkered tablecloth.

Manda admonished him from her post at the stove, "The table is not for sleeping, *m'ijo*; please sit up straight." And then in a softer voice, she told him, swaying in a waltz-mimic, "The serenade is a gentleman singing love songs to his lady."

Joaquín grinned at her sight, and she grinned back at him. Papa grunted to himself, "Hmph! How old is that kid anyway [referring to Juaníta's husband]? Sixteen, at the most. And she's married to

that *chamaco pendéjo* [stupid child]. He parades around the neighborhood in a pair of Levi's jeans from which he has removed all the belt
loops with a two-edged Gillette blade. Imagine . . . he has the time
for those kinds of *pendejadás* [wastefulness]."

"He's got a tattoo, Papa," Joaquín chimed in, "right here on his
arm. It says 'Janie.'" He thought about Janie's skin — a waxen light-
brownish that reminded him of the creamy almond ice cream that
came in the chocolate-dipped bars. Her scent, he imagined, was sweet
and erotic, just like Ms. Johnson's, his second-grade teacher.

Joaquín's thoughts turned to what Manda had said: *Gentleman?
Lady?* In his mind's eye, he imagined the characters from the only
reference he could conjure up: *la chalúpa,* the Mexican Bingo. There
were no numbers to be had on *la chalúpa,* just colorful caricatures on
the cards, including the "gentleman" and the "lady." There was a certain comforting familiarity in that: *el catrín* [the dandy]; *la dama* [the
lady], the frog, the spider, and the sun and the moon. Dressed in a
black and white formal, *el catrín* was the dandy white gentleman with
his overindulging etiquette. *La dama* was an equally white, virtuous,
upright lady. The lady wore a green olive business suit and a fash-
ionable lady's hat, like something from the Roaring Twenties.

The rolling pin distracted his thoughts. *Cluck, cluck.*

"My favorite serenade is *Despiérta*" [Awaken], Manda continued,
acting out a sigh, "as sung by Pedro Infante. I just love his movies,
especially when he plays a singing cowboy."

Cluck, cluck.

Manda's voice was a soft, soothing velvet as she sang to Joaquín,
lullabying him from her post by the stove.

> *Despiérta . . . Dulce Amór de mi vida* (Awaken . . . Sweet love of
> my life)
>
> *Despiérta . . . Si te encuéntras dormída* (Awaken . . . If you're in
> slumber)
>
> *Escúcha mi voz vibrár bajo tu ventána* (Please hear my voice reso-
> nate beneath your window)
>
> *En está canción te vengo a entregár el alma* (With this song my
> soul I'll deliver)
>
> *Perdóna . . . que interrúmpa tu sueño* (Forgive me . . . for inter-
> rupting your slumber)

Pero no pude mas (But I could help myself not)

Y está noche te vine a decír te quiéro (And this night I have come to say that I love you)

Cluck, cluck.

The *cluck* was made when the pin rolled over the end of the tortílla dough and onto the uneven wooden rolling board, every morning's serenade—*cluck, cluck.* The *cluck-cluck* metronome. The first *cluck* was a middle-C *cluck;* the second was four notes lower, a G *cluck,* created by the uneven board as the rolling pin struck it. *Cluck, cluck* every morning—a two-note serenade.

Joaquín peered up at his mother, grinning warmly, and she grinned back at him, having disregarded her order that he not rest his arms on the table. Ignoring her altogether, Benáncio parted a flour tortílla in two, Bedouin style, and used the two halves to stir and mix his breakfast of eggs and beans. He then scooped up a healthy portion of the mixture on the piece of the tortílla he held on his right hand, helped along with the portion of the tortílla he held in his left hand. This liquid amalgamation he now forced into his mouth so that he could barely chew and wiped the corners of his mouth with the back of his thumb.

"That's in the movies," Benáncio retorted, as he shifted the egg and bean golf ball to one side of his mouth so that he could talk.

Joaquín turned his head to look up at his father, whose voice had taken on a serious tone.

"In real life, a *serenáta* is just a bunch of *pinches borráchos* [damn drunks] who've been kicked out of the *cantína* [saloon] at closing time, and they spend their last dime bringing the equally drunk musicians home with them." He laughed heartily.

A smile broke on Joaquín's face, and he turned in his mother's direction, as if seeking some cue from her. Manda intently focused on her tortíllas.

Benáncio continued, "And the women put up with the crap; *se hacen pendéjas las viejas*" [they play along].

Joaquín straightened his back against the chair and stared straight ahead. His father reminded him so much of the brusque mustached Mexican men of the Mexican movies who spoke with so much male confidence that what they spoke could not be questioned. Manda remained at attention at the stove.

Benáncio nodded and concluded, "They play along with the *sere-náta* as if it were something meaningful, but it's just a farcical testament for the whole world to witness."

Joaquín knew his father could not stand for hypocrisy. Every act and every utterance, he psychoanalyzed. Niceties, pleasantries, and apologies were meaningless expressions. For him, a warm salutation was issued by someone making a play on you, who either wanted something from you or was overly pretentious. In either case, Benáncio could see right through you.

"Ay, Diocíto, mio" (Oh, my gentle God). Manda reacted in a half-serious, half-humorous mood. She looked to the heavens and held her outstretched arms, palms open upward, as if to plead, *You see what I have to put up with?*

Joaquín settled back a little, realizing that Manda was not taking Benáncio seriously. The boy's attention then shifted to the prior year's Moctezúma calendar on the wall, the one Manda had brought home from the corn mill. He turned his head and rested it on his right shoulder as he surveyed the piece. The poster colors reflected brightly in the dimly lit kitchen, reflecting the light from the one bulb hanging from an electrical cord.

The picture induced an angst in him. In the Moctezúma print, a doleful sun had abandoned the world and all that was left was a desolate palette. Joaquín searched for a horizon, but there was none. Neither blue, nor gray, nor white, the sky appeared to him more like an ominous and endless wintry sea. A pre-Columbian Indian chief in full colorful war regalia mourned the death of his female companion. A great battle had apparently ended, and the warrior is defeated, helpless in his gloom.

Troubling Joaquín as well, as he began to fiddle with it, was the retractable, drill bit–like, what-cha-ma-call-it (*"la chingadéra,"* Benáncio called it) that was attached to the can opener. Everyone in San Felípe had the same manual can opener, but no one had ever told him what the retractable *chingadéra* in the middle was for. Joaquín was convinced it was not for picking your teeth, which was the use Benáncio was then making of it.

And also rattling in his brain and now surfacing was the "Easter Bonnet" song from music class that had kept harassing him the past week, the gramophone mechanical lyrics playing neurotically over and over in his brain:

"In your Easter bonnet, with all its frills upon it . . . the photographer will snap us, and we'll find that we're in the rotogravure . . ."

What is a rotogravure? Could someone explain that, please? Please! Joaquín's brain could find no niche in which to file this thought away.

". . . and we'll find that we're in the rotogravure."

The file was incomplete, and his brain kept scrolling for some file to close before it could disengage.

Cluck, cluck.

Benáncio was right, after all, once Joaquín got to thinking about it. In San Felípe, men did not love women; they couldn't — it would be a sign of such utter weakness. A man never hugged his wife. There was need for distance between a man and his wife; distance between a man and his children. He thought about his friend Lupe's father who ate at the dining table by himself, alone, while Lupe's mother served him and all the children waited outside until he finished. And he knew that lovers could never be entirely trusted. Wouldn't they eventually puncture your heart with dull daggers and then spit in your wounds? Weekend lyrics sung at *El Salón* [dance hall] next door taught him as much. The wailings of the *tríos* and the *conjuntos* through their ballads and *corridos* left him no doubt that underneath it all, women could be treacherous beings — dagger-wielding, false-promising, heartbreaking, drinking-causing wretches. Watch out for them.

But there were occasions, he was learning, when women were thought worthy of admiration. This was when they were still pure, naïve and malleable, like his neighbor, Janie. But they were also admirable in their old age, like Janie's mother, when, as mothers of sons, they remarkably gained a cryptogenic quality of becoming Madonna-like. That's when they deserved to be serenaded by a band of off-beat, drunken musicians.

"Que boníto, le trajiéron serenáta." [How lovely, she was serenaded].

And drunk was precisely when the men of San Felípe were allowed to share their embellished and exaggerated love-offering.

"I understand that Doña Miránda has lost her mind," Manda told Benáncio very matter-of-factly under her breath. Joaquín thought of Jovíta Miránda, who lived just across the back alley — a lovely, chubby lady as old as the moon who could cook up the most savory chicken *caldos* [soups] using the chicken neck, tail, and small wings tips.

Benáncio nodded agreeably and told her, "If you ask me, that woman's been half-crazy all her life."

"No, seriously, she's complaining daily about her old man's infidelity." Manda shook her head in disbelief. "Rumors are," she said, "that Doña Miránda's outbursts cannot be explained. Now, what possible infidelity could this woman of eighty fear from her withering spouse? Not even her children can comprehend that. Reportedly, one minute, Doña Miránda can be perfectly calm and presumably sane, but in the next, she loses it all and will rant uncontrollably at her equally aging husband, even throwing at him whatever object is readily within reach."

Benáncio shrugged his shoulders and mocked. "I understand she'll also call him a *puto* [whore], which really baffles Doña Miránda's daughters, who swear their daddy is nothing short of an angel." He turned to Joaquín and rolled his eyes.

Joaquín smiled cautiously.

It was natural as day, Joaquín had learned in school, that as people get older, their "far" memory withstands time better than "near" memory. He imagined Doña Miránda as a young Juaníta. When she learned of her husband's infidelity, her disappointment had turned into anguish, and then it turned into rage. But her pain had been set aside as she gave birth to each of her children. Her children needed her, and they needed a father. That rationalized everything. Time passed, and with age, Doña Miránda's husband finally grew into a man worthy of her. But Doña Miránda had been mortally wounded. Her husband's youthful infidelity was part of her far memory. That painful scar had been etched in some special place in her mind.

Cluck, cluck.

These thoughts, including the dandy beau and the lady, the Moctezúma print, the what-cha-ma-call-it *chingadéra*, and the *rotogravure* ventured in and out of Joaquín's mind as Benáncio parted tortillas in two and Manda played her every morning serenade. Glancing over to Manda by the stove, Joaquín wondered whether Juaníta, when she would become old and withering, like Doña Miránda, would be tormented by her far memory. Still humming her serenade, Manda turned to catch Joaquín's gaze. Her face was radiant. Benáncio parted another tortílla in two and wiped his plate clean.

10

Summer of '65

JOAQUÍN TURNED FIFTEEN THE SUMMER OF '65.

The red Ford truck stopped. It was the last leg of the trip. Joaquín had earlier seen a road sign that read "Corpus Christi 70 miles." The live oak belt lay behind them and toward the south lay the South Texas prickly desert. The Gypsy-like caravan of Ford and Chevy pickup trucks and sedans pulled into the Texas roadside park. Anxious to stretch their legs, Joaquín and Bennie jumped out from behind the canvas tarp that covered the truck bed even before the truck came to a complete stop. Bennie was a tad darker and shorter by an inch. They both wore jeans and white T-shirts. Joaquín's sunbrowned hair was shoulder-length after a three full summer months of growth. Bennie sported a clean crew cut. Manda followed much later, making her way down the sturdy plank, favoring her left hip as she walked.

"We've got a loose kumalong," Joaquín pointed out to Don Armándo, who stood by the wood plank. "The walls have been making a racket all the way from Victoria."

"I'll get Shorty to tighten it. Anybody get hit?"

"No, sir. It's just that the walls move a lot, and the chains get loose and that kumalong can bang up somebody."

"Well, we're almost home."

"Yeah, but it would be nice without the risk."

"Shorty will see to it. Shorty!"

As the lines formed at the men's and ladies' restrooms, Manda pulled her two boys away from the others out toward a small, dry limestone creek bed meagerly landscaped with two yucca plants and a Sabal palm.

Hardly a thought about Benáncio had entered Joaquín's mind that summer. Benáncio had stayed behind in San Felípe, and Sis had stayed behind as well. She had graduated high school that spring and gotten a job at the San Felípe hardware store. Now, Manda and the boys were returning from the Michigan strawberry and cucumber fields with a few hundred dollars in their pockets, ready for the start of a new school year. Manda had run the numbers their first day in the strawberry fields and shown Joaquín her calculations:

> *A tray of strawberries translates into a hamburger, fries, and an orange drink. Twelve trays should produce a pair of jeans. School lunch for the kids costs 25 cents a day times three kids times five days a week times four times a month times nine months. That makes $135, or 153 trays of strawberries.*

On that particular day, the strawberry fields had yielded sixteen trays: five for Manda, four for Bennie, and seven for Joaquín.

Benáncio had been at work when the red Ford truck arrived in San Felípe to collect them some four months earlier. Joaquín had hoped (to no avail) that his papa might make it to the departure. *Would it make a difference anyway?* Joaquín wondered. Their goodbyes had always been awkward—for the two boys and for their papa. It was unfamiliar ground. *Are we supposed to hug? Are we supposed to say, "I love you, Papa?"* The questions whirled in Joaquín's brain.

Now, on the return trip, it was Joaquín whom Manda pulled close to her.

"Your father's not going to be home when we get back, m'*hijo* [my son]."

Joaquín's focus was elsewhere. Not the least bit suspicious, he asked her, "Oh? Where is he?" shading his eyes from the relentless south Texas sun, waiting for Manda's response.

"No, I mean, he . . . he's gone," Manda answered in a sigh that was short of sincere. "*M'ijo,* we've divorced."

There was no blame or anger or resentment in her voice. She faced Joaquín under the hot Texas sun, her entreating eyes probing for some reaction from him. "Gone away . . . forever?" was all he could muster.

She nodded.

Joaquín frowned, and the tensed muscles of his face weakened. The sweat beaded at his forehead, and he sniffed as if his nasal passages were cluttering. His breath became weighted down, and he turned to breathing through an open mouth to help quell the cry. Without a handkerchief, he swallowed his snot and spit and tears.

Bennie just looked on, his face reflecting slight concern—and that was all.

"It's okay, Son. If you're worried about me, don't be," Manda whispered near Joaqin's ear, attempting to comfort him by offering a reassuring hug.

Joaquín stiffened up. He stared at her, searched into her eyes, his glassy eyes roaming, grasping out for pity. *I knew it. I always knew it . . . that he would eventually leave.*

Manda reached out for him with her arms in a consoling gesture. Joaquín moved away and shook his head. *Don't!* He felt as if his entire soul wanted to cry out — to scream, to break windows, and to tear up stuff and stomp at the ground.

Manda sighed empathetically and, turning to Bennie, offered, "You will pardon me, my sons, but I am all out of tears."

Joaquín cringed, rotating his head back as far as he could.

Still, Bennie looked on. He had crossed his arms across his chest and taken on the look of an interested observer.

Taken aback to those early days as a child, Joaquín recalled those nights when his mother's contained sobs would distract him from sleep. The bed he shared with his brother would creak and sway a little when he would sneak out of it to slip into bed with Manda and snuggle right up against his mother's fold, like a pup seeking the reassuring warmth of its mama's soft middle. Between her sobs, Manda would acknowledge Joaquín with a hug and kiss the back of his head. There was nothing he could do for Manda; Joaquín knew that. Yet, there was something about him just being there, close to her, with his naïve empathy, which seemed to calm her, strengthen her, and give her resolve. Manda seemed to be consoled by this simple gesture of company, and they would both eventually fall asleep.

But by that summer of '65, Manda was all out of tears.

11

The Autopsy

"SPECIAL DELIVERY!" shouted one of the two male assistants struggling with the gurney, his voice muffled by the surgical mask. It was a ludicrous attempt at small talk. Springing from the side of his neck, this short, stocky one had a tattoo of what appeared to be an orange tiger, presently half-hidden by the surgical mask. He was breathing heavily from his effort to move the cadaver from the gurney to the autopsy table.

The doctor did not acknowledge the remark, and nor did the other assistant—a tall, nerdy one with a Chicago Bears woolen cap. The assistants slid the dark bag holding the cadaver from the gurney on to the stainless-steel table.

"Female, Caucasian . . . I'd say between fifteen and eighteen years old," noted Dr. Mitch Kant into his tape recorder. A white cap was hastily attached to the coroner's head with his surgical face mask at his neck. Vapor came out of Dr. Mitch Kant's breath as he spoke impatiently in the frigid room that was the New Frankfort morgue. With his left hand, he assisted by pulling the zipped plastic bag from under the body and handed it over to a chubby woman who nodded to him in altar-boy fashion.

The assistant who had made the comment slipped the translucent rubber gloves off his hands and arched his eyebrows, as if inquiring, "Did anyone get it?" The woman took a position beside the doctor, eagerly surveying the body as well. On her feet were new black and white track shoes. An oversized Notre Dame sweatshirt concealed most of her green scrubs, the hood hanging behind her neck. A Formica tag pinned to her sweatshirt said "Armstrong," and at her feet was a black gym bag.

"We need to work around this injury here." The doctor motioned to the much shorter Armstrong, pointing to the back of the cadaver's head. "No need to shave this one . . . just make it a short cut."

"Wanna save the hair?" she asked.

"Yes, obviously."

"How 'bout, uh, just shave it up to here, maybe . . ." Armstrong made a semicircle with her finger, recommending the shave around where a head wound appeared.

The doctor paused for moment, "Naw, no need to."

"Dat it?"

"Yep."

A cadaver would *speak* to him, the doctor would jest to his friends who cared to listen to the details of an autopsy. Although he said it jokingly, the doctor couldn't have been more serious. As a visiting professor at the medical school, Dr. Kant would introduce his students to autopsy procedures in an amusing way. "An autopsy allows a cadaver to express itself forthrightly and unashamedly," he would begin. "It does so in a way that a live person would never imagine doing. For when else can a person afford the expense of such a comprehensive physical examination or willingly submit to such thorough and minute medical prowling? If there is but a small and insignificant scar somewhere on a body—the result of some adolescent sibling rivalry—it will show up on the coroner's report. If macaroni and cheese remains undigested in the cadaver's gut, that'll be on the coroner's report as well. The weight of your heart, by golly, and when else will your heart be weighed? Who would possibly care? We do. That's part of the protocol. Colored photos of one's genitalia? Yep! The only photographs to ever be taken of one's genitalia, even from different perspectives and angles, preserved for posterity during an autopsy."

The body had come in late in the afternoon and had been accompanied by a forensic entomologist named Sarah Henderson, who had insisted on waiting for the coroner to provide him with specific instructions. After two hours of waiting, Henderson accepted the secretary's explanation: "Unlike other coroners, Dr. Kant keeps irregular hours. The good doctor will come in whenever he is good and ready, so there's no use waiting around for him. He might be here in an hour, or he may decide to come in and start on the autopsy at three in the morning." Henderson wrote down instructions and left these, as well as some trays and glass jars, for the good doctor whenever he saw fit to arrive.

There was an obvious injury to the right side of the head. Dr. Kant referred to it as "a deep laceration of the right occipital-parietal area." The full extent of the wound would reveal itself in time once he reflected the scalp with his fingers. To do so, he made a straight line incision into the scalp from one ear to the other. Dr. Kant noted a substantial amount of fluid around the head wound. Sarah Henderson had indicated that as well and noted in her report that a large portion of her specimen had been tainted by the brain fluids since they had oozed onto the soil by the time she arrived where the body was found.

The coroner then moved to the head of the table near the victim's head, placed his thumbs under the scalp flap and his fingers in the exterior, and then exerted as much force as he could, pushing his thumbs between the scalp and the gubgaleal connective tissue which adhered the scalp to the skull. He pushed the scalp down over the forehead to the bony forehead ridge, the supraorbital ridge, over the eyebrows. Somewhat loose already, the back flap required less effort. This revealed the skull, now ready for removal of the skull cap. The skull cap was exactly that — a round top to the skull, which was removed in all autopsies by jigsawing and cracking and chiseling.

Using a bone saw, Dr. Kant and the coroner's assistant first scored the calvarium, which left a nice straight line around the head. Then, the assistant took the skull chisel to gently finish the separation. The coroner then removed the skull cap, prying it from the covering of the brain called the dura mater, exposing the brain. He then removed the dura mater.

A protrusion on the rear of the skull cap matched a laceration on the brain. Dr. Kant noted that this had been caused by a V- or L-shaped object. The wound could have been a puncture wound, he said, but was certain it had not been made by the acute angle of an object. The surface of the object that had come in contact with the skull was shaped more like a right angle. In other words, the doctor noted, it had not been a knife or the sharp edge of an ax or shovel that caused the laceration. But whatever it was, the edge of some heavy object coming into contact with the head was the cause of death.

Dr. Kant also reported severe bruising in the area of the left eyelid and over the right eye. He wrote, "The skin above the orbital ridge is lacerated from multiple blows, and the bleeding from that area has been significant." At her throat, he reported his findings as, "The cadaver shows dark bruising that could have been caused by hands in a choking action."

There was nothing particularly telling about the organs. Dr. Kant felt she was a very healthy young woman. The pelvic examination revealed the girl had never delivered a child. In the vagio-genito area, however, Mitch Kant found injuries which startled even the experienced pathologist. The bruising had been initiated outside of the sexual organ, and the labia majora and labia minora both showed signs of tearing by the force of some foreign object — no simple male organ was responsible for this damage, of which Dr. Kant was certain. Instead, some sort of projectile had been used, quite possibly the same cruel object that caused the fatal head injury. There were obvious signs of repeated contusions where the projectile had been used numerous times to penetrate the poor girl in a rough and violent fashion.

PART II

The Corn Mill/*El Molíno de Nixtamál*

COUSIN NINA WASN'T DOING WELL these days, and Sis told Joaquín so.

"She's not getting any better, is she?"

"No."

"Then if she can't help me now, when?"

Sis sighed her abdication and nodded. "Just know that she's not well and tires easily."

Around the large backyard of Nina's home, her extended family partied on her seventy-sixth birthday. Someone had placed the large blue and white umbrella behind her to provide some shade. The sweat beads that had earlier formed on her forehead now trickled like tiny tributaries, joining at the brow and parting at the nose. She reclined on the lawn chair and gulped for breath, allowing a wistful smile to form on her round face. She then took a small plastic spoonful of the white cake with white frosting, swallowed and motioned Joaquín to get closer to her.

"There was never any real courtship between them," Nina recounted to Joaquín. "There wasn't any time. You see, your mother had probably never even kissed a man before she met your father. But Benáncio swept her off her feet," Nina whispered, enjoying that sweet memory.

Joaquín tried to paint a picture of his mother in his memory. By that time, she was already a woman close to forty, he told himself. He had once seen his mother's picture in the splendor of her youth. It had been from the time when Manda lived with her Aunt Terésa in *Saltíllo* in the old country. Terésa was a *partéra* [midwife] who delivered babies just blocks from the downtown cathedral. Taken one Sunday morning in an itinerant photography studio at the *plaza* across the street from the cathedral, the brownish print had yellowed a bit. In first communion white, exhibiting a porcelain-like fragility, the girl, with an appropriate sad pose on her face and the long black hair, clung to a gray cross. The photographer's smoky-

white backdrop had been draped to create shadows, which added a
certain air of mysticism to the portrait. And his mother's eyes, out-
lined for the occasion, seemed to Joaquín, like an El Greco's portrait, to plead piously with the heavens. In the photo, Manda's skin
was tight; her nose, like Joaquín's, just a bit long. Her black hair,
dark and glossy like a raven's wings, was slightly wavy.

Saltíllo, Coahuíla, Mexico, circa 1922. False Romanesque columns
carved from the *Sierra Madre cantéra* limestone adorned the cathedral's entrance. Massive carved oak doors opened blankly toward
the *plaza* below. Once majestically erect and polished, its weathered
planks were now bound and tethered with copper braces. For more
than 200 years, the cathedral's morning shadow's embrace had extended beyond the *plaza* across the street and out over the original
Spanish town site. When Manda was just a teenager, Catholic cler-
ics and their supporters fought the anticlerics on these streets in
fashion similar to that of their distant cousins, the Spaniards, who
were fighting their own great civil war.

At the cathedral, a smaller-than-life wood carving of the crucifix-
ion was strung from the trusses away from the main altar where the
Virgin took center stage. Jesus' eyes turned upward in an unrelent-
ing, absorbing plea — a challenge that remained etched, fixed, frozen
in time, permanent.

She was thirty-seven when Joaquín was born. Her children would
never learn any part of her youth: how she attended Mass every day,
that she had been raised by an aunt in Saltíllo and had enjoyed
whatever privileged lifestyle was available at the time.

His inner voice told Joaquín that by that time, Manda had focused
on a solitary objective in her mind — children. But why at her age
would she take on such enormous responsibilities? He reflected for
a second and pictured Manda with a boisterous effect on her face,
playing with him and his brother Bennie, teaching them to count in
Spanish:

Dos y dos son cuatro (two and two are four),

Cuatro y dos son seis (four and two are six),

Seis y dos son ocho (six and two are eight),

Y ocho, diez y seis (and eight become sixteen).

But what I need from Nina, he told himself, *is from a time before then. Who had Manda been? Where was Benáncio from? They were gone so quickly from my life, and even when they had been there, the times they spent with each other and with us kids was so short and always under enormous distress.* In his mind, Joaquín had always jokingly referred to the circumstances of his childhood as the *affliction,* for he had but few pleasant memories from that time. *Why so few?* He recalled as a child regarding it as normal, but it could not have been. He had never delved beyond that.

Joaquín listened intently as Nina recounted the story, interrupted first by one of her great-granddaughters, who insisted on sitting on Nina's lap, as if to regard Joaquín from that vantage point, and then just as quickly losing interest in him, and then as Nina called on two of her sons to stop arguing. "It's a party, boys," she counseled them. Embarrassed, her two sons heeded her advice.

Before she had her own children, Nina often babysat Sis and Joaquín. By the time Bennie came, Nina was already too old for babysitting services. On her seventy-sixth birthday, Nina recounted to Joaquín how Manda and Benáncio had met.

On a particularly humid, sweaty South Texas Saturday, as Manda tended store at the corn mill and kept an eye out for young Nina, the lyrics of a tune gravitated to her, playing in her brain, and she unconsciously, quietly hummed its poetry:

Pasástes a mi lado (You passed right by me)

con gran indiferéncia (with such indifference)

Tus hojos ni siquíera (Your eyes hardly)

Volteáron así a mi (noticed me)

te vi sin que ve vieras (From a distance, I observed you, but you never turned to me)

Te hablé sin que me oyéras (My heart spoke to you, but you never heard me)

y toda mi existéncia se ahogó dentro de mi (and all that I am died within)

"There's something special about this man that sets him apart from the rest of the wetbacks," Manda whispered to herself—a habit she had picked up as the only child growing up in a strict household. Everyone in San Felípe called them "wetbacks." Those rugged, stringy souls with suspicious faces and cedar-bark hands were either legal workers—*los bracéros*—or illegal workers—*los mojadítos*. But who could tell them apart? Manda had first noticed him outside through the large plate-glass window of the Tortillería and Molíno de Nixtamál (tortílla and ground corn mill). She stood at the glass counter tending the line at the bulky National Register cash register and occasionally glimpsing toward the window. Behind her, a large calendar of the Tortillería de Nixtamál San Felípe threatened, *"Requérda A Pearl Harbor"* [Remember Pearl Harbor].

Outside, the man picked through the seams of his thin wallet and seemed to be taking inventory before coming into the store for a purchase. Perhaps it was the way his clothes fit him—simple clothes, Manda observed, but neatly pressed. *A man who cares how he looks.* She felt herself smiling and wondered whether anyone could tell. This man was tall, and she liked that. At his thin waist, the tip of his well-used burgundy leather belt was tucked in behind the belt loop. Dark brown dress trousers matched quite well with the tan, checkered long-sleeve shirt. Given the August heat, though, Manda wondered how uncomfortable it must all be.

Behind Manda, the hopper noisily swallowed the *masa* (corn meal dough) mixture whole and churned out *tortíllas* for those who could afford them. Two young women helpers stooped over the hot griddle. The oldest one, eighteen at best, whom they called "Panchíta," always helped Manda at the mill on Saturdays. Panchíta put on a full-length plastic apron, took nixtamál mix between her hands, and formed large basketball-sized pale yellow balls of the bulky dough mixture. Still in high school, Carmelíta's job was to cut white butcher-paper lengths from a roll hanging from behind the counter. As the customers paid for their order of nixtamál or tortíllas, Carmelíta wrapped them in the butcher paper.

Without turning, Manda called out as she rang out ten cents on the cash register, "Panchíta, be sure we have enough nixtamál boiling!" The money drawer at the bottom of the register drew out automatically as Manda turned the handle. At the same time, a wide strip of paper with the printed total rolled out of a slot at the top of the machine.

"Ten cents, please," Manda smiled at the short, thin man next in line. Peering from under a weathered straw hat with a chinstrap tied behind the neck, the *mojadíto* miled back with smoke-yellowed teeth and winked at her. She smiled through one side of her mouth, shook her head ironically, and handed him the dozen warm tortíllas wrapped in the white sheet of butcher paper. She then wiped the sweat beads from her brow with her long white apron.

"We have enough *maíz*, Mandita," Panchíta yelled out over the churning sound of the equipment, "but we don't have enough lime."

Manda turned to her in response, arching her eyebrows and crooking her mouth. *"No hay para que gritár, m'ija, si no estás en el rancho"* (no need to shout, honey, you're not out in the ranch). Manda's aunt, the midwife, had despised any shouting in her clinic back in Saltíllo, in the old country. When the ranch hands and their families came to her clinic for care, they all seemed to be shouting at each other when they spoke.

"That's the way they have to call out to each other in the ranch," her aunt had told her. "Out there, people do their chores some distance from each other. One may be feeding the chickens, and another the cows. To be able to communicate with each other at a distance, they shout. In this clinic, shouting is neither necessary nor acceptable."

Manda excused herself from the counter and measured four cups of lime and poured it into the sulfur-yellow mixture that was bubbling in a large cauldron. She then turned toward the plate-glass window to renew her constant vigil over Nina, her ten-year-old niece, who had wandered outside. She loved Nina so, but she told herself she could never love Nina as much as she could love a daughter of her own. Every time she hugged a baby, she imagined it being her own, its warm face up against her bosom, its beady eyes probing up at her face, meeting her eyes inquisitively and finding confirmation, smiling a smile that could only be described as innocent and authentic. She pursed her lips and sighed.

Outside, a group of *mojadítos*, some wearing filthy field clothing, mingled about, sharing their grilled *maíz* tortíllas. Some just added salt and devoured them as if it was their first meal in a long while; others passed greasy fatback pork rinds between them and slurped their Coca-Colas, which they had purchased with their Saturday paychecks, their lips and fingers glossy from the oily fat. Busily around the men, picking up empty returnable glass bottles and the trash they were creating, was Nina.

Manda had minded store at the Molíno de Nixtamál since she had arrived from Saltíllo. The business had been what her father had envisioned when the family first arrived from Mexico in 1905 with his oldest daughter, Rebécca, in tow. Relying on the latest innovations, the corn mill converted the rock-hard kernels of corn into the *masa* that women shaped into the staple of San Felípe life. White *maíz* was boiled in a mixture of water and lime powder until softened and then ground by a motorized mill into the sandy dough. *Maíz* was sold by the pound to the women of the neighborhood, who could smell the sweet scent of the freshly ground *maíz* and scurried daily to form a long line at the *tortillería*.

America had beckoned. The Mexican radio station announcer touted the benefits that awaited the *braceros:* "Come one, come all to the plaza at the center of Lináres on Saturday! Sign up as a *bracero*. Go to America where jobs are plentiful and wages are good. The Mexican government will protect your interests while you are in America."

From under the hood of a 1936 Chevrolet, Benáncio struggled, fiddling with the spring of a carburetor. Lináres, Nuevo León, was just up the mountain from Monterréy, Mexico, up where the old goats grew fat while *lechónes* (baby goats) were weaned for Monterréy appetites — where daily echoes of carpenters' axes resonated just before the warning shouts of "Agua" (Timber)! and the telling thunderous crash of the most superior pine in Mexico. Unlike the others from Lináres who immediately left for the United States, Benáncio had been reluctant. But eventually, he, too, left for the United States.

Handsome, over six feet tall, and with an impressive Roosevelt-style, gray Stetson felt hat on his head, the tall man lowered his head as he walked through the front door of the *Molíno*. Now, he awaited his turn in line at the cash register. Towering over the rest of the men and clean shaven (except for a well-manicured moustache), Benáncio's features were unmistakably Arabic.

Without looking up at him, Manda asked, "Are you with the group that stays at Don Gabíno Flores' place?" Don Gabíno had contracted fifty *braceros*, whom he accommodated at his truck garage, which he had converted to sleeping quarters.

Benáncio was fumbling with his money when Manda spoke and did not seem to have heard her.

Manda was one of three sisters who owned the corner general store and the corn mill, and the three were very well-respected ladies, as Benáncio had learned. The oldest one was close to forty-five, and everyone called her "Señoríta Rebécca." Rumor was that Señoríta Rebécca had been left very weak from tuberculosis and would rarely make an appearance at the general store, preferring to stay in her second-story bedroom next to the breezeway. It was also rumored she was the brains of the operation. It was Rebécca who had final say-so to approve credit purchases at the corn mill and the grocery store next door. The neighborhood's favorite sister, had a vote been taken, would have been the middle sister, Queta.

"Did you know, Joaquín, that Mama's name — her legal name, I mean — was 'Henrietta'"? Nina smiled, as if even after all these years, this fact still amazed her.

Joaquín frowned as if to indicate, *"No . . . go on. Explain that."*

Nina glowed as she began to tell the story. She reached for Joaquín's hand and held it as she began. "Her Mexican name was 'Enriquéta,' and that's why everyone called her 'Queta' for short, but she got her given name, Henrietta, from a rancher's wife in Poth, Texas. Seems the family had traveled to pick cotton at this place just south of San Antonio."

Joaquín smiled and mouthed the word "Poth?"

"Oh, let's leave that for another day," she said. "Let me continue before I forget." Nina smiled and went on. "Now, Benáncio knew that here, in front of him at the cash register, was the youngest of the three sisters. His friend Praxédis had described *la Señoríta* [miss or lady] *Manda.*

"On this day Manda held her wavy black hair down with a hair net. She had clear olive skin and thin lips. She looked up at Benáncio, inquisitively meeting his gaze, cuing him, anticipating his response."

"A dozen tortíllas? Perhaps?"

A modest Benáncio responded cordially, his white teeth gleaming, "Oh, please forgive me, Señoríta, I could not tell if you were addressing yourself to me." He stammered, "No, no . . . I stay with a friend of mine and his family just outside of San Felípe. Praxédis, perhaps you know him."

"Oh, Praxédis Garza. Of course!" Manda could count on her right hand the families that lived along the main road south to the river. They all had a credit line at the store. "Well, welcome to San Felípe, Señór. I hope you are enjoying your stay."

"I think so," he answered, sounding as formal as he could.

"Ten cents, please." Manda gave Benáncio change for a quarter.

He looked at the loose change in his hand. "It's expensive, eh?" Benáncio complained mildly as a disappointed look came over his face.

"Absolutely not," Manda began with a resolute tone, and then reproached herself to the point of sounding apologetic, "but the price of corn has increased dramatically, and still we have not increased our prices."

Benáncio swallowed nervously. His voice faltered. "Señoríta, in Mexico, I would have paid no more than two or three centávos for the tortíllas."

"*Sí* [yes]. That's true, but you're not in Mexico, are you?" She smiled as she said it, being sure to address him with the informal "tu" instead of the "Ustéd" she had formerly used.

"Hmm," he smiled back, and as he opened the door to walk outside, he heard Manda addressing the next man in line, "Ten cents, please."

13

Santander Beckons

NEARING PRAXÉDIS' WOOD HUT, which he saw in the distance bracing up against the levee of the irrigation canal bank, Benáncio followed the path down from the canal and stopped to shade himself under two giant pecan trees. From the lower vantage point, he could still make out the hut's corrugated tin roof as it sloped down, almost brushing the canal bank. The soil under the shade was damp from a recent irrigation flooding, and as the southeasterly breeze bristled past, Benáncio felt its cool caress. He removed his hat and wiped the interior band with his handkerchief. His eyes narrowed with apprehension, and he recalled how as a boy, he had prayed that God would change his life and give him the opportunity to grow up with his absent father. A complaining grunt sounded from his throat as he chided himself. But he could not help himself, and his thoughts turned to the journey which had first brought him and his father to this area just south of San Felípe. The year was 1923.

"Go ahead, Benáncio. Light it," someone yelled at the boy as he struggled to keep the match lit by cupping his hands. Benáncio flipped the lit match at the mountain of drying brush. A huge crackling bonfire erupted, lighting up the early dusk sky. The flames barely missed Benáncio's face as he quickly turned and screened himself with both arms as he ran. A sizzling sound, not unlike a drop of water dancing on a hot skillet, hissed as the sap from the burning brush boiled and vaporized and spit. Benáncio smelled the repulsive scent of branding iron on cow hide. As he ran from harm's way, he could hear the men, his coworkers, laughing and jeering—and all at his expense.

When he stopped running, his father was near. Benáncio heard the old man's gruff voice. "Come here, son. Let's see how bad it is." Benáncio was fourteen.

Benáncio looked up to the towering six-feet-two figure with the trim moustache and the neat, cropped black hair. Aloft on the man's back, attached with a thick leather strap, was a heavy straw hat that

curled up at either end and was wide enough to shade his broad
shoulders under the highest sun. Don Gonzálo whipped Benáncio
around toward the bonfire light for a better view of his son and let
water flow from his canteen onto Benáncio's face. Its coolness com-
forted Benáncio, but the young boy felt the skin on his right cheek
taut, as if it had shrunk and tightened. A good portion of Benáncio's
hair on the right side of his head had been consumed by the flame.
Benáncio felt the thin, crispy, singed cinders that had been his hair
drop to his ear and shoulder as his father ran his large hand over the
right side of his head. Against his young skin, the calluses on his father's weathered palm felt like the cracked and creviced bark of a
huisáche.

Don Gonzálo then rubbed his hand against the young boy's right
arm to remove the crisp, charred hair on his arm and smiled at him.
"A que cabrón tan pendéjo" (Oh, how stupid can you be), the old man
teased.

"Ay," Benáncio yelped, writhing in pain, realizing that the odor of
burning cattle hair and leather had been the smell of his own burnt
hair.

Staring back up to his father, he was met with that all-too-familiar,
piercing stare, which he and his older brothers had been raised with
—that cold stare that declared, *"There's no crying allowed here!"*

Benáncio exaggerated his manhood and offered what he believed
his father wanted to hear. "It's nothing," he said. "It just hurts a little." Don Gonzálo grabbed Benáncio firmly by the neck. While painful, Benáncio took it as his father's genuine expression of affection—
a rare but welcomed display by the old man.

The following day, the crew cook handed Benáncio some creamy
white lard, which he scooped from a twenty-gallon can. "This will
ease some of the pain," the short, portly cook advised him. "Just put
it on like cream." But Benáncio noticed that a scab was not forming.
By day's end, his pain became unbearable. He reserved his crying
for the few and precious secret moments when he got away from
others to relieve himself.

Don Gonzálo's eyes had a fiery look in them, giving Benáncio the
impression of ready weapons, the old man's cocked gun or well-
sharpened blade, ready to tear through any enemy. If there was one
place in the world where Benáncio was certain to feel secure, it was
next to the powerful and confident Don Gonzálo. Back at their
mountain village in Lampasos, Mexico, the old man and his sons

would sit together for Mass in the small church. Benáncio's mother sat next to the old man. All of the sons had their father's fiery eyes, and it was a sight to behold them transfixed on the altar throughout the entire Mass. Each one of them was obedient to their father — even the oldest, who was now twenty-five.

Nina and Joaquín separated while Nina's extended family sat down for barbeque. Nina ate slowly and kept a vigilant eye for Joaquín. When she was through eating, she summoned him over.

"En los días antíguos" (in the old days), she began, "from the area of present-day San Felípe, the prickly brush blanketed all the land south." She stretched her hand and pointed south. "About seven miles to the point where the river shifts southward and then horseshoes back around. There, the north bank rises about twenty feet above the normal water level. Let me tell you a true story, Joaquín.

"Across the river, a sandy beach nurtures the high grasses on which the Mexican cattle and goats feed. In the shallows, the sereneness of the river current barely sways the reeds. But the sereneness is misleading. The undercurrent of the narrow river has claimed thousands of unsuspecting swimmers. All this area immediately south of San Felípe, down to the river, was the *dezenraíze,* the area of root plowing."

Don Gonzálo had explained the *dezenraíze* to Benáncio as the two had made their way down the mountain road from the village of Lampasos to the city of Caderéyta, about a hundred miles south of the border. All along the barren road, cut through the side of the mountain, which served as the main thoroughfare, they passed mud houses, shanties made of mesquite branches for walls and then plastered with gray-brown mud or the sturdier rubble walls and roofs of corrugated tin. At each ranch, the word was the same: the men had left for America to work on the *dezenraíze.* A historical Spanish provincial capital, Caderéyta had been the gathering point in northern Mexico where the newspaper had announced American labor recruiters would sign up the *bracéros* traveling to the United States.

Don Gonzálo was animated, making circular motions with his arms as he described the *dezenraíze* to Benáncio. "You initially prune the prickly brush to allow the men to get to the roots. A round trench

is dug around the roots with a pickaxe and shovels to allow space for
the men to swing their axes. Debris from the trees is allowed two
days to dry, and then it is piled back into the trenches and burned in
huge bonfires. All plant life is devoured by the fire — mesquite, huisáche, acacias, ebano."

"Do they leave any trees to shade the goats, Papa?"

"Very little."

"Why do they have to uproot all the trees, Papa?"

"They don't raise goats; they need to leave the land clear for planting crops."

"But we plant crops, and we don't uproot all the trees."

The old man smiled. "Oh, but we don't plant crops the way the
Americános plant crops. They plant crops as if they desire to feed the
entire world."

Hundreds of men uprooted the brush from sunup to sundown.
Following closely behind the *desenraíze* crew were the hundreds of
other Mexican workers who would eventually complete the system
of canals to irrigate the new fields.

Benáncio's older brothers had remained back in Mexico in the
ejído (rural communal use of land), each entrusted by Don Gonzálo
with duties of maintaining the *ejído* while he was gone. Don Gonzálo
had insisted on making the trip alone initially, telling his wife, Mercédes, that he wanted "to test the waters up north."

"Lo que Díos mande," had been Mercédes' predictable response.
"Come what may, *Díos por 'delánte"* (God willing).

Benáncio's mother had urged that Benáncio go along with his father. "You won't have a woman to do the washing and the cooking,"
she warned. Since God had not favored them with a girl, Benáncio,
the youngest one and the closest to his mother, had learned to wash
and could cook well enough.

"Can you fry eggs just like your mother, *cabrón?* "(young buck or
goat)," the old man challenged.

"Identically," Benáncio answered, a naïve, confident look on his
face.

"A que carbón, este," the old man said, bursting into a guffaw. Mercédes looked on from the small hearth with a reserved smile on her
face.

Herself a tall woman, Mercédes limited her wardrobe to long gray
or black calico skirts that reached to the heels of her shoes. A long
white or gray cotton blouse completed her daily attire, and a light

shawl covered her shoulders. The sleeves of her blouse reached out to her knuckles to cover any part of her arm that might appeal to a man. Her long, straight hair was always kept in neat braids, which were then coifed in the back of the head. Even into her late eighties, her clothes portrayed her as pious, something that struck Joaquín as odd on the few occasions when he did get to see his grandmother. In her entire lifetime with her husband, Mercédes was never permitted to put makeup on her face or blush her lips. That tradition carried on until her death.

Among his mother's last instructions before Benáncio left Lampasos with Don Gonzálo, she warned. "Remember, *mi'jo*, do not speak to anyone unless spoken to." Benáncio already knew that, of course, and he so reminded his mother. But Mercédes urged extra caution, "Yes, but in America, you do not want to say anything that can be misunderstood. The *Americános* are very intelligent people, but they are also very bad people. *Gringos* are the meanest people in the world. *Son unos mendigos.* They always seek to take advantage of you." She also reminded him, as if he needed such reminding, of his father's moodiness and of his temper, especially if he took alcohol.

El Norte (the North) beckoned. Across the border in America, there were jobs for strong men with the desire to work hard. For several decades, cotton had lured many Mexicans to Texas. As a young man, Don Gonzálo had made the annual trip to *las piscas* (the cotton-picking season) as far north as the Petronila ranch near Corpus Christi. This time around, there had been promises of better pay. Don Gonzálo and Benáncio made the trip from Caderéyta, where hundreds of other men had also waited their turn at a makeshift recruiting station. Almost two centuries before, Caderéyta had been a colonial desert outpost from where the Spanish explorations northward to found Nuevo Santander (original Spanish royal reference to the area of South Texas) had begun.

When Don Gonzálo and Benáncio arrived at Caderéyta, they were both impressed by the opulence of the city with its clear water mountain stream and its neat red-brick-lined streets no wider than the space needed for two horse-drawn carriages to pass. Every building around the town square was meticulously kept up, and their white-washed, stucco walls were painted in earthy tones with their thick, carved, stained doors and embellished windows and balconies, broadly edged with borders of bright colors reminiscent of their Andalusian (southern region of Spain) ancestry. Bougainvilleas of all colors and miniature red rose bushes lined the central business district sidewalks, and in the balconies, flowers of every variety and hue bloomed from earthy clay pots. The brass doorknobs and knockers of the homes of the numerous merchants were Medieval figurines of wild animal faces and of grotesque gargoyles.

The walk down the mountain trail had taken almost two days. Their packed lunch was gone by the time Don Gonzálo and Benáncio arrived. At Caderéyta, a short, stocky Mexican, who kept a smokeless stogie precariously in his mouth as he shouted out instructions, signed up the recruits, writing their names on a hardbound ledger. As Benáncio and Don Gonzálo settled in at the end of the long line, Don Gonzálo whispered into Benáncio's ear, "Beware of any Mexican who smokes a cigar." For a time, Benáncio fiddled with the warning, not having understood why a Mexican who smoked a cigar could not be trusted. Eventually, he forgot all about it.

The caravan of trucks pulling the trailers loaded with human cargo made its way northward along the dusty, desert road. As they neared the border, the wagons were hitched to horses, which pulled them the last leg of the trip to the Los Ebanos ferry at the Rio Grande. At the narrowest point in the river, a small wooden hand-pulled ferry got the men over to the U.S. side in several trips. From there, the crew walked up the bank and followed a narrow meandering path cut through the brush until they reached the railroad tracks after a three-mile trek. The new, dark creosote crossties seemed to have just been laid. The following morning, the men were loaded onto a flatbed train car for the two-hour trip east to San Felípe.

14

El Desenraíze

HIGH IN AN OCEAN SKY, gray and black smoke billowed upward and hovered like a massive cumulus cloud — an invisible ceiling flattening the mass on top. Below, a vast battlefield emerged under a pitiless sun. Hundreds of men marshaled pickaxes, shovels, and mule teams. Tractors and dredges on metal wheels tore crisscrossing trenches into the shallow, fertile cover of the prickly desert. Joaquín made his way over a land in transformation, a pickaxe on his shoulder, avoiding deep gashes torn out of the ground as if they had been bombarded by an invading army. Embers still glowed in some of the pits where charred tree trunks appeared like so many burning crosses. Small fledging dusty whirlwinds attempted flight here and there in the parched plain, and just as quickly dissipated.

By a Sabal palm grove, along the edge of a *resáca*, a young, blonde, handsome *Americáno* dressed in starched khaki shoved back his safari hat and bent behind the sighting glass on a wooden tripod to survey the vast, root-plowed stretches of flatlands. He removed his hat and communicated orders to a Mexican who wore a dark fedora and chewed on a stogie at the edge of his mouth. The Mexican walked a few paces and spoke to three Mexican *mayordómos*. The Mexican *mayordómos* departed, one on horseback and the other two in a Model-A Ford. Minutes later, these men addressed large crews who would then disperse throughout the vast defoliated ground.

As an area was slashed and burned, the *Americáno* would instruct the crew to drive long iron stakes into the ground. Against the backdrop of hundreds of Mexicans wielding shovels, *taláches*, and *machétes*, the planting of each new stake brought a smile of accomplishment to the *Americáno*.

"The men were given two meals — one at twelve noon, and another at sunset," Nina told Joaquín. "Each man was responsible for his own breakfast. Most carried around a small Dutch oven to bake their *pan*."

Benáncio was tall for a fourteen-year-old, and he felt he could swing an axe as well as any man. He knew that using an axe required a scientific approach. It wasn't the strength of the man, but the sharpness of the blade and the selection of the proper location and angle at which to cut that mattered. A blunt blade created a pounding effect, and the thrust would reverberate to the man's shoulders and arms and soon tire him out. The thrust of a sharp blade at the right angle was almost pleasurable, as the blade cut through the young brush. Benáncio had been allowed to work on the *desenraíze* because Don Gonzálo promised the *mayordómos* to keep him at the same pace as the men. So, in Benáncio's way of thinking, he was actually contributing something rather than just "being in the way," as his father so frequently reminded him.

The *desenraíze* permitted no waning in a man's stoicism. More than once, the old man questioned aloud whether Benáncio should have even joined him. "At least you have a roof over your head," the old man would often remind him whenever Benáncio's face showed the slightest complaint. Benáncio would silently mock his father since ironically (at least for the time being in the *desenraíze*), they had no roof over their heads. "Someday, *chamaco* [kid] I will tell you about the Battle of Zacatécas [a major battle of the Mexican Revolution]," an old man wearing a revolutionary hat complained to Benáncio. "In a hundred years, I never would have believed that I would ever again be as beaten at the end of the day. Here, every day is a Battle of Zacatécas."

At day's end, Benáncio and Don Gonzálo were left alone to cut through several stout roots of a massive mesquite that had grown on the slope of a *resáca*. Its roots branched out like tentacles reaching out to grip hold of the desert floor. The trunk would eventually yield ground.

"Imagine, Son, how many deer and *javalínas* [peckering] have fed and found shelter under this tree. See the bumblebee tunneling in that branch and sap dripping from its torso? This is an oasis for the animals and the insects." Benáncio shook his head. "Up there . . . see the row of holes the woodpecker has burrowed? Those are traps for the insects he feeds on. I wonder what this land will look like in fifty years."

Benáncio's accident with the fire occurred on the fifth week on the *desenraíze*. A few days later, on a Saturday, which began as if overnight the clouds had dropped to the ground and dampened the shallow soil and the men's beddings and then suddenly disappeared and the sun had been left to bore unmercifully upon the men the remainder of the day, Don Gonzálo had been unseasonably charitable, or so Benáncio had sensed. On several occasions that day, the boy and his father had given each other warm smiles, in spite of the harshness of the stew-damp soil which had impeded their efforts all day long. It had been only for a few seconds on each occasion. But for the first time in his life, Benáncio had sensed a warmth from his father that he had often shared with his mother. How could he describe it? A special silent bond existed between him and Mercédes. A certain *miráda* (look) that expressed contentment, he would often see in his mother's eyes. That sympathetic silent expression between the two was a momentary communion revealing itself briefly. For that reason the sensation was obscure to others. But it had bound the two of them together forever. He now hoped that this special bond would develop between father and son.

Benáncio's instincts warned him, though, that it was safer to be reticent in his relationship with his father. For he knew that between men, and especially between a father and son, there always existed some degree of distance. Still, he truly suspected that the old man's feelings about his son had changed. And he wondered whether their ties were strengthened by being away from home in this foreign land. That must have played a role, he felt, just as well as his own stoicism in the *desenraíze*. He became determined, although guardedly so, to venture beyond the well-set distance his father had required of all of his sons. And so, that night, he resolved to attempt to engage his father in a conversation.

Preparing for night, each man searched out his own comfortable niche in the clearing in which to settle. The ritual reminded Benáncio of his dog, Bigótes (so named because of his long whiskers) surveying his lair, sniffing it out just one last time for self-assurance, and then dancing around this way and then circling back around on top of the spot the other way, feeling out for the precise characteristics of the spot in which he had last slept to find the precise contour in which to lie down. He seemed to want to lay down in the precise place which had given him such pleasure the previous occasion. Bigótes' eyebrows would twitch like an old man's gray untrimmed eyebrows as he appeared to recollect, Now, *did I have my head facing this a-way last time or that a-way?* before he would finally curl up, take a deep sigh, and fall asleep. *Humans are no different,* Benáncio thought, *Just creatures of habit, feeling out for the right hardness or softness of the pillow and bulge in the mattress.*

Benáncio selected a grassy spot on an incline, spread the tarp, and placed their travel bags as pillows. At their feet, a small campfire sparred with the breeze, feeding on the *huisáche* firewood. As night settled around them, the musings of the other men lessened. Benáncio summoned enough courage to talk to his father. "Papa, are we earning a lot of money here?" It was a question Benáncio had been anxiously wanting to ask since their first day at the *desenaraize.* Don Gonzálo smiled.

"Yes, *mi 'ijo.* This kind of money, you would never earn in Mexico." Don Gonzálo then asked in a low voice so that workers nearby could not overhear, "How would you like to live in the city, Benáncio?"

"*Si.*" Benáncio gave his father a smile of approval. "Are we going to be rich when we go back, Papa?"

Don Gonzálo turned to him in a serious mood, and Benáncio knew that he may have tread too far. "Not rich!" came back the gruff voice. "You never want to be rich in this world. The rich get rich by their cruelty to others. But we are going to have enough money to buy a small piece of land in the city. Just you watch."

Benáncio had always enjoyed his father's stories about the city, which the old man would occasionally share with the boys. As night fell on the *ejído,* Mercédes would work up the meal at the hearth. Smoke from the kerosene lamp scented the home with its distinctive essence. Dinner was eaten under the light of the glass lamp which dangled from the center beam of the thatched roof. The older boys would join the old man at the table. Benáncio would find the old wheelchair, which had been a fixture in the home since he could recall, and eat off a plate on newspaper on his lap. After these meals, Benáncio could listen in on Don Gonzálo's colorful tales. This was the picture that now formed in Benáncio's mind.

"There are schools in the city," Don Gonzálo promised, "where the children wear uniforms to class. The Mexican Revolution has made those things possible," he proclaimed. "In cities, there are things to buy—boots, shirts, hats—and there are restaurants where you sit at a table and people actually wait on you. For recreation, there are carnivals and *fiéstas.* And the girls! Ah, the girls. In a city, there are all kinds of girls—light-skinned girls *[Güerítas]* and dark-skinned girls *[morenítas]. Llenítas o flaquítas, como te gusten* (Chubby or thin, take your pick).

"Benáncio, do you know how to tell if a girl likes you?" Lying on his back, the old man was staring straight up into the night sky. He took a long drag on his cigarette. Benáncio turned to his father with a surprised look on his face. Back home, his older brothers often spoke about the girls they preferred, but his father had never discussed women with any of them.

"No, Papa, I don't."

"*Pués,* first, you never stare at a girl."

"Never? Why, Papa?"

Don Gonzálo sighed, "Because she's going to think you're *sonso* [stupid]. You don't want her to think you're *sonso*, do you?

"No, Papa."

"When you go to the *plaza* [public square or small park] steal a quick look at the girl you like the first time she sees you. But be discrete. *M'entiéndes?*" (Do you understand me?) Benáncio imagined his father's wink.

"What if she doesn't even return the look?"

"*Pués,* if she doesn't even notice you, don't waste your time, *mi ijo.*" The old man's eyes glistened in the moonlight. "But, if she does once or twice look in your direction, *agárrate papasíto* [grab on for the ride], that's your signal! You should then walk around the plaza in the opposite direction to her. Then, when you meet up in the next turnaround, introduce yourself."

A pensive smile formed on Benáncio's face, and for a second, his thoughts turned to the girls from the *ejído*, and he wondered to which one of them he might be attracted. Something in his father's unusual look earlier had seemed to convey an unspoken pride. Or was it that the old man was sincerely offering him fatherly advice? Benáncio sensed it and smiled.

Pulling the large *serápe* up to his chin to insulate himself from the chilly night, Benáncio tried to clear his throat. The last few days, the weather had turned cooler, and meant that Benáncio's nose would clog up, forcing him to breathe through his mouth. In the sky above, Orion had earlier begun its trek across the night sky at the east and now seemed to have exploded and covered most of the sky. Benáncio could make out three large stars behind the bare branches of a large ash which had been spared from the pickaxes.

Between them, Don Gonzálo secured the leather pouch in which he kept the money they were earning in the *desenraíze* and continued to share innocent strategies with Benáncio about girl-chasing and how the prettiest girls came from Caderéyta.

"Is that the way you and Mama met, Papa? At the plaza?"

"No *mi'ijo*, your mother and I . . ." The old man paused and sighed for what seemed to Benáncio several minutes but was only a few seconds. "Your mother and I met under different circumstances. *A dormír*" (To sleep)!

As the field hands searched for space in which to squat and have their lunch the following day, one of the Mexican *mayordómos* approached the crew that Don Gonzálo and Benáncio had been assigned to. "Today is the last day of work for you. *Mañana se me van*" (Tomorrow you will leave). The *mayordomo* chewed on a cigar stub. He reached into his pocket and retrieved a wad of dollar bills and handed each of the men some of them. Don Gonzálo's face wrinkled, and Benáncio knew his father was wrestling with how to react.

"Ni las gracias se dan aquí" (Not even thanks are appropriate here)? Don Gonzálo complained.

"Here, we *pay* you for your work," the cigar smoker quipped, staring over his spectacles. "You're the ones that should give us thanks," he bore into Don Gonzálo. Benáncio felt his skin taut with contempt. Benáncio saw the muscles in Don Gonzálo's neck and his arms flex as the anger grew within him. Benáncio watched as the *mayordomo* taunted his father. He knew this was a standoff.

He was grateful when Don Gonzálo edged back and announced, "*M'ijo*, at first light, we leave for Mexico."

15

The Murder of Don Gonzálo

REFRESHED, BENÁNCIO MADE HIS WAY back up to the canal bank. He thought about Manda. *Why hadn't a woman at her age married?* She was attractive. So she must have had her share of proposals. It must be that she was living a lifestyle more comfortable than most women in the village of San Felípe. Women like her, he surmised, often saved themselves for a rich man. As he neared Praxédis' house, he heard the barks of two dogs and then saw them come up the slope of the canal, their noses high in the air. Praxédis shared his one-room house with his wife, Esperanza, and two thin, dark boys, his sons, Lazaro and Gregorio. The two boys reminded Benáncio of a young Praxédis, a boyhood friend to whom he was now indebted for providing him temporary shelter.

He removed the Stetson hat and toweled the sweat off the hat band again cautiously, as he figured how to deal with the dogs, which were now on their approach toward him.

Surrounded by a *mesquite* corral to keep in the horses, the one milk cow, and the goats, the house had remained unchanged since Benáncio's stay there some twenty years earlier. Back then, his mentor's, Pete's, dogs had been raised in a small fenced area with baby goats, to imprint with them. This had made them loyal defenders of the goat herd and they would defend the herd to their deaths. Benáncio hoped that Prajeris' dogs had gotten used to his scent and would back off as soon as they caught a whiff of him. He was right. The dogs recognized his scent and dropped their ears, swaying their tails in a friendly welcome.

It smelled of farm animals behind the corral gate. Strands of barbed wire held up by mesquite boughs served as a gate and expanded like the bellows of an accordion. A cow and two goats rushed up to the gate to meet him. The cow lost interest. The goats followed him all the way to the door, their aging udders undulating from side to side. Innocent, yet inquisitive, their eyes searched his for compassion, and their sniffling nostrils expanded in search of that whiff of corn *tortíllas*. Benáncio tightened his grip on the white butcher paper package and called out for Praxédis.

Benáncio recalled the circumstances under which he and the man he would come to know as "Uncle Pete" had met.

A northern wind blew in the night of the last day he and Don Gonzálo had spent at the *desenraíze*. Rather than wait until the following morning to leave for Mexico, Don Gonzálo decided that starting on the trip immediately made more sense. "Walking will keep us warmer than sitting in the cold all night," the old man judged. During the night, the two made their way southward toward the Rio Grande.

By dusk, the two had left the *desenraíze* behind. A full moon lit their path as Benáncio followed the tall dark figure of his father.

Several hours were lost when Don Gonzálo guessed on the wrong path. But by dawn the pair discovered a well-worn cattle *brecha* (path) through the thick brush. They were certain this led south to the river's edge. After several hours, the old man set his sight on the glow of a distant campfire. In a clearing by the river, two cargo wagons and a 1922 Model T had been circled next to a *cochéra* (a small cover). Shuffling of cards and the loud banter of men sounded like a card game continuing from the previous evening.

Three men huddled around the windbreaker made of thin corrugated metal sheets hastily nailed to produce a cover at one of the corners of the *cochéra*. The men sat at the makeshift card game table, which consisted of a flat board on an overturned rusty wash tub. Each was well covered with a thick woolen coat. Two of them shared a green woolen U.S. Army bedspread over their laps. From the high bank, Benáncio peered down to the beach that lay across the river. A tall weeping willow swayed serenely as the north wind blew over the tallest of the branches.

"Good morning, friend!" one of the men shouted in a gruff smoker's voice — the oldest by his appearance. He shuffled the cards as he glanced over at Don Gonzálo, as if he had been expecting the pair. He wore a dusty cheap black fedora. Unlike the others, this man appeared to be better dressed and had a pen in his coat pocket. One of the other men, who wore a large black cowboy hat, placed his cards face-down on the table and walked past Benáncio without uttering a word. A third one, called "Chon," gave them an acknowledging nod of the head. At an ironic attempt at hospitality, the old man with the cards pointed to a greasy metal grill over some dying embers and offered the guests, "If there's anything left, you can have it." There were a few small pieces of meats burnt to a crisp and some flour tortíl-las that had curled up and hardened on the gril. Benáncio waited for word from Don Gonzálo to take food from the grill, but the go-ahead never came. Within earshot, the man who had gotten up re-lieved himself and belched.

Chon stared at Benáncio's head, pursing his lips as if about to in-quire about the cause of the bald spot on his head, but refrained. Be-náncio, self-consciously, ran his hand over his head. Under his sleeve, he felt the throbbing pain in his arm.

Don Gonzálo warmed his hands over the fire and told the man with the fedora, "We're looking for someone to cross us to the other side, Señores, do you know where we can cross?"

"Do you have any money?" the old man at the table inquired, dis-guising his interest by repositioning the cards in his hand. For a mo-ment, Benáncio thought he recognized the man in the fedora as one of the Mexican *mayordómos* at the *desenraíze*.

There had been something ominous in the way the question had been posed to Don Gonzálo, Benáncio surmised, and he felt the im-pulse to interrupt his father and say, "No, we don't have any money," but it was too late, and Don Gonzálo was answering, "Yes, I have some money. Do you know someone who can get us across?"

All the men at the table were at attention now, and Benáncio be-came uneasy, sensing a silent scheming among the men as they gave each other cautious, conspiratorial looks — like a pack of wolves co-ordinating their attack on an outnumbered prey. Don Gonzálo felt it, too, and Benáncio knew it because Don Gonzálo gazed at him discretely, edged back, and advised the group that he would prefer to continue down the river and look for a crossing.

"No, my friend, you don't need to do that." It almost sounded like an order. "Chon here, he has a canoe, just about half a mile away. You'll go get it, won't you, Chon?" The man with the pen was now definitely acting like a *patrón*. Chon got up from the table. He was a little man, smaller than Benáncio. As he passed by, Benáncio noticed Chon's features showed that he was a man who had had his share of violent scrapes. A scar ran across the right side of his face, begin-ning just above the middle of the forehead where a bottle, a knife, or some other sharp instrument had carved its mark and permanently removed the hair, the hair follicles, and a piece of the scalp. The scar continued down to the eye, which it had miraculously missed, and down over the cheek, curving toward the lip. It appeared to have healed without the benefit of any medical attention and gave the appearance of the baker's cut on the top of a French baguette. Chon looked filthy, and Benáncio knew Chon was lying when he agreed to go get the canoe.

"No, but thanks anyway," Don Gonzálo insisted, and no sooner had he finished that Chon came flying at Don Gonzálo with a flurry of punches to the face. The others joined in, and Don Gonzálo screamed at Benáncio in a voice that sounded of sheer fear and horror. *"Corre*! Benáncio, *corre"* (run, Benáncio, run)!

Benáncio never stopped running. Occasionally, he would look back over his shoulder to see if someone was chasing him. He ran wildly, crashing through the prickly brush. His boots sheltered his feet from the cactus needles, but his cotton pants and coat were no match for the brush. As he ran, the *huisaches* and mesquites whipped into him, letting their fury tear into his soft flesh. He felt the warm blood on his cheeks and tasted it. Chon's face imprinted in his brain, the face of a coward. And as he imagined the unimaginable — that his father was being killed or already dead, he moaned, "Oh no! Oh God, how can this be? How can this be happening to me . . . to Papa?"

At some point he felt no more physical pain. The fear that gripped him became his natural analgesic.

Benáncio could not tell how long he had run. He had run northward, away from the river. In the distance, he saw a raised levee and walked toward it in the hope that from that higher point, he could get his bearings. He felt a pain under his ribs and wondered whether it was from hunger. The last meal had been the prior afternoon. The levee was actually the bank of an irrigation canal. He drank until he ached and decided he would run no farther.

His thoughts turned homeward. *Why did we ever have to leave the ejído? For this?* Then came the guilt. *I should have stayed and defended my father.* Maybe all that the attackers wanted was the money, and once satisfied they would have allowed the pair to cross the river. But no. Surely, these men were the river robbers that everyone had warned them about, vampires who preyed on the migrants who crossed the river to find work in America. And besides, Papa had ordered him to run. Papa knew best.

Nighttime came, and Benáncio remained on the canal bank, shivering — not from the cold, but from utter fear. His eyes puffed up from the tears and fear and damage done by the prickly brush. He was certain that it was only a matter of time before he, too, would perish. And he welcomed it as he prayed, "Please, dear God, take care of Mama and my brothers . . ." Not a full day had passed since his father had shared warm thoughts with him.

———⟫⟪———

"Pete" had been what the manager of the irrigation company called him. But his saint's name was Pedro. It was Pete's job as canal rider for the Icarus Irrigation Company to ride up and down the canal banks to make sure the check valves along the bank were properly operating. His loyal mare, *la llegua coloráda* (the red mare), knew the routine so well that at each valve, she would edge closer to the bank so that Pete could get a good view of the flow into the valves without having to get off. At sixty-five, Pete rode straight in the saddle, the thick fingers of his left hand guiding the reins effortlessly.

"Ándale chulíta, vamonos" (Come on, cutie, let's go), Pete patted the mare, and she acknowledged his kind words by snorting and shaking her head. But the mare stalled, and her ears shifted forward and sideways as they searched out like radars trying to pinpoint the exact source of a faint sound. Pedro looked around cautiously. As Pedro flipped his cigarette butt into the canal, he saw Benáncio lying on the other side. He first noticed the young boy's blood-stained, tattered clothing and hands and face, which were splattered with the dried blood. He jumped into the canal and swam to the other side

16

Manda Marries the Wetback

"MANDA, MANDITA . . . *por favór*" (please, come now), Rebécca shuddered, "You can't marry that man! You just met him, for heaven's sake. *Hay Diocíto!* He's a wetback!"

Out of habit, Rebecca had a tendency to tap her breastbone whenever stressed. During her bout with tuberculosis ten years earlier, breathing had become difficult for her, and she had picked up the habit of tapping. Presently, that was the way Rebecca reminded her sisters that she wasn't particularly healthy.

Manda's jaw tightened. "I'm going to marry him, Rebecca. I've already asked him to marry me."

"*Oye nomás, Díos Mio* . . . Enriquéta! Enriquéta! Please bring me a chair. I may faint."

Enriquéta was at Rebécca's beck and call. She obliged, but her face seemed glowing with a sincere joy for Manda. A defiant Manda stood in front of Rebecca, her arms crossed.

Rebecca offered what Manda knew was Rebecca's perennial logic. "Manda, we're a team—you, Enriquéta, and me. You have a home here. You know that perfectly well. No man controls you. *Que le pasó a Enriquéta*" (What happened to Enriquéta)?

Manda turned to Queta, who wasn't about to listen to Rebecca's caustic complaint about her own marriage. Queta turned and walked away, her lips pursed into a strain.

"Exactly six months was the time it took Queta's young groom to return to his home—back to his mother," Rebecca carped, "but not before Enriquéta became pregnant with Nina. Need I say more?"

Whenever Rebecca was bothered, as she was on this day, she was also prone to swallow with great difficulty, as if her tongue were swollen. But she would never lose her temper. None of the sisters ever did. Even when angry, Manda knew never to cross that invisible line from which there might be no retreat. But she felt this was as good a time as any to say her piece, even if she risked crossing the invisible line. "No one controls you, Rebecca. And no man controls me," she told her. "I agree with you. But you, Rebécca, you do control me. You control my entire life. We are slaves to this store and to the *molíno*."

"Now wait a minute, *hermaníta* [little sister]. This store is our life. We work hard, especially you and Enriquéta. I've never complained about that. I know you both work harder than I. Of course, I haven't been well for years. But this store has given us a roof over our heads. There are many people in San Felípe who would kill to be in our position. You must know that!"

Manda began to roll her eyes. Then her Aunt Terésa's admonition prevailed. "A proper lady remains dispassionate, when facing great difficulty. Her expression should never reveal frailty or immaturity."

Manda wanted to make it known that she had made up her mind, that she hadn't walked over from the corn mill next door to ask Rebecca for her blessing, but to advise her that she was going to marry. After all, she was all of thirty-four.

"The store and the corn mill are precisely what I am fed up with!" Manda wished she could have taken back that remark as soon as she blurted it out. The store and the *molíno* had been their father's dream, and Rebecca had embraced it as her own. And Rebecca was right, after all. The store and the *molíno* were their lives.

Rebecca swallowed. An injured mood overtook her face.

"Rebecca," Manda began again apologetically, "the folks in the neighborhood are now getting around in cars, and they can shop for their groceries anywhere." Rebecca's left eye began to tear and her face began to reject Manda's every assertion. But Manda continued pleading, as if the entire matter was resolvable through mere logic. "They no longer need us. For the store to compete, we have to keep providing credit and you, in your condition, have to share in making grocery deliveries. We are losing money by insisting on operating the store. The corn mill's profits subsidize the cost of maintaining inventory at the store."

Rebecca's sight focused on Manda's eyes, and a painful frown grew on her face as she negated Manda's statements with the motions of her head. The older sister's maternal instincts usually prevailed, and she was not about to let Manda undertake a disastrous course. Except for those two years she'd spent at the tuberculosis hospital, Rebecca had run the businesses and supervised the household with a firm hand.

"You are wrong," Rebecca whispered, as if forcing back her rage. "You are so wrong."

Manda approached a few steps and raised her arms to her face emphatically. "Rebecca, the store's clientele has been almost exclusively *mojadítos*. You know that. Just yesterday, I was listening to the radio. Some congressman is proposing a law to repatriate all the people from Mexico who are here. All the men must leave or be taken away. Those men are the only customers who pay cash for what they buy. Sooner or later, the store is going to have to close."

Rebecca bent forward in front of the reciprocating fan and wiped her brow with the back of her hand. Her wrinkle lines were few and were well-powdered-up. Just then, a group of children interrupted the discussion, noisily coming in one end of the store, ordering some gum, and then rushing out of at other end, with Queta following their every move. "It's one o'clock," Rebecca instructed, and as tradition required, Queta and Manda closed the two doors to allow for the day's *siesta*.

When it was Rebecca's turn, her voice shrilled. "Manda, there are ten, maybe fifteen at most, households in North San Felípe that can boast a late-model car. We are one of those families. Besides," Rebecca complained, "unlike me and Queta, when have you, Manda, ever experienced what it is to labor in the cotton fields, and from that work to save enough to create a business—a business that has survived in San Felípe for close to twenty-five years?" Her voice trembled as she pleaded, "This store is the product of our father's, Queta's, and my sweat!"

"I know, Rebecca, but . . ." Manda swallowed, sniffed, and bowed her head in the same way she had done as a child dozens of times before her aunt Terésa, whenever she was brought forth to make amends for some infraction. "But this store will never give me children. I am thirty-four years old. I don't want to live the rest of my life torturing myself wondering what life would have been with children." A short distance away, Queta listened in, her hanky muffling her own sobs. Manda had been spending her nights drifting off to sleep while thinking of names for her children. "Two boys and two girls," she had told Queta. "That's all I can have. My Aunt Terésa once told me that women beyond the age of forty should not have children."

Years of resentment converged on Rebecca's face. *How long has it been now?* Rebécca had pondered the matter with Queta when she realized that Manda was spending time with Benáncio. "Remember, Queta? Papa taking us to the train station in Mexico where we waited for hours for the delayed train?"

Queta sighed. "I do remember. Imagine! It's only been nineteen years since we first met our baby sister." Shortly after Manda was born, their mother had died, and Manda had been returned to Saltíllo. The first fifteen years of her life, Manda had spent growing up in Saltíllo with her uncle and Aunt Terésa. Aunt Terésa was a very successful midwife in that once-Spanish colonial city, and their Uncle Placido was the rector at the renowned, private technical college, the Ataneo Flores Gomez. Letters from Saltíllo had often come in cute little envelopes with a printed return address, Rebecca recalled. Inside, the rector's letterhead even included a telephone number. How envious Rebecca had felt every time a letter arrived from Saltíllo. It would be a very proper letter, typewritten, with all the formal greetings and salutations.

When Manda wrote her sisters her letters fell into that same style. Occasionally, pictures of Manda would be included. In one, she sat on one of the benches at the park across the Saltíllo cathedral. In another, during some wedding, a pre-teen Manda posed as she walked down the red-carpeted, curvilinear steps of the Spanish Casino as she held onto the balustrade. In yet another, Manda sat facing the steering wheel of a Model-T. How Rebecca had resented her younger sister's lifestyle every time one of her letters arrived.

With Queta at a distance, feigning disinterest by dusting the colorful cloth sacks of flour stacked high, Rebecca forewarned Manda, "Don't forget these words, little sister. I will never repeat them to you ever again. But you will remember them, Mandita. Believe me, you will remember them. You are bound to suffer because of what you're doing. Mark my words. You are marrying a wetback who will marry you solely because it will keep him here in this country. And then, and remember this well, my little sister," she paused and even took her sight off Manda as if reconsidering what she was about to say and then turned back at Manda, "when he no longer needs you, he will desert you."

The Manor House at Lover's Lane

IF YOU WALKED SOUTH on the west bank of the Icarus Canal, you would eventually reach Lover's Lane. You could get there only by walking on the canal bank, for the narrow paved road that ran along the canal was gated. Lover's Lane was the well-manicured portion of the canal bank that had been landscaped with curving magnolia trees on whose trunks were carved the initials of hundreds of lovers. Next to the paved road was a high chain-link fence with signs attached every fifty feet or so which read "No Trespassing" or "Private Property." And, set back some four hundred feet from Lover's Lane was the manor house. Everyone credited the owner of the manor house with having created and covering the cost of maintaining Lover's Lane. No one knew who he was, but rumor had it that he was a powerful lawyer who had inherited thousands of acres of agricultural lands just south of San Felípe.

By the time Joaquín was old enough to walk the distance to Lover's Lane, only a few of the trees were left. A few limestone blocks that had lined the canal bank as a retaining wall were still visible here and there. It had been years since anyone had referred to the place as Lover's Lane.

Joaquín's nights often took him to the manor house, his dream inhabitance. Like a jigsaw puzzle which he was powerless to avoid, the dark existence which he felt there seemed to parallel and co-exist with the world of his waking hours. His appearances there were always as his younger self, and usually as an adolescent. Each evening, he fitted a new piece of the puzzle. So each night was a new revelation.

Legend had been that the husband had come home to Manor House to find his wife with another man and had shot her; waited for their daughter to return home from school, shot her as well; and then blown his brains out next to the swimming pool. The town's only lawyer had kept the estate open in hopes of selling the property. The surviving heirs had never been close enough to the family

to care about the inheritance, so the house remained empty and unkempt for several generations.

Nothing had stirred. Shaded on all sides by elderly ash and mature pecan trees, the manor house protected its secrets. Swaying gently in the crosswinds, several palm trees towered, like sentries, high
above the green canopy. From the public roadway, it was apparent
that the four white Mount Vernon columns that held up a flat curvilinear porch roof at the second-floor level had buckled and the porch
roof had detached from the house and torn from its grasp a small
Spanish-design false balcony that now dangled from a rusty reinforc-
ing steel bar. The cedar shake shingles on the two massive gables had
long ago lost their dexterity, and the South Texas sun had blistered
and fried-curled them. Sparrows had taken refuge in the spacious attic, using the spaces between shingles as entryways. A running Wis-
teria trim along the gables had long ago succumbed to mildew. Gloom
and gray had so overtaken the façade of the house that one tended to
overlook it unless carefully peering through the thick foliage and
making out the outline of its walls. The two-story structure had remained mysteriously still, silent, and undisturbed until Joaquín (in
his dream) had gained access through an attic window.

So completely shielded was the house that light penetrated only
through the space left by a slight parting of the thick dining room
curtain, the result of a single hook in the curtain rod having been left
unhooked. Only when the sun passed directly above, eluding the
shade trees and the palm trees, could light intrude into the house
through that small opening in the curtain.

Joaquín made his way throughout the cavernous first floor of the
house. Plastered ceilings at fifteen feet were sectioned off by false
wood beams. At the first opportunity, he raised the flap of the thick
curtain, and a swath of light revealed a mahogany dining room table
suitable to seat twenty.

The movement set off a whirlwind of dust motes, and Joaquín
moved away just in time to avoid breathing them in. In the dining
room, the long table remained formally set with flatware and china
in place for some dinner which Joaquín surmised had never occurred.
Through the years, the expensive needle-threaded table liner had
withered and paled, losing its dexterity, and its brittleness dissolved
in his fingers. A matching buffet still held the cut-glass salt and pepper shakers and a punch urn and cups on a stainless steel tray. Joaquín lifted a crystal tumbler, which left a hefty ring mark on the

dusty buffet. Like a burglar who wipes away his fingerprints to avoid being caught, he promptly returned the glass to its rightful place.

At his feet, Joaquín walked on fine dust, which had sifted into the home over the years and now felt to him as soft and velvety as corn starch. He stopped before the stairway and surveyed the dining room. He imagined that all of the accoutrements would have been withdrawn from safe storage exclusively for the most special of occasions, when the hostess would have wanted her guests to share her very best—and her very best would have brought on fond memories and nostalgia of times past, of weddings and birthdays and other solemn celebrations. But, like the dining table, the urn and the cups, too, had remained unused.

Joaquín had shared the dream with Bennie once, many years ago, when both were still in their early twenties and Joaquín came home from law school. Bennie was already married and offered him a bedroom for several days. Joaquín went to bed late after studying for his finals, and his dream (he had never referred to it as a nightmare) returned on that first night.

"And when I make it to the second story," Joaquín told Bennie, "there in the bedroom with walls dull and blank, is one solitary thing: a portrait of a blonde, but her eyes have been scratched out—or, rather, cut out as if to remove her identity. There's a stench . . . oh what a horrible stench!"

In Joaquín's dream, the unpleasant scent wafted around him. Bearable at first, the palpable stench of human decay finally settled around him as he stepped in front of the portrait. He took shallow sips of breath through narrowed lips as a trapped miner who knows the air is poisoned and in desperation hopes that, by not smelling the stench, he can overcome its lethal effect. But some of the stench was swept into his nostrils, and Joaquín felt his gut recoil in advance of ejecting whatever foul poisons the brain suspected were attempting to invade his body. Joaquín would sense his body shivering uncontrollably (and trembling in the bed was what had awakened Bennie that night).

"And on the floor below the picture is a doll—a bald one, mind you, as if someone has pulled out all her hair. But she seems to have been arranged just so, as if there is some connection between the doll and the picture. She's dressed! This doll is dressed in some home-made clothes . . . raggedy, you know. Then, coming from nowhere, I hear a girl's voice cry out for help," he continued. "I run down the stairs, and I see the kitchen door is open. And I fear that someone may be waiting outside for me, like it's a trap. But I take my chances. As I run toward the fence, the brush slashes my arms and face. And listen to this . . . it actually *hurts* me in my dream. I feel pain as I'm running. And then, I wake up."

Bennie was on the edge of his chair adjusting his glasses. "Man, you hardly took a breath telling me that story."

"That's because I know the dream so well," Joaquín had told him. "I was never inside that place, yet there seems to be this insistence in my dream that I return to the dream and to the house in that dream, that I somehow keep going back until I can get close enough to the portrait of the girl to figure out who she is. But every time I get close to it, I cut and run."

Not only did the Manor House come to occupy his nights like a never-ending movie, it was now occupying a good portion of his waking hours. The unidentifiable blonde, the bald doll, and house had combined into a daily preoccupation. *Is there some significance to it all?* He closed his eyes and tried to shake the sight: the incessant, zealous sound of flies, some hovering over the woman's corpse, awaiting their turn, while others with bodies too pregnant with flesh for prolonged flight congregate in every orifice, their neon turquoise backsides flashing in the sunlight.

PART III

18

Mexico Lindo y Querido/*Home Sweet Home*

"QUE PASÓ? WHY AREN'T YOU READY?" Benáncio's voice was calm but firm. He waited for Joaquín's answer. Bennie sat across the kitchen table from Joaquín. He had no shirt on and was wiping his bare chest of some pancake syrup. It was Saturday, and Benáncio had just finished spit-polishing his brown Stacy shoes and buffing his gray Stetson. Joaquín lay down the fork on his plate. His eyes pleaded with Manda to come to his aid.

"The boys don't want to go anymore, Bene." Manda bowed her head as she said it.

Benáncio gave Joaquín a look of disdain and curled his lips. Joaquín knew with his better judgment that he should keep quiet and weather the storm. Benáncio remained silent as he seemed to be considering his options. He turned to Bennie, who had kept his sight on his father throughout.

"*Y tú*, Bennie? Don't you want to go?" Benáncio's voice had lost its confidence. His tone faltered as if he were confirming a final act of betrayal.

Joaquín knew Bennie was far too naïve to understand the magnitude of the event that was taking place among them, and he prayed that Bennie would say "yes," that he would accompany his father, Benáncio, to Mexico on this Saturday morning as the boys had done every Saturday for as long as Joaquín could remember. *Say "yes," Bennie*, Joaquín prayed. *After all*, he concluded, *Bennie has always been Papa's go-to-guy. Right?* Joaquín prayed again. *Come on, Bennie, please do it for us. Aren't you the guy who Papa can always count on, regardless of the circumstances? He can always count on your smile and on your unflappable, agreeable nature. You are like the pup who awaits for a signal to show his master his unfettered loyalty, right, Bennie?* Joaquín glanced up at his father. The hurt was obvious on Benáncio's face.

But Bennie was not interested in joining Benáncio either. "Naw," he said while gulping down a portion of the pancake and giving Benáncio an innocent and precocious smile, which Joaquín felt on any other normal day would have been so appropriate, but not today. Today, the circumstances before them required Bennie to jump out of his chair and cheerfully tell his father he would be ready in a few minutes. That would have been it. Perhaps that would have left the door open. *Perhaps I should have volunteered to go with him*, Joaquín would often wonder. One more door seemed to have closed on that day.

"Pos, vayan mucho a la chingáda" (well, you can all go to hell), had been Benáncio's final farewell on that occasion.

It was all the little things of his life that Joaquín had forgotten. For years, he had recalled his life as a horizontal line, quite like a timetable on which significant events (his critical path) were marked in some bold way along the line and lesser events were marked in less bold ways. The lesser events had disappeared from memory. Like the autobiographies of victorious conquerors, the earlier part of his life seemed to have been relegated to nothingness; for in his mind, his earlier life had been a life full of small things, teensy-weensy, in-significant, non-historic, non-public sorts of things (like growing up and scraping your knee and getting a bloody nose), hurtful things he may have said or heard, gestures that at the time may have appeared to have been meaningless, those sorts of things that don't show up on resumes or acceptance speeches. His real existence had practically begun at the beginning of law school, and that was all that mattered, all that anybody cared about anyway. *"How did you get here?"* is all they ever wanted to know. In other words, *"Give me the short version of who you are now. What is your education? How cool is your job? Can you indi-rectly let me know how much you earn in a given year?"* Wasn't it all just a human's version of the lower species' smelling each other's rear ends? But he did not begrudge that way of thinking. That's the way it had been for the past twenty-five years. That had always been his goal. He had become what he dreamed he could become. So, why had all the little things suddenly begun to matter to him? And why were they growing in significance? The longing that grew was now for these personal nuggets, these shiny trinkets that were of no value to anyone but him.

"Pos vayan mucho a la chingáda" (Go f— — yourselves)!

Joaquín chuckled almost aloud as he was reminded of the occa-sion and was then struck with the painful thought that the more Be-náncio had withdrawn into his way of life, the more rejected he must have felt.

While Joaquín sat there hoping to retrieve his memories whole, he knew it would all be for naught. He relied, therefore, on drawing out scenes, scents, or emotions — the pieces of his life, like pieces of the puzzle that was him. It was tedious work. But this journey that he was about to undertake would provide him great insight and some answers. During his journey, he anticipated, he would have the benefit of being right there where it all happened. What his unaided mind alone could not recall, his scent would decipher, and his eyes would absorb and his touch would feel a place and time that once was. Joaquín could not bear to wait. He leaned back into the plane seat and shut his eyes. *You have not been this calm for a very long time, my friend,* he told himself. His visit would be a well-deserved vacation. That is what he had told Bennie. His life to this point? Moral. His debts? Minor and manageable. His regrets? None. *What else is there to life?* he asked himself. He had anticipated revisiting places he had visited as a teenager, and now, he would actually do it. He smiled. What are the chances the trip would bring him in contact with someone who might have been around at the same time? Was that possible after thirty-some years? He just could not wait to get back to the strawberry fields.

It was the only picture they had ever had of their father. Joaquín brought the small passport-sized black-and-white glossy of Benáncio closer to his face. Sis and Joaquín had rendered it lost many years before when Sis had wanted to duplicate it. Benáncio had come to the marriage with the clothes on his back and had left in same fashion. But for that picture and their thin memories, they had nothing of his existence.

Joaquín stared at his father's features there in black-and-white. Benáncio returned the probing stare, his neatly trimmed moustache barely clearing his upper lip. He was always very neat. Always! There was that secretive and apprehensive focus in his father's eyes, that Mediterranean stare that Joaquín had grown up with and so admired and unconsciously emulated. That stare brought on memories of his father's animated articulation: the cuts and slashes that he administered with his hands as he punctuated his sermons. He advocated. He condemned. A political evangelist, he never relented.

His father's stare had been such a part of their young lives that it would also register on their own faces and show up in their own photographs.

Joaquín turned his wrist and pushed his arm out of the shirtsleeve to reveal his watch. He would be arriving at the Houston airport within the hour. Momentarily, his thoughts turned to his cousin Nina.

"Cancer, Joaquín," she had whispered. "We all seem to carry it."

Joaquín canceled his trip for another week to attend Nina's funeral services. He closed his eyes again and fell asleep.

"Que Viva Mexico, lindo y querido" (Long live Mexico, wonderful and beloved).

In his memory flowed the music. The low bass strings of the *guitarrón* (large bass-type guitar) led in solemnly, and two strings followed. There were a guitar and two trumpets, a tenor's voice singing phrases which he had never paid much attention to or understood, except that part about *". . . if I should die, bring me back to Mexico . . ."*

> *Voz de la guitarra mía al despertár la mañana* (Voice of my guitar at wake of morning)
>
> *Quiere cantár Su alegría a mi tierra Mexicána* (wants to sing its joy to my Mexican land)
>
> *Yo le canto a sus volcánes* (I shall sing to its volcanos)
>
> *a sus pradéras y flores* (and to its valleys and flowers)
>
> *Que son como talismanes del amór de mis amóres* (which are like talismans of the love of my loves).
>
> *Mexico, lindo y querido, si muero lejos de ti* (Mexico, beautiful and beloved, if I should die far from you)
>
> *que digan que estoy dormído y que me traigan aquí* (tell them that I am asleep and tell them to bring me here)
>
> *que digan que estoy dormído y que me traigan aquí* (tell them that I am asleep and tell them to bring me here).

Joaquín recalled the irony of Benáncio's ambiguous love-hate, much like the singer's professed love. Benáncio embellished his own undy-

ing attachment to Mexico, to the *volcanes* and *flores,* but more obsessively so, like that of a son's unyielding love for a mother. And yet,
Benáncio could never discard his irrepressibly harsh criticism of
those who held dominion over his motherland. A mythical Mexico
lived in Benáncio's heart, a Mexico full of an adolescent's romantic illusions. Oh, how the smells and sights from across the border must
have remained enticing to his father. Joaquín knew this as an adolescent, although he could not put those thoughts into words at the time.

Although Mexico remained alluring to his father's thoughts, rejuvenating nostalgic memories, the rationality in him surely knew he
could never return. Manda expressed that. "Like so many other
Mexicans in America," she told Joaquín, "your father is a calculat-
ing man and has resolved that on balance he'd rather dodge the
blows here in America." She had a way with the Spanish language,
painting elaborate pictures with her words to describe the Mexico to
which the homesick Benáncio would never return. "The poor who
have left Mexico," a group she never presumed herself to be in, "will
never blame their mother country. But deep down inside, their
Mexico is a skeleton, stripped bare by vultures who tore off the tendrils and the tendons. That Mexico's soft joints were chewed and de-
formed by the teeth bites of small mammals, its bones sucked dry of
marrow by maggots and beetles and aphids. What is left for the
poor? It is clear that there is nothing left for your father back there.
Absolutely nothing."

If anyone was proud of his Mexican heritage to a fault, it was his
father. So why should Benáncio have felt any guilt about that? Yet,
Manda was so assured that in his heart, Benáncio had betrayed Mexico and abandoned his people. "He might have slightly crept away
from where he feels he belongs," she said. "He admits this to himself
but tries to convince himself he has never ever fully let go, ever fear-
ful that the centrifugal force may weaken and send him out into
outer space, into a no-man's land."

Manda feigned naïveté, which helped her keep the peace. She acknowledged Benáncio's sermons with her nods and heard his endless
complaints patiently as a silent counselor until Benáncio expelled all
his toxins, for the time being. Benáncio never sought counsel. Joaquín knew his mother knew Benáncio better than he would ever
know himself. She confidentially shared this with Joaquín. She explained that his father must remain close to the Mexican border so

he could sense it, so that he could measure its distance securely with his outstretched arm, like the diver who keeps reaching back for a hand-hold.

Joaquín recalled his mother's colorful illustrations. "He thus fancies himself that he has not abandoned his beloved Mexico; that he has not yet sold his soul to the *Americános*, but that he remains Mexico's loyal son."

———※———

How many others out there in America are like Papa? Joaquín wondered as a boy. *Do their children do as we? Saturdays, we dress up and head for Mexico, across the river. We get all spiffed up there—a haircut, a shoe-shine, and a stroll around the plaza—in that order.* It was a certain familiarity—an inherited memory—that seemed to welcome and embrace Benáncio.

Joaquín stirred in his half-sleep, lullabyed by the drone of the plane's engines.

It was a remarkable transformation. Only on Saturdays was Benáncio ever in a good mood, and Joaquín could sense it. On Saturdays, Benáncio was a different person altogether. These were the only occasions when his father could put up with the boys and their childish antics. He smiled from under his Stetson felt hat, which he had brushed, leaving not a scratch or a dent on it. His Stacy shoes sparkled in the light. He could even tell a rare joke or two, his moustache twitched, and coins jingled in his pocket. *We're heading to Mexico, to my turf.*

Benáncio took the point. His stride was tall, firm, and confident. He prided himself in knowing the exchange rate, which changed with every streetwise entrepreneur that offered his wares to the threesome. He advised caution with the street hockers in overflowing bazaars. *"Que no te hagan pendéjo"* (Don't let them rip you off), he snarled at the boys, but never took the time to explain what it meant to be made a fool of, which confirmed to Joaquín that by the end of the day, someone would have taken advantage of them because of their defectiveness. And Benáncio would be embarrassed because, yet again, his sons would have failed to measure up.

No one ripped Benáncio off—at least not there! At Mexican immigration, he generously dropped a couple of *pesos* with the male desk clerk, who discretely slid them into the middle drawer of the desk. Joaquín and Bennie traded furtive glances. *Is this charity, a tip, or a bribe?* Their father nodded his head at them, as if to say, *"Miren, hací se hace pendéjos."* The boys responded as nervous foreign tourists on their first European trip.

Minutes later, they began the uphill climb to the center of town. Chaos and disorder ruled the day. Up to the *plaza* they hiked, across streets that didn't quite intersect at right angles, across streets at odds with each other; here a narrow catwalk, there a wide thorough-fare where every driver knew it was every man for himself.

"This is where all the crooks are," Benáncio reminded them, point-ing to the government palace. Joaquín looked at Bennie, and Bennie returned the look which meant, *"Gosh, as if we would forget since our last visit."*

"It's a government palace?" Bennie complained as they walked by the large office building, a cement block and concrete box, rectangu-lar and efficient, bulking up against the narrow sidewalk where it pompously crowded and shoved each passerby into the street. The boys had to take special care because the sidewalk was cracked and uneven. Telephone poles and guy wires had been deliberately placed in the pedestrians' way.

Other obstructions projected from and protruded through the walls along the sidewalk — an open window that swiveled out at head level and a barefoot Indian woman who sat begging on the narrow path, encroaching on the pedestrians' path. The barefoot Indian beg-gar woman huddled up against the stucco wall. A smudged dark face peered up from under thick black hair with the same texture of the broom corn sticking out of the wicker container next to her. She begged at Joaquín, *"Una caridad, por favór"* (Some charity, please).

"Here," Benáncio turned and handed Joaquín a dime. "Give that woman a dime."

"You're going to give her a dime?" Joaquín protested. "Why don't I keep the dime?"

"Because you don't need a dime!"

"But I do need a dime," Joaquín pleaded with a dismayed look on his face. He turned to Bennie as if there were something his brother could do, but Bennie deferred. "I need a dime," he begged at Benán-cio, his voice cracking. "I don't have a dime."

"Give her the goddamn dime, will you!"

Joaquín's injured eyes turned one more time to his father, as if imploring, *"I, too, need your love. I, too, need your charity, Papa."* Benáncio nodded his disappointment at Joaquín, as if he had been tested and failed miserably.

The woman raised her hand in supplication. An infant peered up from under the black shawl across her belly. Joaquín swallowed and dropped the dime on the woman's shawl. For the first time, she peered at his eyes, and hers was an unsympathetic, detached look. Joaquín wondered if she expected more. She then lowered her sight, as if a profound thought has seized her. *"Gracias,"* she whispered without looking up and nodded her acknowledgment. That matter settled, the boys hustled in single file up a steep incline to the *plaza,* a fuming Joaquín behind Bennie.

Through the high, narrow, screenless windows of the government palace, the boys saw men in plain khaki uniforms.

Clickity clack, clackity clack echoed through the concrete caverns, emanating from antique black Royal manual typewriter keys, which were being punched by these government men. Loyal political party workers, they typed thirty-five words per minute with their two index fingers. These jobs were essential stepping-stones. Low-level *políticos,* these men bided their time there at the outer rim of the power sphere, where the gravitational pull weakened and often hurled its human satellites out into the dark wasteland. Benáncio explained all of this on endless occasions. He despised them all, his countrymen. *"Bola de lambiáches* (Bunch of brown-nosers)," he accused, his nose up in the air in Victorian fashion.

There was so little here that Benáncio seemed to appreciate. *So why do we have to come here?* Joaquín wondered often, as yet another sermon loomed ahead. Atop the hill was the *plaza,* which Benáncio explained separated the religious from the secular, the church from the government palace—a balancing act which created a neutral, demilitarized zone. At one end was the common *plaza* space—an open area framed with quarried rough *cantéra* limestone blocks, on which the public could find repose. Self-standing simple *cantéra* columns that bore no load and were either an incomplete part of some future structure or a geometrical sculpture surrounded the plaza. In the center, a small area was landscaped with anemically thin orange and lime trees whose trunks had been whitewashed to keep the bugs away. The trash of the day had been accumulating next to the trees.

"The church purports to offer refuge, sanctuary, consolation, and reassuring ritual. Souls of the faithful poor found tranquility here." *Is it sarcasm?* is Joaquín's first thought. Benáncio's words had become lyrical . . . "*Sanctuário . . . consolación . . . refúgio,*" and there was the expectation that finally, something sincerely moved Benáncio. But in Benáncio's next breath, Joaquín knew would come the letdown. Reality would seep in, and cynicism would raise its critical head. "'Disregard the temporal,' they are instructed by the Church," he chides Joaquín in an angered whisper, wagging his finger at him, "their reward awaits them in the hereafter—tomorrow . . . always *mañana.*" Benáncio half-turned to regard the city hall which they had just passed, laughing cynically at the joke which he probably intended to share with the boys. In between laughs, he jested, "And at the other end stands the government palace—a lab. A social experiment gone awry where mad scientists are eventually replaced—by even madder ones. Ha! Ha! Ha!"

The *Peluquería Modérna* (the Modern Barbershop) sat atop the hill as well, across the *plaza,* sandwiched between a well-supplied liquor store and a colorful fabric shop, whose wares the proprietor had brought out to the sidewalk for display.

"Welcome, Benáncio."

The short, stubby barber, whom Benáncio addressed as "*El Maéstro,*" grinned, as he clipped a customer's nose hairs. *El Maéstro's* smile displayed two gold teeth around the front upper left side of his mouth, which gave him the appearance of a cartoon character. His gold teeth seemed to betray *El Maéstro's* false camaraderie, like a warning beacon against false sincerity or lurking danger.

The barber's white smock was open at the chest, and there was a fourteen-karat gold chain with a gold *Peso Centenário* dangling from it. A thick, slick wad of wavy hair seemed rigidly in place on *El Maéstro's* head. But on the barber's bold chest, there was no hair. Neither was there any hair on his arms, nor any sign of beard growth.

As if intuition had begged him, Bennie turned to Joaquín. Joaquín cautiously raised his hand to his mouth as if to cover a yawn and then broke it at the wrist. His hand dropped listlessly, and he wiggled his fingers. *This guy looks like a sissy.* Bennie gave Joaquín a confirming nod.

"What's it been, a month?"

"*Sí,* about a month," Benáncio reminded *El Maéstro,* "and I brought these *ixquíntles* over fighting and screaming. These two happen to think that American barbershops are better than ours over here. What do you think, *Maéstro?*"

The barber didn't touch it.

How treacherous, Joaquín thought. *Papa is divulging the family spats to this Maéstro, sissy guy. And what are "ixquíntles"?*

Joaquín pushed Bennie into the barber chair first. As they waited in the barbershop, Benáncio headed catty-corner to the lottery booth across the street.

"Are you going to get your *cachítos,* Benáncio?" *El Maéstro* asked him.

"Yes," Benáncio answered, his smile full of confidence. Not able to afford a full national lottery ticket, Benáncio usually purchased percentages from several numbers. Disinterested, Joaquín slouched into an old sofa with a sagging middle.

"Even a *cachíto* can make you a millionaire," the barber mocked. The remark went right past Benáncio. The barber turned to Joaquín, attempting to make conversation with him. "The lottery requires so little investment, yet the payoffs are potentially very huge." Joaquín glared back at the barber, a grimace on his face, gesturing, *"Who's talking to you? Butt out, mister!"*

When Benáncio returned from the lottery booth, *El Maéstro* turned to Joaquín and struck up a familiar chord. "You know . . . ," the maéstro formed a confirming gesture with his mouth and nodded, "your father hates the church and the priests." *El Maéstro* was ostensibly addressing Joaquín but actually prying at Benáncio's ego, coaxing him into the political discourse, which Benáncio was famously known for in the barbershop.

"And the government as well," Benáncio added from his seat by the large picture window in the shop. His face took on his typical serious and cynical mood. A waiting customer took a brief, meek peek out at Benáncio from behind his newspaper, as if mildly distracted, and then just as quickly dissimulated.

"Benáncio, did you hear about the apparition of the Virgin in the knot of a mesquite tree?"

"I did." Benáncio's face was incapable of holding anything back. On this occasion, his face showed sarcasm as he chuckled.

"That's the Catholic faith!" he mocked. "Always looking for signs, always looking for evidence, and finding it in tree knots, in the formation of clouds, and even on a *tortílla.*"

Joaquín remained silent. He had heard it all before, of course. He chose to focus on the *plaza* across the street. Teens promenaded counterclockwise around the large kiosk in the *plaza* center.

Benáncio asked rhetorically, but directing his complaints to the barber, "What have all of these *cabrónes políticos* brought to the Mexican people? Nothing! Nothing but poverty and treachery."

"Well," the barber began to answer with a polite note of disagreement in his voice as he stopped his work to make a point, "you must admit, Benáncio, that the Revolution did bring music and culture, a national university, and the mural art genre."

Benáncio's response was a mere nasal "he'h" followed by a brief pause as he considered "the mural genre" that the barber spoke of. "The mural art? The so-called people's art!" Benáncio huffed his revulsion. "Like the Revolution and its *corridos* [ballads], that 'art genre' has now become an empty political slogan, my friend." Benáncio motioned his contempt, waving his arm to indicate *"Good riddance."* An overly pious look then overcame him. "The ballads no longer call us to revolution," he proclaimed to the invisible masses that he often addressed. "They've become homages to slimy politicians and glorified criminals, and nothing more."

Benáncio took off his hat and used it to fan himself before continuing his sermon. "For me, Cardenas has been the greatest president Mexico has ever had, maybe will ever have." He paused to gather his thoughts. "Under Cardenas, men became free thinkers. Under Cardenas, we could develop morals based on human needs and human virtue and not on Catholic fear, shame, and guilt." *Mexico Lindo y Querido si muero lejos de ti.* Cardenas had been gone for thirty-nine years as of that year, 1961. But for Benáncio, Cardenas lived on.

El Maéstro delighted in Benáncio's contentious discourse as some sort of amusement. He signaled that Joaquín was next on the barber's chair.

Benáncio inspected Bennie's haircut much too seriously, but eventually nodded his approval. Bennie couldn't have cared less, and Joaquín said to himself, *Let's get on with it! It's a damn flattop!* Benáncio returned to his chair and picked up the Mexican newspaper. Joaquín's face showed his disdain. He hated it all — the politics, the talcum powder, the obnoxious, sweet-smelling hair tonic, and the smelly Mexican cigarettes.

"I didn't want any hair tonic," Joaquín screamed at the barber.

Patiently, the barber answered, "You can remove it when you get home."

Patience aside, Joaquín fumed at *El Maéstro's* insensitivity.

"Mexico could have been the greatest nation in the world had it not been for Don Porfirio," Benáncio preached as he unfolded the Mexican newspaper and began to scan. Mexico could have been great, but it was doomed, according to Benáncio. Don Porfirio Diaz had abandoned the presidency in 1908. To this day, Porfirio Diaz has been reviled and revered by Mexicans, depending on which side their bread is buttered.

At 32,000 feet, the captain allowed the jet to cruise on automatic pilot in a direct path to Chicago. Aided by the humming rhythm of the plane engines, Joaquín promptly fell into a comfortable snooze. From the aisle, an animated male flight attendant in a white, short-sleeved shirt and light blue vest distributed cellophane-wrapped cold ham and cheese sandwiches. He paused, looked in Joaquín's direction, and made a comical sad face. He then continued with his duties.

Every Saturday, Benáncio straddled the *plaza.* Round and round he swirled on the carousel, joining his countrymen in this ritual, Joaquín imagined, crowding into the small, demilitarized space in the *plaza,* the zone between the church and the government palace, which over time kept getting smaller and smaller. Even as he cursed this place, the keeper of memories, Benáncio must have been searching for answers there. *The answers must be here! Somewhere, but only here!* He had to find solace in the familiar. Once atop the hill, did he rationalize to himself that he continued to be a Mexican? Did he long to return, and did he promise that one day, he would return? He must have, for how could he explain that he had abandoned his beloved Mexico and voluntarily exiled himself.

Nothing was lost on Joaquín. As on many other Saturdays, the boys had been brought to Mexico, to Benáncio's nostalgic Ganges, to soak in its purifying waters and to take in the sounds and the smells and the spirits. The breath had to be taken deeply to hold them until the next time. This ritual was intended to bind son to father and father to tribe. It was the morality of custom, affinity, and a reconfirmation of Benáncio's own communion.

Joaquín refused the baptismal bath. *We're not Mexicans! Never have been and never will be! But what are we?* Joaquín often wondered. *Aren't we Americans?* he asked himself. *Yes,* he answered. *We are the hated pochos [foreign-born Mexicans] who live on the other side and speak a strange tongue that only we understand. They mock our Spanish—the Texas cross-*

breed, Tex-Mex. *We are both lesser beings as violators of the unwritten code and yet, lucky Américáno sons of bitches, by virtue of the accident of our birth. Our Mexican cousins tell us as much. Yes, we are Americans. But where's our silver spoon?* he queries.

As Joaquín followed his father around the *plaza* and eventually into the bazaar, his eyes surveyed peripherally, intensely aware of every pair of eyes that suspected or hated or envied. But their eyes never met his. As if in a funeral procession, Joaquín did not wish to delve into the hate-pain.

Who are they? he asks. *Who are we? Does Papa suspect or hate or envy us as well?*

They continued deeper into town, into the belly and the bowels, far away from the safe and secure glass counters and silver crafts of the tourist traps, Benáncio always in the lead. Around him swirled the scents of raw meats and nude chickens, which dangled by the neck from nooses, their thin, limp legs stretching out from wrinkled skins the color of lead-poisoned Gion geishas. Pungently sweet and sour, foreign and almost repugnant, the smells reminded Joaquín of the putrid Mexican cigarettes his grandma used to smoke. He could never help being somewhat repulsed. But why? As hard as he tried, he seemed incapable of fulfilling for his father even a simple obligatory gesture of gratitude. Why could he not embrace what his father embraced?

The captain calmly blared out the expected temperature at Chicago and the speed of the jet. Joaquín stirred in response but remained asleep. As his dream progressed, the jittery shifting of his eyeballs was noticeable through his thin eyelids. *Where is home for us?* Joaquín wondered. *What are we?* He could not help but believe that he was one of the lucky ones—the son of a wetback who traded in his Mexican heritage for a shot (just a shot) at *up north*. Yet, other thoughts were never far, and these were the ones that choked and suffocated him, pulling him into the still and deep waters. Would he forever be portrayed as one of the barefoot child entrepreneurs, the men-children who hock Chiclets and garlic cloves along dusty roads in Mexican border towns or the seagull-children who perch on the piers at Cabo San Lucas and greet the *Américáno* tourists, bidding down the price of their inventory and their labor, bidding against each other for a few *pesos? Why has it always been so important to me what the Américános think of me?*

Joaquín begged Benáncio, "Can we go home now, Papa?" Benáncio tried to swallow his disappointment, but it still showed. It - remained in Benáncio's eyes, in his squints, in the mashing of teeth and in the thick lump that bulged in his throat.

And so, they returned to America, to the here and now. To the land of "Don't touch . . . stay out . . . keep quiet . . . fragile . . . flammable . . . we reserve the right to say no to anyone . . . no Spanish allowed." *It sure is good to be back home,* he imagined. *Darn good!*

Hijos de las Hurácas/Sons of the Grackles

"WHY IS IT SO HARD FOR PAPA to understand that we wanna have our own haircuts?" Joaquín whimpered.

Joaquín and Bennie were making their way to school—tardy this time—through the narrow passageway between the canyon-high south white stucco wall of the *Teatro Riálto* and Tino's Pool Hall next door. It was so narrow that only the slimmest of kids could take this shortcut. The early morning fog was especially thick this morning, so they had to be careful not to step on the shards of broken beer bottles or the turd mines strategically placed in their path by the kids of the bar maids that lived in the rented shanties along the alley.

Bennie shrugged his shoulders noncommittedly. Often, his loyalties seemed divided between his father Benáncio and his brother Joaquín.

Joaquín ran his hands over his head for assurance that he still had a flattop and pressed his eyeballs through his eyelids as if he had just awoken from a nightmare. At school, everyone could tell whether a haircut was the product of the downtown barbers or the crude hacking of a kitchen butcher.

Joaquín's eyes were red, as he spewed his anger. "But why should Papa care? He wears a hat, except to sleep. No one ever sees his hair. But even if they did, who cares? No one at that age cares about how they look, much less about their haircut. And why does he have to wear that hat all the time? Why does he have to wear a moustache? I hate it!"

On television, no one had a moustache, except maybe the bad guys. No one on television wore the type of hat Benáncio wore. "Papa always gets his haircut at a barbershop, across the river, in Mexico. So, maybe he does care about *his* haircut," Joaquín posited. "It's *our* haircuts that don't concern him."

Porcupine quills grew out of their heads—a black thicket of dense and tensely strung strands that stuck out rigidly once chopped. Their hair deserved professional help, Joaquín felt. Bennie remained silent

as he followed behind, making sure he didn't step on Joaquín's shoes
or the turds. Joaquín hated it when Bennie stepped on his shoe heel,
especially when it made his shoe come off.

"The trimmer is for the short hair only, Papa," Joaquín had pleaded
quietly the day before, only to receive no response from his father.
"The barbers just use it on the back of the neck, usually. I've seen it,"
he insisted desperately. And there was silence still.

A light chill had blown in through the window screen. Joaquín sat
by the open window, a worn-thin, discolored towel around his neck.
It was Sunday in March. From the chinaberry tree came the competing lyrics of two mockingbirds, like two blues guitarists, each intro-
ducing a new riff at his turn, challenging the other for its rejoinder.

Joaquín's sobbing in the bedroom had drawn Bennie in from the
kitchen. Bennie peered around the corner, crouching, slithering almost, along the floor, to avoid being seen by Benáncio.

Still in his underwear (for it was Benáncio's delight to read the
Mexican Sunday newspaper in his boxer shorts), Benáncio was giving Bennie his back, crouching over Joaquín. On top, Benáncio wore
a half-eaten-by-silverfish sleeveless ribbed undershirt. In his left
hand, he clasped and steadied Joaquín's head in an eagle-like vise-
grip. Manda's thick black-framed, *I Love Lucy* eyeglasses dangled
from his nose as he attempted to focus on Joaquín's head. The much-
feared stainless-steel manual hair clipper was clutched in his right
hand.

"Why can't we go to the barbershop, just this once?"

"You think money grows on trees?" This was Benáncio's response
to every request, regardless of how large or small. It always had to
do with money growing on trees, or rather, not growing on trees.

"No, it doesn't grow on trees, Papa, but I'll work for it. I'll pay you
back."

"*Habér* [now], keep still, or I'm going to clip your scalp like I did
last time" *(Te voy a trasquilár)*.

"No, don't clip it. I'll be quiet."

Joaquín stared right through Bennie, anguishing desperately over
the sheep-shearing he was been subjected to. Tears and sobs anticipated the ridicule that would certainly follow for days (or perhaps
even weeks) at the Mexican elementary school.

Bennie nodded agreeably as he walked behind Joaquín through
the dark, narrow crevice created by the two buildings. The stench of

human excrement and urine was unbearable. He pinched his nose.

Barbers used the trimmer to trim the soft peach fuzz that grew in the back, just above the neck line. But Joaquín's pleas had gone unheeded. In Benáncio's hands, the trimmer was a pair of shears, and the boys' heads were overgrown wool. Knowing he would be next, Bennie readied for his father's shearing. He anticipated the cold steel and the coarse blades that would nick the scalp when Benáncio would be unable to follow the contour of Bennie's skull.

"*Aaaay, aaaay,* you nicked me, Papa, you cut me!" Joaquín whimpered in self-pity.

"*Chingáda madre!* [Damn!] I told you to keep still, didn't I? Manda, get me some alcohol."

On Monday morning, before the boys left for school, they shared one last desperate look in the mirror, hoping against all hope that by the grace of some unknown but benevolent power, their hair had grown back overnight. Joaquín whimpered one more time.

They arrived at class intentionally late to avoid the early-morning jeers. By lunchtime, the taunts began,

"*Pelón Pelácas, Pelón Pelácas, Hijos de las Hurácas.*"

20

Diphtheria Soup Line

SUMMER WAS COMING TO AN END, and as was required by Texas law, all school children would be subjected to a battery of inoculations — diphtheria, polio, smallpox. The health clinic was free, and the shots were mandatory. Manda was recovering at the hospital; she had lost the baby. In her absence, Benáncio had been burdened with the responsibility to take the boys "to the shots," and Joaquín knew Benáncio dreaded the responsibility.

Doctor James had never complained about Manda's medical bills, which had over the past five years become his largest account receivable. It had begun with Bennie, a tough delivery, and then Manda got pregnant again in spite of Dr. James' advice. But Dr. James appreciated the small installment payments that Sis and Joaquín delivered every Friday. Like clockwork, Manda subtracted from her weekly pay what she figured her needs were for the week and turned over the rest to her creditors. Dr. James was always at the top of her list. Most times it was only two or three dollars, but the handsome tall German nurse with the frizzy blonde hair made it a point to always show her appreciation. She'd tell Sis in her strong German accent, "Honey, now you be sure to tell Manda that we appreciate these payments, okay?" Sis would nod timidly up at her.

"If she cannot pay, Dr. James will wait, okay? Be sure to tell her that." Sis would nod again, and then she'd turn, shoving Joaquín along in front of her as they made it out of the front door of the clinic.

Every one of Manda's kids had been delivered by Dr. James, even her last one, who had not survived the ordeal. Only if Manda could not herself diagnose one of her kids' aliments would she even think of spending money on doctors. She told her children that doctors were around to treat serious problems and not your run-of-the-mill complaints. For stomachaches and a touch of insomnia, she'd prepare some chamomile tea or ask Joaquín to tear off a few leaves from the ungrafted sour juice orange tree, which she'd boil into a tea and sweeten with a touch of honey. Rice water would settle a baby's stomach faster than any store-bought medication. There was no shortage of home remedies in Manda's arsenal.

Their arrival at the county free clinic was early, Benáncio having to get to work on time and the boys having to get to school. The line snaked down the sidewalk up to a single screen door. An aging sign in small black letters said, "Precinct One Health Clinic." Below it, someone had taken a piece of cardboard and written with a pen in barely noticeable lettering—"Form One Line Here." In the small reception area, the line proceeded orderly by sliding on three wooden benches, first this way, and then that way until it reached the receptionist's desk. Benáncio took off his work hat. The imprint of his hat on his head remained as evidence of his protective shield that, with a modest bow of the head, concealed his eyes from view. Joaquín knew without the hat Benáncio felt completely naked and the entire world could see—his small, round belly which he always kept tucked in, his pale and hairless legs, and the strangely bulbous second toe which extended out beyond the big one. He was vulnerable without that hat on his head. Benáncio's eyes were open windows to his soul. He reluctantly made his way behind Joaquín to the receptionist's U.S. Army surplus green metal desk.

He was well aware of his father's obsession with being early and first, if at all possible. Benáncio was always in some kind of hurry to get to somewhere—to work, to drop the kids off at school—to just do it and get out. Benáncio hated crowds. As he waited there in line, Joaquín sensed his father's impatience growing on him. On some nights, Joaquín could hardly get any sleep as his inner clock alarmed him every fifteen minutes—"Always be ready . . . on a moment's notice . . . never be late . . . Papa waits for no one . . . It's late! You've overslept! Papa left without you, just as he threatened!"

"Next!" came the order from the nurse at the receptionist's desk, and Joaquín felt his father's angry nudge from behind. In response, Joaquín and Benáncio made their way toward the receptionist's desk. The receptionist craned her neck, taking umbrage at the sight before her, and searched boringly for some invisible assistant, as if some logical explanation were due her. *God, is this necessary? Do I have to put up with this shit?* She made no eye contact with Joaquín or Benáncio. The receptionist must feel she is worthy of a greater station in life, Joaquín intuited. The woman withheld any acknowledgment. Joaquín took that to mean that an acknowledgment would only serve to give them the false impression that they were equals in her human realm. *But, as far as she's concerned, we aren't,* Joaquín felt. *Never will be, and it is her undeserved punishment to have to deal with our lot.*

Joaquín stepped up to the desk. Benáncio stood at his side but slightly behind Joaquín, hat in hand, which he held by the brim like the defendant about to be rebuked by an indignant judge. Focusing on a broad smiling President Ike, who hung there on the wall along with the Great Seal of the state of Texas behind the receptionist, Joaquín sensed Benáncio's will to make himself invisible. Benáncio's suspicion and wrath (and envy) for America were always exaggerated

"Name?" the receptionist blurted out, as if it were a spontaneous physical reaction directed at no one in particular. She still refused to look into either Joaquín's or Benáncio's eyes.

The receptionist was a middle-aged Mexican, and probably a mother, Joaquín figured. *A high school graduate? Very likely since she has this terrific office job. She can probably vote.* Benáncio couldn't vote; he wasn't a citizen. *With the money she earns at this job, she can certainly afford the poll tax. To top it all, she probably owes her job to the county commissioner or the county judge.* Benáncio had explained to Joaquín how these things worked.

The clerk had teased the hair she had left into a flip, which she kept aloof with that new beauty product called hairspray. Lacquer oozed out of a can and glued into permanency whatever concoction one could conjure up with a head of hair. Her protruding eyeballs — likely the early stage of Graves Disease — she had accentuated with broad strokes of eyeliner. Still bothered, she toyed with her thick wedding band with her thumb and little finger as she impatiently waited for Joaquín or Benáncio to respond.

Joaquín sensed that this woman relished the insatiable sense of power that vibrated from the top of her balding head down through her spine, innervating her body. Here he was, made to feel every bit like a beggar, and he knew his father felt every bit like a beggar too, having to face this government bureaucrat dispensing free inoculations to his children at the diphtheria soup line. Joaquín stared reprovingly at her and did not answer as he searched into the deep recesses of his mind, flipping the pages of his thin, elementary English dictionary for the words to rebuke her. But nothing came beyond total impotence. Nevertheless, his mind screamed at her, *"Chinga tu madre"* (screw you).

"Name!"

Joaquín's stare remained fixed and lost in the maze of the woman's eyes as his brain interpreted the scene for him: *The receptionist refuses to acknowledge our humanity. We are like pariahs, and she dare not risk one ounce of her superiority to lower the standards of this fine government office by speaking to Benáncio in Spanish. Castrate him . . . he deserves it.*

Benáncio shoved his fist into the small of Joaquín's back, which pulled Joaquín back into reality. "Oh, my name's Joaquín. This is my father. Here's his driver's license and our shot record card."

"Okay. You go in that door and get your shots," the receptionist said as she pointed to the narrow hallway that opened into a nurses' station. And to Benáncio, like directing a small child, she ordered, "You'll have to step back and find someplace to stand." Joaquín translated for his papa, who stepped to the back of the crowded reception area to wait. She stood up and ushered Joaquín into the nurses' station. Bennie followed. Her gait was that of a ponderous, bulbous jelly mass waddling its way through the narrow hallway. Behind her, Ike retained his mischievous smile.

Benáncio pulled the '52 green panel Ford truck into the elementary school driveway. Janitors were opening the doors to the classrooms and turning off the night lights. A single car was parked in the teachers' parking lot.

"Thanks, Papa," Joaquín told him.

There was no response from Benáncio, who kept his sights on the road. Joaquín took it as a sign that his father was still fuming from the episode at the clinic with the condescending receptionist.

The air turbulence around the airplane woke him, and Joaquín rubbed his eyes and contemplated portions of a dream from which he had just been torn.

So much of my father's skepticism was born from a constant worry of impending doom, he thought. For Benáncio, it had always seemed behind every unknown, there had to lurk danger. Joaquín could always sense that fear, anguish, and hostility that accompanied his father. *Where was the bravado, Papa?* had been Joaquín's silent challenge to his father on the occasion of the shots, for Benáncio could be so eloquent in his domain, sermonizing under the porch at Don Magín's corner grocery store where he held court, where Joaquín would imagine riding with his father and Pancho Villa's *dorados* and leading the Revolution to the heart of Mexico City. Oh, how proud Joaquín had felt when the men at Don Magín's would yield to his father's oratory! Yet, Benáncio had melted into defenselessness before the government bureaucrat at the diphtheria soup line.

Belínda Disappears

"I'VE BEEN THINKING ABOUT MICHIGAN a lot lately, Mama. Sometimes I think I've gotten over it." Dahlia's tone was barely audible. Out of habit rather than real sentiment, she sniffed. She took the cup from her mother's hand and poured coffee into it.

"No, that's not true. I have gotten over it. It's just that I can't get over the fact that we've never known what happened. I think if I just knew that Belínda was off living in some secure place with a family of her own, that'd be fine. I wouldn't need to see her. If she didn't want her children to know their grandmother, that's fine. I just wanna know that she's safe."

Dahlia's elderly mother stared out of the small clear window above the kitchen sink at nothing in particular and nodded. Dahlia returned to the bed, holding the cup of coffee with both hands, and began to recall the fateful day in Decatur.

We could have been mistaken for sisters, Dahlia surmised; she smiled as she sipped on the cup. Belínda did have her mother's clear face and lanky, shapely figure. Their eyelashes were long, and along with their eyebrows were an inviting sight. It was not unusual for other women to share with them their admiration for those eyelashes and eyebrows. But there were unique differences. Dahlia was a brunette; Belínda, almost completely blonde. While it was apparent that Dahlia was older, just how much older was difficult to discern. This wasn't something that Dahlia made up. Everyone assumed that Belínda was her younger sister, and legally she was.

"Mama, remember when Belínda would pose for her high school portraits she would become so beautiful and so charming? She was a natural. But how I dreaded those mornings when she left for school or when she returned with that persistent brooding painted on her face. Always!"

"*Díos Mío*, it was the same with your father." The old woman took a deep sigh as she continued, "I think your father was so preoccu-

pied with Belínda when she was a baby. He used to carry her around
and feed her and even change her, which most men would never do—
but he did. That was all fine, but when he became moody, I think he
may have passed that on to her. There was nothing we could do
about his depression."

"She would never lose that accent." Dahlia's complaint was not
serious, and she shrugged her shoulders as she thought about it. She
recalled that Belínda's English did not bear Dahlia's own strong accent, but it was colored with the same noticeable inflection in the
style of those Mexicans who did not learn English as a first language.
She was defiantly confident and intent on her ways and so easy to
tempt. Belínda was known to guzzle a few beers with the boys at
parties while most girls would be squeamish at such conduct. When
pot was still eyed with strict caution by most kids, Belínda had already had her hits. Dahlia had known it and covered it up. Belínda's
quick temper had been storied. As a middle school student, she had
broken a cheerleader's nose in a fight. That incident not only ended
her own cheerleading career, but she had also gained the rather dis-
graceful reputation of being *"la gringa loca."*

By reminiscing, Dahlia reestablished intimate ties with that day
in Decatur during that summer of '66. It had been that day which
had come to define her life. She tuned in to that Decatur morning
often, returning to the initial calm in the cabin the two shared with
Dahlia's parents somewhat in the manner that one tunes to a favorite
radio station for nostalgia and those regretful what-could-have-beens.

In her memory, it was an unexpected, but welcomed calm that
morning. At the entryway, covering the door opening to the ten-by-
ten wood shanty, she imagined an old homespun threadbare quilt,
pale from use. At one corner was a propane gas, two-burner stove,
and she could almost catch a whiff of the toasty scent of flour *tortíllas* billowing with hot air on the griddle. Her memory omitted most
of the day and quickly defaulted to the late afternoon. The late summer nights in Michigan arrived earlier these days. Shadows were
chilled and nights required blankets. Afternoons grew darker by the
minute. Whatever light remained filtered in through a small, four-
pane glass window at the rear of the hut. As the scene formed in her
mind, Dahlia closed her eyes and kneaded her forehead with three
fingers of both hands, the thumbs at the jaw under the ears.

Dahlia's memory veered. A few hundred feet away was the edge
of a vast strawberry field, and next to it was a thick wooded area.

Spreading across the top of a rise in the land, the green field sloped down toward the strawberry pickers' camp. The day before, as she recalled, Don Eduardo huddled his crew, and standing on the Ford running board, he announced, "On Sunday, my brother Armándo and I are taking our crews (or whatever remains of them) to Newton, Indiana." A few in the crowd nodded their consent. A tomato crop beckoned, he told those who cared.

"There'll be work through the first several frosts up to mid-October, perhaps into November, if the weather keeps. Those who wish to end the season here in Decatur, I just want to tell you how much my family and I appreciate you being part of our crew, and I wish you luck."

The indenture had lapsed for the crew. But Don Eduardo had asked everyone to join him in Newton and was prepared to tender a bonus. Dahlia's family had signed on for the few additional weeks of work.

That Friday morning, Dahlia had awakened to the voices of children playing football in the large open area by the huts, which they shared with Don Eduardo's trucks. But by late afternoon, a violent argument had erupted between Dahlia's father and Belínda.

Dahlia pictured herself on one side of the room. She squirmed uncomfortably on an Army cot, her head on the pillow on her knees. Next to her, with her arms crossed defiantly in front of her, Belínda stared straight into the eyes of her raging grandfather who stood shouting down at her.

"You wanna end up just like your mother? Be a good for nothing?" the old man shouted, pausing as if he genuinely expected Belínda to respond.

Behind Grandfather, Grandmother cowered in the corner of the small room, wringing her hands.

"Go ahead!" the old man taunted, staring at Belínda, his face contorted with scorn.

"You think I'm doing this for myself?" he screamed. "Well, think again, young lady. All of this is for you . . . because you're destroying your life." He hovered over Belínda, balancing himself with the help of his cane.

Grandfather's accusations were generally directed at Dahlia as well. Making use of every opportunity, he reminded Dahlia that she had turned out to be the greatest disappointment of his life. Each time he spoke, he wounded her. But Dahlia would much rather shed blood and be done with it forever than have to renew her penance every day of her life.

Dahlia had brought Belínda into the world when she herself was just a teenager. And that mistake had soured and changed the course of their lives.

Belínda refused to withdraw her stare and remained fixed on the old man's eyes, as if prepared to counterstrike. Behind the old man, her head bowed, Grandmother shifted helplessly on the crate she used as a chair. She fiddled with two of the buttons that lined the front of her dress, a nervous fear in her eyes.

The silence and sobs of the women were something the old man had always taken as their assent to his berating. He shifted his weight around the cane and was silent momentarily. Then, as if reminded he had not finished, he continued the assault. "Well, your grand-mother and I can't put up with much more of this," he complained in his slurred speech. "Look at her," he demanded as he craned his neck, aiming toward Dahlia. "Look at your mother!" he raised his chin in disdain, "Thirty years old. What has she ever done of any value in her life except have you?"

A brief pause followed as the old man again sought his balance. "Why are we in this place at our age?" he asked rhetorically, paus-ing as if he had lost his train of thought. "We're trying to get you to learn to earn a living so you don't end up like her."

Still nothing from Belínda who remained tense but guarded. Next to her, Dahlia muffled her sobs on the pillow on her lap.

Grandfather continued his diatribe. "I saw you flirting with that one — the one they call *Blue. Pinche Peládo feo* [Ugly son of a bitch]. He's as old as your mother, for heaven's sake. You're just a baby."

Belínda finally erupted, "I wasn't flirting with him!" It was not immediately apparent whether the disdain on Belínda's face was for her grandfather or for Blue. "He's my friend," she declared, spitting out the words through tears flowing down to her lips. "He's every-body's friend in this camp except for you. And inside, in his soul, he's not as ugly as some people I know."

"Ah, *sí*, well I guess you can take off with that son of a bitch, Blue, and see if he or his soul will feed you." He turned to walk out of the cabin. *"Ya me voy"* (I'm leaving).

With her ice-cold, blue eyes expanding, Belínda stared right back at the old man.

"I don't need any of this," she screamed. "I've heard it all before, and I'm sick of it. Believe me, if I could, I'd leave right now. That way, I'll stop being your problem."

The old man turned back to her, as if on a dime, and, in a sarcastic tone, told Belínda, "Well, no one's stopping you." No sooner had he begun the sentence when Dahlia joined the fray.

"Don't tell her that," Dahlia begged weakly through her tears. Her voice resonated with a plea for mercy as she had done all her adult life. But then, it took on a threatening tone.

"Who do you think you are, God almighty?" she shouted. "You're always judging us, but never yourself. I am tired of it all, Papa. You're just a drunk! That's what you are — just a pathetic, sad old drunk."

The old man's jaw stuck, and Grandmother let out a desperate wail.

The one humiliating mistake in Dahlia's life had become her lifelong tragedy. She had done penance for her sin for close to sixteen years, but was there no end to her punishment? Despite the passage of time, she relived that event like a naïve and infatuated teenager. So innocently it had all begun. Every winter back then, the small carnivals and circuses would join the bird migration south to seek refuge along the Texas-Mexican border. Here, fair weather allowed them to operate without much interruption. Even if the carnival season should prove unprofitable to the carnies, there was always farm work that could be relied on to supplement the receipts from the carnival shows. Carnies earned a little extra by joining the ranks of the field workers, working next to the Mexicans — oranges and grapefruit in the fall; cauliflower, cabbage, and carrots in the late winter; onions in March; and tomatoes in the spring.

She met the boy on a warm February Saturday night. Lupíta was with her that night. *Lupíta was my best friend then,* Dahlia recalled with a grin. She wondered momentarily, *What ever happened to Lupíta?* but forced her thoughts to return to her mission. Lupíta and Dahlia were "two peas in a pod," as their mothers used to say, and on that night, the two peas were out at the carnival. Lupíta's mother drove the girls in her '48 Ford, an Army green thing that resembled a wooden keg with wheels.

He caught Dahlia's attention immediately as she and Lupíta waited for their turn to ride the Ferris wheel. Everything about him was so rugged: tall and lanky, limp blonde hair, a square jaw, and blue eyes.

Tears welled up in Dahlia's eyes as she recalled the boy with the well-worn, greasy jeans and a checkered shirt, his sleeves rolled up thick above the elbows. In her memory, the boy's eyes displayed a certain innocence, perhaps even frailty, which one could detect in recent migrants to urban life. It was the type of aura that comes from growing up in the tranquil environment of a farm or a ranch. She imagined the mechanical organ-grinder music and the screams from delighted children behind her on the merry-go-round and the swirling saucers.

"It's like I'm the only one who can make his sadness go away," she would later volunteer to Lupíta.

No *Anglo* boy had ever looked at Dahlia that way before. And as she recalled the event, to this day, it made her feel so special. For it was as if she, out of all the other Mexican girls, had been singled out. And she just knew that at that moment, every other girl waiting in line for the Ferris wheel envied her. *They were so jealous then, weren't they?* She shook her head, smiled, and broke into tears.

The carnival shipped out two weeks later. "I will write to you," he had said. "And I'll be back," he had promised.

Dahlia could only protect the secret of her pregnancy for a while — five, five and a half months. But when she began showing at the age of thirteen, Dahlia had no options. Alone and afraid, she sought comfort and compassion from Lupíta. But within days, everyone in town, it seemed, knew about it and delighted in her pain. For years after that, mothers with daughters Dahlia's age could point to a real-live next-door example to lend credence to the reasons for their stern admonishments to their daughters. It had been set in stone for generations. Only a reckless girl would draw that type of shame on her family by disregarding the conduct insisted on and expected of women. At home, Dahlia's parents were the last to find out. She was sent off to a nunnery, where she would deliver Belínda, who would be adopted by Dahlia's own parents.

Grandmother looked around to her family in desperation, and then to the heavens. Unable to suppress her pain, Grandmother's soft sobs had become painful wails. She felt the brittle seams that barely held *her* family together, now tearing at every stitch. That terrible fear of a future unknown — her nightmare — was now becoming reality.

Belínda was startled as well at Dahlia's reaction. For a moment, mother and daughter stared at each other, sobbing. The hurt that Belínda saw in her mother's eyes came from the depths of her soul.

Dahlia had never before stood up for Belínda or herself, for that matter. Belínda knew she was the sad result and constant reminder of an illegitimate union. How many times had she heard the admonishments? Such relationships are improbable; everyone knows that. "What can you expect from a *gringo?*" mothers had often warned.

Belínda's own resolve seemed to be strengthened at the sight of her mother. She gave the old man a defiant look and countered, "Don't worry . . . I'll be gone soon. Maybe I'll go to Chicago with Blue."

Belínda's retort had sounded so self-assured, as Dahlia now recalled, as if Belínda might have been uncertain where she was going, but there was no question that she would be leaving—and soon.

The old man's face grew concerned as his daughter and granddaughter ganged up on him. As long as there had been no challenge to his impudent threats, he could intimidate the women at will. But now, the prey had turned on him. He responded by raising his cane, threatening Dahlia. But Belínda's swift move caught him off balance. She easily toppled him and quickly disappeared through the covered opening.

"Get away from me," the old man shouted at his wife, who came offering to help him off the floor, and he dragged himself to the door opening to the small room. Once there, he lifted the flap of the old bedspread that covered the entryway to the wood frame hut. Inside, he left his sobbing wife and Dahlia. As he made his way down the two steps from his hut, from his left and his right, he must have felt the peers of several men and young boys standing or sitting next to their own huts. He gave them all a *"What the hell are you looking at?"* sneer and hobbled with the help of his cane into the woods in the back of the huts to relieve himself.

Grandma had counseled, as had become her self-ascribed burden, "Your father will get over it in the morning. Everything will be okay then."

Later that night, certain that the old man was snoring, Belínda had returned to the cabin. Belínda cuddled up to Dahlia in the narrow cot, put her long arms around her mother's neck, and whispered, "I love you so much, Mom. You watch . . . it's going to work out." She promised Dahlia she would sign up for school in Indiana so that she wouldn't miss a day of school. "No one will know me there or care about my reputation," she told her mother, who stared at her with a blank look.

"Hey," Belínda insisted, moving her lips closer to her mother's ear to reassure her. "I'm gonna try especially hard. I'm gonna sit up on the front row of class and make a bunch of friends. It'll be a fresh start."

Dahlia had remained silent on that occasion and prayed, *Oh, my daughter . . . if I could only believe you.*

As was the case on every other Michigan morning, on Saturday morning, the three women headed back to the fields. A few field hands picked cucumbers, staying behind Don Eduardo's slow-moving truck, from the rear of which dangled a thick wood ramp. The truck would slow down when someone needed to walk up the plank and empty a can full of cucumbers. Dahlia recalled Belínda walking up the plank that last day to empty her can of cucumbers. Always the flirt, she was wearing a gold cap she had borrowed from one of the men and her sunglasses.

Yard of the Month
Pepíto, the Blue-Gray Chihuáhua

AS MANDA EXITED THE PASSENGER side of Joe Farmer's 1959 Ford station wagon, she could already hear the Chihuáhua barking inside the home. Two tall ash trees along the driveway shaded the red brick home from the west. The Farmers had landscaped the flagstone sidewalk up to the front door entrance. Tiger lilies, a pair of firecrackers, and elephant ears framed the two steps up to the pair of walnut-stained doors. A hummingbird flirted with one of the flowers on the firecrackers, its turquoise-blue breast glistening. A "Yard of the Month" poster was tacked to a stake in the yard near the front door.

The fall rains had washed away the desert dust from the plants. Rejuvenated, the tiger lilies glowed greener, as if they were freshly waxed. *I won't be needing to wipe the rubber plants*, Manda thought to herself. *Poor Mr. Farmer is so naïve. He has no concept of the time required to properly clean a house. He makes it a point to remind me to please wipe the rubber plants once I finish my other work. As if there are actually enough hours in the day to finish with the Farmers' housework.*

"Manda, the kids have practice this afternoon, and today's our busy day at the bank. I'll try to make it home by four-thirty to five." Mrs. Farmer clerked at the bank. On busy days, bank clerks were expected to stay around until the day's transactions were all posted and balanced. Today, Manda would be at the back end of Mrs. Farmer's schedule and would have to wait for her ride home until Mrs. Farmer was done.

Back at home, Benáncio and the kids would have to make do at dinnertime by warming the food Manda had prepared. She smiled, for she had raised a good family. There were no complaints from the kids since that had been their practice from early memory. Her thoughts turned to Benáncio, and she swallowed as a knot formed in her throat. For Benáncio was the breadwinner, and he insisted on sitting at the kitchen table while Manda kept the supply of flour *tortíllas* coming. He liked them right off the griddle.

She knew she would fail him again as she so often did, and again he would complain that all her work as a "maid" for the *pinches grin-gos* was all for naught. "It isn't worth it," Benáncio growled, bottling up his anger until the point of eruption. At that point, he would grit his teeth and make a fist and strike the table at full force.

Manda would never disagree with him. "I'm looking elsewhere for a job, *Viejo*. I've been on the waiting list at the packing shed for a year now . . . you know that. Once I get that job, *vas a ver* [you'll see], *Viejo*. I'll be home by three, and I'll cook great dinners for all of you."

But Manda would never be called for the packing shed job. "Up North" remained always in the back of her mind. If the children were ever going to make it through high school, there simply had to be more money.

Pepe was the Farmers' two-year-old blue-gray male Chihuáhua, and he must have known Manda would soon be entering the front door. Otherwise, his bark would have taken on that frenzied tone. But it was Manda because it was Wednesday, and Wednesdays Manda spent her days at the Farmers. Tuesdays belonged to the Trents. Thursdays were for the Robinsons. Manda had always felt that Pepe somehow knew all of that.

The folks over in the south side praised Manda. They liked her cleaning. They liked her ironing. They liked how she left a kitchen spotless and rearranged the innards of their refrigerators, removing all of the spoiled fruit and the crud. And mostly, they liked her be-cause she was trustworthy. They told each other that and often won-dered what would happen if she were to get sick or grow too old to work. She always showed up for work, never complained, never took anything that didn't belong to her, and she always had a smile for them. They shared her, accommodated each other. If the Robinsons were going to host a party on Friday, Mrs. Trent would accommo-date the Robinsons and lend Manda to the Robinsons so that their home could be ready by party time. *Is Manda up to it?* Yes, Manda was always up to it. That's why they liked her so much, because Manda was always up to it. All they had to do was drive by the house and honk their horn and there she was at their beck and call. Benáncio hated how Manda would leave whatever she was doing and run out to the car as soon she heard the honk. Even if she was eating or dying her hair, she'd drop whatever she was doing and get out there as soon as possible.

As Manda entered the Farmers' living room, the Chihuáhua circled anxiously and then jumped up on its hind legs, begging to be picked up.

"Okay, okay, my baby. I'm here," Manda humored Pepe as she wiped her feet on the doormat and hung the umbrella on the wall tree. She pulled off the oversized man's gray canvas overcoat and hung it up in the hallway closet. Pepe jumped up to her arms as she bent over to pick him up.

"How's my Pepíto?"

The fidgety pup continued its excited welcoming.

"Hay, mi'jo [oh, child] those eyes of yours! If only you could talk, you would say you love me. *Pos yo también te quiéro mucho* (Well, I also love you very much). Manda allowed the pup to lick her nose.

It would be four-thirty in the afternoon before Mrs. Farmer would return from her own job at the bank, so Manda began with the kitchen. The Farmers' kids had probably rushed off to school this morning since they hadn't finished their breakfasts. But they had at least left no milk in their glasses. *Such a waste,* Manda thought. She inserted the carton cap on the glass milk bottle and returned the milk and the butter to their proper cubby holes in the refrigerator. She gathered the dishes. As usual, Mr. Farmer had left his cigarette butts in the ashtray. After finishing the dishes, she headed for the bathroom.

Like a trained Arabian stallion, Pepíto marched step for step by Manda's side. But at the bathroom, she closed the door behind her. Pepíto wailed and scratched at the door. Undoing her blouse, Manda stared at herself in the mirror. Peering back at her was a woman with a small frame and large hands. Gently feeling one hand with the other, she ran her fingers over her calluses. Grinning ironically, she recalled how she and Benáncio had promised that someday, they would be able to afford wedding bands, but that had been so very long ago.

Looking back up at the mirror, the reflection returned a nervous smile at her. She undid her blouse slowly, revealing the left side of her chest.

The German nurse had translated for Doctor James. "Manda, the doctor says that they have to remove the breast."

"All of it?"

"Yes. They're hoping it hasn't spread to other parts of the body."

"Chinita!" [Darn!]. Manda buttoned her lips. That had been the extent of her complaint.

"How much does it cost?"

"Well, it's expensive. You're going to have to go to the city hospital. Dr. James will only assist. They will have to get a surgeon."

"Do you think it will be more than $250? That's all the savings I have."

"Oh, Manda," the German nurse hugged her, and they both wept.

Inside the Farmers' bathroom, tears came. Manda swallowed. "Please, Lord, tell me it's all been a bad dream." But it wasn't a dream — only the ugly surgical scar remained on her flat chest. After placing the false sponge breast in the bra, she snipped the bra on. And then Manda wept, and then she screamed until her eyes puffed. Outside the bathroom, Pepíto had not stirred. Inside, he could hear Manda's cries and offered his own low wailing in support. Drained of her strength, she sat on the commode and got her breath back.

Lifting her chin, she walked out of the bathroom and then let Pepe proudly lead her into the master bedroom. *Next year, for certain,* she vowed, *we're going up north, before it's too late.*

Mexican Pulp Fiction/*Muchos Huevos*

JOAQUÍN ALMOST KNOCKED OVER the two boys who were shooting each other up with water guns on the sidewalk in front of the R. Gonzalez Gas Station on Main Street. He raced by the Montez restaurant, a hole in the wall, which teenagers preferred because their jukebox always had the latest Billboard hits. His heart was pounding—he could almost hear it—and he felt its thumping in his throat and in his ears. At the corner, the broad sidewalk ended, and Joaquín barely missed hitting the light pole as he dashed by a group of men pitching dice against the wall of Don Chencho's *Mueblería* (furniture store), risking their Saturday paychecks. The bugs had gathered to worship the fluorescent night-lights. Accordions whined out *redóvas* (redowas) and *guapángos* (a traditional fast Mexican dance) through the open doors of the half dozen or so *cantínas* (saloons) on main street.

Clearing the tears from his eyes with the back of his hand, he let out a hateful growl and felt the carotids tighten as he set his sights on the next streetlight. One more streetlight, and he'd be home. As he sprinted down Third Street, which was now paved, he tuned out all sound; he felt himself moving somehow in slow motion.

A part of his brain had shut down, and the other part was on autopilot, scheming every minute detail. He would enter through the kitchen—quietly, of course, so as not to call attention to himself. Then he would make his way to the upright metal gym locker Manda had acquired from the Army surplus store. At one corner, Benáncio kept his prized possession in a rigid round box—a Stetson felt hat. But in the round box (and only Joaquín knew this), Benáncio also kept a gun and six bullets.

The house was empty. What a surprise! What a blessing! Joaquín anxiously loaded all six bullets into the revolver. The gun felt light, almost like a play thing. He untucked his shirt and stuck the gun in his denim pants. The nickel-plated steel felt cold against his crotch. He headed back to Tino's pool hall.

The son of a bitch had pulled the chair from underneath him while Joaquín stood up from a game of dominos to get a Coke. When Joaquín returned to sit down, he sensed the chair was missing, but it was too late, and he sputtered uncontrollably backward as he tried to regain his balance, but he was too far off-balance. And he slipped and hit his head on the edge of one of the pool tables. The son of a bitch laughed at him while Joaquín lay on the pool-hall floor. It was Saturday night, and the pool hall was packed. Joaquín was thirteen.

As he ran back to the pool hall, Joaquín visualized how the act would be played out, how good it would feel. He would walk into the pool hall and yell out for everyone to hear, "Hey, you son of a bitch, I'm gonna kill you like a pig!" A couple of bullets in the chest would knock the bastard down. Then, one in each eye. He would then force the barrel into the son of a bitch's mouth and drop the last two. Damn, it would feel good! Bodies riddled with bullets . . . Mexican pulp fiction . . . payback time. No one died like that unless they deserved to. A ballad would be written about Joaquín — *"Ese vato tenía muchos huevos"* (That dude had guts). Men would drink in the *cantinas* of San Felípe to honor the boy who turned into a man to guard his honor.

Joaquín couldn't keep the pace. He had to slow down. He took a deep breath. His heart pounded against his rib cage. The street lights seemed to continue endlessly now, and his vision was blurred. His legs were no longer receptors for the electric pulses from the brain. Instead, they took on a life of their own.

Exactly thirty days later, Johnny Castellaños got slapped in the face by Toro at Tino's pool hall. Toro was a bully. It was about closing time. Johnny and Joaquín were inseparable. They were playing nine ball. Johnny ran out of the pool hall and returned (within minutes, it seemed), brandishing a shiny black cannon of a gun. Johnny shouted to Toro from the swiveling front doors, "Hey, son of a bitch! I'm gonna kill you!" The pool hall emptied. Joaquín remained and walked parallel along the pool tables, matching Johnny step for step as they made their way toward the back where Toro sat on a *keeno* pool table sipping a beer.

"You're not going to kill anyone, man." Toro appeared half drunk and not a bit preoccupied.

Johnny pointed the gun at Toro's face, and Joaquín's heart thumped, *Two in the chest, one in each eye, and the final two at the miniature punching bag in the back of Toro's throat.*

"You son of a bitch bastard, *chinga tu madre, bastárdo*. You deserve to die like a dog!"

In Joaquín's mind, the scene was taking too long to play out. The threats were ballooning, and there was a sense of desperation. Somehow, he sensed that the rage was cooling. *Shoot the son of a bitch now, man. Shoot!* Joaquín's heart cried out.

"You know what I'm gonna do, Johnny? I'm gonna walk over there and take your gun, and then we're gonna have a beer. Okay, man?" Toro sounded remarkably in control of the situation.

"I don't wanna have a beer with you, you son of a bitch." Johnny wiped the tears with the back of his hand. Joaquín looked back toward the front of the long hall. The two *cantína* swivel doors were wide open, and the front of the crowd could barely hold the rest from spilling into the hall. Faces were piled upon faces, pressed against the broad picture window that faced Main Street. *The entire world is watching*, thought Joaquín, *and Johnny is having a spat over having a beer with this guy? Shoot 'im*, Joaquín's brain blared out. *You'd better shoot. Heck, shoot him in the leg. Do something.* Joaquín could sense the embarrassment that Johnny would have to face if he didn't shoot the son of a bitch. *"Se rajó!* He backed down!"

No one was ever shot at Tino's pool hall in San Felípe. The gun incident was never reported to the police, and Joaquín never made it back to the pool hall the night of his own discontent. There had been just enough time for Manda's admonishments to take hold. But at the age of thirteen, given a few less minutes, Johnny would have shot the son of a bitch, and so would have Joaquín.

Vamonos Pa'l Norte (Let's Head North)

A RUGGED LANDSCAPE OF SLEEPLESS nights and overindulging had long settled on the old trucker's face. Don Armándo's ears had thickened into tough leather, and black thickets grew from within their deep fertile pits. His nose had taken on a bulbous shape; its texture appeared bulky and cratered. Porcupine-thick hair grew out of his nostrils, which appeared like large openings to a dark abyss. And in the area below the eyes (where cheekbones had once been apparent), unattended blackheads had long ago grown into the fatty landscape.

The day had come. Joaquín and Bennie sat on the floor in Sis' room on either side of Manda. She sat on an old rocking chair. The sofa on which the old trucker Don Armándo sat was a sturdy emerald green vinyl. False seams, false pleats, and false buttons were detailed into the vinyl pattern. Manda had picked it up from the foreclosure salesman. She wanted it in the small room just off the kitchen, which doubled as the living room and Sis' bedroom.

An animated Sis had complained, "Emerald clashes with the hot pink in my room." That was not acceptable to Sis, she complained. Sis knew all about those things — about etiquette and styles, which she absorbed from all the books and magazines she read. Manda calmly suggested to her, "*Mamasíta,* as soon as you have the means to match the decor of this room, then you may certainly do as you please. For the time being, the vinyl sofa will have to do."

Thick, callused corns on Manda's little toes showed where the frayed canvas on her shoes had thinned into holes. She tried covering them. Bennie gently felt the bulging vericose veins on his mother's leg, tracing them up the back of her leg to the crook in the back of her knee until she prodded him out of it with a sidekick to his ribs. Embarrassed, he turned to Joaquín, who had been observing Bennie's every move. Pursing his lips into a sneer, Joaquín poked his tongue at Bennie, nodded his head up and down as if to say, "*Ándale pendéjo*" (Serves you right).

"Good coffee," Don Armándo whispered into his cup, blinking his eyes as if the coffee had revived him.

Joaquín and Bennie did not overlook the great difficulty Don Armándo was having steadying the cup of coffee, which Manda had brewed for him. Even from a distance of about five feet, they could smell the raw breath that emanated from his deep alcoholic pit. Don Armándo's painful eyes betrayed his attempts at maintaining a pleasant smile. He turned to Manda and offered in a somewhat strained, but deliberate, low-key sales pitch, "There are cherries up in Kalamazoo, *Señora;* strawberries around Decatur and Dowagiac." Almost at a whisper, he continued, as if the mere sound of his own voice brought pain. "Eventually, the cucumbers will ripen, *uh, uh, uh* . . . up in *uh, uh,* up in Mount Pleasant and New Lothrop, all around Saginaw."

Manda nodded, mulling over the bargain.

The old trucker chewed on a thin *tamál,* which Manda had toasted on the grill and spread some hot sauce on. Then, he took another hot sip and savored the coffee as it left a hot trail down his esophagus. Rejuvenated, the old man breathed out a gratifying "Whew," reacting to the hot sauce. His thin moustache twitched, and he began shooting off names of exotic-sounding places. Joaquín turned to Bennie, his eyes gleaming, as if their luck had dramatically changed.

The old man continued, "From there, we head south for tomatoes around Mudpool and Newton and up around New Frankfort—that's in Indiana. There's plenty of work there."

"Will the children be able to attend school if we stay beyond September?" Manda needed to know.

"Sure, and the law requires it in any case. And the schools are very close to where we'll stay—very good schools, I might add."

"Can you promise me, Don Armándo, that you will help me get my boys registered for school? They can't miss a single day." Bennie rolled his eyes at Joaquín. If she could get a firm commitment from Don Armándo, she was certain to hold him accountable.

Fascinating, Joaquín thought. Manda had invited Don Armándo to tell her and the boys about all these exciting places *"up north"* where she planned to take them as soon as school ended for the summer. That's where their future lay, according to Manda—*"up north."*

For as long as Joaquín could remember, Manda had marveled about it and about the missed opportunities. "Once you're older," she told Joaquín, "that's where we're headed." And the stories the neigh-

bors told! *Up north* was where the Castellaños had gotten the money
for their white picket fence and their new pickup truck. There was
money to be made up there. Some people came back in new-model
cars all the time. They could afford new clothes and television sets.
Joaquín wondered whether Benáncio knew of Manda's plans, for
she had decided the boys were old enough. He knew Benáncio was
not to going appreciate her enterprise.

"We're more equal *up there,*" Manda told Joaquín, and he wondered what she meant by that.

"Another group goes up to Colorado and the Dakotas for sugar
beets," Don Armándo continued. "Still another heads west to the
Valley of California, after a few weeks in Colorado. Everything grows
in California. You name it, we've picked it."

Don Armándo was a trailblazer, and Joaquín had visions of a
wagon train. At the trail's end, Joaquín pictured a pastoral setting in
which he could walk around, smugly confident, picking red shiny
apples and cherries. As he snatched each fruit from the tree, a cash
register rang up dollar signs—*ding ding.* Money grew on trees *up
north,* and they would be "more equal." He couldn't help but share
Manda's excitement.

"If California is not quite ripe," Don Armándo shrugged his shoulders, "no problem. We head up to the Oregon border. There were
even some people from San Felípe who went east, where they were
needed in the poultry plants and pig farms."

The old crew leader's story lengthened that afternoon. He had an-
nually delivered the flock to Michigan in his Ford truck. He knew
the territory like the veins on the back of his calloused hand, he assured them, having led many others before. And, he, in turn, had
learned the route from other trailblazers who had come before him.
He warned that they should take on the trip only what they absolutely needed. Don Armándo advised that the Michigan and Indiana harvest season was three, maybe five months, tops. The family
would have to travel in the back of the truck. "But, it's real comfortable back there," he told them.

The waxed, brown, military-style tarp over the raised sides of the
truck cargo bay would keep the rain from soaking the passengers
and their few belongings. "And darn, if it doesn't rain each and every
time," he warned them, suggesting that was better than sunny skies
for the long trip. The remainder of the flock would follow in their

Ford and Chevy pickups. A caravan of vehicles would head for Michigan by late May. Joaquín was set on getting a geography lesson from the tarp flap opening in the rear of the truck. It would be a good three-and-a-half-day trip, Fords and Chevys permitting.

This time around, there had been no flock, only one bird — a Boeing 737 with a two-hour layover in Houston. During the flight, Joaquín had caught up on Kurt Vonnegut's *Timequake*. Vonnegut had shared his insights on brain matter, analogizing the brain to a "gelatainous sponge" whose steady life-blood infusion is the universe that surrounds it. Without this stimulus, the sponge dries up; it stops weaving the electronic pathways and circuits that form a person's internal information highway. Although very entertaining, Vonnegut could not explain why Joaquín's memory was not cross-referencing and cross-linking to a time some thirty-three years before.

25

Los Pachúcos

THE PACHÚCOS APPEARED WEEKENDS at the San Felípe billiard halls all spiffed up as colorful bantam roosters, slick pompadours with ducktails, suspicious chins jutting out, as they surveyed their bailiwick. They wore colorful, single-tone, long-sleeved shirts, neatly pressed, but from a bygone era, from an era of zoot suits and of Cab Calloway. Their thin bodies were clad in waist-tight khaki pants with long belt loops adorned by extra-thin belts with flashy silver buckles. Glazing with heavy starch, the pants bell-bottomed out and were then choked tightly at about the ankles. Metal taps on the soles of their shoes trumpeted their grand approach.

On late thick-sticky summer nights in San Felípe, window and door fly screens invited the breeze in from the Gulf of Mexico. As Joaquín lay in bed, he focused on the distant and approaching cadence of the metal taps as some *pachúco* made his way on the macadam surface on Third Street. *Tap, tap . . . tap.* Even the chirping of the crickets seemed to subside, as if they were an audience threatened or awed by the presence of the *pachúcos,* as the taps made their way down from Main Street over to the *barrio* by the canal.

26

If You're Nothing, You're Nothing

LATER IN THE EVENING, after Benáncio had returned from Don Magín's corner grocery store after an evening of to what a passerby must have appeared to be an evangelical meeting of sorts, Manda was waiting with her proposal. Joaquín knew what was coming, for she had promised to give Don Armándo an answer the following day. When he heard the kitchen screen door whine, Joaquín went into the kitchen.

"Bene, I have spoken to a trucker by the name of Don Armándo. He says we can join his crew this summer to pick strawberries in Michigan."

Benáncio's eyes responded initially and left no doubt that Manda's suggestion was incredulous. "You already put up with huge insults at the places you work," Benáncio complained. "What need do you have to put up with more?" He would not go, he said. "I refuse to work like a wetback." Unlike him, Manda must have had an immense capacity for being insulted, Joaquín discerned from his vantage point, for she was willing to put up with whatever *El Norte* offered. Benáncio shook his head with great disappointment. "I cannot imagine myself accepting those conditions." So thoroughly consistent in his reasoning was he in rejecting any suggestion by Manda. He framed his objections on principle, and therefore unassailable by mere logic. *It was an insult to his manhood to work under such conditions in the strawberry fields. Or, by working in the fields, one perpetuated the abusive working conditions for farm workers.* His objections had no end.

"Bene, we'll all be working and saving."

"Saving? Saving for what?"

"So the children can go to school. I want them to work their way up. I want them to be somebody."

"That's not the way it works." He stared at her as if she were a questioning child testing his better judgment. "You do not work your way up from nothing. If you're nothing, then you're nothing. Today, tomorrow, the next day — nothing every day!" With Benáncio's side-

ways glance at Joaquín, he let Joaquín know the lesson was meant
for him. Manda's face told Joaquín to disregard his father, as if it
were just another one of those moments that they all had to get
through.

She wet her throat before she continued. "Benáncio, you always
tell me, 'I'm the best framer around. If I could read blueprints, I
would run circles around every s.o.b. supervisor I've ever had.' That's
the difference — a slight difference, but a difference. That s.o.b. makes
five times your salary and does not have to hammer a single nail. Am
I wrong?"

Joaquín continued to listen to the argument from his post in the
hallway to the bedroom just outside the kitchen.

As he recalled the incident, Joaquín understood his mother's con-
venient explanations to him dispelling Benáncio's rejection of her
ideas as simply his father's character flaw. Only now was Joaquín
beginning to fully understand the depth of his father's injured psy-
che and how unarmed Benáncio had been in the world that was
America — how so unprepared for the onslaught, his soul so bruised
that it would never recover. His parents' arguments (like the one he
recalled in the kitchen before that first summer trip to Michigan)
had given him the greatest insecurity and anxiety. Whom could he
rely on for answers? He sensed the powerlessness all around him.
And from childhood, he had the presentiment that Benáncio could
not cope; that, at some point, he would have to leave.

PART IV

Airport Nightmare

STANDING IN FRONT OF HIM WAS A little blonde girl, perhaps three or three and a half years old, garbed in a tutu. *How long till Halloween?* was the first thought that came to his mind. She regarded him with large blue eyes that reminded him of doll eyes. Her bangs had been diligently brushed and straightened and were cut in a straight line on her forehead. *Someday I'll have a cute kid like this,* he thought. A precocious smile through the girl's two rabbit teeth sought his compliment. Joaquín abided her. "You're such a pretty little girl," he told her and winked as he nodded at the young man in his twenties whom Joaquín assumed was the girl's father.

Behind her, the young man trailed the girl, following at some distance as she waltzed confidently from passenger to passenger, as if soliciting, and making believe she was receiving, every passenger's undivided attention. Unable to keep his eyes off of her, Joaquín folded up the newspaper, placed it in the seat next to his, and followed the girl's antics. What he did find odd as he glanced around the waiting area was that other waiting passengers not otherwise engaged in their own reading were not as engaged as he was. In fact, besides him, no one seemed to have even been aware of the girl's antics.

They're not dissimulating! he told himself, turning in both directions as if to make sure. If he didn't know any better, he might think that the girl was invisible to the other travelers. She danced gracefully, pirouetting on occasion, curtsying on others, and at times manipulating her small hands in flamenco fashion. The miniature dancer moved from seat to seat and smiled up inquisitively at travelers as if asking her subjects, *Don't you think I am just so pretty?* Yet there was no visible reaction from any of them — no acknowledgment. Undeterred, the girl reacted as if she had indeed received a reply or a compliment, and she moved on to the next traveler.

A sudden dimming of the lights brought back a brief memory of his youth. That had been Joaquín's only experience with a lunar eclipse, and he recalled the perceptively instantaneous silence and slowed-down pace of his world during that brief moment. Dogs could not bark; people had gone dumb; all that was space had turned to a shadowy, dusk orange. Suddenly, a chill surged into his space and lingered around Joaquín's ears and neck and on his calves just above his socks. Joaquín tugged at the collar of his coat up to his ears. From a distance, the girl turned and stared at him. The scene changed. He sensed a dark vacuum around him — like an abandoned cave — and felt the glare and heat of a spotlight on his face and a few feet away, another ray of light shone on the girl.

Joaquín searched around with a suspicious, forced smile on his face, but the shining spotlight would not allow his pupils to tell what lay beyond him. It was the motion that attracted his attention back in the girl's direction, and he saw her making her way (floating in midair) toward him as a single ray of light fixed on her. Thin and hoary, patches of hair attached to sparse clumps of scalp, which here and there clung precariously to her skull. Dark sockets had replaced the girl's blue eyes. Like mysterious openings to dark and ominous pits, they had a magnetic draw on Joaquín, whose mind searched for an explanation. *Did someone slip a drug in my coffee? Is this a nightmare?* He drew back. At her neck and chest were the dark imprints of palms. Matted heavily with dried blood, the girl's dress appeared like some long-discarded rag, half-digested by maggots and termites. Joaquín's eyes expanded as he felt a strong, suffocating scent, thick and overpowering, like an anesthetic gas, fill his lungs. He held his breath, fighting off its deadly choke hold, but he couldn't. He tried shutting his eyes in desperate panic and opened his mouth, but no sound came, and there was no air to breathe. He lost consciousness.

Consciousness returned slowly. The girl was comfortably in her father's grasp as he came in Joaquín's direction. She was holding a raggedy bald doll under her free arm. Joaquín searched for answers in the faces of other travelers. *Has anyone else witnessed the scene?* The looks on their faces didn't indicate that. The girl in her father's arms smiled at Joaquín, and just as he was about to return the smile, the precocious smile of an innocent little girl was replaced by a cunning, sardonic smile of a seductress. Joaquín reached for his eyeglasses and felt his fingers numb and unable to grasp their frames. He grabbed the glasses awkwardly and rubbed his eyes with the back of his thumb. His sight then turned upward toward the ceiling, not in search of anything, but as if expectant that some godsend might remove the scene from his sight. His breath had thickened, and he could no longer stand.

28

A Commercial Elevator Ride

JOAQUÍN'S SMILE WAS PENSIVE. He straightened out his back in the plane seat and raised his arms. There were audible pops in his shoulder joints. He leaned back into the seat and searched his memory, which shifted back to the summer of '66, back to the bumpy ride in the bay of the red Ford truck.

The area in the back of the red Ford truck was not much larger than a commercial elevator. Bodies slid into the few nooks and honeycombs still available under the tarp; belongings were arranged and rearranged and stacked and shoved into areas already cramped with the few parcels of clothing and beddings, which Don Armándo permitted his crew to bring along; children were sized up to determine the spaces they would occupy and usually ended up making the three-day trip across their parents' laps or crammed in between legs like sardines in the tin.

Sometimes somber faces, sometimes pleasant smiles, he witnessed them all, seeking to absorb their features, forming his first impressions as each face was temporarily picture-framed by the four sides of the trap door in the rear of the truck as each of the pilgrims entered for the long journey. Some had made this journey before. He listened as they renewed old friendships. Young men his age, already dressed for their first day in the fields in boots and crisp, long-sleeved khaki shirts, searched around like canines in the darkness of the bay of the truck, sniffing out their temporary abode. Their brief glances served as introductions. There would be time to make friends later, but not now. Everything was still formal, still distant.

The women also entered through the trap door, eyes cast piously downward, shoulders in, embracing their own humility or hierarchy, sliding their hands protectively down the back of their long dresses or pants to their buttocks as a symbolic rejection of preying eyes. The males, young and old, acknowledged them, silently lowering their eyesight or turning away from the trap door.

A grin showed on Joaquín's face. He reset the tray on the back of the plane seat in front of him and slid the book he was reading into the seat sleeve beneath. *Was there any farting in the back of the truck?* he wondered. *I bet not,* he answered himself. That would simply not have been acceptable. *Smoking?* He pressed his lips as he thought about it and settled the issue by assuming that a smoker was probably allowed to stand by the opening in the back of the tarp flap so the smoke could escape. *What about human odor?* Certainly there would have been no baths during the trip.

He recalled during at least one trip the nauseating effect of the gasoline fumes and the nonstop coughing caused by a tickling-feather sensation at the windpipe. A panic had resulted, and Don Armándo had been forced to place a tarp on the floor of the truck bed to keep the fumes out. But other than that one event, he could not recall anyone complaining during a trip. Even the youngest of the children seemed to have been well behaved and well mannered in the face of the torment that was the three-day trip to Decatur. Their behavior was impeccable. *How remarkable,* he thought.

After piling their belongings up against the front of the truck bay, Joaquín and Bennie had arranged a niche for Manda. They stuffed a fat pillow with a piece of discarded flat sponge to soften the bone-jarring ride. Bennie snuggled into it for size, and the boys agreed that it would serve its purpose.

"That corner by the trap door is ours," Joaquín instructed Bennie. "At all times, one of us has to be on the truck to protect that corner. If I have to get off to go to the john, you gotta stick around. If you go, I have to stay." Bennie agreed in deference, as if he had a choice in the matter. Joaquín had assured himself the spot closest to the rear trap door of the truck, on the narrow wooden bench built up along the interior side of the cargo bay wall. It was a matter of first-come, first-served in the commercial elevator. He would see to it that at the end of every stop, Bennie or Manda would scurry back to the truck and reserve him a spot before anyone else got on board. Sleeping would be impossible. Joaquín and Bennie would sit on the benches like soldiers, their backs erect, until they could no longer stand it. Then they would stand until someone would volunteer a bench space in exchange for a standing space. All during the trip, Bennie would keep his transistor radio close to his right ear.

"There was an old couple with two girls — a woman in her early thirties and a pretty blonde, who appeared a little younger than me. Do you remember them?" Joaquín had asked Bennie during his last call before he left. Bennie had slid in the desk drawer and was staring thoughtfully through the open door of his office toward the receptionist's station. He trapped the phone between his ear and shoulder and held the yellow legal pad flat as he wrote, "Blonde". "I don't remember a blonde," he told himself.

"Sure," Joaquín insisted. "They must have joined us somewhere en route. I can't be imagining it." But Joaquín couldn't quite picture where that had been. "Maybe they were with Don Eduardo's crew," he pleaded with Bennie. "You remember how the two crew leaders would pick up their crew throughout the Valley, and then the cars and pickup trucks would join up at a pre-arranged meeting place, at which the caravan would begin the trip?"

"Yeah, I remember that. But, it's been many years, and I'll be honest with you, I just don't think there was ever a blonde."

<hr />

What a beautiful and alluring creature was the first thought that entered Joaquín's mind. *What is she doing here? Is she coming along?* He stared at the girl from behind the tarp that covered the bay of the Ford truck, certain that she could not see him up above. She was so close he could tell she had blue eyes. The girl stood slightly behind the two other women, one of whom was old and too emaciated to be healthy, he thought. The old lady stood quietly, as if waiting for instructions, and he figured she was probably the old man's wife. Joaquín had dozed off during the trip and now had no idea which town they were in. If the foursome were planning to come aboard, there would no space for them. The old man had raised his voice, and Don Eduardo seemed to be shrugging off a complaint and insisting that they get on one of the trucks. Joaquín did not pay attention to the other woman except to note that she could have been the blonde's older sister.

He checked the buttons on his shirt and found they were all in their proper buttonholes, and he tucked the shirttail neatly into his pants. He began finger-combing his hair until he realized he could not recall whether he had earlier parted it on the left or on the right. He tried to visualize himself and imagine what would be the blonde's first impression of him.

Was that natural blonde hair? It had to be. Even from this distance, he could tell. She had none of that lifeless, frizzy, fried yellow peroxide-bleached hair that reminded him of grain sun-drying on the stalk. This girl's blonde hair was natural, and there was no doubt about it. In the classroom, he had sat behind several *gringas,* and their blonde hair was never evenly blonde. On them, the blonde mingled with shades of brown in a very blended, aesthetic way. That's how this girl's hair appeared. The strands of her blonde and shades of brown were in harmony. She enthralled him.

———————

Exactly where Joaquín's recollection ended and his imagination began had become increasingly fuzzy for him. During the last week before his flight to Chicago, he had begun to recall everything about the blonde. Yet, he could not remember ever before having recalled the blonde. Had his memory lapsed for all those years and now his far memory had returned? Had there ever really been a blonde? Could he be certain after all these years? Why wouldn't Bennie have remembered? The girl's father (or whom he assumed to be her father) was over sixty years old, he figured, and there was nothing blonde about him or the others in his family.

By the time the Ford truck arrived at the house where the blonde had stood by the curb, the windows of the small wood frame home had been shuttered. A sheet of plywood was laying on the porch, and Joaquín figured it would be nailed across the door as soon as the family boarded one of the two Ford trucks. A cane helped the old man along as he led the trio of women, who carted their belongings to the street.

He ran through several options on how to introduce himself to the blonde. He wondered whether now was an opportune time to change his name. This was not the first time he had thought about it. He had flirted with a name change before, ever since Juan Castellaño had changed his name in the second grade to Johnny. He personally liked the sound of "Jake" because it was one syllable, like Tom or Jim or Bill.

He shuddered. *But what if the blonde is not even part of the family? She's not!* He cringed. *Why are none of the others blonde? She's just a friend of the family and simply came by to bid the family good-bye. What a twerp! I should've known.*

He was disheartened and withdrew to the bench in the truck, crossing his arms over his chest. *What could I have been thinking? What would Papa have said if he had witnessed the spectacle I just put on?* Thank God Papa was not here. *This whole "Jake" thing was probably a mistake. Papa wouldn't have stood for that.* He imagined his father's ridicule . . . *"Que pendejáda! Still denying that you're a Mexican? Sucking up to a gringa?"*

Relationships of that type were unsafe, and his instincts should have told him so, he chided himself. Why did he have to keep correcting himself? Sure, his intuition told him, that no one would have disapproved if a Mexican penetrated any *gringa,* but only if it were a symbolic slap at those of her ilk. *Why is that?*

───※───

Having made his way to the edge of the parking lot of the vast truck stop, Joaquín stood alone, brooding, by the narrow landscaped strip, balancing himself on the parking lot curb, his fists sunk into the pockets of his blue jeans. He had not been able to get the blonde off his mind, and against his own earlier admonition, he kept constant vigil, hoping that he had been mistaken — that the blonde had indeed joined the convoy and would at any moment exit one of the trucks or cars.

Just north of Texarkana, the parking lot at the Texaco truck stop was in constant flux as tractor trailers maneuvered in and out of the parking lot. He watched as on the busy interstate, hundreds of eighteen wheelers idled impatiently as some unknown obstacle slowed traffic ahead. The collective sounds of their engines thundered in the distance as their air brakes spewed angry breaths. A late spring shower had cooled the late evening and turned the spacious asphalt surface into a canvas of flowing and form-changing reflections. Sporadic reds flared up from the brake lights, and yellow-oranges blinked nervously from the turn signals of the tractor trailers backed up like one giant centipede, growling on their exit to the backed-up roadway. But Joaquín could derive no pleasure from the fluid array of water, oil, and light, and with a thrust of loose pebbles sought to destroy the reflection.

About two in the morning, in need of rest, Don Armándo had parked the red Ford truck some distance from the gas pumps of the truck stop. The remaining caravan of pickup trucks and cars had stalled at the intersection. Presently, the vehicles were distributing themselves among the neighboring parking spaces. A few minutes later, Don Armándo's younger brother, Eduardo, maneuvered his own truck into a parking space and joined him for an update. Just then, a canary yellow '55 Chevy, a two-door, hard-top minus the front bumper and sporting shiny baby moons on its wheels, revved up by Joaquín and parked next to Don Armándo's Ford. Out came a short, stocky man puffing on a cigarette and finger-combing his goatee. He motioned Joaquín with his body, *"Que pasó?"* (What's up?) Joaquín nodded that nothing was happening.

"Frsst! Shorty, over here," Don Armándo whistled from the center of the parking lot, where he had gathered with some of the elders of the caravan.

"The caravan's intact," Shorty reported to Don Armándo. Armándo returned an acknowledging nod. "For a change," Shorty complained as an afterthought.

"On this wagon train, Shorty's the scout," Don Eduardo told the elders who had gathered to share a smoke. "Weeks ago, he scouted the entire road trip and mapped out the route for the caravan to follow. Now, his job is to make sure no one gets lost, and if they do to round up the stragglers."

Don Armándo took the short cigarette butt out of his mouth and ground it into the pavement. He then stretched his neck and pulled at the crotch of his pants. "God almighty," he complained, making a face, "these hemorrhoids are killing me."

Eduardo gave everyone a tired acknowledgment and bid them goodnight. Don Armándo made his way to the back of his truck and shouted into the cargo bay, "There's bathrooms if anyone needs to go." Bennie peered back at him, ungluing his eyelids and reattaching his radio earphone to his ear. Don Armándo then proceeded to walk around the truck with a flashlight, shining the narrow beam of light on the wheels and the tires. With the back of his fingers he felt each of the wheels for any unusual heating.

"Hey, *ese*, my name's Blue. What's yours?"

"Joaquín," Joaquín answered, surprised and a bit timid.

The dark, wiry figure which called itself "Blue" had made his way from Don Eduardo's truck. On his huge head, Blue donned a gray fedora. *He can't be much older than thirty,* Joaquín felt. Yet, he noticed on the forehead and around the eyes of Blue's face wrinkle lines, which all at once seemed to convey concern, anguish, and suspicion. Blue's smile was thin and uneasy. Tatooed into the cleft in his chin was a scraggily blue cross.

They shook hands. Blue had no last name. Just Blue.

"Me regálas un frajo carnál?" (Can I have a smoke, brother?)

"Sure. Take two—one for you and one for your ear." Joaquín smiled cautiously. It was tradition in San Felípe (though its provenance was unknown) that if a person asked for a smoke, you gave him two. Blue's hand came up attached to an arm that was so long Joaquín imagined Blue could easily scratch his knees without bending.

"Préstame la lumbre" (Let me borrow your light). Blue acknowledged the additional slight imposition, his straight white teeth showing. His breath emitted a licorice-alcohol scent.

"Simón" (Sure), Joaquín told him in a tone that meant *"Don't worry about it"* and tapped the cigarette lighter on the palm of his hand, which was supposed to force the liquid fuel toward the wick. He then clicked it open and cupped his left hand around it to shield the flame.

"I'll pay you back as soon as we get our first paycheck," Blue promised as he savored his first puff. The extra cigarette Blue inserted over his right ear. Blue's long, greasy hair covered it.

"First trip?" Blue asked.

"No. This is my second."

"Alone?"

"No. My mom and brother are with me. Last year, my dad came, but he didn't like it at all. And this time, my sister found a job back home, so she didn't want to lose that opportunity. She stayed back home too."

Blue nodded as if he understood perfectly.

"You?" Joaquín asked.

"First trip." Blue answered. "Never picked a thing in my life, 'cept my nose. Now I'm gonna pick strawberries."

"It ain't that bad."

"Still bad, though?"

"Still bad, but not that bad. You'll get used to it."

Blue formed a sneaky smile as he blew out smoke. "No, I won't," he promised.

Joaquín smiled in response. Joaquín arched his back and moaned, "I've been trying to get some sleep on that narrow bench. My back is killing me."

"Oh, man, tell me about it. When the truck left the freeway earlier, it made a quick stop, and the kumalong hit me in the back of the head." The walls of the truck hold were held up with chains stretched across the bed of the truck, which were shackled by a heavy, clanging metal kumalong. Blue pulled off his fedora gently, and a bloody white handkerchief dropped to his hand.

"Are you okay?"

"Yea, Junior let me borrow this handkerchief. I guess I owe him one." Blue threw the handkerchief into the bushes. "Met Junior yet?"

"No, who's that?"

"He's my cell mate, man. We spent the weekend at the Nueces County Jail."

Joaquín frowned.

"Yea, Junior's been all over, man—Michigan, Indiana, California, Oregon, Ohio, Minnesota, Florida. This guy's picked every vegetable and fruit you can imagine. Matter of fact, that's why I'm on this wagon train. We were sitting in the jail lunchroom last week, and we get to talking." Blue smiled and shook his head dismissively. "Imagine the guys who just the night before were pumping their iron are now cooking your breakfast. Yum. Yum."

Joaquín remained distant, wondering still what type of crime Blue was in jail for.

"So I tell Junior, 'Man, I feel like eating cauliflower. Just boiled, you know, with salt and pepper.' Junior looks at me with those beady eyes and says to me, 'I've picked cauliflower, but I've never tasted one.' And I tell him, 'You picked the stuff and never even ate one? Never even tasted one?' 'That's right,' he says. And then he starts on me about all kindsa shit this guy's picked."

The flight attendant stretched across Joaquín to collect a paper cup from the seat and barely nudged him. There was a slight shift in his breathing in response, but he otherwise remained asleep in his seat. Conflicting images in Joaquín's dream fought to dominate his focus. An unnatural fear surged into him, and he anticipated what was coming. He quivered. In the plane seat next to him, the startled passenger rolled her eyes in a startled countenance and then slid her body away toward the window in a protective mode. *Flash!* Eyes, cunning, with eyelids lowered, invaded Joaquín's dream screen—an assailant fixating on its prey. *Second flash!* Blue's face distorts into one huge cleft chin with a giant scraggily blue cross tattooed in the center. Just as quickly, Joaquín's dream reverts back to the scene at the Texarkana truck stop.

Blue lit his second cigarette with the first, took a puff, and looked back at Joaquín. "*Ese*, what do you think?" Blue smiled cautiously as he pondered his own inquiry. "You think there's enough work in Michigan to keep a *vato* like me out of trouble?"

Joaquín did not immediately answer. He smiled awkwardly. His eyebrows seemed to ask, *"What? Me give you advice?"* Blue's eyebrows repeated the question, and Joaquín finally answered him. "Man, in Michigan there's no time to get into trouble, not where we stay. If you want trouble, I guess you're going to have to go out of the camp and work hard to find it."

Joaquín's body jerked, foreboding the panic invading his dream. *Flash!* A fiendish smile is cast on Blue's face through sharply filed teeth — shark teeth, row after row of shark teeth. *Flash!* That scene disappears.

"My name's trouble, little man," Blue told Joaquín through a row of straight, bright white teeth.

Joaquín never saw it coming, and when he realized it, he guessed that all things heaven-sent occurred that way — without warning, deserved or not. He had been the last one back on the Ford truck, and true to form, Bennie had protected his seat on the bench. Much to his great surprise and delight, the blonde was on the truck.

Like gazes in an elevator, Joaquín's late-night glances at the blonde were furtive, shifting to avoid being caught overly observant by the blonde's father. Next to the girl, the old man cradled a sterling silver flask close to his chest. He took sips discretely. Whenever the old man snoozed off, Joaquín worked in a few more secret glimpses in the direction of the pretty blonde. If the old man caught Joaquín's gaze at the blonde, feigning innocence, Joaquín would simulate working out a crick in his neck or continue his glare (presumably innocently) foolishly in the blonde's direction. He felt that would give the impression that Joaquín was doubtlessly concentrating on some object on the wall behind the girl.

Later that night, everyone in the back of the Ford truck seemed to have gone to sleep except for Joaquín and the girl. Bennie feigned sleep, closing his eyes as he listened to the radio. As the glow from streetlights on one side of the road angled into the bay of the truck, Joaquín's face was illuminated. He could be seen looking in the girl's direction. Then, light would enter from the other direction, and the blonde girl's face would appear from out of the dark bed of the truck. Refusing to reciprocate, she would look away from him. Then the truck would come upon another streetlight, and Joaquín's face would reappear from out of the dark, as if a single theater light beam had been fixed on his face (and he would be looking in the girl's direction), and then the girl's face would reappear while his disappeared. Then, it would be dark for several minutes. Then, the entire scene would be repeated. Through the second day of the trip, the blonde had never once looked in Joaquín's direction. He fumed. His face said it all. *"How can she stand not to look at me?"*

"Her name's Belínda, *ese*," Blue volunteered at the next stop.

Joaquín feigned indifference. "Who are you talking about?"

"La chavála, bro'" (The girl, bro') Blue pinched the tip of his nose, thumbed his lips, and looked away over his shoulder, avoiding any lengthy connection with Joaquín's eyes. The occasional, detached, over-the-shoulder aversion when talking to someone was classic *Pachúco* posing. This detachment was very cool — unspoken, unwritten, perhaps rude or strange to those unaware, but very cool. Joaquín made a mental note: *Men should never look into each other's eyes long enough to risk learning or disclosing more than they need to.*

"Simón, la güera" (Yeah, right, the light-skinned or blonde), Joaquín admitted. Why deny his interest any longer?

How could she? Joaquín wondered. Why hadn't she responded to him? A simple smile, some acknowledgment, would have sufficed. Why had she slighted him? Besides, what did she have in common with Blue and not with him? As Blue averted his eyes again, Joaquín focused on the blue cross in his cleft chin, which jutted out so that Blue's fat lower lip wasn't quite plumb with the upper one. His core reaction was to pity Blue. Here was a grown man, after all, whose entire estate probably consisted of the clothes on his back. He was not even educated. For all he knew, Blue was married with kids of his own. Perhaps he had even abandoned them. Maybe he was a hardened criminal. *Why does she not like me?*

"She's a good kid," Blue avowed, as he ground the cigarette butt against the paved parking lot and then spit a wad out ten feet, which didn't go unnoticed by Joaquín. Spitting like that took practice. Joaquín could spit pretty well, but he had never quite mastered the art of spitting. To be a *Pachúco*, a really cool *Pachúco*, one had to spit well. If you couldn't spit well, the *vatos* would roll their eyes or turn their heads and glance over their shoulder in a detached sort of way or jut their jaws out and think to themselves, "Este vato, *he can't spit worth a shit.*"

He could not help but pry into what kind of relationship Blue and Belínda may have developed in such a short time and off-handedly asked Blue, "She's kinda quiet, isn't she?"

"Ta media friquiada" (She's somewhat freakish), Blue told him in a somber voice.

Belínda is a little weird or crazy. Joaquín nodded in acknowledgment. *A rational girl would have at least made eye contact with me! Of anyone on this wagon train, I should have attracted her.*

As Joaquín was finishing his conversation with Blue, Don Armándo honked his horn twice. Midday, and the lunch break at the roadside park was over. Passengers lined up single-file, up the plank at the back of the red Ford truck. Glancing in the direction of the truck, Joaquín caught sight of Belínda in the midst of other passengers. Taller than most, she stood out in her faded tight jeans, cowboy boots, and plaid red and white cowboy shirt. Metal snaps on the pockets and cuffs of her shirt sparkled in the warm sunlight. He felt a shiver as he noticed her piercing him with her cold-blue suspicious eyes. *What does she see?* Joaquín pondered. This was the first time she had acknowledged him. Belínda's stare had made Joaquín feel awkward, as if he were an *intruder* on her space. He felt threatened, even intimidated, by that bitter and contemptuous stare.

29

El Negrito/Negasúras

COOL MOISTNESS FROM THE HEAVY, early fog caressed his face and settled on his shoulder-length hair. He shuddered with juvenile excitement. From the peat moss, a strong odor akin to that of freshly pulled mushrooms rose, and Joaquín took in the sweet, musty scent. His bare toes tingled as they acclimated to the massaging moist sand. Atop the green canopy, at thirty or forty feet, a mild breeze began to rustle in alternating waves. Trees swayed gently, but an occasional strong breeze wrenched the trees, and eerie creaks echoed through the forest. His eyes quickly acclimated to the shadows. As he turned back, Joaquín noticed the thick understory at the edges of the forest that created a fortress-like barrier.

In the distance, at the tunnel's end, daylight was visible — but hazy, though, like the blurry desert mirages back home. "Shhh." Walking in front of Bennie, Joaquín signaled and pointed toward a thick oak in the distance in the midst of a circular clearing. Bennie edged back a little and began moving around the giant oak, tiptoeing on his bare feet, his trusted weapon readied for the battle.

The flight attendant returned to find Joaquín asleep; his head listless, with his chin resting on his chest.

In their mid-teens, Joaquín and Bennie were after brown squirrels. They had armed themselves with slingshots they had imported from San Felípe. Carving slingshots from mesquite wood was just one of Bennie's varied hunting skills. His trademark was the notches he gouged into the ends of the "Y" to secure in place the rubber bands that attached the sling to the wood. He carved the rubber slings from discarded tire tubes and tied them down with industrial-grade rubber bands.

These slingshots were the boys' *"negasúras,"* but Joaquín was not aware that *"negasúras"* was not even a real word at all, but instead, Tex-Mex transliteration (slang, if you will) for *"nigger-shooters."*
"NIGGER! NIGGER! NIGGER!"

Abruptly, the scene changed in Joaquín's dream! He stirred in his seat, and let out a barely perceptible moan. The woman sitting in the passenger seat beside him shifted her eyes sideways toward Joaquín without turning toward him and just as quickly disregarded the interruption and returned to her novel.

Dreams did not always play out as well-orchestrated scenes progressing logically from act to act, at least not for Joaquín they didn't. His dream scenes erupted without warning or sequence, much as random, emotional outbursts, disconnected geysers triggered at will in the deep white-gray matter of the brain. The night crew were his culprits: the janitors, and the garbage collectors, the auditors, and the cops on the graveyard shift. Their tools were the compression software and the tape in the back-up computer server. The night crew saw it all, at the end of the day, into the late hours of the night. With the brain at rest, uninterrupted, they cruised its thoroughfares and residential streets, under freeway overpasses and abandoned hallways and desktops, detaining juvenile curfew violators and elderly insomniacs mistaken for perverts, picking up the remains of the day, filing them away in drawers and boxes and nooks and crannies. Receivables and payables were totaled and ledgered for future retrieval. Into the "D" drives and the "G" drives and the "Z" drives it all went, and once compressed into the network, where it was indexed for multiple recalls under "scents," "sights," and "sounds." Evaluated thoughts, an algorithm determined their destiny in the deep recesses of the brain, way down deep in the gray and white matter.

The year was 1959. A properly Southern-mannered white lady with her hair done into a coifed bun tinted to a blue-gray hue interrupted her third-grade class in San Felípe. Joaquín looked around wondering what he was doing in this dream scene. But that semiconscious moment was fleeting, and in the next moment, the dream became reality.

"There has never been a more horrendous word than 'nigger,'" Mrs. Jackson instructed her class. The teacher's normal stare — that confident Victorian piercing that was so familiar to Joaquín — had disappeared from her face, which now contorted into painful feebleness. Mrs. Jackson let out a desperate sigh, and tears flowed. She searched for something above Joaquín, or rather, something beyond him — something this word had stirred in her memory. Nothing had ever set Mrs. Jackson off before. Pulling at her teal woolen sweater, almost timidly, she pouted. She turned to the heavens again, setting her sights higher this time, and breathed deeply; but it didn't help overcome her emotion. She had to excuse herself.

Joaquín turned to Johnny Castellaño on the next row. *"Que pasó?"* (What was that all about?)

Johnny Castellaño explained that a girl classmate had shouted that word, "nigger," at a boy.

"At whom?" Joaquín asked.

"At Poncho," Johnny answered.

Poncho was a chubby classmate, an unusual trait among San Felípe boys, and he was also very, very dark-skinned. Poncho was not very popular. Boys from his neighborhood called him *"Mayáte,"* meaning a shiny black dung beetle. By boldly accenting the second syllable *(ma yá te)*, they made the utterance sound even more despicable. Using its hind legs, the *mayáte* rolled up dung balls into which it inserted its eggs. The dung was the food supply for the young *mayátes*, which had voracious appetites.

Joaquín had never seen a Negro, not up close and personal. His world was inhabited by only two Negros—one of them was the saint, San Martín de Porras, who had an uncanny resemblance to the actor, Sidney Poitier. Holding his hands out in pious fashion, San Martín offered, "Come to me, and I will console you." Joaquín knew all about this because Manda kept a laminated picture of the saint tacked just above the lintel of the door between the kitchen and Sis' room. San Martín spoke Spanish, which he picked up in Haiti or Peru or some such place.

The other Negro was a caricature in the Mexican bingo game— *La Chalúpa.* *"El Negríííííí . . . ííito,"* the barker would call out, surveying the players.

Joaquín would take a pinto bean and mark the *Negríto* on the two cards he was playing, but all for naught. The winner yelled out, *"Chalúpa! I've won."*

Not *"Negro!"* That utterance was too harsh and unkind, just like *"mayáte."* Joaquín cringed at the sound of *Negro* for reasons which he could not yet explain. Perhaps the *Negríto* was an orphan or had been cursed with an incurable disease or was just unlucky. He just didn't know yet. Adding the "ito" to it just softened the blow—but then, it also condescended. Mexicans love diminutives; can't get enough of them—so "ito" is no different. They're just so handy, those efficient linguistic manipulations—perhaps an inheritance carted over from the Iberian Peninsula. Diminutives allowed Mexicans in San Felípe to limit their dictionary to a few essential words. They could say so much by saying so little and act out the rest with intonations and assorted facial and bodily expressions.

There was only one *Negríto* remaining in Joaquín's minuscule world—a burlesque dancer, a Bojangles with blue trousers and a yellow striped shirt and a snazzy cane with a hook handle, a Cotton Club dancer with Louie Armstrong's eyes and pronounced lips. From his cubbyhole on the *Chalúpa* game card next to *el catrín* (the gentleman), *el Negríto* always smiled at him, bearing pearly teeth. In the next row down on the card, *el borrácho* (the drunk) stumbled with a bottle of *tequíla* in his hand. Next to him, *la ∂ama* (the lady) walked erectly in her office attire. And in the frame below her, *el músico* (the musician), short and portly, *a la Botéro*, posed with an upright bass. *El catrín* was white, as was *la ∂ama*. They were all caricatures in Joaquín's childhood game, *La Chalúpa*, and formed a part of his informal pedagogy.

La Chalúpa was Joaquín's primer. *Chalúpa* images taught him. Like invisible chiggers, they had bored through the optic nerve and embedded microscopically in his sensibilities, somewhere down deep where his memory core lies. There, they had scarred his brain ever so slightly—just enough to induce his black and white hemianopsia.

In Joaquín's mind, the scene abruptly changed yet again: *The overnight crew at work.* He saw himself running through a dark wood, stumbling, tumbling, and panting. *Los Negros* were chasing him! Angry faces, protruding snouts, with sharp teeth—overlapping rows of sharp teeth like those of werewolves or sharks (he couldn't quite tell)—snapped at him in his hallucinatory state. Out of breath, he had to slow down in the twisted darkness; feel his way through snaring hawkweed vines; take care that he did not trip on the dead fall.

Calm returned.

Sʰhh . . . Under the calm green canopy, Joaquín startled the squirrel, which sought refuge by scampering up the backside of the thick trunk of the tree. In a squirrel's world, this tactic succeeded when it was being chased by a sole predator. Playing its game of hide and seek, the squirrel worked its way opposite the side to the predator until it was out of harm's way and could return to the shelter of its hermit hole. Instincts! But Joaquín worked his way toward the backside of the tree, and the squirrel returned to Bennie's side of the tree. Bennie rarely missed at such close range with his trusty *negasúra*. Joaquín removed the squirrel's tail and pinned it on his hat and discarded the rest.

After a healthy walk, a camp came into focus in a distant clearing beyond a vast field of strawberries: ten small, white cubicles, pitched roofs, geometric hutches set out neatly in a row, Ford and Chevy pickup trucks, a decaying yellow school bus, and a makeshift pit privy. *The strawberry fields! Michigan!*

Joaquín's plane began its descent to "the windy city." On the speaker, the flight attendant warned the passengers in a well-rehearsed, low baritone voice, "Please bring your trays to the upright position." Joaquín lost focus.

30

The Road Atlas

BLANKETING THE HOOD OF THE SUBARU rental was a road atlas. Joaquín's black computer case weighed down one of the map's corners; his cell phone another. U.S. Interstate Highway 94 was a bold red line on the map that snaked from the airport through downtown Chicago, past that huge Catholic church with the two towers near where that painted wall used to be (the one with the sports icons the likes of Michael Jordan and Mike Ditka) to Niles, Michigan, on the southeastern end of the lake.

"What's in Chicago?" Bennie had asked.

"It's my annual tax law conference. It keeps me on top of recent developments in the tax laws."

"Sounds downright boring."

"Not really. Besides, it's one of the conditions to keeping my bar membership, but I also take advantage of the change. Two, three days is enough to recharge my battery. I enjoy the scenery." Joaquín had enjoyed shopping the windows along Michigan Avenue up to State Street at the far north end of the retail district where the trendy shops were—where he could pick up something to read at the Temple University bookstore or sit across the street at the Water Park or at the second-story coffee shop he liked. He'd find the latest sushi innovations, real Italian food, and catch a show at Steppenwolf or at Second City.

Joaquín pointed to Niles, searching with his finger for the county roads north to Decatur. He had devised his plan for a temporary detour to Decatur, Michigan, when he paid the advance registration fee for this year's legal conference.

"I'll start out for Michigan early the morning after I arrive in Chicago," he told Bennie. It was Michigan that was on his mind. "Say it'll take me four, maybe five hours. I may have some time to spend looking around at least for part of the afternoon on the first day and then all day the second day." He felt that might be enough time, but he had not shared with Bennie what he would be looking for. Rather, he had left the perception that he was approaching the visit very much like a leisurely tourist.

The airport incident had put a new wrinkle on his already confounded dreams and recollections. *Why was an emaciated body of a dead woman straight out of a sepulcher showing up in this mental screen?* He recalled the clear signs of violence on her body and her gown. *Who was the precocious child, and what was she doing in my dream world?* These memories kept creeping back into his consciousness in a most haunting manner.

Joaquín checked his watch as another airplane took off on the runway behind O'Hare's international terminal. "One-thirty," he whispered, as he calculated what was left of the day.

Anyone could have missed the unassuming Monroe Street entrance to the Palmer House Hotel as I did, Joaquín reasoned, and he then had to swing around Monroe Street under the El and come back up on Wabash. He had stayed in the hotel half a dozen times, but this was the first time he had driven in Chicago, which is no easy feat.

Busying himself in his hotel room later in the afternoon, Joaquín spent a few minutes reviewing the file notes and drafts of pretrial motions his legal assistant had prepared for the Mejía Mata case. From the window of the small study, his only view was the other rather unattractive hotel tower. Joaquín shrugged. *At least nothing will distract me from the work,* he reasoned. He drew a Heineken from the courtesy bar, pulled out the comfortable leather chair, and stretched on it using the bed as a footstool.

"Mejía Mata is guilty of the cocaine possession . . . no doubt about it," Bob Peters had written in his file memo. "Every effort should be made to plead him out and the best terms advocated for his punishment," he urged.

Joaquín agreed, nodding his head. He took a gulp from the bottle and wished he had some cheese and crackers to go with it.

His associate's memorandum asserted that a Newton, Indiana, arrest was simply too far removed to be considered by the Court in setting punishment in the case. Peters' addressing of the issue had been elementary. He was well aware that Joaquín's limited experience with criminal cases required that no legal detail should remain unaddressed.

What a strange coincidence, Joaquín thought. Mejía Mata was once arrested in Newton, Indiana, of all places—for burglary of a vehicle.

Joaquín called Peters.

"There's no issue of probable cause," Peters advised. "There's sufficient evidence to arrest the guy."

"So, why the motion? And why at this late stage?"

"Why not?" Peters responded. "Maybe there were mistakes made. I'd leave it in."

"I suppose his other arrests will increase his sentence, then?"

"If he has any other arrests (and he does), this will increase his sentence by as little as six months or up to several years, depending on the severity of the prior criminal activity. The sentencing guidelines are a no-brainer. This guy's doing time. It's just a matter of how much, sir."

"Bob, I agree with you. We should tell our guy to plead guilty and focus our efforts on the sentencing phase. I don't want to learn any more criminal law than I absolutely have to."

Joaquín crossed his ankles and stretched his back and neck.

"Sir?"

Joaquín had momentarily lost focus as Peters continued his update.

"Yeah, Bob, go ahead. I'm here."

Peters advised, "Mejía Mata has been calling from the county jail and insists on talking to you about the case. I don't think he likes me."

"Bob, why don't you figure out what the sentence will likely be, go visit the guy, and take copious notes of everything he says? Get him to commit to his guilt—again. Tell him I will visit with him as soon as I get back."

"He's very insistent that he needs to talk to *you*." Peters sounded a bit distressed. "And he says if you don't talk to him, he may just want to complain directly to the judge."

"Aw, shit," Joaquín complained and then went silent. He sighed. "Tell you what . . . Arrange a collect call from him to the office, and then have the office patch me in. I think that'll work. Let's agree you'll call between four-thirty and five-thirty on Friday, because that's when I plan to return to Chicago."

The Fly in the Milk/*Mosca En La Leche*

MILLER'S WAS CONVENIENTLY LOCATED just outside on the Wabash Street entrance to Palmer House. It was a small place with a bar and black-and-white glossies of celebrities on its wainscoted walls. Famous for pork ribs, it was a second home to many of Chicago's finest. But regardless of the sign on the door proclaiming its pork rib fame, Joaquín preferred Miller's Greek salads. *Feta cheese and anchovies,* he imagined as he made his way out of the hotel. His mouth watered at the thought. He considered Miller's for an early dinner. After all, he was a bit on the moody side, and Miller's was quiet and reserved—the kind of place where people kept their voices low and with a built-in sense of privacy. The only view offered by the window was the El stop above and pigeons roosting in the nooks of the metal structure. But custom was hard to break. Joaquín's first meal ever in Chicago had been Italian, and he had since made it a tradition that his first meal of every Chicago trip begin with Italian. And there was nothing Italian about pork ribs and Greek salads.

Leaving the Palmer House, he felt the cool breeze coming in over Lake Michigan. Its effect was rejuvenating. He headed in the direction of Michigan Avenue through the crowded sidewalk. Overhead, at a jewelry store, a large round clock marked the hour at a quarter till five. Joaquín marveled at how the cacophony of a downtown Chicago fall afternoon consorted into the lively din of a fine-tuned idling motor—the clattering and shrieking metal of the busy El above, police car sirens, the pounding of street maintenance equipment, and the choral murmur of voices all working together in some sort of strange urban melody. He felt the city's rhythmic vibrations enter through his toes and reverberate in his entire body. The city grew on him quickly. Yet, somewhere in the distance, Joaquín made out the sustained dissonant blaring of car horns. *An impromptu tailgate pep rally,* he gathered, and dismissed the sound.

They aren't nightmares, he had tried convincing himself. Yet, *they* had returned with sustained frequency. His perennial bad dream from childhood had not recurred in many years. That dream he had long ago deciphered and in so doing had convinced himself of having overcome its power over him. But the dreaded dream was back. An invisible force suddenly gripped him. The space around him became thick and heavy, and he felt as if he was walking in a swimming pool with the water up to his chest. Others in his dream were unaffected by this force. Self-assuredly and with confidence, they walked freely, right past him, deliberately moving to some place up ahead where everyone was headed. The *force* affected only him. It impeded *his* forward motion. No one noticed or rendered aid as he grabbed onto objects in his path for leverage to pull himself forward — a car door handle here, a shrub there — only to be drawn back by this overpowering *force*. He was drawn back in the direction from where he had begun, and he held on to avoid the overpowering rejection. The force was not external. Rather, he felt it in his body, as if he was being directed by something within him which he was powerless to overcome.

Struggling against the irrepressible wave until the breaking point, Joaquín would finally wake up. Being awake and in control reassured him. *It's been a dream . . . only a dream.* At night, though, he could not control the random independence that a part of his brain took on in a dream state. The dream was a reflection of a weakness he once had, he was sure of it — something of his own inferiority complex, which he had long ago overcome; which he had defeated and suppressed; which he seemed reassured this dream would not rekindle.

L'Strada was almost empty. Not Italiano enough, and unadorned, the dining room was not particularly appealing to him. And, at subsidewalk level, a patron's only view was that of busy pedestrians making their way above on Michigan Avenue. Since his first visit here years before though, Joaquín had felt at ease here. Sinatra was always crooning in the background, never overbearing, and could be tuned in or out depending on Joaquín's mood. And after dinner, he could always count on a good cigar or catch a bit of sports at the small bar set off to the side by the entrance.

"Is a banquette available?" he inquired of the maître d'.

"Certainly, sir," the maître d' answered, and Joaquín took the utterance to be more Bronx than midwestern. Joaquín selected the banquette at the far corner after reassurance from the maître d' that group diners were rare this early in the evening.

"*Provécho, señór,*" The maître d' dipped his head and gave Joaquín an inquisitive look.

Joaquín started in on the bread with a thick helping of butter and a glass of cabernet. His mind drifted. For many years he had carried the resentment against his father! *And, justifiably so,* he argued with himself. Joaquín's neck muscles tightened at the thought. Joaquín had often dedicated hours at a time searching the deep recesses of his own mind. But rarely could he form a glimpse of pleasant times with Benáncio. Gritting his teeth in frustration, he punished himself. *What happened to us?*

"*Paréces mosca en leche*" (You're like a fly in the milk). His father's stare was scornful and penetrating. Joaquín had slipped into a game among a group of Anglo children who were playing kickball while Benáncio read the Mexican daily. Joaquín knew that Benáncio's stare meant he should immediately return to the concrete park bench where his father sat under the shade of a massive ash. But he had no clue of what he had done wrong.

A few months pregnant, Manda had been full of excitement for months in spite of a serious case of diabetes and high blood pressure. Dr. James had objected to the pregnancy since it risked the lives of both mother and child. Still, Manda had promised Joaquín that he would have a baby sister. But Manda had taken ill the previous night, and Dr. James had required that she stay at the hospital. That morning, Benáncio and Joaquín made their way over to the park across the small hospital while the hospital staff got ready to discharge Manda. The Baptist church down the street used the park for its recreation program, and the first-grade class was out for recess from Bible school.

As he lay there on the cool carpet of grass looking up to the sky imagining cloud figures in his mind, he was distracted for a few seconds by a noisy cicada somewhere in the hundreds of branches of the ash tree. He pictured "*The fly in the milk.*" Desperately, the fly fluttered in a figure-eight in the thick creamy milk, contrasted against the perfect white canvas.

The gruff prominence of Benáncio's arching eyebrows, wrinkling his forehead, seemed to warn of his unbearable urge to whack Joaquín silly.

⸻

Joaquín's breathing became audible. He set the cabernet on the table and rotated his neck as if his shirt collar had become unbearable, and he forced his shoulders back.

⸻

"Fly in the milk." The expression escaped Joaquín. *What does he mean?* No reaction came from Benáncio to Joaquín's weak attempts to engage him by trying to distract him. Benáncio stared straight ahead, averting Joaquín's eyes, squinting with a ferocious look of disappointment on his face, and never even acknowledging that Joaquín had returned to the bench as instructed.

What pathetic conduct have I engaged in this time? Joaquín wondered, edging closer to his father on the bench. *Maybe it wasn't so bad an infraction this time, and Papa will eventually give me a hug?* But Benáncio pulled away.

⸻

The waiter brought a fresh glass and poured more of the cabernet. Joaquín nodded at him. *I guess I just couldn't make it out at the time. I was too young, and naïve—so much still that I did not realize that my actions constituted consorting with the enemy.* Joaquín's thoughts returned to the fly, continuing its struggle but eventually tiring out and being swallowed up whole by the white canvas.

⸻

Two weeks later, in the backyard, just beyond the kitchen, Joaquín carted a pair of washed jeans up to the clothesline. Manda was hanging up the wash. She kept two large soot-black cauldrons of boiling water just outside the kitchen, which she used to fill an old, round electric washing machine. The machine sat on four legs, each of which rolled on a black coaster. Sis heralded it as "the twister" because when they turned it on, it shook and twisted and shuddered until it traveled so far that its extension cord would unhook from the electric socket. Manda would then have to recruit the boys to push "the twister" back close to the kitchen electric socket so the machine could start its gyrations all over again.

"*Mi 'jo*, be sure to keep checking those blue jeans. I want them just moist enough to iron. Don't let them dry up on you, now." Manda shaded her head with the gingham blue *guarde soleil* she had sewn for the upcoming cotton-picking season.

"Okay."

Manda had taught Joaquín that since the socks and jeans took longer to dry, they must be hung on the east clothesline, where they would be the first to benefit from the warm southeasterly breeze. Manda handled laundry and pressed shirts for some of the business-men from across town. Businessmen's white shirts, sheets, and pil-lowcases were light and a breeze to hang up. Bennie always volun-teered for that job on account that he was the youngest.

"*Los patrónes* [the bosses] are coming for their shirts first thing in the morning," Manda reminded herself. She complained, *I'll have to work late into the night if I'm going to be ready for them.*

A moist and cool pillowcase that was strung from the clothesline flapped into Joaquín's face. The breeze kept it there. He breathed through his mouth and felt the air, cooled and filtered through the linen, expanding his lungs.

"Mama, what do people mean when they say 'there's a fly in the milk'?" Joaquín was giving his back to Manda as he hung the pair of jeans from the cuffs.

"*Platicando, pero trabajando,*" (talking, but working), she preached at him, and he rolled his eyes in response.

"So?" he insisted. "What does it mean?"

"It's a *dicho, mi'jo,*" Manda answered.

"It's a *dicho?* What's a *dicho?*"

"A *dicho* is a saying—a way of making an important point, but by analogy."

"What's an analogy?"

"By example, *mi'jo;* as in comparing two things."

Joaquín's anxiety showed. He dropped his shoulders listlessly and turned around to her. "Like what?"

"Well, there are many *dichos,* Son. There's one that says, 'Tell me who your friends are, and I'll tell you what you are.' Makes sense, right? You'll learn that one in school—Aesop's fables. And another that says, 'Only he who totes the load knows what he carries.'"

Joaquín mulled over Manda's response as she handed him the legs side of a pair of Levi's and they wrung it free of the rinse water. He patted some of the cool water on his face as his mother took the pair from him.

"What does it mean to be 'a fly in the milk'?"

"Oh, that's a good one. We use that whenever a person insists on bothering a group into which he is not welcome — for instance, just like a housefly is an unwelcomed guest. That is where it comes from."

Joaquín frowned but remained silent.

Manda explained further, "It refers to a *morenito* [dark-skinned person] who's trying to fit in with the *güeros* [the light-skinned persons]. In other words, it means that he's trying to be part of something of which he simply cannot be."

"That's what it means?"

"Yes."

In his dream, Joaquín made his way diagonally across rows of parked cars. Up ahead, from a venue of some sort, came the roar of a cheering crowd. Then, the force entered him. Messages from the brain could not reach his limbs. The invisible force drew him back, and the world was soon leaving him behind. *Papa is leaving without you.* Others on the way to the venue found the trip effortless. Hard as Joaquín tried, he could not gain. Grasping at car tires, door handles, and bumpers, he struggled to pull away from the thick, sucking, invisible force that drew him back. Down he went into the thick milk in slow motion, his arms useless against the gravitational pull that had drawn him back.

Great Aspirations/Mary, Quite Contrary

A WOMAN'S VOICE CALLED OUT Bennie's name on the intercom. Heads turned from the teachers' table at the school cafeteria. The voice asked that Bennie return to the office. He gave the teachers at the table a half-bothered, half-apologetic shrug.

"Master Sergeant, you have a call on Line Two," the school office clerk advised him mockingly as she handed him the phone. "I always had this feeling that you were a military guy," she told him.

Bennie took the phone by the clerk's counter. He nodded at the clerk, "This will be a short conversation." The receptionist moved away to offer some privacy but remained within earshot. He recognized the sound of Joaquín's voice. "Sergeant Major, this is the president calling from a gas station between Niles and Decatur. I'm lost." Joaquín chuckled as he hugged the phone between his left shoulder and his ear. In his left hand, he held a large Styrofoam cup of steaming coffee, which he blew at in a desperate attempt to cool it. With his right hand, he retrieved his calling card from the public telephone.

At the other end of the line Bennie chuckled in return. It had been years since Joaquín had referred to himself as the "president," a term he used ironically to mock himself.

Ike was president at the time. At the northside elementary school in San Felípe, the classrooms were reserved for the Mexican kids. Ike's black-and-white portrait smiled at each of the children from above the large green and white alphabet chart that ran along the full length of the blackboard.

Mrs. Garfield searched around the room of second-graders for candidates. Her shy students fidgeted in their seats, except for Joaquín, whose eagerness to volunteer showed on his face.

"José, wouldn't you like to grow up to be a policeman?" Mrs. Garfield smiled. The teacher had been anointed to dish out jobs, and she was having a wonderful time at it. José turned to the other students, giggled through gaps left by missing baby front teeth, and shyly shrugged his shoulders.

"Sure you would. José is going to be a policeman. Class, give him a hand." Her charge joined in and gave José a round of applause.

The children clapped their hands eagerly and looked at each other proudly. Joaquín clapped, impatiently waiting his turn to be called upon.

Mrs. Garfield beamed as well. She just couldn't help herself.

In the next row, Mary turned to Joaquín. Mary was a small girl — a girl with that type of frame she would certainly never grow out of; she was destined to be short all her life. Mary bit her lower lip in her cute, coy way. With a wit sharper than a knife, Mary's posture was that of a military cadet, matched only by the contents of her Big Chief tablet, which contained page after page of neat and erect letters and numbers.

"Mary, don't you want to be a secretary when you grow up?"

"Yes," Mary's response was whirling in the air even before the teacher could finish the question. She would be the secretary. *Sure, why not?* She counterfeited a smile for the teacher and then turned to Joaquín with a look that told him, *"I know this bullshit game; play with it."* Her instruction was lost on Joaquín.

A sincere smile formed on the teacher's face. She beamed proudly again as she surveyed her charge. She nodded to herself as if to confirm, *This is what teaching is all about.* She seemed to be holding back a tear. The children's faces confirmed that she was getting through to her students, providing positive role models, teaching them cognitive skills. *Her children,* as she referred to them — since she really had two sets of children, or so she told her class — the ones at school and the ones at home — her children had great aspirations. She even once shared with them that she had told her home family just how proud she was of her school family. In fact, this class was perhaps her best ever. This made Joaquín feel warm inside.

When his turn came, Joaquín was dying with anticipation.

"I'm going to grow up to be the president of the United States of America." Joaquín looked the teacher straight in the eye with that great anticipation of the warm fuzzies that a child senses from a mentor's praise. *What can possibly top that?* Joaquín's upright posture in the chair said it all . . . from sea to shining sea!

As if on cue, the class went dead silent.

"Y este?" (What's up with this one?)

Mrs. Garfield was caught off guard. Her raised brow was not deliberate. After all, she was a trained professional, learned in the ways of ministering to children with such adolescent illusions. Just for a second, she looked at Joaquín in silent astonishment and then formed an inauthentic grin. To Joaquín, the look meant, *"You little shit, lower your sights a bit."*

Actions speak louder than words, and the eyes rarely lie. So it wasn't a game after all. His classmates caught on to this and ribbed him for weeks.

"Joaquín is going to be president! Joaquín is going to be president!" Joaquín had turned to Mary who refused to look back at him. After all, she had done her share and warned him to follow her lead: be a fireman; be a policeman; be a secretary. That would have made the teacher proud, but Joaquín could never help himself.

Joaquín often joked about the incident, but in his younger years, late at night, he had these strange dreams: the invisible *force*. It came from nowhere to torture him. His body fell under its control. Every step he attempted degenerated into slow motion and required great effort of mind, as if the muscles in his legs received but faint messages from his brain, which they were unable to interpret. And Joaquín went nowhere in his dreams as others passed him by, oblivious to his dilemma. At other times, his dreams found him in some public place completely bare, but no one noticed. He sought cover from his nudity but couldn't hide from himself. The torture ended only when he was able to wake himself.

"Yes, sir, Mr. President, talk to me."

To Joaquín, Bennie sounded less than enthusiastic.

"Hey, I'm sorry to bother you again. But something's been bugging me, and I thought you might be able to fill in some blanks in my memory."

"Well, let's try." Again, Bennie's response was not engaging.

"I know this is going to sound strange," Joaquín wet his lips and hesitated, "but did we ever have a friend up in Michigan?" He paused, then added, "Do you remember an anglo girl . . . a blonde?" The query came out uncomfortably slowly, too slowly for Joaquín, whose voice had cracked, and he wondered whether Bennie could tell how embarrassed he felt just making the inquiry.

"Oh, yeah," Bennie mocked. "You and I both, we dated a lot of blondes in our time. I thought we discussed this earlier, though. I don't recall a blonde."

How could he blame Bennie? Bennie must have felt that the circumstances called for sarcasm as the only appropriate response.

"Come on! I'm serious, here," Joaquín implored.

Bennie's silence confirmed he was backing off.

"There was a blonde!" Joaquín's desperate voice pleaded. "That's all I remember. I don't know where she came from, but there was a blonde. At some point up in Michigan, there was a blonde!"

"I don't recall a girl," Bennie told Joaquín. "I'm sorry. We've been over this before." Bennie's voice was firm and implied conclusiveness.

Joaquín remained silent.

"What's this all about, man? Are you okay?" Bennie's voice was firmer.

"It's about something that's very important to me. It is goddamn crucial to me. Otherwise, you think I'd be wasting your precious time? Well, maybe it's nothing." Joaquín seemed to be thinking aloud to himself. There was a note of disappointment in his voice. "I just could have sworn there was this girl. But it's not . . . it's not that important." He drifted at the end, hoping that Bennie would insist on hearing more.

History Lessons at the Kitchen Table

BENÁNCIO'S VOICE THUNDERED in Joaquín's memory, "The carrot Hidálgo held before them was not freedom and democracy and a new state. *No, señór!* It was the *moreníta* [the brown Madonna], the Virgin of Guadalúpe."

At the kitchen table in San Felípe, Joaquín received instruction about the Mexican War of Independence as he stood in front of Benáncio's favorite chair. Benáncio pointed with his finger to make the point. "The Virgin was the Indian Joan d'Arc, the mythical lady in blue, who exhorted the Indians to rise up. And rise up they did! Therein lay the problem."

"But why was the Virgin the problem, Papa?" Joaquín asked, a perplexed frown on his face.

Benáncio returned a scornful stare, as if Joaquín was nothing more than an insolent child. "Don't you see?" Benáncio bristled as he stared into Joaquín's eyes, demanding his absolute allegiance. He lifted both fists up to his face and punctuated each word. "Listen, there were no principles involved!" He swept his right hand in front of his face and shook it to mean "good riddance." "The Indians were blindly following an image the church itself had created."

Joaquín stared.

"Initially from *Dolóres*, and then from other villages, the revolting Indian peasants gathered behind the Virgin's standard and banner. Growing in their collective hatred for everything that was Spanish and therefore, oppressive, they moved on to the Spanish *haciéndas*."

There was fire in Benáncio's eyes as he said it.

"At each *haciénda* and village, the Indios and their Mestízo offspring sought to divest themselves of hundreds of years of abuse, degradation, and exploitation by destroying whatever Spanish life they could find." Benáncio spoke as if he pictured himself in the scene, a brave young fighter joining the fray. "They fought with sticks and stones and whatever sharp or blunt instruments they could find."

"And the children, Papa?" A young Joaquín winced, anticipating Benáncio's answer.

Benáncio was in full stride. "They grabbed the children by their feet and whipped them around and cracked their heads open on stones. Why allow them to grow up and use the yoke on you?"

It had been an innocent question by Joaquín who had imagined children left to fend for themselves as orphans, but not for his father who, in usual stride, declared it self-evident. Tears formed in Joaquín's eyes. He had missed the entire point of the exercise.

It had all occurred a hundred years before Benáncio had even been born, but he spoke about it as if he'd been there.

"The peasants had finally said, 'Enough is enough!' The defect was in the Spanish blood! It had to be destroyed."

In Joaquín's pre-adolescent memory, as the Virgin's banner passed, in the swath it cut, it left behind rubber baby dolls strewn everywhere on the roads to Mexico City. Ripped from their mother's breasts, the babies were banged about like so many rubber dolls — headless baby dolls. It was an unending heap pile, littered with the thousands of bodies of dolls whose heads had been busted open. Limbs had been torn from their bodies, ripped from them like chicken wings. Some were missing their colored pupils, detached from their swiveling eyeballs as their heads were bashed in against the limestone outcroppings. They deserved it, right? All for the sake of the Virgin.

But there was more. Benáncio mocked, "The flamboyant *Padre Hidálgo* had enjoyed his share of temporal virtues and vices — good *vino*, women, and an occasional dice game." He told Joaquín how Hidálgo had been motivated as much by the Spanish church's assault on his family's own special privileges as by revolutionary dogma. A satisfied smile formed on Benáncio's face as he concluded, "Sadly, contrition would not be enough to save the cleric. Hidálgo lost his head a long time before he was deprived of it."

Benáncio was still not finished. "The Virgin never spoke to the Indios directly," he complained, and shook his head. "Instead, she communicated her will only through the intercessionists, like the learned Father Hidálgo. *Pon atención!* And so, when the *Indios* got to the center of power, Mexico City, they did not know how to take it, for it was beyond their reality."

Indeed, at Mexico City, Father Hidálgo withdrew as leader of the *Indios*. He could no longer provide answers. Sadly for the Indians, there had never been a plan — just a spontaneous overflow. It had been for the *here and now;* it had been for the emotion and for the purification *(aquí nos vamos a dar en la mera madre).*

"Son, the Mexican history books won't admit it, but Father Hidálgo had abandoned the Indians, betrayed them. He ended up begging the Inquisition for forgiveness. He apologized, claiming he had been misguided."

The 1816 rebellion was short-lived, and indeed, Hidálgo did confess and apologize to the Spanish Inquisition.

The only heroes Joaquín had identified with Benáncio had eagerly toppled. *Why was it so important for him that I know that?* Joaquín asked himself.

Crabs and *Igualádos*/
We Should Be More Like Jews

BY EARLY OCTOBER, the sonorous wails of the *chichárras* had abruptly disappeared. The year was 1961. Next door, Janie (the former vanilla beauty dipped in chocolate) was bursting at the seams with her third child and had shed all those features which had so attracted Joaquín. Earlier in the afternoon, the boys played two-on-two football until dusk at *El Salón* with Johnny Castellaño and his cousin Louie, another rare little fat kid. They later joined Benáncio at Don Magín's corner grocery store. Joaquín invited himself into the circle of men under the spacious tin-covered porch, finding a space on the concrete floor next to one of the two *mojadítos*, who balanced on their haunches. The *mojadítos* reeked of a tortuous musk, which Joaquín rated somewhere between that of a *javalina* and the unforgettable foul odor of a bat cave. Squirming his way through, he sought the niche between Don Silvéstre and the steel column holding up the tin roof where he could still keep an eye on Bennie.

Don Silvéstre was on his soapbox. Like Benáncio, Don Silvéstre was one of the men regularly attracted by the fluorescent light at Don Magín's. It wasn't clear that Don Silvéstre was a Mexican, that is, until he spoke. Life in the shoe shop before his retirement had kept him away from the sun, and now the sun made him pink like the underbelly of a suckling piglet. Short and pudgy, cherry cheeks, a receding hairline, and wire-rim glasses bore him a close resemblance to Tom Thumb's father.

As Bennie sat next to his father, Don Silvéstre coughed up a snarl of phlegm and spit it a good fifteen feet into the *calíche* roadway. He wiped his mouth with a red bandana and took his place on the wooden bench by the front door to the store.

"We Mexicans are like crabs!" Don Silvéstre grieved, as if he'd just been betrayed by his closest of friends. He shook his head, sighed, and looked to the heavens in feigned disbelief. Benáncio listened intently.

Manda had long ago instructed Joaquín and Bennie on the virtues of corner-store etiquette—"Just sit quietly and don't bother the adults, boys." Joaquín crossed his eyes and put on a curious face, which remarked implicitly, *"Yikes! We're crabs?"* Bennie chuckled under his breath in response.

"How do you mean, Don Silvéstre?" Benáncio's interest was genuine.

"Well, if you have ever been crabbing, you know that crabs in a bucket will not keep still. They will always persist in climbing out. But they keep slipping down the slick sides of the bucket." Don Silvéstre had a point and everyone nodded at the profundity of his assertion. Joaquín frowned again. "The crabs will pile on top of each other, and as one of them is just about to make it out of the bucket, there's sure to be another crab that will grab it and pull it down." Don Silvéstre took another sigh, deeper and, this time, more profound. Indeed, the weight of the entire world seemed to be a burden on Don Silvéstre's shoulders. "That's us, the crabs," Don Silvéstre concluded somberly, searching around for sympathy.

At first, Joaquín pictured brown crabs clawing at each other in a number-five galvanized tub—the kind that could hold about seventeen gallons of water. Just as one crab was about to make it out over the brim, two other smaller crabs grabbed it and yanked it down. Then Joaquín imagined a tubful of slithering, shiny black snakes. He shuddered at the thought.

Benáncio puckered his lips. "I've never been crabbing—" he began. And that was an understatement. Benáncio had never even seen an ocean. Benáncio tended to pucker his lips just as he was about to say something profound, just as a conductor would tap his baton to get the orchestra's complete attention. He began to pucker, but Don Silvéstre wasn't ready to yield the soapbox. His pause had been simply to gather his thoughts.

Benáncio yielded, and Don Silvéstre continued, this time more animated than before. "That's the way we Mexicans *[nosótros los Mexicános]* are." He tapped his chest with his open hand to include himself in the blame. "We're always pulling each other down. We cannot help each other up. No! Drag 'em down. Why is that?" he asked, his face showing genuine perplexity. "Why are we like that?"

Don Silvéstre asked the question rhetorically, even acknowledging Joaquín and Bennie in his discourse, as if offering even them a stab at explaining why Mexicans were like crabs. Joaquín's eyes perked up. *Perhaps there is no answer to this apparently centuries-old dilemma. Has an unexplainable defect, of sorts, entered the gene pool somewhere along the line? Are we all like that?* Joaquín turned to Bennie with a confused look, his hands open for suggestions, and Bennie peered back at him with a blank look. He seemed to have no clue either.

He had been chomping at the bit for his turn, so speaking with booming authority, a certain bravado in his voice which demanded one and all to listen and obey, Benáncio took his turn at the soapbox. "What we *Mexicános* need is to be organized, to act as one and to help each other." He would occasionally turn in Joaquín's direction. *"Dicen que en la unión está la fuerza."* (They say that there is strength in a union).

"They say," prefaced all dubious declarations uttered at Don Magín's. It was a skillful way to avert responsibility for an assertion.

"They say there is strength in a union . . . *organization!*" That's what it would take, according to Benáncio. Benáncio saw the world in very clear and simple terms. Joaquín knew that, and that in Benáncio's world, there was *them* and there was *us*. And the *us* of the world needed to get organized, for alone, there was no power. *"They* are against you! *They* hold you back!" It was that simple.

What is this "organization" supposed to accomplish? Joaquín wondered. *Just how do you organize all these crabs that are so instinctively at each other's throats? And what do the crabs do when they get organized? Do they build a ladder to get out of the tub? And once they're out of the tub? What then?* The questions whirled in Joaquín's brain.

But Benáncio had not finished. "Answers can be provided by a genuine leader," he declared, raising his finger in the air as he said it.

All the great patio philosophers at Don Magín's nodded their agreement.

"We need a true leader," Don Silvéstre chimed in, surveying the audience for any thoughts on the subject.

"But not just any leader," Benáncio demanded, and stared in Joaquín's direction.

Everyone nodded again in unison.

Joaquín imagined his version of the leader that the Mexicans yearned for:

> . . . *a good and moral leader, a giving leader, not a man of bone and flesh who could succumb to temporal vices, or who would have any personal ambition, but a leader without sin, a perfect leader, a messiah,*

someone who could be there for us, all the time, at our behest, to serve our needs, not his. Ours. Yes! That is our problem, we need organization and a perfect leader, someone who can lead the crabs! A benevolent King Crab!

"They say that the Jews always give each other a hand up," Don Magín added as an afterthought. He scratched the inside of his left ear, which appeared to give him great pleasure. "They say that the Jews are very well organized. Their advancements as a people come from being organized. We Mexicans, too, need that kind of organization."

They all agreed. *They needed to be more like the Jews.*

<hr />

The cold beer came. Disappointment showed on Benáncio's face. He knew the congregation would lose focus after some beers.

The crab metaphor grew uncontrollably that night. Don Silvéstre never got around to complete his story, for his anxiety and obsession with the crabs took the better of him.

"As soon as a Mexican begins to scratch out a lifestyle just a wee bit better than the rest, what happens?" Don Magín challenged again.

From the corner of the tin-covered porch, his back up against one of the round steel columns, Don Lupíto, who had remained silent throughout the discussion, now grunted to get everyone's attention and lifted the brim of his hat. He had an answer to tender, "*Pués*, the other crabs will come out to pull him down."

Is it envy? Joaquín pondered. That seemed to him to be precisely Don Silvéstre's point.

"But on the other hand," Don Lupíto pushed away from the column and posited, "what if the only way a crab can escape the bucket is by his own wits?" Don Lupíto seemed to be posturing himself, for of all the men, he was a self-employed entrepreneur of sorts. Benáncio often complained to the boys that Don Lupíto made a good living off the backs of the wetbacks as an intermediary for the vegetable farmers.

Don Silvéstre wouldn't let Don Lupíto go unanswered. "Ah, and the one who makes it out by himself, will he ever look back? Will he ever lend a helping hand to the others? Or will he sell out?"

There were crabs all around. Crabs trying to make it out of the slippery bucket and other crabs holding them back. And the ones who made it sold out! The bleak metaphor lodged deep in the gray matter of Joaquín's brain.

"Igualádo!" Benáncio angrily blurted out as a scowl formed on his face in reaction to Don Lupíto's comment, and at that very moment, Benáncio turned to Joaquín, shooting him a stabbing stare.

Who was this *Igualádo?* Joaquín learned that night under the porch that there would always be that one person who insisted in believing that he could be equal to *"them."* Such insistence was, of course, utterly naïve, it was pointed out, and was perceived as the *Igualádo's* sorry attempt to abandon the rest (the *"us"*), for he believed that he could gain equality and acceptance from *"them."* But he was wrong; for all must enter the temple as one, or no one enters.

"We should all know that," Don Silvéstre complained, making sure that the message was not lost on the boys. "It is inconceivable that anyone can ever be equal to *them*," he argued.

Alone at the small bar at L'Strada, Joaquín stared blankly at the silent screen of the television mounted on a sturdy metal arm behind the bartender. He sipped on his third single-malt scotch. It was not only the word *"Igualádo"* that had described this traitor and treacherous human being, he reasoned, but the utterance itself, how each syllable was accented and intonated and spitted out for effect. *No language in the world can match Spanish to so eloquently convey in one single utterance the utter and despicable disdain which the men at Don Magín's could conjure up for the Igualádo. Was that the disdain Papa had for me?*

Yo M'echo La Peséta (I'll Do the Time)/ Los Vatos Feós

OUTSIDE, THE BREEZE HAD CALMED, and the sky had taken on a gray overcast. The day had cooled enough to make it a comfortable fall-like day. Much in tourist mode, Joaquín paused to admire the color-ful tulip arrangements placed on the street medians and hanging from ornamental light poles and growing from massive sidewalk flowerpots on Michigan Avenue. Warm in his chest and light on his feet, he credited the cabernet for the sensation.

Across the street, a motorcycle patrolman was single-handedly halting the progress of a motorcade of young Mexicans parading on Michigan Avenue. Curious onlookers had begun gathering on all four corners of the intersection and appeared to wonder among themselves what crimes may have been committed. After lining sev-eral of the parade participants up against the concrete center me-dian, the patrolman began to issue each driver a citation. At the head of the parade was an older model Cadillac, a black convertible with the late 1950s wingspan. A yellowing pinwheel, a plastic red, white, and green flag of Mexico, was attached to the car's antenna. Like a trapped, discarded plastic grocery bag, the flimsy plastic fluttered busily as the breeze began to pick up.

Opting to observe the action from a safe distance, Joaquín backed up against the protective sidewalk railing for a comfortable vantage point. Just then, an older model van (a straggler from the parade) barely missed hitting him. Balancing on two tires as it made the turn, the van almost emptied its passengers through its side sliding door. Bouncing back to all four tires, it completed the quick illegal turn and screeched back westward, toward the Chicago River and the retail district.

Inside the van, a chorus cried out angry slogans. *"Viva México Putos* [Long live Mexico] . . . *Viva La Revolución* [Long live the Revolution] . . . *Viva la Virgén de Guadalúpe* [Long live Our Lady of Guadalúpe]!"

The cop turned to the screeching van and peered over his aviator's sunglasses as if mildly distracted. As does the hunter who has

bagged his limit for the day, he disregarded the van. The sounds
from the loudspeaker on one of the pickups in the parade which remained even as the officer issued the citations were from an off-the-
cuff version of a *Diéz y Siez de Septiémbre* celebration. Joaquín had
heard it before, across the border in Mexico, at the *plaza* at a *Diéz y
Seiz de Septiémbre fiésta* during his childhood weekend visits with Benáncio. He surmised that the caravan must be the source of the honk-
ing he had earlier taken to be the sounds of a high school pep rally.

With red bandanas on their heads which sported 1950s-style crew
cuts, the men in the parade mingled by their cars. The angry looks
on their faces matched the homemade tattoos on their arms, their
sleeveless undershirts, and their low-riding khaki pants.

"Feós, los cabrónes" (ugly bastards) Joaquín muttered.

The iconoclast of the group had shaved the sides of his head but
left some hair on the top and scorched it with peroxide. These proud
warriors were anxious to do battle.

"Bién feós" (really ugly), Joaquín muttered again.

On this day, the sixteenth of September, 1810, an upper-crust,
Mexican-born, Creole priest named Miguel Hidálgo y Costílla had
led the call to arms for the liberation of Mexicans from Spain (the
Grito de Dolóres). And in remembrance, much to Joaquín's chagrin, a
Richard Rodriguez skit had come alive on Michigan Avenue — a ren-
dition of Sergio Leone's spaghetti western, *The Good, the Bad and Los
Vatos Feós*.

"Look at me and eat shit," the *macho* facades lashed out to taunt
the uninvited audience. *Or is it to taunt an invisible enemy?* Joaquín observed cautiously, his arms crossed, one among a crowd which had
now doubled in size. *Aren't the Spaniards gone — have been gone for 150
years!* Joaquín snickered to himself. *Whatever Spanish blood remains
unshed now murmurs in your gelatinous sponges. Who's your enemy now?*

Joaquín recalled having once defended a young man for assaulting
his older brother-in-law. The memory of that event now penetrated
his consciousness. The medical expert's report had been telling:

*The victim received approximately twenty-five blows to the head, face,
neck, and shoulders with a blunt object such as a baseball bat. The right
eye socket [knowing its evidentiary value, when the doctor had his notes
transcribed from the voice recorder to his typed narrative, he identified —
for prosecutor and the jury's benefit — the occipital orbit as the eye socket]
had to be reconstructed. The victim is blind from that eye.*

"How many years do you think I'll get, *ese* [dude]?" The young defendant had asked Joaquín, scratching the hairline at the back of his
head as he said it, and Joaquín could never forget how much the
tone was like that of a credit applicant inquiring of his banker about
the interest rates on a personal loan.

Joaquín's response had been noncommittal. "Well, I was hoping
that since this is your first felony conviction, perhaps we could try to
convince the judge that you should get a short sentence . . ."

The defendant's expression remained unchanged. "Some guys in
here, in this jail, tell me this judge could hand me a quarter." He
knew that in prison terms, a quarter is twenty-five years.

"He could. The evidence against you is pretty telling. Frankly, a
jury is going to be scared half to death of you when they hear the
doctor testify and the prosecutor holds up that bat."

"Yo me'cho la peséta carnál, me vale madre" (I'll take the quarter,
brother. No sweat).

At six in the morning, the first day of the trial, Joaquín delivered
a white shirt and tie to the county jail for his client. The thirty-six-
person jury panel had been seated in the courtroom earlier than
usual, and the prosecutor, defense counsel, court reporter, and
bailiff waited for the judge and for the defendant. As if on cue, the
silence was broken. The two large, paneled walnut doors to the
courtroom opened, and the sheriff's deputies escorted the defendant
down the center aisle as he shuffled through in typical dull orange
garb stenciled with a number 41 on the back, with clanking chains
on his ankles and cuffs on his wrists.

Joaquín frowned. *Where's the white shirt and tie!* And that was not
the half of it. The defendant had shaved his head, revealing numerous scars where the hair follicles had been carved out or pounded in
with sharp or blunt objects. And as he was brought to the defense
counsel's table, the boy could not hold back issuing one final silent
declaration of defiance to the world in order to leave no question in
anyone's mind that he neither needed nor wanted a damn thing from
anyone. Turning to the jury panel before taking his seat, he gave the
jury panel a *"Suck on this"* sneer.

"Look at me and eat shit!"

Try explaining to this kid of seventeen (Joaquín recalled his attempts) who cares diddly-squat about what this jury panel will do to
protect society from this monster — this kid with the asymmetrical
face who has guaranteed himself the quarter in prison; who within

his first twenty-four hours in prison would be raped through every fissure in his body. *How did he get that way?*

"Me vale madre, yo me'cho la pinche peséta."

"How did he get that way?" Joaquín whispered as he recalled the incident. As his thoughts drifted back to the scene currently unfolding before him on Michigan Avenue, he adjusted his weight to the left foot.

"Aw shit, you need a parade permit for this?" came the complaint from the leader of the parade. The *vatos'* advance at the corner of Michigan Avenue and Randolph had been stymied by the motorcycle patrolman. Mexican flags had been lowered; frowns developed; the body language summed it up. *"Quién fue el pendéjo a quién se le olvidó el permiso"* (Who was the idiot who forgot to get the parade permit)?

The sound distracted Joaquín. A wrecker truck removed the black convertible. "I thought this was a free country, man!" The weak and pathetic, overly sensitive challenge emerged from a short, stocky *vato* who had shed his shirt. He directed the complaint to the lone patrolman in a Cheech and Chong heavy-duty Hollywood/Puerto Rican/Mexican vernacular, a higher pitch in the voice, a telling acknowledgment of the overwhelming superior force. As the young man turned, Joaquín noticed that tattooed on the full length of his back up to his neck was the icon of the *Virgén de Guadalúpe.*

Joaquín tried to understand his pathos. *Why does my brain make these connections? Why should I feel pity for the* vatos feós? *They are not me, and I am not them.* He surveyed the crowd as it began to disperse. Clutching mommies' and daddies' hands, children-spectators watched *Los Vatos* from a distance, ingesting and absorbing from this morality play: *those* people are the bad guys. As the crowd dispersed Joaquín remained in the center of the expanding concentric circles of observers. They blinked and nodded, assuring each other, thankfully acknowledging, that peace had been restored to Michigan Avenue. There was no longer any threat. Joaquín nodded. *Today,* los vatos *have made everyone's job easier. Like caged colorful songbirds, they confront their enemy from behind the bars they've raised against themselves, from behind the masks they wear. They whistle harmless* chinga tu madres *at the free world which they push just beyond reach, harassing it with their tattered, bantam rooster plumage, delighting in the temporary terror they cause.* He tried to understand his pathos. *Why am I insensitive this way?*

A few blocks away, the statue of Beníto Juarez, the liberator of Mexico, looked out toward Lake Michigan.

Joaquín headed to his hotel.

Palmer House Nightmare

THAT NIGHT IN HIS CHICAGO HOTEL, Joaquín pre-packed his bags for the trip the following day. He included some of the extra miniature soap so daintily arranged in the basket in the bathroom.

In Joaquín's dream, a solitary figure approached him. Partially eclipsing a bright light, the silhouette's features were unmistakable: a loose-fitting, long-flowing dress, some sheer material covering the shoulders and the arms, and long hair and shapely hips. Occasionally, its graceful flowing gait allowed the glow from behind to shine through, temporarily blinding him. He squinted.

The light behind her dimmed. It became apparent that at waist level, in front of her, the woman steadied a candle with both hands. Shadows were cast around her. As Joaquín's pupils adjusted, he searched out the woman's features. Her hair was long and straight. Blonde? Yes, blonde. He could tell that now because, as usual, at some point in this dream, he always realized that he knew the path the dream would take, though he was never immediately conscious of it, as if a passageway in his brain needed clearing before he could recall this detail.

In the next minute, he knew exactly what was coming. The hands would be those of a young woman. *How young? Sixteen or seventeen? Can't be older than that,* he guessed, as he had before. What's it been? A hundred times? A thousand? But now, for the first time, his dream was much more revealing.

Above him were what he initially took to be the floor joists of a second story. But Joaquín realized he was in a barn or some other rough structure, and these were the joists of the floor of a long, narrow hayloft. A distant musical wail distracted him: barely audible. Joaquín squinted in his sleep, searching for a recognizable melody from his youth. His heart sputtered like an infant's heartbeat at the nostalgic sound of his mother's lullaby.

"Hey, Blue, how you been?" Joaquín asked in wonderment that Blue had not seemed to have changed in all these years. The abrupt interruption went unnoticed by Joaquín. Even Blue's clothes were the same: the skinny, unkempt, stiff, new Levi's jeans, a dark brown corduroy coat loose over his torso, and a dark fedora over a healthy stalk of greasy black hair. Blue was dancing with a woman down in the barn floor.

Blue turned up at Joaquín sitting in the loft and grinned at him with threatening blade-sharp shark-teeth, his nose jutting out because of his underbite, a scraggily cross tattooed in the cleft of his chin. Blue pulled his dancing partner away, and the woman hid her face. But her features were unmistakable.

Why is she dancing with Blue? Why is Blue pulling a rod from his pocket?

The night crew was working overtime, searching into the deep, dark voids, unraveling old mysteries locked in Joaquín's brain. His original dream returned. The blonde had thin lips and a small mouth. *I need to see her eyes!* No lipstick and no blush. Her eyes were shadowed from the light glowing from the candle below at her waist. A scent of gardenias or jasmine—a scent of innocence—overwhelmed him. Following himself in this dream as an omniscient observer, Joaquín knew he was capable of waking himself at will. He had, after all, done it all his life.

The blonde lowered herself to her knees. Kneeling in front of him, cradling the candle between her hands, she began to move closer. The girl raised the candle up toward her face, and her long neck came into view for the first time. Purplish-black bruises on her neck appeared as the candlelight ascended to her face. Joaquín needed to wake up, but he couldn't. As the light reached the girl's face, scratches began to appear on her face, neck, arms, and the back of her hands. Blood had dried into a dark tar as it soaked onto her gown from a visibly torn piece of her scalp. As she raised the candle up between their two faces, Joaquín was aghast; the girl's eye sockets had no eyes.

Suddenly, he perceived a sensate blending of her body with his, a sort of osmotic merging with his own physical being; or, perhaps, as if his body had become fluid and was flowing into her cold corpse. He began to have difficulty taking in air. Joaquín's breath thickened, and his mouth opened to scream, but he could not scream.

Joaquín pulled the trigger on his dream. But unlike in other cases, he could not wake himself up. He struggled in the bed, violently shaking his arms and legs, knocking his head into the headboard and tripping over the bed lamp as he got to his feet. His eyes remained closed all the while, and still, he was unable to wake himself up. Luckily, the hotel operator at the Palmer House was on the phone with his wakeup call. Joaquín took in a few deep breaths and stared at the ceiling. He could feel the pounding in his left temple. He looked around as if searching for something he had misplaced.

Leaving Chicago

IT WAS FIVE-THIRTY IN THE MORNING. Two hotel valets, wearing un-starched, hastily pressed white shirts and buttonless black smocks were waiting by Joaquín's rented Subaru on the Monroe Street entrance to the Palmer House. Their uniformed supervisor, looking every bit like a military officer, gave Joaquín a salute as Joaquín downed the last portion of a blueberry muffin and sipped on a steaming cup of coffee from a large paper cup. He winced as the heat from the coffee penetrated his hand.

In spite of the early hour, Chicago was already swinging: metal shrieking on the El overhead; valet whistles summoning taxicabs; homeless street people milling about in varying states of absence, temporarily abandoning their overnight abodes, beginning their daily wanderings. Joaquín looked up and saw an overcast sky, but was sure it would turn into a warm day.

He slipped the valet a five-dollar bill. *"Mil gracias, señor,"* the valet dipped his head.

In short order, Joaquín was on Highway 94, following the bold red line on the map, heading southeast. In the highway median between incoming and outgoing traffic lanes, the train stops with green pagoda roofs were bulging with passengers working their way into the city. On the car radio, a disc jockey warned of heavy rains further south and of the traffic jam on incoming lanes at around 159th Street, "Traffic is backed up all the way to the Indiana state line."

How long did I tune out? He could remember nothing of the past half hour and became jittery upon the realization that he had been driving as if in a trance. The large highway sign communicated with red icons and black icons: a knife and fork, a gas pump. He regained focus. He was angry at himself. Why was he trying to deceive himself? *God, what am I doing here?* His eyes watered. He felt nauseous. *If*

I could just find the place, he figured. There should be a forest nearby, a wooded area that he would have visited. Maybe there would be some familiar reminders. His breath thickened. *If the murder happened, it happened there.* What was he saying? Was there any doubt left that there indeed had been a murder and that he had at the very least witnessed it? He had to know. Pulling the sun visor down revealed the mirror behind it, and Joaquín caught his reflection. A pallid, unshaven face stared back at him. The crease in his forehead had deepened into a scar, and fatty folds had grown dark under his eyes. He acknowledged for the first time just how much he had aged in the past few months.

It all began with the high school reunion invitations. Why would anyone have even remembered him? His stay had been but a few weeks, and he had never graduated from Newton. But there they were: invitations for his twenty-year high school reunion, his twenty-fifth, and his thirtieth, all in one brown envelope, which was unsealed. They had been delivered to his office. No one at the office could remember who had delivered the envelope, but inside were the sealed letters. He could not imagine why these letters would have never been returned to their original senders, and the local post office was as confounded as anyone when asked to consider whether the letters had been circulating within the postal system for all these years. His guess was that someone had received the letters by mistake and was now delivering them. In any case, that was what had gotten him excited about Newton, Indiana, and returning to Michigan. And he was now certain that his nightmares and the intensity of the events of the last few weeks had been brought on by those invitations.

Did I kill her? That question had become Joaquín's distressing occupation, and he fixed deeply into his eyes as if searching for an answer. At that very moment, the car's right-side tires left the paved surface of the road, and the loud crackling of the graveled shoulder startled him.

There's no way I would have done that. It's not me. I need coffee. The counter on his odometer remarked that he had put in a mere fifty miles since leaving Chicago. He slowed the car and pulled over to the side of the road anticipating the exit ramp to the fast-food restaurant, but he was indecisive and kept driving slowly on the shoulder. From habit, he tugged away at the cuff from his left wrist and saw the time. It was seven. From somewhere in his consciousness, an alert sounded. It was indescribable, except that he perceived it as akin to all the admonitions that his mother had ever issued to him as a boy. The alert beckoned him to cease it all; to pack up and return to Texas . . . Now! But against the great preponderance of an addiction, which this venture had become, such admonition was futile. *I have to know.* The memory of the blonde lingered unmercifully and now completely dominated his thoughts. One second he was recalling his teenage trip in the red Ford truck, and in the next, he imagined his hands around the girl's neck, squeezing desperately to snuff out her life. He imagined putting all his weight and effort into the act. Suddenly, a voice from inside his head cried out, *She won't die! She won't die!*

PART V

All Moist and Crisp and Cool and Ready to Eat

"WHEN A MAN LOVES A WOMAN, *she can do no wrong . . .*" Lyrics wrenched from agonizing pain accompany a wailing church organ pleading for the audience's empathy and compassion. The bass line tendered a down-in-the-dumps gloom that never eased. Even the simple, austere beat of the drumstick on the drum rim triggered a memory of a painful soul.

. . . trying to hang on to what he's got . . .

On the opposite side of the highway, just outside of Gary, the on-coming cars flicked on their headlights. Up ahead, the highway curved gradually to the right. Joaquín turned on the windshield wipers as a dark wall of rain appeared. Driving straight east, in a near trance, he was taken in by the music flowing from a Chicago radio station.

If she is baaaa . . . ad, he can't see it . . .

An image of a tall, muscular, handsome black man formed in Joaquín's brain. (For a moment, he connected to a warm early evening on Beale Street in Memphis, where he had once listened to the blues while nursing warm beers in an alley that had been converted into a makeshift stage.) A Sony transistor radio dangled from the black man's belt. Lip-synching in perfect sync with the muffled wail from his miniature music box, the black man shared a confident smile between lyrics just like a professional entertainer would. Joaquín and Bennie disregarded the chilling drizzle soaking them as the enter-tainer brushed off bees with his left hand and held an imaginary mike with his thumb and three fingers of his right hand. His pinky was in the air. Mud was caked on both of his knees and boots, but the show went on.

Hundreds of pickers had fanned out over the strawberry field. Still, the morning mist veil kept them vaguely visible, appearing like ghostly images in a scary movie. But Joaquín could hear them—the

indecipherable low bass male mumblings, a distant wail of a tired
and inconsolable infant, and the innocent, secure screeching of contented children.

Decatur, Michigan; the year was 1967; the place was a strawberry
hunt. Imaginary demarcation lines on the strawberry field separated
the crews of blacks from the Puerto Ricans and the Puerto Ricans
from the Mexicans. Nobody ordered it that way; that was just the
way it worked out. Bees were on the hunt too, for their addiction to
strawberry flowers or the berries themselves left them to regard the
strawberry pickers as intruders. When threatened, the bees would
attack a strawberry picker's hands. Manda offered Joaquín a pair of
latex gloves for protection. At first he dismissed the threat and refused
the gloves, but the bees convinced him otherwise. He settled on a
pair of baby blue and a pair of the screaming yellow. He then spent
the better part of the morning amusing himself as the bees attacked
the gloves, ass-backwards, and jettisoned off, abandoning their
stingers and assorted bodily tissue, forever attached to the gloves.

"*. . . for such a good thing he's found . . .*" The lyrics wailed from Joaquín's car radio.

Yes! A link, Joaquín thought as he slowed the car down in the rain
on Highway 94, just west of Gary, Indiana. He smiled at his reflection in the rearview mirror and told himself, *It's the summer of '67. It's
Percy Sledge's rock hit, and we're in Decatur or nearby . . . in a strawberry
field.*

Decompression had begun. Joaquín tried to picture the *Negrito's*
face. His brain formed an image. An unwieldy, bushy pompadour
was molded by a nylon hose, rolled up just above the singer's ears.
Others, on their knees, straddling the rows of strawberry vines,
urged the singer on: "There you go . . . Sing iiiiiiit, bru . . . tha!"
Joaquín had never seen a *Negrito* up close.

Definitely a link, Joaquín thought as he searched for a freeway exit
that might lead to a cup of coffee and a dump, though not necessarily in that order. Coffee and a muffin had that effect on him, and he
knew his digestive tract required that he find a john soon. On the
shoulder of the highway, a reflecting laminated green road sign read,
"Gary, Next 5 Exits."

They had all heard the stories about the *Negritos* long before leaving for Michigan that first summer. *They are a shiftless lot, and loud.*
The *dichos* in San Felípe abounded:

"Paréce cena de Negros" (Sounds like a bunch of Negroes at dinner), they would say whenever there was a group of people noisily speaking over each other.

"Esa chamba es pa' Negros" (That job is for Negros), they would say about jobs that were too hard or messy.

"Me traén como Negro" (They're treating me like a Negro), they would proclaim when presumably treated unfairly or unjustly or unduly harshly.

But Benáncio would have none of it. He fiercely and publicly rooted for the underdog. On Friday nights, he would walk the three blocks over to Don Nicásio's furniture store on Main Street for the Gillette Friday Night Fights. He'd stand outside on the broad sidewalk fighting off click beetles, black beetles, crickets, and mayflies with the other men, watching the fight through the plate-glass window. If he felt like rewarding the boys, he'd take them along.

On those evenings (and on many others), Joaquín would observe his father entranced in the bout, admiring how at over six feet he towered over the shorter men. There was no doubt that Benáncio knew best. Of all the men Joaquín had ever observed, *his* father understood that world that existed beyond the fence line. It was his father's confidence in what was right and wrong that was most admirable. If the match pitted a black guy against a white guy, deep in his gut, Joaquín hungered for the black guy to win, and he wished the white guy nothing short of a battering. It was payback time — Benáncio's faith demanded. In a fight like that, it was *them* vs. *us*, and in his blood Joaquín knew black boxers fought for the *us*. Benáncio was never deterred. "You'll see," he would predict, "some day, when given the chance, the Negroes will succeed at swimming, tennis, bowling, and even golf. Just give 'em half a chance."

Joaquín couldn't help feel that his very own condition seemed to be locked in step for step with the condition of the Negros. For every time a half-ass black boxer lost to a white guy, it seemed to set the Mexicans back several generations.

> *...When she is baaaaaad, he caaaaaaan't seee it ... She can do noooo wrooouuuoonng. Trying to hang on to what he's got ...*

Back in the strawberry field, the *Negrito* had a broad smile on his face. Drizzle had distorted his pompadour, flattening it on top. Turning to the boys, he bowed proudly, exaggerating by bending his back at the waist as Olympians do. Joaquín clapped his latex-clad hands and whistled. It made him forget about the cold drizzle and the mud and the bees. Back in Texas, Manda often sang as well when she was out on the cotton fields with the boys. Her favorites were the hits from the Mexican movies. Joaquín and Bennie would giggle as Manda sang and play-acted dancing in the middle of the cotton field, mocking a polka or a waltz for them under the desert sun.

As the Michigan sun burned the fog, the mist veil lifted. The fleeting spirits had become hundreds of crouched or kneeling bodies that had packed onto this field, scrambling, competing for the few strawberries that had ripened overnight. Straw cushioned their movements, sticking to their mud-caked knees as they dragged their weary and sweaty bodies along row after row.

At the center of the field, a busy, shaded area served as a makeshift packing shed. Under the shade, a tall, burly man in his forties, sporting bold black sunglasses, gave all the body language needed to convey that he was no doubt *the* man in charge. Surveying the field around him far and wide, a permanent pissed-off frown on his face, he clenched his fists on his hips as he searched for that one sorry son of a bitch who insisted on bringing him bad strawberries.

Joaquín turned back to Bennie, a distance of about ten feet between them: "Man, that song's so cool." Bennie nodded in agreement but seemed more interested in the girl about three rows to his left. She hadn't turned to see Bennie gawking at her, but Bennie could tell she was focused on Joaquín. The girl had a thin face and high cheekbones. A black scarf pulled above her ears was tied in the back of her head in a very Aunt Jemima–esque fashion—that is, before the pancake syrup company removed the scarf from its mascot and gave her that Doris Day hairdo.

Clear skinned and very dark, she sat in a very ladylike way, on her side, as if out on a Sunday picnic. She searched the plants carefully, picking only the ripest, reddest of the strawberries. She then carefully arranged them in the tiny balsa wood containers. Admiring her artwork, she would then stand up, neaten herself up (she remained remarkably unblemished by the mud), take a short step, and settle back again.

Bennie signaled Joaquín with his eyes toward his left where the girl was working. Joaquín turned to see the girl and gaped for several seconds. His eyes growing, he turned to Bennie. Feigning pain and frowning, he bit his lower lip and mouthed, *"Mamasíta"* (Beautiful). Fond memories indeed.

On the freeway to Gary, the windshield wipers on Joaquín's car couldn't quite keep the time with the beat flowing from the car radio. Yet there was something rhythmic about them that enlivened Joaquín's senses. The brain was searching, linking. Thought nodes were exploding.

Back at the strawberry field, the masses of pickers packed strawberries into small balsa wood grocery-store containers like little gift packages. Shoppers could find these in the well-lit produce section, all moist and crisp and cool and ready to eat. These the workers toted to the makeshift shed, eight containers to a tin metal carrying tray. Several men were charged with culling the containers by removing all the green or rotting strawberries. On his first attempt at compensation, Joaquín was turned back without any, having lost half his tray to the culling judges.

"Culéros," Joaquín complained under his breath about the culling judges as he headed back from the culling station.

Backed up against the makeshift shed was a red cold-storage semitrailer. In the distance, other trailers noisily lined up behind it, waiting their turn to get loaded. A huge, hairy, heavyweight wrestling champion was the apparent driver of this cherry-red beauty decked out in chrome. Awaiting his shipment, the driver killed time by polishing the chrome on his baby. There was chrome on the side rearview mirrors, the hood vent cover, the door and hood hinges, the hood ornament and the grill, the bumper plate, the headlights, the turn signal bexels, the wheels, the lug nuts, the three horns on the cab, the upright muffler, and the running boards, which had been welded onto the gasoline tank! He even had chrome baby moon caps on each chromed wheel. Even the edging around the rigid rubber mud flaps had been chromed; and, of course, that included a chrome cutout of the babe in the tanning pose so common to these manly machines. These strawberries were going straight to market, and the heavyweight bouncer was going to get them there safely and in style.

A unique payroll accounting system had been devised for the strawberry pickers. A full tray of strawberries entitled Joaquín to a plastic token, something like a Las Vegas dice chip. At certain intervals during the day, the old man in the Ford truck (the lead swallow from Capistrano) exchanged cash for tokens. His profit was imbedded in this token exchange. It was nothing more than a pyramid scheme — a plasticware conspiracy. The top Mexican worked for the strawberry company. The top Mexican recruited the old men in the Fords and Chevys, the head geese called "crew leaders," who, in turn, recruited the pickers.

Joaquín's need to take a dump badly took hold, and his imagination and dreaming logged off for a while.

39

Barefoot'n

"HI, I'M MABEL. THIS IS GERALDINE," Mabel told Bennie and slid sideways around him on the narrow path to get back to where Joaquín stood. Mabel was the *mamasíta* Joaquín had been gaping at in the strawberry field a week earlier. She was about their age. She was a lanky sort of girl, very slim with a short torso, but taller than both of the boys. She spoke as if in a hurry. Her shorts were awfully short and tight, but Joaquín decided it was not in a way that one would call vulgar. *If the girls at the Texas camp would dress that way . . . well, let's put it this way: girls in our camp would never dress that way.* And her blouse was a little red-checkered thing, like something from Li'l Abner. *But it's not vulgar at all, either,* he reasoned again. Geraldine was a chubby girl who wore spectacles, a ponytail, and a simple cotton sleeveless black and maroon dress that buttoned in the back. They were all barefooted.

Bennie had not bothered to ask just how or when the invitation had been made. Mabel promised Joaquín the Mississippi camp was just a skip, hop, and a jump away. They met along the pathway, closer to the Texas camp where Mabel said the girls would "come to fetch" them. Mabel was definitely the alpha of this pack, as she led them down the path at a steady stride, pulling Joaquín behind her with her sidekick and Bennie, struggling to keep up. They came up against a moist depression. Bennie turned to Joaquín in wonderment as Mabel jumped effortlessly around the mud. They avoided the mud but were not able to keep from arousing the hungry mosquitoes, which attacked them without mercy.

In the rear of the pack, Bennie couldn't help glancing back over his shoulders for familiar signs in order to find his way back to the Texas camp, as if he were Hansel searching for bread crumbs. But, his ambivalence waned when the two girls distracted them into conversation.

"Mabel's the best dancer in camp," Geraldine told them, in what sounded awfully like a rehearsed presentation. Geraldine lacked the confident inquisitiveness, which Mabel displayed every time she glanced at Joaquín. But there was a noticeable sophistication in the way Geraldine stood with one hand on her waist and the other in the air, which she used like a wand to spin tales.

"Are y'all good dancers?" Mabel asked.

Bennie looked at Joaquín as if he cared to answer. Joaquín declined with a frown.

"Like soul music?" came the inquiry from Geraldine.

"In Texas, we dance another way," Joaquín answered.

"Oh, really? What y'all dance in Texas?" Mabel asked.

"Ah," Joaquín paused, "we dance . . . you know . . . polkas and waltzes mostly."

"Waltzes?" Mabel was not so much asking, but rather seemed to be struggling to recall if she had ever even heard of such a thing.

Geraldine giggled. "Like in *Gone with the Wind*?" That brought on a frown by Mable as if Geraldine was being out of line.

Joaquín buttoned up, hoping that would end the whole dancing discussion.

They walked for several minutes after Mabel took them off the beaten path on an alleged shortcut. Bennie slapped Joaquín in the back to get his attention to look back. When he did, he gulped. It was getting dark, and in the middle of the woods was no place to be after sundown. It would be impossible to find the way back to the camp. Nevertheless, they trudged onward behind Mabel and Geraldine.

"Did you say you wuz Mezcun?" Mabel inquired from her lead without turning, appearing half-interested.

"Yes, Mexican."

"Is that anything like Latin?"

"Yep."

Mabel halted the caravan, a bit surprised, and asked in a shrill voice, "So y'all can speak Spanish?"

"Of course."

"Well, say something in Spanish, then," she challenged Joaquín, as if he should have disclosed this fact long before.

Joaquín's jaw jutted out, "Okay . . . *eres muy hermósa . . . preciósa*" (You're beautiful . . . precious).

The *mamasíta* turned to Bennie and shoved his shoulder playfully, threatening, "Hey, whad'ee say?"

"He said you are very beautiful." Bennie shrugged his shoulders as if to say, *"You asked for it."*

"Aw, come on now . . . he didn't say that," she answered, turning to Joaquín coyly. "Did you?" Mabel asked with a bit of blushing disbelief.

Joaquín bit his lower lip and nodded. The *mamasíta* stared at him for second, as if to say, *"Get outta here"* and then threw her head back and giggled.

"I'm gonna be a professional dancer," Mabel told them, holding her chin up.

"Uh huh," Geraldine confirmed on cue while Mabel stopped again emphatically. The three stopped in their tracks behind Mabel.

"Goin' to New York Seedee," Mabel confirmed. "Got me an aunt there," Mabel said to herself as if she didn't really believe it. The way she pronounced "aunt" sounded British to Joaquín.

They finally came to a broad clearing in the thick woods, which appeared to Joaquín like a camp scene out of some Western flick. Unlike the Texas camp, this camp was circular with the common open space in the middle, surrounded by white cabins. The cars were parked next to the cabins. The center of the circle was open ground made barren and dusty from all the car and foot traffic. A large balding black man, well into his years, wearing dirty denim overalls and resting his cap on his lap, surveyed his bailiwick from a discarded sofa next to a large covered but otherwise open washroom where several women stood washing clothes. He jiggled a toothpick in his mouth with his lips, somehow indicating that he had every intention of sitting there and digesting his dinner for the next several hours. This was his flock, Joaquín figured. There were no chairs here, so folks sat out in front of their small white cubicles after a day's work in the strawberry fields. They sat on steps, cans, or crates, on the open bed of a turquoise-colored 1953 Chevy pickup and on the hood of an old yellow bus crudely painted with the name of the Baptist church that was probably its former owner. As the foursome made their way down to the middle of camp, Joaquín could not help the strange feeling that he was being viewed like a trophy or some object taken as a spoil of battle and was now being paraded in the victor's homecoming.

Next to the common washroom, there was a jukebox. The boss man watched the foursome intently as they sunk tokens into the music box. Along with everything else in this camp that wasn't securely fixed to the ground, this music box also belonged to the big boss man. Before long, Joaquín and Bennie were "barefoot'n" with the *mamasíta* and her friends in the middle of the camp.

In time, the youngest of the children come out to join them. Shy at first, they soon encircled the foursome, edging closer. They rocked to the beat. Joaquín couldn't tell though, if they were smiling along with him or laughing at him. The children seemed to want to discover, to touch, to feel, and to sense him and Bennie. A little boy approached Joaquín, as if on a dare by his friends. He felt the sun-bleached hair on the side of Joaquín's arm with his small hand and then reached up and touched Joaquín's shoulder-length hair. Mission accomplished, his hand on his mouth, he turned to his friends with a half-mischievous, half-victorious giggle, as if to say, *"See, guys, it don't bite."* Joaquín also desired to touch and feel their skin and the texture of their hair.

Clap your hands and stomp your feet . . . we're barefoot'n.

Joaquín was feeling so cool.

On his rental car radio, the song "Barefoot'n" ended. Layers of emotions, which had been sealed away for three decades, were finally being peeled back. There was a distinct gleam in Joaquín's eyes as he caught sight of a pair of highway signs on the side of the road. One sign was a blue shield with white and red letters that read "U.S. 94."

Back at the camp, the jukebox music suspiciously stopped, and the *mamasíta* brought her hand toward her mouth in a sign of astonishment. "They're back!" she warned. There was something that had been bothering Joaquín while they were skipping, hopping, and jumping over to this camp with this *mamasíta* and Geraldine. He just hadn't been able to put his finger on it. But now, he saw in Mabel's face what it was that he had overlooked. He knew at that very moment who the girl was saying was back — the guys!

As if a wild thought had just entered her mind, Mabel abruptly asked, "Y'all wanna see the largest tree in the world?" Joaquín and Bennie were on their second frolic with the two girls from Mississippi, but this time, a safe distance from the Mississippi camp.

"Yeah, let's show it to 'em," Geraldine signaled with her head, as if to indicate, *"Follow me."*

Joaquín recognized the familiar path to the huge oak where they had ambushed the brown squirrel. The foursome surrounded the tree as if on a guided tour.

"I'll bet this tree can see for miles," Mabel fantasized.

Joaquín's eyes inspected the tree, following the girth of its trunk up to its broad branches that extended upward until the weight at the farthest reaches arched them down close to the ground. Mabel glanced at him attentively all the while.

"Imagine the stories this tree could tell," Geraldine wondered aloud.

Bennie turned to Joaquín. "How old do you think this tree is? I'll bet it's at least fifty years old."

"Fifty? Try like three hundred," Geraldine countered quickly before Joaquín could venture his own guess.

Joaquín nodded, concurring. But never to be undone, he added, "Yeah, it's at least two hundred years old."

Mabel approached Joaquín. There was a mischievous look on her face, which she was angling toward him. "A tree has hundreds of eyes and ears all over," she whispered near his ear, as her eyes expanded. Joaquín frowned at her, as if distracted, pulling his face away from her as he did it, evaluating her from head to toe.

"It does," she defended herself, turning around and facing Bennie for support. "Imagine . . . it can see and hear all around, and it has all those secrets from all the years it's been here."

Joaquín shook his head in mild disbelief. "Boy, this tree was here during the Revolutionary War."

"Wow!" Geraldine gasped.

"And during the Civil War," Joaquín added.

The mischievous look returned to Mabel's face. "I know a way to get the tree to talk," she proffered, smiling at each of them.

"What? How?" Joaquín scowled, a suspicious frown on his face.

"No, it's true," she said, placing her right hand over her chest, indicating her solemn pledge. "All you gotta do is put your hands together around the tree. Let's do it."

Bennie turned to Joaquín for a cue. The look on his face was nothing short of reluctance.

"Come on," Bennie urged Joaquín. "Let's see what the old tree has to say."

Mabel prodded him as well. "You've got to talk to it, and then you've gotta listen to it. My mama says that back where she grew up in the Mississippi Delta, they had a large tree like this, and they always talked to it. Asked 'im things. They would ask it to talk back. They used to say, 'Grandfather tree, Grandfather tree, why don't you tell me what I can't see?" Mabel looked around, surprised that no one had joined her. "Come on now, y'all . . . ," she begged, and motioned with her arms as a conductor. She then cued them on with her head, as a schoolmaster would. "Grandfather tree, Grandfather tree . . . I said come on join with me," she urged. "Reach around it now, boy, girl, boy, girl," she urged, pairing them off, placing Geraldine between Joaquín and Bennie in a circle around the tree.

"Grandfather tree, Grandfather tree, why don't you tell me what I can't see?" Geraldine joined in.

"Grandfather tree, Grandfather tree, why don't you tell your secrets to me?" Joaquín finally submitted, and the four of them chatted in unison, "Grandfather tree, Grandfather tree, why don't you tell me what I can't see? Grandfather tree, grandfather tree, why don't you share your secrets with me?" The chorus continued as they circled the tree and held hands in merry-go-round fashion, circling the tree until they tired, became dizzy, and fell to the ground, breaking the circle. For a strange second, Joaquín felt as if something had been revealed to him, as if he himself had stood tall where the tree stood and had actually seen beyond. Joaquín remained on the ground, appearing stunned, resting on his elbows. He looked around in a daze and caught Bennie in his sight, fixing on him contemplatively, as if he was trying to recognize his brother. It was a look he used to have as a kid when he woke up too abruptly from a deep sleep.

Joaquín tried to explain to Bennie, "I felt like I had left my body and was actually inside the tree and could see everything around me. I saw all kinds of strange things."

"*Puro pedo,*" Bennie told him and pulled him up so they could catch up with Mabel and Geraldine, who were already on to something new.

Taking a Dump in Gary

"WELCOME TO GARY, INDIANA," said the sign on the highway. From the overpass, Joaquín surveyed the vast landscape of padlocked galvanized steel, aging red brick, and cold smokestacks. Joaquín's bowels were about to burst, but he worked at remaining as calm as possible. Any relaxing of the muscles might have proven catastrophic.

He took the exit ramp onto a thoroughfare parallel to a wide and desolate plain of railroad tracks and came to an intersection. It was still early, and there was little traffic on the road. To his right, the ten sets of empty railroad tracks on the empty switching yard and the overpass next to it were a proscenium beyond which lay a distant world of which only rooftops were visible. He stalled the car on the tracks like an experienced buck pausing on his instincts before crossing a vulnerable path. But he had to take a dump soon, and there was little time to waste. He proceeded through.

On the other side, the place lacked the imprint of safe and secure, mall-bound, franchised suburbia that he was accustomed to. None of the comforting trademarked color schemes, labels, or emblems that were emblazoned in middle Americana's sensibilities could be found here. "The franchises must be down by the freeway," he moaned, "where it's familiar and easy in, easy out, and where mall goers can shop in the comfort that they will not be reminded of the other worlds that inhabit their universe beyond the fence line."

There was no traffic on this broad boulevard. And in the sidewalk cracks, tufts of grass had found safe haven. Ambivalence set in. But he had chosen this path, and it was just simply too late to turn back.

As Joaquín drove deeper into the neighborhood, he pondered whether this part of Gary burned during the hot summer of '68. Abandoned and boarded up, vintage 1930s and 1940s storefronts on either side of the street were set out wall-to-wall on narrow lots. Even the tax man must have abandoned any effort to collect a levy from their owners. He'd seen it all before . . . Dallas, Washington D.C., and on that Amtrak ride from New York down to D.C. where you get a better picture of what the industrial East used to be from the railroad tracks. Like rotten apples in a barrel, the buildings decayed a little more each year, and the decay spread like a virus. Whatever businesses did manage to operate here required little capital — things like beauty shops, laundry services, and dry cleaner drop-off establishments. The largest inventory was up on the right at the bus stop, the J & B liquor store, which was already open for business. A fleeting thought came and went in Joaquín's head . . . *A Raisin in the Sun.*

Man, I gotta go, Joaquín cringed. In desperation, his brain factored in whether there might be an abandoned alley where he might take a dump. *Am I safe here? Should I venture further?*

Long gone were the days when Joaquín rooted for the black prizefighters through a plate-glass picture window at Don Nicásio's. The thought went through his mind, and he wondered why. Was it the thirty years of American cinema, the twenty-four-hour CNN news worm, and twenty-seven years of filing federal income tax returns that had made sure of that? An ambivalence jerked at him. There were *gangstas* out there, and with big guns.

Joaquín ventured further. Sagging roofs, buildings beginning to list, rotting, back-alley second-story ladders, precariously thin and weathered, their nails, loose and rusty were the only playgrounds for children. Tar and asphalt siding with the offset brick patterns (in a sorry attempt at a *terra cotta* look) on the homes with dilapidated stoops reminded Joaquín of segregated huts in south Lamesa, Texas.

His mind wandered as he sat mesmerized, staring at the red light at an intersection. In the 1950s, on Saturdays, the family would drive in for groceries from the cotton fields around Sparenberg and Klondike — not quite towns on the Texas *mesa,* but rather zip codes denoting farm-to-market road intersections. Welcoming them as the road curved north into the town square of Lamesa, Texas, was the Negro shantytown. A segregated clay-red flatland devoid of flora or fauna (save for the sturdy tumbleweeds, which grew in abundance) was reserved for the small huts with the tar and asphalt siding. The only integrated venue in town was the long line at the rear of Murphy's slaughterhouse, where the Mexicans and the Negros would line up at dawn on Saturdays with their galvanized washtubs to receive the calf bowels that Murphy disposed of.

A lone patrol car approached Joaquín at the intersection light in the bleak Gary neighborhood. The cop gave him the obligatory sniff and then went about his business.

There was silence. Nothing opened until lunch time, including the public library, which probably had an immaculate john.

He knew he had power over his body, but he also knew all too well that when all rational options were tried and failed, the brain could default into the severe emotional modes, and the blood would gush to essential body parts. Joaquín's panicked brain blared out, *my only option is a shit in the pants.* Such was the experience for Joaquín this morning in Gary, Indiana, almost resulting in Joaquín shitting in his pants. The only time he had experienced that had been his first day of school at the San Felípe elementary school, and that was clear back in September 1956. Joaquín knew no English, and the teacher knew no Spanish. The brain defaulted; Joaquín shit in his pants.

Set back apiece from main street was what appeared to be a recycled hamburger joint, its once-red sign now discolored. The facade of the building was covered with white acrylic paint baked on light sheet metal squares. There was even off-street parking, and through the large floor-to-ceiling curtain glass wall, Joaquín could make out people milling about inside.

Behind the counter, a large, self-assured woman turned from the griddle and eagerly welcomed Joaquín, "Come on in, honey." She wiped her face with the back of a meaty arm. "Cup of coffee?"

"Come on in, honey?" When was the last time a waitress anywhere gave me that kind of welcome? What happened to the mamasíta? The Negritos in this joint are mostly old and appear sullen, sitting at distances from each other, as if distributed here and there into weighted tables to balance out the place. It's clear they're human fixtures in for their daily ritual of coffee and familiar conversation. I can't just go straight to the john, Joaquín considered, *I've got to order something.*

After nervously ordering coffee and a BLT sandwich to go, Joaquín finally built up enough courage. "Do you have a bathroom?" he inquired of the woman behind the counter, a trace of impatience in his voice.

"Down that way to your left." She pointed and then warned, "It's nothing special."

The john was not immaculate, but it sure was special, because it beat a shit in the pants.

On one of the stainless steel-stools at the bar sat a big fellow, crouching protectively over his breakfast. *Younger than me*, Joaquín guessed. Prematurely balding, the customer's dark green khaki uniform advertised that he must drive or operate some kind of manly equipment — like a forklift, a crane, or something mechanical like that. As Joaquín walked past him on the way back from the john, the man glimpsed up and acknowledged Joaquín's presence.

In the background, Muddy Waters began to work on his *mojo*. Joaquín sipped on a cup as he waited at the counter for the order. The coffee tasted great. *It's all in the cream*, someone once said. Gone was the nervous scowl on his face. No one had attempted to rip his throat from ear to ear. *Did that actually pass through my mind?* He began to feel at ease.

Block after block of this part of Gary was abandoned, but the dilapidated structures along the wide boulevard told of a once-thriving commercial center. This had once been a place where hard-working folks could spend their money on Fridays and Saturdays. But that was when U.S. Steel monopolized steel, and the mills spewed out orange poison on a twenty-four/seven schedule in three shifts a day; and the blacks, Poles, Ukranians, and Croatians had the luxury of turning down overtime, which, in turn, gave the English-speaking Mexicans from Texas an opportunity for jobs. Then the Asians went into steel. Gary took it on the chin, and those who could do so left.

He imagined what the streets of this neighborhood might feel like with clusters of boisterous teenagers clinging to every street corner. But most were gone, for they had left to search for better opportunities elsewhere. The first journey for better opportunities by his own family had been out to West Texas. He turned twelve that summer, and it had been disastrous. He recalled the scene. The twelve-year-old knocked on the screen door of a farmer's home. Behind him on the dirt road was the 1953 red panel truck with his papa at the wheel, a concentrated, frustrated, desperate stare on his face. Bennie was peering at Joaquín as well through the passenger door, his elbows over the door. Next to him, a brown dog's face with its long red tongue to one side salivated voraciously, looking once in Joaquín's direction and then up at Bennie with a slightly inquisitive look forming in its canine eyebrows. In the background, the scene was an endless, rolling West Texas dark plain recently planted with cotton. In the vast blue sky was the dissipating contrail of a jet plane.

"What can I do for you, young man?"

It was the West Texas twangy voice of a farmer who just got up from the dinner table, and his steps on the wooden floor of the living room got louder as he approached the front door where a skinny Joaquín awaited.

"Sir, we have four workers available to start right now. We will do any work you need." Joaquín finished the offer even before the farmer came into view. He knew he had to issue the proposal in full to the farmer, for Benáncio would want confirmation that all the relevant information was presented in the offer: *Did you tell him there's four of us? Did you tell him that he needs to hire all four of us? What about the pay? Did you . . . ? Did . . . you?* The dark screen door opened, and the farmer pushed back his cap and dipped his head in a neighborly fashion toward the red panel truck on the dirt road.

"My boys are coming up next week from Pecos," the old man said, scratching his ear. "Why dontcha come back in two weeks just in case?"

Joaquín smiled and thanked the man.

The motor of the red panel truck heated up and needed to cool down every hour or so. "Has to do with the timing chain," said Benáncio. But unlike the timing chain, Benáncio could never cool down, especially after the sixth rejection of the day, and he snarled at Joaquín even before Joaquín opened the door to the truck, *"Que dijo el hijo de su chingáda madre?"* (What did the S.O.B. tell you?)

"He says that he has his own crew coming in from Pecos. He doesn't need help," Joaquín told his father.

"Are you sure you told him that there were four of us? Are you sure . . . ? Did you tell him—"

Joaquín was brooding as someone dropped a quarter into the coin slot of the jukebox. *It's just one more example of how Papa pushed me ahead as his shield against an unknown world, and I was willing to play the role. Yet, he resented even that accommodation. Not once did he acknowledge the role that I played, for that would have been an admission of his shortcomings.* The bitterness resurged in Joaquín, and he chided, rebuked, and accused his father: *Your twelve-year-old kid opened doors for you, and you resented that. Every opportunity you got, you got even. You got even by belittling me. How you loved to show me up as you weighed your vast experience with my sixth-grade education and announced yourself the winner every time. You were the wise one, and I could never measure up to you as you gloated in the comparison.*

"What happened to this place?" Joaquín invited himself into the silent conversation in the restaurant, attempting to appear familiar. "Everything around here is abandoned and boarded up."

The big fellow reacted to Joaquín's comment by sipping on his cup of coffee and shaking his head as if to say, *"Damn straight."*

"Oh, it's coming back, honey," the waitress begged to differ from behind the counter, giving Joaquín a friendly frown that said, *"Hey, don't knock it."* "Why, we're getting new businesses coming here all the time." From the corner, the jukebox clicked, the compact disc holder rotated and finally settled. Etta James was introduced to a smattering of applause.

In the corner, a short man, in his early seventies, dressed in a Chi Chi Rodriguez two-tone, burnt orange, polyester combo and sporting a cool and collected Duke Ellington face, fell for Joaquín's familiarity routine. He interjected, "When was the last time you was here?" The Duke spoke from deep down in his throat, a certain tension in his vocal cords.

"Back in '64 or '65," Joaquín lied through his teeth in his West Texas country twang, as if this was somehow going to ingratiate him with his hosts for whom plain English wouldn't do. But Joaquín was not *here*. He was *around here* in Indiana, but never in Gary, so far as he could recall.

"Man, back in sixty-fo', sixty-fiiiive," pondered the Duke for a second. "Hmm . . . this strip was where da action was, man; that's probly what you rememba." The old man puffed on a Camel and crossed his leg over his knee the way only women, European men, and Chicano *vatos locos* could. The Duke fondly recalled the strip, with its neon lights, its cheap beer, and its Motown sound. Joaquín could tell all of that just by the way the man blew out the smoke.

"That's right," Joaquín promised himself this would be his last embellishment. "We had some fine times around *here*," he drawled.

The Duke took a deep drag and smiled as he slowly exhaled those fine times. "Yeah!" the Duke smiled to himself.

Spam, Sardines, and Vienna Sausages/
Roadside Stop

AT NILES, THE RAIN RETURNED, lightly and innocuously, but at a steady pace. The traffic was beginning to back up as, ahead on the road, a flag woman with a bright red cross across her chest and a yellow hard hat signaled the traffic into a single lane.

The interrogations kept mounting. *What have I forgotten, and what have I attempted to remove from my consciousness?*

As he traveled north on a narrow, curving road, he surprised himself. This very meandering road through the downtown area, a small park to his right (he questioned whether the ball park had already been there in 1966), and shortly thereafter, the large trees in the neighborhood on both sides of the road creating high cupolas sparked his memory—as if it were all just yesterday. He pressed his lips into a smile, acknowledging with obvious contentment much as a pup acknowledges a scent he is familiar with by wagging its tail. All of this he recalled as a scene from the opening in the tarp at the back of the red Ford truck, and he lowered the window of the car to allow the raindrops to strike his face. As the traffic cleared just north of Niles, darkness came. His brain continued sieving out idle memories, searching for that one granule that might trigger a more complete recall.

They would have reached Niles, Michigan, on the third day of the trip. *Assuming none of the vehicles in the caravan broke down,* he added as an afterthought and sighed.

Occasionally, a state park offered travelers accommodations, including bathrooms and showers. But those amenities were rare, and even when they were available, they were intended for tourists. Don Armándo preferred to rest at truck stops since they offered plenty of parking space and he could avoid the questioning stares of tourists who cringed at the thought of sharing the state park facilities with migrant farm workers.

The first trip to Michigan had been memorable, for it was their first time out of San Felípe. Joaquín and Sis had purchased a Rand McNally road map to follow during the trip. St. Louis had been nothing like what Sis and Joaquín had imagined before the trip: clapboard storefronts and wooden porches on dirt streets and an occasional freckle-faced Huck Finn–type kid running around barefoot. And the Mississippi was even mightier than Mark Twain had described it. But it was Indiana and Michigan which was the *Americana* their consciousness had been infused with from their very first day in grade school — the one they had marveled about, where life seemed almost perfect among the solitude of a spacious rural America, where topsoil was measured in feet and little boys dreamed of playing high school basketball and little girls dreamed of becoming homecoming queens; where a man could breathe *his* air and claim *his* space up to the blue heavens; a land inhabited by fattening cattle and red barns and grain elevators and uniquely confident, stoic men, who never bought a cap in their lives but wore them obsessively, advertising to each other brands of farm equipment, or fertilizer or seed or cattle feed; artists, in a way, whose canvasses were the sky and the open spaces on which they never tired of creating green and lush symmetry.

But it had been that second trip, in the summer of '66, that had drawn Joaquín. For the characters that remained in his memory were from that trip. In particular, there was Junior, his implicit mentor, whom he tried to picture.

Late into the night on the second day of that trek to Michigan, the convoy of Ford and Chevy trucks stopped along a lonely stretch of a highway right-of-way. Don Armándo had left the main highways, and was now traveling the smaller thoroughfares. There was no telling which state they were in at this point . . . Missouri? Illinois? Indiana? But Texas was left far behind. From the rear of the caravan, Shorty made his way through the line of pickup trucks along the highway, stopping by each truck and speaking to each of the drivers. Joaquín and Bennie awaited his instructions at the back of the Ford truck. When he reached them, he told Joaquín, "Beyond the right-of-way, you'll find a nice area to lay down a blanket and get some rest. Pop says we'll stay here until the sun comes out."

Disembarking from the commercial elevator had become a deliberate feat, especially for Manda. She complained about her hip. "Let me rub it a little," she begged and strained. Joaquín stalled and returned her a cautious frown. She gave him a reassuring smile. "I just need to warm it up," she said. Others in the back of truck coughed as they disembarked and complained of becoming disoriented by the consumption of gasoline fumes. Joaquín massaged his own comatose legs back to life, pumping out the blood that had settled during the ride.

Manda and Bennie followed two women with their complaining children in tow. A cloudless crescent-moon night accompanied them, glowing serenely on the dark landscape. There was a well-kept pebble path that cut through a narrow palisade of tall evergreens. The path then opened into what appeared to be a vast, lush blanket of grass. Word spread throughout the caravan that this was the place to stretch out crimped limbs.

"Hurry, children!" a woman's voice called from the lead. And the tired and sleepy wails of her children followed. "María, you need to change that baby's diaper. I can smell him all the way from here," she complained.

A younger woman's voice answered from out of the dark, *"Está bién."*

The family with the blonde girl and old man mingled around a small mound. Joaquín couldn't quite make out their whispers, but he could tell the old man's wife was trying to settle him down. Bennie chose a spot close to a couple with two teenage children — a girl and a boy — and unfurled a thick quilt. Manda muttered something to him about how Providence had helped them find such a comfortable spot. "It reminds me," she said, "of Mr. Farmer's lawn back in San Felípe, the year he won the 'Yard of the Month' award, except that this even seems more lush and manicured." But Bennie was too busy listening to the WLS radio station out of Chicago and did not hear a single word she said.

In the distance, someone had the good sense to light up a small campfire and brew some coffee.

Joaquín found himself a spot as far away from the crew as he could. Much later, once all had settled in, he could make out Junior and Blue giggling their way up the path, and he wondered what could possibly be so funny this late at night. Even Don Armándo, who would never abandon his truck, joined in and camped out as well. Don Eduardo remained on the side of the road guarding the convoy of vehicles. Shorty plunked down in his '55 Chevy.

Sporadically throughout the night, Spam, sardine, and Vienna sausage cans were opened and discarded; children were nursed and diapers changed; and bodies were relieved along the palisade of trees.

At first light, Joaquín was up, already skillfully rolling his first Buglar. He held the paper at either end between the thumb and middle finger as he thinned the tip of his tongue to wet the gummy end of the rolling paper. Lighting the cigarette took effort in the strong breeze that had developed. At fifteen and soon to be sixteen, Joaquín had been smoking for five years. The drag went deep, and as he exhaled, he was reminded for the millionth time just how bad a habit he had acquired. Strewn throughout the area occupied by the crew were the discarded cans of baked and ranch-style beans. A skinny dog guardedly ventured toward the cans and licked their insides. In the distance, from the area of the palisades, walked a woman holding a half roll of toilet paper. Don Armándo, a chain smoker, left a dozen or so cigarette butts ground into the grass.

A short distance away, the man Blue called Junior was also already up, black hair slicked back. On top of a small mound, Junior faced the slight breeze head-on. The breeze was trapped in his pink short-sleeve shirt and ballooned it in the back. Junior covered his mouth in a Marlon Brando cool sort of way, laughing to himself, as if trying to keep from waking the others. Junior noticed Joaquín and *zzzed* through his teeth for Joaquín to come on over. Joaquín joined him.

"*Wachate, ese* [Look, man], we're in a golf course," Junior whispered, a sly grin on his face, his beady eyes as red as ripe cherries.

"What?" Joaquín surveyed around him, a quizzical look on his face. A green-emerald manicured fairway extended out before them. With the morning light, it was now obvious to Joaquín that the caravan had occupied parts of a green of the local country club. In the distance, large homes rose above the pine trees like a New Mexican pueblo.

"So this is what a golf course looks like?"

"*Simón, calzone.*" Junior walked toward the edge of the green, knelt on one knee facing the hole, as if figuring out how to best play a shot. Joaquín picked at his ear.

"How far, *carnál?* Say about an eighteen-foot putt?" Junior stepped off the distance to the hole.

"From there to the hole, you mean?" Joaquín's only knowledge of the sport of golf was that a Mexican by the name of Lee Treviño played the game.

"Yeah!" Junior mocked impatiently.

"Yeah, I'd say about eighteen feet."

With his left hand, Junior pulled an imaginary putter out of his right side, like one draws a sword, and walked to the edge of the green with the imaginary putter on his right shoulder. "This is Arnold Palmer, now," Junior whispered, mocking a television sports announcer. "Palmer has an eighteen-foot putt for the win."

A few awkward practice swings followed. Junior feigned missing the hole and followed the route of the ball all the way across the other edge of the green and looked up at Joaquín, frowning and shaking his head in mock disgust.

He then set to tee off. During one of his swings, he superficially hit his toe and jumped around on one foot, holding the other foot in his hand.

Joaquín laughed in response.

"What, man? You think it's funny?" Junior mimicked a tough guy and looked at Joaquín in a serious hurt way. But once he got the cautious reaction he sought to elicit from Joaquín, Junior smiled at him in a *gotcha* fashion.

"Wrong ball," Junior cried out, as if that explained the difficulty he was having. He then bent over as if to replace the invisible ball on the green. Facing the deserted fairway as if teeing off, wiggling his butt a few times, he finally took a few slow, measured practice swings with an imaginary driver. In one final graceful motion, Junior lifted the club, did a mock backswing, downswung, and perfectly followed through, keeping his left arm straight as his invisible driver struck the invisible ball. His eyes followed the imaginary ball as it looped high on the fairway, and as it came down his head movement tracked the course of the imaginary ball in the air as if it were veering to the left. An anxious look formed on his face. "No, no, to the right," Junior instructed the ball. "Right into the hazard! Man!"

From a distance, Bennie whistled to Joaquín. Everyone had begun to clear the area.

"They call me Junior, *ese*. What's your name?"

"Joaquín."

"Never played golf, eh?"

"No."

"Me neither."

The two strolled back through the path.

Corn Chips out of a Cellophane Bag/
The Brownie Holiday Flash Camera

"I TOLD YOU SO," Bennie laughed at the other end of the telephone line. "Are you really there — in Decatur?" Bennie's voice sounded enthusiastic. Just a few weeks earlier, Bennie had told Joaquín how to get to the camp, assuming it would still be there after thirty years. But as usual, Joaquín seemed to have disregarded Bennie's advice.

There was a gulp at the other end as Joaquín downed some coffee, and then he spoke. "Yes. I spent the entire afternoon yesterday and started off this morning around Decatur, driving up and down the rural roads. Can't recognize it. Not a thing."

"Decatur must have grown a lot."

"No, not really. The town is still very small, but I have no reference to where our camp was. The area around here is huge. Besides, remember the fog?"

Bennie paused for a second and then agreed, "I remember the fog. I dreaded those cold, foggy mornings."

"It's very thick today, and I can't see anything beyond the roadway anyway. I'm at a gas station that appears familiar. I was hoping you could orient me from this point on."

Picking strawberries meant a daily morning drenching as they did battle with the strawberry plants and the bees. And in early summer, it was still nippy on those early Michigan mornings. Straw was placed around the plants to support the weight of the strawberries and to keep them suspended and from coming in contact with the soil. This allowed them to redden evenly and to prevent rotting as well. Shoppers wanted full-bodied, shiny, red, crisp strawberries.

"What's the name of the gas station?"

"Its a Gulf station on the west side of the road."

"Wrong one."

"It can't be," Joaquín sounded a bit distressed. "I seem to recognize the area, although the fog doesn't help."

"As I have often proven to you," Bennie reminded Joaquín, "I have been blessed with a great memory. You're looking for a curve in the main road to Decatur. It turns to the right. The gas station you're looking for is on your right, on the east side. I recall that there was a convenience store, and not a gas station. One of these family-owned things. It was set back a piece from the main highway, maybe a hundred feet or so."

"Yeah? Well, this is on the west side of the road and built right up against the road almost. It must be the wrong one."

"Just listen to me. I know where you're at. The place can't be more than a mile or two from the camp. We used to walk over from our place to the convenience store. It's a shady road between the camp to the store."

The cashier at the Gulf station confirmed to Joaquín that a couple of miles up the road, there was a curve, in fact — and a pretty dangerous one at that. *That must be it.* Joaquín got another cup of coffee for the road.

He proceeded north on the lonely county road. Up ahead, just beyond an intersection, a portable yellow sign with black letters and a large red arrow pointed away from the highway. On his right-hand side, through the fog, Joaquín could make out the fluorescent lights of a drive-in grocery store. Set back beyond a huge parking lot with access to the highway and the intersecting road, a wooden structure with a porch in the front peered out of the fog through two large plate-glass windows.

The rental car was littered with Styrofoam coffee cups, half-eaten hotdogs, and a mess of road maps. Joaquín made a mental note that at the next rest stop, he would fold the maps back to their original, neat, retail form. He hung his glasses from the rearview mirror of his rented car and then exited.

Hunched up against the front wall of the store, two raggedy Mexican men-children shared corn chips out of a cellophane bag. From underneath sooty baseball caps, their eyes shot a quick, apprehensive stare at him and then drew back. The pair acknowledged Joaquín by dipping their heads. Their suspicious peers from under their caps were hardly noticeable — not threatening, but distant somehow.

Didn't Papa used to do that? Joaquín wondered and faintly recalled that the dipping of heads was more of an acknowledgment than anything, a neutral and noncommittal gesture.

He adopted a gait intended to show he was oblivious of their apprehension and greeted them warmly, *"Hola."*

They dipped their heads again.

Inside, the store shelves were narrow and cluttered. Large convex mirrors framed the intersecting walls at the ceiling, providing the cashier multiple views of the shelves. Behind the counter, a young male storekeeper, about thirty, volunteered that his parents used to own the place.

"Yes, they once had gas pumps, but they removed the underground tanks back in the late eighties when they found out they were leaking. They decided then that they really didn't wanna hassle with gas sales anymore."

"Are there any farm workers' camps in the area?"

"Yes. There's a workers' camp down the road a bit, less than a mile. Just catch this road and go east."

This must be the place. "How long has this camp been there, would you know?"

"Ever since I can remember. Before I was born, I figure."

The store owner sold his last three disposable cameras to Joaquín.

Cameras in hand, Joaquín walked a distance away from the store, toward the intersection, intent on getting a wide-angle shot of the grocery store. He had promised Bennie plenty of photographs.

As he focused the camera on the building, the lens framed the image of the young men. He stared at them, at their familiarity, with the oversized coats and caps, with their thick fingers and dirty fingernails. The men stirred and grew uncomfortable. A memory began to emerge. A window to a thought node opened, and Joaquín felt his heart sputter. Even before the complete picture had formed in his mind's visual screen, a lump developed in the deep recesses of his throat. Drawing back the camera, he returned to the car and sat there, leaving the door open, a picture of exhaustion. The crease in his forehead felt sweaty. Nervously undoing his tie, he looked about desperately, as if in search of an escape route. But the look in his eyes told of no place to run to.

Coming from nowhere and from everywhere, a memory which he believed he had long ago erased from his consciousness tenaciously surfaced. There they were, Joaquín and Bennie, some thirty years ago — two raggedy, Mexican men-children, eating out of cellophane wrappings at the curve on the road between Decatur and Dowagiac, *dignos de lastima* (worthy of pity). Wearing a beat-up cowboy hat, Joaquín stood just behind Bennie. On his right hand was Benáncio's banged-up black lunchbox. The furrow in Joaquín's brow had already matured. Bennie's burr haircut was showing, a black thicket that had been carelessly logged, leaving ghastly chopped trunks at different angles.

Joaquín sat in the car in a contemplative mood. *How could we live like that?* Through the windshield of the car, the two men stared back at him. Oblivious of the men and the rental-car open-door warning device, which had been buzzing for some time now, Joaquín sighed deeply. He undid the paper cover of the two throwaway cameras on his lap. In the back cavity of Joaquín's throat, a lump formed. He swallowed. His nose began to run, and his eyes watered. A new lump formed, quicker this time. He swallowed again, this time with difficulty. *This wasn't the way it was supposed to be. Did I come all the way for this?* he questioned himself. Joaquín had envisioned something more like a homecoming of sorts, a welcome back after his long journey. Hot sweat began to ooze from the back of his neck just at the hairline. He felt it and sensed he was about to black out. His heart was working overtime. He could feel its thumping in his jaw.

Joaquín and Bennie peered into the lens of the curious camera. It was a noncommittal peer — a cautious, calculated, concentrated stare through lowered eyelids. It was a black-and-white glossy Kodak, the type that freezes the image and lasts forever.

Sis with her camera. At $4.95, it had taken Manda almost a whole week's worth of cotton-picking, but Sis had finally gotten her prize: her Brownie Holiday Flash. The black box had seen better days. Yet Sis waved the boys into alignment with the image periscoped through the lens and then instructed, "Hold it." She pressed the tan button down, rotated the film, and prepared to take a second. "Say cheese, y'all!"

Their peers responded appropriately, *"Que 'cheese' ni que la chingáda."*

The lid had been forced open. Working overtime, the night crew had been prying into storage bins of a past which no longer existed, or perhaps never did exist — at least not in the way Joaquín remembered it. *Did I conveniently imagine, rationalize, and re-invent the past to suit my needs?* The previous day, he had overlooked it, he now admitted to himself, overlooked the youthful anger that had accompanied those summer days in Michigan. Yes, he had preferred to recall the music with all that soul that covered up what life had really been like. But these men-children now reminded him of that world.

Joaquín and Bennie had made their way to this place from the farm labor camp down the road. Benáncio and Sis would not join them the following year. Huck Finn and Tom Sawyer, *negasúras* in their pant back pockets, they hunted brown squirrels along the paths in the green fortresses around the strawberry pickers' camp. Back at the camp, there were five of them this time around: Joaquín, Bennie, Mama, Papa, and Sis. Nine other families had made this trip as well, leaving boarded-up frame houses back in San Felípe.

Sitting in the rented Subaru, Joaquín looked at his watch. "Barely eight in the morning," he whispered. *Am I on Central Standard Time or Eastern Time? Does it matter?* He remembered that one full working day had passed and he had yet to call his office. *Or has one full day passed?* Joaquín needed a smoke. Returning inside, he asked the storekeeper for a pack of cigarettes.

Once outside, Joaquín flipped out the cigarette butt and approached the young men diplomatically. *"Vengo desde Texas. Yo aquí trabajé cuando era chavalón. Me permíten tomár el foto?"* (I've come from Texas. I worked around here as a kid. Do you mind if I take a picture?) Joaquín had intentionally avoided speaking Spanish since his college years and surprised himself that the words came out so fluently.

The two Mexicans mistakenly assumed Joaquín was interested in a picture of them. One traded glances with the other. They shrugged their shoulders like shy second-grade students; one innocently grinned at the other. The other passed the buck, *"Pos tu"* (Well, you decide). But it was too late. Joaquín gestured politely with his hand that they shouldn't bother. *Click, click, click,* he took several snapshots.

The Detroit City Entrepreneur

DETROIT WAS GOING UP IN SMOKE. The governor had called in the National Guard. *LIFE* magazine photographers captured the blazes on the glossy cover of the last of the oversized magazines. A new art genre was rampaging its way into the American culture: ghetto graffiti. *Burn, baby, burn.*

Joaquín repositioned his rear end on the open door threshold of the cabin as Bennie looked over his brother's shoulder out toward the middle of the camp where a few boys played football. The cabin was a ten-by-ten square pine box with an A-frame roof and was one among many lined up along the pond. Just after noon on a warm Saturday, and the folks had come in from the fields and were readying for a trip in the back of the Ford truck to an afternoon of grocery shopping in Saginaw.

"They have every right to rebel," Benáncio had often preached each time the news reported that the blacks were rioting. Joaquín was reminded of it as he turned the pages of the black-and-white glossy oversized pictorial page of *LIFE* magazine. A young black man's eyes confirmed being surprised by the photographer as he hurled some object through the plate glass of a storefront.

Joaquín flipped through the pages of the magazine until something caught his eye. Wearing a loose-fitting black pajama, a Viet Cong guerrilla posed in an action shot, running nimbly through a jungle path. The photographer's vantage point was from above, the photo staged from a tree branch perhaps, and the impression was that the Cong could move nimbly undetected through the thick jungle. Joaquín shook his head as if a mild complaint were being birthed there. But just as quickly, he disregarded the thought and turned the page. On another page, a colorful centerfold of the smiling Detroit Tigers "boys of summer" jumped out.

Neatly cut out of a forest down around where Lake Michigan and the Michigan and Indiana borders meet, the strawberry pickers' camp was sheltered from the civil war. A narrow, tire-rutted path had been shaped through a wooded swath along the highway. It quickly veered intentionally within the woody area and disappeared from the view of the highway, opening a few hundred feet later into the labor camp which the path both led to and surreptitiously concealed.

Lined up on either side of the field were the white cubicles the strawberry pickers called cabins. All the doors to the cabins were open, and there was a sense of urgent goings-on in each of them. Joaquín could pick up mild bickering from one direction, the wails of a button accordion from another, and the clinking of beer bottles from still another. A line of women with galvanized pails had formed at the red water hand pump.

"Detroit beat the Yankees yesterday," Joaquín began to tell Bennie, and just as he was about to add that this might be Detroit's year to win the pennant, he was interrupted by the blaring of a loudspeaker.

"Sugar pie, honey bunch . . . you know that I love you . . . I can't help myself . . . I love you and nobody else . . ." A large cherry-red Cadillac convertible with a white ragtop was pulling up to the strawberry pickers' camp and very deliberately making its way to the highest point in the open field, interrupting the lively game of flag football that had developed. Joaquín narrowed his eyes and peered at the car, a cautious look on his face.

Out of the car walked a tall black man, a white Panama hat on his head. A perfectly tailored pair of pleated wool and silk blend pants draped the man's long legs. Each pleat was fitted perfectly, offset and flatly in place atop of another. The pants were of a subdued rust color and tended to glitter on the side on which the sun struck them, and they matched an equally subdued, brown-olive shirt that this fellow must have spent a week searching for, for it matched his body perfectly. A thin, doe-skin belt dyed to an elegant auburn sheen graced the outfit. There were narrow cuffs on his pants, thoroughly pressed blade-sharp and stiff, and on his feet an accenting pair of English-woven burgundy shoes.

No sooner had the visitor in the Caddy closed the car door than was Shorty quickly on his way toward him. Manda motioned with her chin toward the Caddy, authorizing Joaquín to go check this out. The man remained by his car as the welcoming committee of curious urchins, mostly children and teenagers, approached him from all directions.

From the opposite direction approached Joaquín and Bennie. The adults of the camp looked on from a distance. At the doorstep of one cabin, a male onlooker, clad only in his khaki pants, stared in their direction. His rotund belly had flopped over the belt, drawing out the white inner lining of the pants. One could fit a good-sized zucchini into his belly button hole with room to spare. Next to him, a thin woman who had not quite gathered all her hair into a rubber band at the back, and now had it all bunched up and dropping over her left ear with loose strands over her face, handed the man a blue towel to dry his hair. In the cabin next door, another curious on-looker chewed on a taco while sitting on a crate in front of his cabin as his wife fetched him some Kool-Aid. A toddler in a soiled diaper and an upper lip caked with snot amused himself next to his young father, who chewed on a small green crabapple.

There was no fat on this six-feet-two frame. A gold-colored belt buckle matched a Rolex watch set in eighteen-karat gold with an eighteen-karat gold fluted bezel. Rolex advertised that this model was pressure-proof to three hundred feet/100M, a feature someone probably noticed.

Short of five-feet-six, Shorty stomped toward the Caddy, his short arms battle-rigid and fists tightened into small balls, an intent of dispatching an intruder articulated on his face. His XXXL-sized plain white T-shirt accommodated a very healthy beer belly. A pint-sized version of a Samoan wrestler, with disheveled hair and a Ghengis Khan moustache and goatee, Shorty occasionally tugged at either side of his baggy khaki cut-offs to hold them up.

"Hey, man, are those things hot?" Shorty blared out at the camp visitor who stood in front of his red chariot with his muscular arms crossed across his chest. Shorty exercised his prerogative to look over the man's inventory in the back seat. The man lifted his Panama hat and gave Shorty a confident grin.

"Whoa! Whoa! Why are you insulting me, man?" the salesman responded in an exaggerated, pained way. A sly grin followed, denoting a mild threat, somewhat intimating, *"Don't you dare screw with me, little man!"* In these situations, it's always a matter of establishing some terrain.

Shorty was caught off guard and edged back stiffly. The salesman stared at Shorty momentarily, then raised his chin confidently. "I don't have to explain nothing to you," he told Shorty. Then, reconsidering, he moderated his tone, "But I'm gonna explain anyway." Now, that was the art of salesmanship.

"Name's Johnny Roland," the salesman said, offering his hand to Shorty, remembering that in his self-defensive posture, he had left out a portion of his salesman etiquette. The salesman's handshake displayed his long, flexible biceps and sinewy arms and the gold Rolex President's watch. "What's yours?"

"Shorty." The salesman drew a smirk from Shorty in return. But at least Shorty had loosened up a bit now that the salesman had acknowledged who the steward of this shop was.

"You see, Shorty, I buy all of this stuff from insurance compnees," the salesman said, pointing to the back seat of car. The rolled and pleated white and red vinyl rear seats of the Caddy were stuffed with television sets and radios.

"Just don't touch the car, boys," he instructed some of the smaller children who were anxious to get a peek at the merchandise. The salesman's face showed genuine pain. "It's just been waxed. I don't need no smears."

He wet his lips and returned to his presentation to Shorty. "You see . . . when a store burns — just like we had in Detroit recently — there's a lot of damage."

The crowd listened with intent looks on their faces.

"Shorty, in a fire, not everything is damaged, you see. Some of the stuff is not even affected. Hell, man, most of it's still in the package." He placed his hand on Shorty's tame shoulder and looked him in the eye. The salesman's hands were a work of art — his long slender fingers those of a pianist who'd never done a day's worth of manual labor in his life.

"You see, bro' . . . the store owner, he don't want the risk." Johnny Roland was teaching the crowd Elementary Business 101. "He don't wanna sell Shorty a TV set that may have some slight damage and then have Shorty return da damn thing the following day. He don't want that. Are you with me, man?" Roland was preaching, and he wanted his due "Amen."

Shorty nodded in agreement and dabbed at his scraggily moustache.

Johnny Roland was on a roll. "So, what does the store owner do, Shoor . . . tie? Only thing he can do, ma' man . . . force the insurance compnee to pay him for those TV sets, right?" He searched into Shorty's eyes for an answer from down deep. "You with me, man?"

Shorty, who was listening intently trying to follow, nodded in agreement again. "Amen." Joaquín was dazzled by the salesman and didn't see Bennie chuckling at his sight.

Johnny Roland was in full stride. "Now, I'm da guy dat goes to the insurance compnee. I tells the insurance compnee, 'Hey, those sets aren't worth much to ya. You're not in da bidness a selling TV sets, man.'"

"'Tell you what . . .'" Roland was now punctuating his sentences with his index finger, which he kept in the air, "'I'll take 'em off yer hands for a percentage.'"

Shorty hadn't been entirely comatose, and he quickly interjected, "What percentage you pay for 'em, man?"

Roland smiled. "Can't do, my friend. That's my trade secret. But I will tell you this . . . I'm offering everything I have at 25 percent of retail, but only fo' tu-day." The sentence trailed off as the salesman punctuated the grand offer he just made Shorty by biting his lower lip, anxiously awaiting Shorty's response.

Shorty was being the kind of leader that the camp needed. He challenged the salesman, "Yeah, but how do we know whether we're paying too much for them or not?"

"Fair question, Shorty." The salesman's eyes swept the crowd, as a politician would say — to connect — and he repeated to them as well, "Fair question. Tell you what I'm gonna do fer you." Joaquín turned to Bennie, sneering and biting his tongue as if to say, *"He's got 'im now, hook, line, and sinker."* "If I sell five TV sets here today — that's five sets, now — at 20 pissant of reetail, I will leave with you, Shorty, a TV set as a gare . . . on . . . tee, but only with you, Shorty." Roland paused and then restated his offer, "But only as a gare . . . on . . . tee. Are you with me, Shorty?" Shorty nodded again in response to the salesman's full disclosure.

Shorty had been made an equity partner by Johnny Roland. The salesman had co-opted him right before the crowd's eyes and Joaquín gave Bennie a roll of the eyes. Bennie puckered his lips and chuckled.

Johnny Roland continued. "It ain't yours yet, man. It's only a gare . . . on . . . tee. Now, I be back Sunday right afta church. Dat'll give you plenty a time to get over to Saginaw and check the retail price of these TV sets. On Sunday, if the prices don't check, I take my sets back, man, and I take your set back too. And acourse, you get a full refund. Now dat's fair?"

"Amen." The nods among the welcoming committee confirmed the fairness of the deal.

Soon enough, Johnny Roland had sold more than his quota of TV sets, and that was the last time they saw Johnny Roland.

The Longing

WHAT LONGING HAD DRAWN JOAQUÍN back to the strawberry fields? Had he hoped to experience a certain affinity with the place?

A narrow strip of asphalt led east from the curve in the highway toward the labor camp. He recalled the camp sitting on a small rise overlooking a mosquito-infested marsh. As he drove toward the camp, fog thickened and hovered heavily among the trees. He slowed to a snail's pace. *The brick homes along the road are of recent vintage.* The aging trees lining the road, like the trees at Niles, were familiar to him. He couldn't explain it, but his memory of trees seemed to be the sharpest. Perhaps it was because on off-days and weekends, Joaquín and Bennie would spend endless hours hunting brown squirrels along this once unpaved road and the other paths that tunneled through the tall forest.

"The road will curve slightly to the left, and there will be a large red barn on your right," Bennie had told him during their last telephone conversation. Joaquín had imagined a stately gambrel-roofed red structure framed by two elder pines. But the barn Joaquín found, like a Greek marble artifact, had only weak traces of its once-bold red coat. An unpainted driftwood gray, the barn stood off the road about 150 feet. One of the barn's stone-adorned walls had crumbled. But at least Joaquín had found another milestone. In front of the barn, a rye grass lawn glistened with the morning dew. And Joaquín decided the lawn was as good as any place to wait for the fog to clear.

A sharp pain just below his rib cage had been bothering Joaquín since early morning. His diet that last two days had not been a healthy one. Now, vaporized gastric juice shot up through his esophagus. Swallowing bitterly, he pressed his tongue against his lower front teeth to produce enough saliva to drown the bitterness. He then reached under the seat and pulled the leftover Sprite from the night before and forced the warm drink down. The fizzle was almost all gone, but it seemed to neutralize the bile. He dozed off.

Still a bit groggy, Joaquín rubbed at his eyes and looked down the thinly paved road. The fog had cleared. He had overlooked it before, but there it was—the high canopy of trees where the boys had once hunted squirrels. He headed toward the road, neglecting the idling car.

The road hadn't been paved some thirty years before. Through the brush across the road, he could tell the ground surface was made of dark red loam, which had felt so cool to his feet as they had explored the wood. His brain was fully engaged, and his heart thumped with anticipation. *The camp should be but a few hundred feet away as the road flattens down below,* he told himself. Joaquín walked toward it, camera in hand, until he remembered that he had left the car idling and returned to drive down to the camp.

Two tall red maple trees, like old and patient weary sentries, framed the entrance to the camp. Aging scars on their perfectly cylindrical trunks complained of metal cuffs that had once sustained the weight of metal gates.

Joaquín was taken aback by the site. Something was very wrong. The neat row of white cabins was gone. In their place lay the littered corpses of mobile homes, scattered here and there in disarray, as if hastily removed to this mobile home cemetery but never properly interred. Victims of prolonged abuse and degradation, their once-sleek bodies showed the scars of angry branding by urban taggers and lacked the least bit of attention. Most were too dilapidated or damaged beyond repair to serve as habitats. But fresh tire tracks in the damp soil told otherwise. And in the air, Joaquín acknowledged the admixture of familiar kitchen scents and other human odors. Around the mobile homes, he noticed the fresh litter of human existence. As he drove down the center of the camp following the drying mud path, the memories began to return.

He rested, his back against the door of the rental car. In his memory of this place, there had always existed a scene of an idyllic rolling hill at a distant misty forest's edge. Something about the forest had attracted him. Its verdant stillness—silent, bold, potent, and mystical—had been overpowering in its allure. There was something in the forest waiting for him. Somehow, he had always known it. He had always known that someday he would have to journey back to this place.

Was it remorse he was beginning to sense? Is that why he was here? He fought with his memory, for he sensed a premonition, by seeking to redirect his thoughts to more pleasant times. He tried to recall the safe ivory towers of his college days when every waking hour had been a celebration of intellect and students of every ilk battled each other safely within the confines of academia over political options and hypothetical nuclear assaults and whether food stamps or bootstraps were the better motivator of those who were of color or born poor. But he lost the battle; his memory insisted on returning to this place, as if some accounting by him was due. *To account for what?*

Joaquín surveyed. He smiled a stupid smile. This place invited ambivalence: memories of a certain mundane, sweet innocence which had been every child's inherent privilege; memories of a teenager shedding his adolescent skin and, in so doing, only further clouding his brow; memories of a mature, subdued desperation that time and place had carved into the furrowed brows of those who had been this way before, to *El Norte*, time and again, longing, searching; and memories of that restrained contempt that eventually germinated in places like this. He felt his jaw tighten, his teeth clench. How he had hated this place, despised everything about it, and promised himself that when he was a man, he would never let anyone treat him the way the people of the strawberry fields were treated.

Joaquín surveyed again. It was all coming back to him. Even the scent of this place now shared its familiarity: the smell of vermicelli *con carne picáda* (ground beef) was in the air—cumen, garlic, black pepper, and tomatoes. Why is it that he has never again tasted vermicelli *con carne picáda* the way Manda used to make it? After all, the magic ingredient that gave it the savory taste was cumen. Or perhaps the taste resulted from the temperature at which the garlic was sautéed? Or perhaps it had been the times that he had savored and which now lured him? Because in spite of it all, there had been good times, he reminded himself. *Often*, he confirmed. Perhaps it had been the peculiar scent of this place and of the people who had inhabited it that had made all the difference; had made it bearable. After all, it had been bearable. No one died here. No one was brought here in chains. Free will had brought them all.

He smiled sincerely this time. He could not resist the irony and shook his head. *With the exception of the mobile homes, this place has not changed in thirty years.* An awkward exhilaration, sweet, yet sour, enveloped him. He imagined the presence of sweaty kids, shirtless and catching their breath, engaged in a spirited game of flag football. At any moment, they could walk out from behind the mobile homes. One of them would shout, "Take off your shirt, Joaquín, so you can be like the rest of us." *Could I, after all these years, still shed my skin? Be like the rest of them?* He turned as if something had caught his attention and imagined another kid's voice asking him to run for the long pass. Junior, his implicit mentor, would show up as well, with his cheap shades, wearing a bleach white, ribbed, sleeveless undershirt and smelling of cheap cologne. Blue, taking measured steps on his lanky limbs, would salute demurely. And Shorty, flipping the football and puffing on a Buglar roll-your-own, would nod his acknowledging *"Hello"* and smile back at him.

Warm and nostalgic, the sensation was brief, for he could not rid himself of an unpleasant harbinger that had begun to annoy him from deep down in his core. *Why have I come here? I never liked like this place!* What he had long ago suppressed — an appendage he had disdained, which in his unconscious he had severed and burned, pulled out its thinnest of roots, down to the remotest of moist tendrils — was now, after all these years, like a creeping vine, snaking back into his unconscious.

Igualádo! Igualádo! Why? he asked himself. *Why would Papa accuse me so? Did I need to be saved from his perceived futility of my ambitiousness?* Joaquín's anger grew as he pictured his father's oratory under the tin porch of Don Magín's corner grocery store. *Was I that pathetic in his eyes?* he asked and was reminded of the *Igualádo*-like Negro in Washington Irving's "The Legend of Sleepy Hollow":

> *. . . the appearance of a negro, in tow-cloth jacket and trousers, a round-crowned fragment of a hat, like the cap of Mercury, and mounted on the back of a ragged, wild, half-broken colt, which he managed with a rope by way of halter. He came clattering up to the school-door with an invitation to Ichabod . . . ; and having delivered his message with that air of importance, and effort at fine language, which a negro is apt to display on petty embassies of the kind*

Is that how Papa saw me? he asked himself. Joaquín frowned and struck the hood of the car with his fist. *I tried to be so like you; to emulate that powerful glare of your eyes; to walk in your gait. But other forces drew me away. My hunger was different than yours, Papa. I don't know why.*

It just was. Desperately, I prayed that some power would enter me and control my being so that I could be pleasing to your eyes, but to no avail. I could not be you, Papa. I tried, but in the end, I had to be myself.

"*Igualádo! Crab!*"

"*Joaquín is going to be president! Ha! Ha! Ha!*"

How could he ever forget his elementary school classmates, the older boys in particular, whose jeering faces flashed into his mental screen, who would make fun of him for days . . . "*Joaquín is going to be president. Ha! Ha! Ha!*"

He closed his left eye, which felt dry, and jerked back at the sensation of a tiny prick on his eyeball. *I have not been el hijo desobediente*, he boldy assured himself. I abandoned nobody. He pushed himself away from the car, bent to pull a bouquet of goldenrods, and began to make his way toward the mobile homes in the distance.

Lured by the strawberry fields, here they were. Thousands of Mexicans. Tens of thousands. Everyone from *el valle de Texas* (the valley of Texas) was here. It was like entire high schools in South Texas had emptied, and students and their families transported *en masse* to the strawberry fields.

Joaquín recalled the conspicuous vigor in Manda's spirit when they had finally arrived here, even as the cancer devoured her body. He felt like both laughing and crying as he confirmed his mother's ploy. He recalled the pain on Manda's small body as she struggled in the fields. The left side of her back had buckled from scoliosis, and she had pulled out what were left of her teeth to fit in her dentures, but she was overjoyed, for she had finally arrived at Jacob's Ladder. What did she need breasts for anymore, she joked. "I'm through with feeding babies." Joaquín recalled how he had been taken in by his mother's inexorable reasoning. "It's temporary," she explained about the hardship of the strawberry fields. "What's a little sacrifice? When you look back years from now, you can say to yourself, 'Look at the reward. But I paid the price.'" It had been her will that had been impossible to question, he now confirmed. For in the balance, her will had always been *terra firma* compared to Benáncio's forlorning hope that some other force—the perfect leader—would someday come to deliver them out of the strawberry fields. Joaquín had never said it, but had always intuited, *Had we been going into battle, it is her I would have preferred to lead me.*

Joaquín rotated his neck and looked up at the sky. A gray cloud, ponderous and thick, temporarily moved aside for the sun to shine through. But this was momentary, and it quickly shut out the sun again. His eyes were glassy. His mouth felt dry and raw. He spit.

Over by the marsh, white clapboard cubicles not larger than the portable lawn sheds for sale at Sears had been provided *gratis* for the strawberry picking season. At night, layers of bedspreads cushioned the discomfort, but the rough pine floorboards were punishing on the bony parts. A butane two-burner was their kitchen.

Two aluminum portable johns had replaced the makeshift outhouse. There had been no pit privy at their Decatur camp when they arrived. The men had stood around giving each other bewildered looks like seamen marooned on a deserted island. Out of frustration, Benáncio had led the digging party for the camp outhouse that day. Seizing an axe which he filed down, he set out to draw and cut the right lengths of wood. Other men eventually joined in and awaited his instructions as Benáncio directed how the pit should be dug and the wood attached.

The makeshift outhouse had been reserved exclusively for the women of the camp. The outhouse was a Neanderthal lean-to, with old bedspreads as walls. Women would head there in groups and encircle the lean-to to cover whatever openings may have drawn a man's peer. Inside the lean-to, the women squatted to relieve themselves. Men scampered into the woods to do their business.

Initially, Joaquín's sensibilities were affected. He pained when it was Manda's or Sis' turn at the outhouse. He imagined the discomfort and the thoughts that went through people's minds at such a sight. He screamed at the top his lungs, "God! I can't believe what we put up with!" *Isn't it amazing how in due time, we fall in step and it all becomes acceptable. Anything can become acceptable, in due course. Everything!*

———※———

He recalled his father's anger and frustrated daily complaints that someone should come around to organize the strawberry pickers because an organization could improve the worker's lives. At some point, Benáncio's self-imposed exile had become unnerving. Joaquín could sense Benáncio's humiliation and it was turning to hostility. "We're like slaves looking for another master," Benáncio complained to Manda in an accusatory tone. *Did Papa see in us servile complaisance?* The living conditions were beneath Benáncio's dignity. His regrets had become a tangible emotion fixed on his face: *Why had he come to the strawberry fields against his better judgment.* He didn't belong here; he didn't belong . . . anymore.

At his corner of the white box, on a two-by-four, Joaquín had gouged his name and his birth date. Someday in the distant future, when he returned to this place, he imagined pointing out to his children, "There it is; that's my mark." He was fifteen on that day. Manda remembered and kissed Joaquín on the forehead as they departed for the strawberry fields. It was a rare show of affection of which they had been robbed—an emotion suppressed for so long that it surprised Joaquín. But he knew Manda cherished every new day now as if her dream had come true. He sensed *her* pride whenever he caught her glimpsing in his direction, as if confirming her great luck that finally, her boys were becoming men, and she had seen the day.

Strawberries ripen from one day to the next. It has to do with the temperature. To extend their shelf life, strawberries have to be picked at the right time. A nice pink will quickly turn ruby red en route to Chicago, New York, or Houston. To avoid losses, the patches are picked a few hours each day. Ripe strawberries are preferred. Machines can't be that selective; only humans can be efficient strawberry pickers. The work started at first light.

"That first week in the strawberry fields is etched in my memory," Bennie began. He and Sis sat at the coffee shop and wondered what course Joaquín's trip had taken. Sis took a long sip from the tea glass without removing her glare from Bennie. A waitress brought Bennie a brown cookie in the form of a piggy. "I remember it as if it were yesterday," he continued. "Dawn is upon us. Still dark," he shuddered. "I hate it. An old school bus has come to a stop. We're passengers. The bus is a yellow, hand-me-down, resurrected for one more strawberry season." He bit his lower lip, proud that he recalled such minute details. "For us, it's high-tech, perhaps the single most modern advancement in strawberry picking." Bennie nodded at Sis. "It sure beats the back of the truck."

Sis sipped her tea, holding the glass with both hands, eyeing Bennie with an unsettled look and uneasiness in her voice. "What was it? 'Bout five-thirty in the morning?" She asked the question reluctantly.

"Yeah." Bennie nodded. "We didn't wish to see behind us anymore," he said and posed as if assuming airs. "It's what's up ahead that matters now. The bus allows us that luxury—that dignity. I remember wondering why in heaven's name it was so important that we be up so early." He chuckled and turned to the ceiling as if trying to picture the scene. "Let me paint a picture for you. Across the aisle, one row in front of me, Joaquín is sitting sideways, the back of his head is up against the bus window, his knees recoiled up in the seat. It's the sixties, you know, and his shoulder-length hair may be in vogue elsewhere, but in the strawberry fields, it's inappropriate."

Sis ventured an aside, "He was so proud of his long hair."

"Yes, he was, but some will whisper under their breath as he passes them on the way to the culling station in the middle of the strawberry field, 'ha de ser joto'" (he must be a queer). Bennie laughed.

"Did you ever tell him that?"

"No! Of course not." They both chuckled.

Bennie took a bite of the cookie, chewed quickly, and downed it with coffee. "I remember one occasion in the bus. The season is right for prickly pears back home—you know, May, June—and in the strawberry fields, it's a time of pimples and beard stubble: boys becoming men. Several seats ahead in the bus sit Junior and Blue. Junior, about thirty, has jet-black hair and beady eyes. Rumors abound that Junior smokes marijuana, but I never thought it was true. Junior and Joaquín have become a pair. Someday, I'll tell you about that. Anyway, Junior crosses his knee the way women and *pintos* [jailbirds] do. On the bus, Junior and Blue whisper to each other. Junior occasionally lets out a squeaky snicker—not quite a laugh, but a put-down, making-fun-of kind of snicker. That's Junior's trademark snicker. Otherwise there's not another sound in the school bus."

Sis smiled and nodded her head as if it was all unbelievable.

"From Joaquín's direction comes a rasp. A match is lit like a candle in the dark. Joaquín's silhouette draws on a Buglar roll-your-own. It sounds like a sigh. He protects the flat cigarette, cupping it between his thumb and index finger. Junior smokes that way too. Here, no one holds a cigarette between the index and middle finger. That's for queers. The smoke is being sucked out of the bus window, which is slightly ajar.

"Slapping of body parts throughout the bus confirms that the pesky mosquitoes have begun to find their marks. They must sense the body heat, because these mosquitoes seem to zero in on any fleshy surface that has been left uncovered. The neck line between the hair and the shirt collar, even in the spaces between the frayed threads of worn bobby socks, offer little resistance to the mosquitoes' warmth radar."

Bennie went for the cigarette pack in his shirt pocket, and Sis gave him a "no" nod. He frowned amicably, decided not to smoke, and returned to telling his story. "It's like Army convoys traveling at night. Streams of car headlights are swelling the field from all directions. You can see them—the Fords and Chevys—as they come down bumpily on the dirt roads and eerily make their way through a curving path in the woods. The headlight beams shoot through the fog, creating silhouettes of the trees. We, on the other hand, have left camp and traveled in the old bus to the strawberry fields."

"Mucháchos, échenle ganas, mientras que dura" (Boys, let's get it while it lasts). Manda was always the self-designated motivator, the Army sergeant, the coach with the whistle. She could either charm Joaquín or embarrass him to get a move-on. Take your pick. "It's picking time; the strawberries are ripe; *que esperan* [what are you waiting for]? *A lo que te traje chencha* (Let's get to the business of what I brought you here for, Chencha), she would prod, using an off-color joke of the day.

Back in San Felípe, Manda had introduced the boys to the cotton fields at ages four and five. "You children go up ahead in the row and pick small piles of cotton for me," she would urge them on and challenge them to see who was the faster picker.

She would follow behind, dragging the plump canvas sack, which resembled a giant, fat caterpillar. A large, colorful gingham red *guarde soleil* covered her head and, like horse blinders, kept her focus. At a penny a pound, she often took home at least a dollar a day.

On this morning, the air was thick with hesitancy. Within the bus, no one was eager to rush the strawberry fields. Bennie had nodded off. Joaquín tried a few last puffs on the cigarette. Manda had been up since four in the morning serenading *tortillas*. Most of the others were still drowsy, savoring this period of repose until the very last minute. But Manda rose from her seat behind the bus driver. She zippered the second-hand-store thick ski jacket, tightened her woolen scarf under her neck, and forced on her head the padded green cap with the earmuffs, which made her look like a short, fat Kamakazi pilot. Favoring her right hip, she made her way down the bus steps. The frosty morning air swooped in. Others reacted with grunts, bothered by the realization that it was time to get a move-on.

Joaquín was watching. Actions speak louder than words. He knew her message: *"Que esperas, papacito?"* (What are you waiting for, son?) He knew work was his mother's obsession, her religious devotion, her therapy. Flipping the roll-your-own out the window, Joaquín turned to Bennie and called out, *"Vamonos bro . . . !* (Let's go, bro'!) Junior and Blue followed them, still muttering.

Not much space on the mobile-home walls had been left untouched by the graffiti artists. Joaquín suspected that sooner or later, someone would appear to inquire about his visit.

Toward the back of the camp, behind the mobile homes, a thick curtain of smoke struggled to rise against the weight of the morning dew. *A sign of life.* The smoke drew Joaquín. Edging his way to avoid stepping on piles of debris strewn about, he made his way between the lengths of two mobile homes toward a smoldering trash heap. Approaching the simmering fire, Joaquín was stunned. Through the smoke, two tiny blue eyes had fixed on him. In the next moment, he realized that they were doll eyes. He stooped and picked up a rubber baby doll. It was bald; all of its hair had been pulled out, but through some of the holes through which the human-like hair once attached, short tufts of blonde hair still clung to their attachments. Its synthetic flesh had begun to melt in the heat, and Joaquín was amazed at how lifelike it appeared. Swiveling blue eyeballs, lifelike, seemed to stare emotionless at him, and for a second, Joaquín was aghast that the doll could not feel the heat that had begun to distort her face. For a second, fragments of his dream raced through his mind, and he was reminded of the bald doll that accompanied the blonde's portrait of his dreams. He discarded the doll back into the fire and lit a cigarette.

What longing has brought me to Decatur, to this camp? In his memory, this place had been full of excitement. This trip would recapture for him that feeling that he had once felt: of innocence and naïve youth. But happy? *Is that true? Were we happy?*

He surveyed. They had first arrived here in June 1965. White paint was still drying on the recently built pine boxes, which they called cabins. With the exception of the mobile homes, as if suspended in a time warp, this place seemed immune to outside influences. *Over there was our cabin,* Joaquín surmised. He searched for signs of a fence line, beyond which used to lay the march, along which the cabins lined up in single file.

The red manual water pump was gone. Much like a first-century Palestine desert well, the pump had been one of the few places where boys could safely talk to camp girls without threatening some father's or brother's *machismo.* Joaquín and Bennie often fought over who would volunteer to carry the water pail to the pump. At present, the only source of water for the camp remained at a new small electric pump. There was no other visible plumbing to the mobile homes.

Children still walk to this place every morning to brush their teeth and wash their faces.

A barely audible soft strumming of *bajo sexto* (Mexican bass guitar) chords interceded in his thoughts: G, C, D minor. His heart was working overtime, and he could feel it beat at his left jaw. Joaquín surveyed around one more time and in the distance caught a glimpse of the tall sugar maples swaying in unison and made out the growing sonorous wails of cicadas. *I worked myself out of this place. What am I doing here?*

His recollections of this place had always been but snapshots, incomplete and unjoined, minuscule frames, memories caught in black-and-white Kodak glossies and laid out in millions of pixels in hundreds of files retrievable only through his emotions, unreliable hybrids suitably rationalized to serve a particular nostalgic moment. But now, the memories were connecting, merging unequivocally, and fusing. He asked himself, *could I have had so much and yet so little in com-*

mon with the people of the strawberry fields? Was he so different from others of his generation? It all began to come back to him.

The guitar chords had become more audible.

> *. . . pobre de mi, pobre de mi* (miserable me, poor me),

The few lyrics he did recall often cried softly of an endless, agonizing pain, of the futility of existence, and they bled out from old and jagged, incurable wounds. An inherited pain — a pain of the prior generation's memory — was kept alive by the men philosophers at Don Magín's corner grocery store; the affliction raising its ugly head. Joaquín's jaw stiffened. The affliction: for as long as he could remember, the fatalism had been there, often barely submerged just below the emotional surface. But it was always implied. Had not Mary Quite Contrary simply reaffirmed the contradiction that their generation had been raised with: "Run fast, as fast as you can! But don't win the race. If you win the race, you lose. Be smart, but not too smart. Too smart, you lose."

And Joaquín knew that for a long time in his youth, he had been imbued with it, had absorbed it. The very first lyrics he had memorized while picking cotton as a boy had said it all:

> *Está vida mejor que se acabe, no es para mi.* (It's best that this life end, it's not for me)

> *pobre de mi, pobre me de mi* (miserable me, poor me)

Have I (we) overcome it? Or does the affliction remain in the host of the inflicted like a remittent malaria fever?

———◆———

The camp was empty again. Joaquín turned, and the scene was transformed. He now stood amid a vast green sea of strawberry vines. The plants reached up to just below his knees. Hundreds of pickers, some standing, others crouching, still others trudging with their strawberry-carrying trays en route to the shaded culling station in the middle of the field, had fanned out as if to equitably allocate the field among themselves. He surprised himself with the realization: *But this is not the scene of a fatalist people; a cemetery of vanquished spirits.* A palpable drone emanated from the field, and as the seconds passed, it was amplified. In his imagination, Joaquín was initially unable to distinguish the source: *From which drones does the drone drone? No, this is*

*not a scene of vanquished spirits. This is a scene of a people on a mission. Lis-
ten to the drone of mass energy. Is it conceivable that there had been a master
plan? Was that possible? Had these wretched souls designed a way out of the
strawberry fields?*

His hearing sharpened. To his right, he could distinguish the voices
of two women engaging in a friendly back and forth. As that sound
subsided, it was replaced by a distant goat-calling whistle, *fristt,
frissst,* and Joaquín imagined two small boys being reigned in by
their father. And then, this image was replaced by the sound of a
melodious, soulful falsetto male duet:

> *. . . if she is baa-ad, he cain't see it; she can do no wrong . . .*

He turned around and found himself in the center of a cobblestone
plaza in Mexico to which his father, lured by the faces of his countrymen and their somber lyrics, had crossed the street to join. Around
the *plaza,* in a counterclockwise slow motion promenaded a throng
of humanity. Their faces evoked a spellbound listlessness on their
endless journey to some venue that must lie up ahead. *Why do they
seek answers only in the past?*

"*Igualádo! Igualádo!*" (Pretentious! Pretentious!) His father chided
him, "Son, you pretend to be whom you are not and end up denying
your own people. Do you believe that you are better than us?"

Joaquín imagined defending himself against his father. "What is
the obligation, Papa, that covenant of obedience, that our ancestors
have entered into which requires that we must enter the temple as
one, or none of us shall ever enter?" But Joaquín's arguments had
remained in his thoughts, because the marathon discussions he recalled having with his father had never taken place.

How strong had been Benáncio's overwhelming nostalgic longing to return?
Joaquín wondered. Every Saturday, he had searched in vain for
that lost emotion that had once connected him to his mother country, that womb which he sought to reattach his umbilical cord to.
Had Benáncio so resented this world to which he had delivered his
children to the point of depriving himself, and depriving his children
of it as well? In the end, Benáncio would give up his quest and would
never again revisit the carousel. And he would not return to his wonderful and beloved Mexico, and he would leave no instructions that
his body—like in the song— be returned there. In the end, he, too,
had stayed in America, sold out his people.

Sensing something akin to an invisible tap on his shoulder, Joaquín instinctively began to turn.

"*Buenos días, Señór, como está?*" (Hello, sir, how are you?) A man's firm voice came from behind Joaquín. Not quite like a welcome, the salutation sounded rather dismissive, like the implied warning before a trespasser is dispatched, like a harsh "*Can I do something for you?*"

Joaquín guessed, *A few years younger than me.* He reconsidered, *Probably in his thirties.* For such a short man, his hands appeared disproportionately large. A wide, flat chest seemed to connect directly to his head. The man's thick hair did not part in a straight line, yet seemed to fall limply toward either side of his head. He had a round face with a large forehead and a resolute jaw. Joaquín learned from him that the people in the camp were from the state of Zacatécas in Mexico.

"That seems like a long way from here" Joaquín offered in a nervous laugh, going through the map of Mexico in his mind to see if he could recall where Zacatécas is.

"Yes. Many miles. It is very far away."

"So, you think Zacatécas is what, say about 2,500 miles?"

"In miles, yes, I think so." There was impatience in the man's response.

Uncertain now even whether he felt an affinity with this man or whether he even desired it, Joaquín was struck. *Have I been driven here by fate to commune with this man? Is that possible? Do I have a message to deliver? Or, is there a message I am to receive?* The thoughts cluttered his mind as he grappled for words, fearing that the man would leave any second now.

"Did you pick strawberries this season?" Joaquín asked in a condescending tone.

"Strawberries? I don't think they grow here. I have never seen one."

"They don't grow here?" Joaquín appeared surprised and disappointed all at once. "You haven't seen any?"

"No, *Señór.*"

"What do people do for work here?" The man's smile betrayed his discomfort with Joaquín's questions. Sensing it, Joaquín grew concerned that this conversation was about to cease.

"I used to live in this camp many, many years ago." Joaquín smiled forcefully at the man, still insistent, hoping this might interest him.

"Oh, yes," the man responded, wetting his lips. It was not clear that the man even grasped what Joaquín had said.

I'm losing him, Joaquín thought. *Don't cut me off,* he wanted to plead. *I came from here. I am like you. You are like me.* He thought for a moment that he so desperately wanted to say these words to the man. *It is my obligation to do so, to instill hope, to enlighten. Don't give up,* he wanted to tell the man from Zacatécas. *Hang in there.* In the deep recesses of Joaquín's mind, he had an overwhelming need, the obligatory urge and responsibility . . . *To commune with this man? Can that be my quest? Does that finally explain the reason for this journey?*

"Many, many years ago," Joaquín repeated, and before he could finish his thoughts, the man's reaction told him that he was not impressed with Joaquín's attempts. Joaquín tried again, "How about cucumbers? Did you pick cucumbers this summer?"

"*Sí,* over there . . . that's where the cucumbers are." The man nodded toward the field in the back of the camp. Joaquín turned and glanced in the direction of the field. The cucumber vines had thinned into an anemic yellow, and a few bees undertook an erratic and pointless search for an elusive flower.

Joaquín closed his eyes and turned to face up toward the sky. He gulped to swallow his frustration. Manda's message had been a constant in Joaquín's young life. Her glance was enough to convey it: always that ironic optimism, in spite of whatever challenging circumstances. *Never for a second stop believing that beyond those gates is a better life for you.* What had once been boring clichés now sound so appealing to him. They flow spontaneously, singing in his distant memory like gently embracing and comforting lullabyes.

Should I offer the man this message? He was reminded of Benáncio's liturgy: we need a leader, but not just any leader, but a person who does not have personal ambition, a perfect leader, someone without sin, to serve our needs. *Did I disappoint him because I could not be that person that he dreamt of being?*

He paused and frowned, recalling the sympathetic condescending tonality of the voices of those who just couldn't help believing they were a notch above and Joaquín was a notch below. It was in their heart of hearts. It was in their voices, in the inflection of their utterances. They were sacrificing their own comfort to minister to the poor and ignorant Mexicans of South Texas. *What right do I have to tell this man anything?* Thankfully, the words didn't come.

On the road, a flatbed truck honked twice and revved the engine.

A company name was painted on the truck door, but Joaquín couldn't make out any of the words except "Lumber." The man from Zacatécas became perky and expectant and seemed grateful that this conversation had been so timely interrupted. *"Adiós,"* he said and smiled (*a full, sincere smile, confident,* Joaquín noticed) and scampered toward the truck. For the man from Zacatécas, there seemed to be no time for sentimental fulfillment. "Look at me," Joaquín had wanted to tell the man. "See how far I have come. Me, from these strawberry fields." But the man from Zacatécas had more important things on his mind. *Things more important than filling that cavity in my ego,* Joaquín admitted. The man from Zacatécas had to get to work, had to board the flatbed truck which awaited him on the road and now wailed for him. The boss man called. *"Que esperas? Chingale!"* (What are you waiting for? Get a move on!) *A lo que traje Chencha.* The flatbed truck moved on and disappeared as the road curved beyond the canopy of trees.

An ironic smile formed on Joaquín's face. It all made sense. A Zacatécan Indian had traveled 2,500 miles to these fields of *El Norte.* Had he come here for any reason other than to bargain the use of his *brazos* (arms) for a price, like the *bracéros* before him, like Benáncio had, and like those of the generation that followed, Joaquín's generation, who had traveled to the strawberry fields? How many years must he have saved his *pesos* in order to come? Years from now, would his children appreciate the great risk and sacrifice that this man had undertaken? And when his children (or maybe his grandchildren) grew into adolescence and became as American as apple pie (for, no doubt, they would), would he resent them for what they had become, or would he look at the accomplishment and consider his efforts proudly?

Joaquín recalled the telephone call he had gotten many years before. "He was very proud of you" had been the message from the other end of the telephone line within a few days after Benáncio had died. Had Benáncio offered his love the only way a man of those times was allowed to? His inner voice told him, *Maybe he has been holding that abrazo* (his hug) *open for you? Why don't you embrace him back?* "How many years have I carried the resentment?" Joaquín whispered. "Is this where it finally stops?" He shrugged his shoulders. "Maybe he left us," he began and stalled. "Yes, I am sure," he nodded reassuringly, "he left us because he must have realized that he could not stop the progress of time and that, like Saturn, he would have destroyed us had he not left. That's what I want to believe.

The sun was out in full force! Joaquín squinted.

How mistaken I have been! This place was not home; was never meant to be embraced, missed, or recalled nostalgically. It was simply a way of life. Nothing more. Manda had known it all along, hadn't she? She never led us to believe that this was the "promised land." Oh, she had longed to come to this place. Make no mistake. But only because this place provided that rite of passage. For she knew there were no shortcuts. She had been so well aware of that. Any deviation would have short-circuited a much larger plan. Manda's was an implicit acknowledgment, a persistent faith that here, in the strawberry fields, would *at worst* be bearable for the first generation. And that was her generation. And she willingly accepted those terms, for that was the price to be paid for the possibility, if only a possibility, of the seemingly endless opportunities granted her children in return. She had made that covenant and lived with the expectation that if she met her end of the bargain, the opportunities would be there for her children.

How clear it all now was. In the strawberry fields lay a miserable world fraught with endless struggle, but it was a world full of adolescent dreams of endless possibilities where children could trade their sweat for plastic tokens and the freedom of abstract thought.

Shooting the Breeze and Shooting Dice/
Echándo Mosca

SATURDAY EVENINGS, DON ARMÁNDO relaxed the rules and allowed dice games and drinking of alcohol at his camp. On that last Saturday in Decatur, as some packed for the long trip back to Texas and others sought an extended stay in Indiana, a heavy rain began at dusk and continued through the evening. In spite of the weather, a spirited game of dice developed once the rain subsided. A pickup truck was backed up next to the light pole at the entrance to the camp. In the bed of the truck, pieces of cardboard were laid out to create a smooth surface for the dice to roll.

Junior was pitching dice, a half-empty dark bottle of Stroh's in his left hand. He wiped the sweat beads from his forehead with the back of his left hand. His beady black eyes looked beadier now and red. For the past hour, as if it were his obligation, Blue had been silently nursing a warm beer, steadying himself against the spare tire attached just behind the driver's side of the Chevy pickup. He existed in a trance now, his eyes at half mast and his Fedora pulled back so that it only covered half of the head. Even stone-drunk, he just kept smiling in a quiet chuckle, as if his brain was connected to some perpetual movie tone, which he was taking delight in. Anyone could tell he was drunk because he had stopped the serious phase of drinking. While his eyes would occasionally acknowledge that he was superficially still with the rest of the men, it was obvious his focus was elsewhere. And wherever it was that Blue's mind visited during those Friday and Saturday night binges, it seemed to be a peaceful place.

The old man, the alcoholic with the two women and the blonde girl, earlier insisted on rolling the dice on a twenty. He got craps. He dropped another twenty. Craps again, and he grumped away. He sat in front of a cabin sulking with a half-empty dark bottle of bourbon whiskey. Shorty and his older brother Jimmie had been lucky this night and were getting on the other players' nerves.

"Nine, canine! Talk to me!" Junior blew on the dice for good luck.

"No viene!" (It won't come!) yelled Shorty, wanting to make a bet.

"Órale chapéte." Junior matched a five. Junior's trademark snicker was missing. "Any other takers?" he threatened. There were none. He picked up the two dice and inspected them briefly in his right hand, manipulating them with his thumb.

"Nueve, se te muéve" (Nine, your butt is mine), Junior jibed and snickered in a move calculated to set off Shorty. Shorty chuckled.

"Este vato!" came a barely negligible complaint from Blue, which surprised everyone.

Not to be outdone, Shorty taunted in kind, *"El chiquis, buéy"* (Your small butt, asshole). That drew a raucous laugh from the others, and Shorty acknowledged everyone's enthusiasm, laughing heartily, poking at Junior.

Half of Junior's weekly earnings were gone. But Junior wouldn't be outdone. He bit his lower lip. "Five more says it does come, *mi chorizíto*" (my little sausage). Junior threw another wadded five-dollar bill on the cardboard and grabbed his crotch. While it was a play on Shorty's name, Junior was likewise raising the bar in the taunting, ribbing game of *la mosca, el relájo,* the insult game which consisted of sparring insults.

"Uy, uy, uy . . . ," some of the others taunted Shorty, trying to coax a stronger comeback from him. Junior looked on calmly without reacting, knowing he had wounded Shorty.

Shorty grinned but avoided passing spit. Yet his eyes admitted that he was considering the consequences. He was in a weighing mode: the ego, pride, violence, pain, and death. The ribbing had thickened, and Junior had placed the ball clearly in Shorty's court. The rules for ribbing one another were unspoken, but everyone knew them. Bennie knew carrying it to the next level could result in dire and unpredictable consequences. How would Shorty react? Was he going to submit? And if Shorty raised the bar, how would Junior react?

Feigning a frustrated impatience, Shorty finally retorted, *"Órale,* shoot the *pinche* dice," to save a little face.

Shorty had blinked! It was the most advisable option under the circumstances. His remark had the intention of diffusing the situation. Everyone knew it, and the ribbing stopped. Injured, Shorty had retreated, and Junior knew the taunting game was over. Junior had won but was gracious, unlike the *matadór.* He let the injured bull walk away injured but still alive. But nothing more was said. Within each of the players, while no one would ever admit it, there was a silent sigh of relief. Even Blue, who had appeared comatose a few minutes earlier, seemed to nod, acknowledging the truce as the better solution.

At about eleven p.m., Joaquín showed up from behind the cabins. Something must have gotten Bennie's attention since no one turned except him. Everyone else was too busy with the hot dice game to mind him. Joaquín appeared dazed and was sweaty. His bare feet were muddy above the ankle, and he carried a muddy shoe in his left hand. Bennie hurried to catch up with him. Shivering and out of breath, he took Bennie aside and complained that he was being chased by the Negroes. "There must have been at least five of them," he claimed.

"Why? Why were they chasing you?"

"I don't know, man. I don't know."

Bennie sniffed at his breath but couldn't smell the Stroh's. He could tell, though, that Joaquín had been drinking. "What have you been drinking, man?"

"Orange vodka."

"How much?"

"A pint, I think."

Bennie got him a towel and some shorts and pumped water out of the hand pump as Joaquín washed himself down. Bennie provided cover as Joaquín slid out of the wet and muddy pants and into the shorts. One of his knees had a large scrape, but otherwise, he appeared to be okay.

At a corner of the cabin, their belongings were tucked in cartons and stacked ready for the following day's trip. As usual, Manda had tucked herself into bed early. Only the top of her head was visible under the covers as Joaquín made his way into the cabin. As Joaquín entered, he disturbed her sleep, her whizzing ebbed and flowed. Completely exhausted, Joaquín collapsed into the Army cot. Fortunately, he had avoided waking Manda up. As he settled in, Manda's normal breathing returned.

Joaquín didn't get much sleep. Retracing his ordeal that night, he recalled being chased through the forest. In the dark, his foot sank deep into the moist, soggy peat of a kettle hole. When he pulled out his right foot, the mud sucked his shoe right off. He dug in with his hand up to his elbow and drew it out. Tossing in the bed at night, he discovered a bump on his head, at the hairline. It felt wet to the touch, and he brought his finger to his nose and lips to confirm it was blood.

All he could remember was being chased in the dark; waking up. *Yes, that is it! I was running from the kids over in the Mississippi camp.* Then, in his carelessness, he had run into a tree and knocked himself out. At some point, he must have lost consciousness for a while, Joaquín figured, as he traced the time. He was able to recall all the events of the day up until four in the afternoon. It had been about eleven when Joaquín had come upon the crap game. Seven hours of his life were missing. And the only thing he could remember vividly was being chased by the Negro kids from the Mississippi camp.

And the Rains Came

JOAQUÍN WAS UPBEAT. The continental breakfast at the Niles Inn had been more than promised, and he added pancakes to the two scoops of scrambled eggs and sausage and had several cups of coffee. He thought about calling Bennie. He needed to share his high spirits with someone.

Joaquín stretched out the twenty-mile drive from the inn to Decatur. He felt no stress. For once, his entire body felt relieved. Youthful? Dare he say it? He was driving back to Chicago that afternoon and wanted to take one final look at the camp and forever say goodbye to that part of his past. At long last, he felt as if his longing had been answered.

The blonde? Maybe the blonde had indeed been a figment of his imagination after all, he surmised. Why else would Bennie have no recollection of her? No, he was certain of it now as he drove past the camp and came back around through another narrower unpaved path, which he did not recall ever traveling on, and parked at the top of a rise, opened the door, and stood there intent, from this vantage point, on surveying the camp, the vast open field next to it, and the woods beyond. He took in a healthy gulp of air.

Waltzing among the treetops, in the distance, the spirited warm breeze wave ruffled the upper reaches of the silver maples, eliciting a contentious chatter from the sea of blue-green leaves. His face became animated as he listened; he sighed. Ebbing and flowing, responding to the wind dance, the leaves fluttered, flaunting their glistening undersides. Then, the chatter readily synthesized into a symphonic movement.

Then, silence.

Joaquín observed the scene as a childlike game of sparring, with the trees at once recoiling, jabbing, feinting, and bouncing against the antagonist breeze. He squinted in the sunlight, supposing that in a few weeks, this entire natural palette would be painted over in an impressionist's sultry reds and manifold shades of burnt orange. The hop hornbeams he envisioned as taking on an illustrious coat of yellow, which, in short order, would pale into its diluted shades. But the resolute oaks he knew would refuse to indulge in this vivid transformation and would retain their sturdy greens.

On the opposite side of the field, the backside of an old barn on the incline of another rise caught his attention. It was the same barn on whose yard he had spent part of the morning of the previous day. One of the double-hanging entry doors on the longer side had partially collapsed and dangled precariously on one of its runners. The black mandrel roof seemed sturdy enough, but the area of the barn on the overhang held up by stone rubble walls showed signs of several crumblings. An opening in the stone wall seemed to him large enough for a person to walk through.

A distant musical wail in his memory distracted him. It was barely audible. Joaquín squinted, searching for a recognizable melody from his youth, from the Mexican radio station about thirty miles down south of the Rio Grande that shot its signal north to reach the Mexicans living just on the northern edge of the river. Then, as if the breeze had caught a whiff of the sound, the music became slightly amplified. A sentimental three-row button accordion cried out in self-pity, imitating a Mexican waltz or a redowa. He couldn't quite tell which, but it penetrated like a somber funeral procession. Melancholic whimpering fifth and seventh chords became lengthened wails stretched out to prolong the pain and anguished memory. *"El Salvador,"* he confirmed to himself, as he cheerfully recalled rather proudly the legendary slow waltz. It had been Manda's favorite. During the 1950s, the folks would dance to that waltz at every wedding and *quinceañera.* Ironically, he would always associate the slow waltz with a New Orleans funeral march. His heart sputtered like an infant's heartbeat at the sound of a mother's lullaby, for he now recalled that had been the music of his childhood.

"Hey!" Belínda greeted Joaquín with a smile as they met at the plank that led up to the flatbed of Don Armándo's Ford truck. She carted a half-empty ten-gallon can of cucumbers on either hand. She had on a golfer's cap and a pair of sunglasses. Her ponytail dangled around her neck. A short distance behind her trudged two women. The older one was on her knees, examining the cucumber vines with her right hand and dragging by the handle a ten-gallon metal can with her left. A few feet ahead of her, the younger woman bent astride a row like a center on a football team, searching among the vines with both hands. All the huddled crew wore colored latex gloves on their hands. Don Armándo had asked his crew for one final sweep of the cucumber field before shutting down the Decatur camp the following day. All morning, a threatening dark squall had loomed ominously just above the maples.

Joaquín had put on some weight, and his hair had grown long since getting on Armándo's truck several months earlier. He never wore a hat.

"Hi," he answered Belínda, caution painted on his eyes, and did not smile back at the girl but motioned for her to go up the plank first. He took in a full view of her shapely hips. It had been an awkward scene for him. Just a few months before, he had acted as if he had been in the presence of one of the most beautiful girls he had ever seen. He had considered all the other eligible boys that he had noticed on the trip in back of the red Ford truck and convinced himself that he was one of the few whom she could possibly be interested in. But what a dreadful night he had spent in the back of the truck being disregarded by her as if he were merely a fly on the wall. And he recalled the following day having actually been intimidated by Belínda's piercing stare during that brief road park stop after the evening at Texarkana. So, Joaquín had given up any chance of befriending the blonde. And it had also helped that Don Eduardo's crew had settled in another camp about a half a mile down the road on the Saginaw highway. He had forgotten about her and would only be reminded of her on those few occasions when he would catch a glimpse of her in the distance as they had chopped cucumber vines or later picked the cucumbers. But he couldn't deny to himself when she had smiled, just then, that she was beautiful and that he would give or do anything to be alone with her.

———◦◦◦———

Once green and lush, the cucumber vines had thinned and withered and no longer sprouted buds or new tendrils. Few leaves remained, and those that did were readily wilting. Only during the early morning hours did the crew search, as if on an Easter egg hunt, for the few, small, pickle-sized cucumbers. With a slowdown in work, the afternoons had become endless. There had been an increasing apprehensiveness in Manda's face, and she had noted her concern to

Joaquín that "Without full-time work, we'll eat whatever earnings
we have saved during the season."

The numerous crews that swelled the Michigan population had
thinned out as crews left for other states or returned to Texas. Don
Armándo's own crew had been cut by two-thirds as well during the
last two weeks. Those who had come in their Fords and Chevys had
the luxury of leaving at will. Even the camps were being shuttered
for fall, and the smaller crews were being shuffled to other camps
that remained in operation. The days were shorter, and the evenings
were cooler. Don Eduardo's crew joined his brother's camp the last
week of their stay in Decatur to finish up whatever work remained
and to join in the caravan on the upcoming journey to Newton, Indiana. Along with Don Eduardo came the family with the blonde.

"I hear you're going to Indiana too." Belínda's flirting was obvious
to him as she came down the plank with the empty cans. Joaquín
knew that only a handful of families had signed up for the Indiana
tour. Because of his age, Bennie would not be joining them. He
would be leaving the following day back to San Felípe.

"Yeah," a surprised Joaquín answered, having been caught off
guard. "Will you be going to school there?"

"Yep. You too?"

"Really? That should be wild. What grade are you in?"

"Eleventh, eleventh grade."

"I'm a tenth grader. Flunked one year—second grade." Belínda
shrugged her shoulders apologetically.

"Yeah, it happens. Well, I'll see you later . . . okay?"

"Yeah, see you later," she told him.

Joaquín turned to return to his place in the field. He knew it had
not been a chance encounter. Belínda's cucumber containers had
been half-full. She had intended to run into him at the plank.

What luck! he thought to himself. But his thoughts were side-
tracked as he began to wonder why all of a sudden Belínda was being so friendly. Why the sudden shift?

"Hey," he heard Belínda's soft voice again, felt her small hand on
his arm, and turned.

"Wanna walk to the store with me after work?"

"Sure," Joaquín jumped at the opportunity without giving it a
second thought.

"I'll meet up with you at the intersection . . . say about an hour after work?"

He felt like jumping ten feet in the air and dismissed his prior apprehensiveness.

——⟫•⟪——

Light was coming in through the open crossbuck loft doors which the blonde had opened. Joaquín and the blonde were in the recently painted red barn with the mandrel roof, their legs hanging from the hayloft. Below, the bay was half-empty, with bails of hay stacked up high against the barn walls. In the distance, threatening clouds were darkening the sky. The scent of the harvested alfalfa stacked up all around them on the loft was overpowering. Sitting just away from the trapdoor, Joaquín and the blonde traded sips from a bottle of orange vodka.

"You dance?" she asked.

"A little," he answered.

In the distance, a twelve-string bass fired up.

"I don't like Mexican music," she said. He was ambivalent. *Is she really Mexican?* he wondered. And he stared at her lips, trying to imagine what her kiss would be like. He could not help but marvel at his exceptional luck. She had so stood out among her family when he had first seen her from atop the truck. She was like a fine thoroughbred, like a competitive blonde collie stands out among a group of mongrels. She had once been untouchable, and now here she was, within reach, wanting him.

He desired to feel her hair, to let his fingers explore her eyebrows and her slender nose. "I like to listen to it," he said about the Mexican music, almost apologetically (and could just as quickly have said, "I hate it," if it made her happy), and he took another sweet sip from the bottle. The blonde displayed her disappointment in his response. Joaquín did not notice.

——⟫•⟪——

Joaquín imagined a makeshift wooden dance floor somewhere outside the barn, near them. On the dance floor, an aging couple attempted steps from memory. But their mechanical movements were delayed by weathered limbs, which struggled and failed to follow the rhythm. They appeared to drag their infirmed legs and feet on the dance floor, unable to lift them and keep up with the beat. Visibly surprised, Joaquín shook his head. Multiple images in his brain began to merge and yet clash inconsistently with each other. The faces of the dancers showed up in his visual screen. It was Blue, the blade-sharp, shark-toothed Blue, the Blue with the chin jutting out, the *Pachúco* with the metal taps on the soles of his shoes, clicking like cleats on a concrete floor. And his partner? It was the woman in white, the young girl of his nightmares — the blonde. *Why is she danc-ing with Blue? Why is Blue pulling a metal rod from his pocket?* The night crew was working overtime, searching into the deep dark voids, un-raveling old mysteries locked in Joaquín's brain. That snapshot folded out of his brain, and his focus returned to the barn.

In the distance, across the field from the red barn, a threadbare white curtain swayed through the slid-open kitchen window of one of the mobile homes. On the roadway, a commercial-sized dumpster over-flowed with trash. The Zacatécan Indian was gone. The camp was empty, abandoned. The irony did not escape Joaquín. *That's exactly how it had been with us. When it was time to move out and head to another crop, we picked up and left. There was never any fanfare. We left little trace of our existence.*

The same bewilderment he had felt the day before had come over him. One minute he had not been able to contain the overwhelming nostalgic anticipation that he was to experience something wonder-ful upon returning, and in the next, the sad realization that it was his brain playing its cruel trick, digging deep for memories and provid-ing only confusing and questionable recollections.

"It's gonna rain. Let's go get lost in the forest. Let's get wet." He could make out the blonde's voice in his memory, and the excitement returned.

"Hey, wait . . . ," he began, but the girl was already through the trapdoor and halfway down the ladder. Outside, the rain had begun. For a second, he feared losing her. Was the scene painting in his memory an illusion?

It happened here, Joaquín whispered to himself and locked the car. In a few weeks, it would be autumn, and by then it would be too late. For the forest he had envisioned had been green. He had to make one last effort before leaving this place forever. Today, there would be no hesitation. He disregarded that he had on his dress shoes and cut across the open field. Then, as he proceeded on a nar-row footpath, the grass brushing against his knees, there grew on him the face of a man possessed. Snapshots of the bloodied blonde flashed across the visual screen in his brain, the palpitations of his heart thumped anew, and he felt the pounding at his carotids. A scent akin to freshly cut mushrooms permeated the air as soon as he entered the edge of the forest. A visible calmness then came over him, and the silence around him became palpable. The only sound he perceived was a light ringing in his ears.

A scene from his teenage life re-created in his mind. He imagined himself rushing through what from the barn had first appeared as an impenetrable green thicket. He kept his eyes on the ground, maneuvering and meandering though minor obstacles in the path: dead fall, broken bottles, aluminum soda pop cans. The green canopy was high, but at the edge of the wood, brush and the overlapping branches of the trees covered much of the tree trunks, making the wood appear fortress-like.

Turning around to make sure she was following, Joaquín smiled at her. She returned the smile, or at least he sensed that she did because visually he couldn't make out her face (and he now admitted to himself that he had yet to recall her face). But even through the haziness of the scene, he could tell the girl was a blonde. Her voice was clear and soft. Joaquín allowed a branch to snap back into her.

"Aah!" she cried and threatened him in a gentle tone, "I'll get even with you." *She is so beautiful,* he said to himself and was grateful that this unimaginable moment was taking place. How would his friends back home react when he told them of his good fortune? What was it about the blue eyes and blonde hair that attracted him so?

Earlier in the day, Joaquín had offered the blonde, "I'll get some beer."

"Who'll get it for you?" she frowned in a questioning tone that he took to mean that perhaps she had better access to liquor than he did.

"Shorty."

"No!" she complained, "I'll get it. Beer will stay on your breath. I'll get orange vodka," she insisted. "It gets you high, and no one will be able to tell."

As Joaquín made his way through the path, the shadows seemed to grow longer, and the remorse began to nag at him. He sensed as if he had been to this place before. He looked around and reminded himself how, from afar, the forest could appear as an almost impenetrable fortress. But when viewed from within, it was apparent how porous and defenseless it can be to intruders and how rather effortlessly one could penetrate into its innermost and remote shelters. *How deceptively inviting,* he admitted. The forest could draw an admiring visitor deeper and deeper into its core. Yet, ironically, light and sky could be so completely shut out. Stillness and eternal shadows prevailed. *Do they intentionally misdirect and confuse? Is it in their nature to do so?* Only occasionally would a solitary tube of light be allowed access where an aging tree had succumbed and created a clearing in the canopy.

A surprised white barn owl shot out in front of him seemingly from nowhere, surprising him with its loud rapid flapping of its wings and then taking one final stroke which propelled it gracefully through the confusing maze of self-pruned tree trunks. His blood pressure rose, and his breath left him. He settled down by bringing his chin to his chest and taking in great gobs of breath. *Something happened,* he told himself. *Things did not work out well.* He swallowed with great difficulty and looked around suspiciously.

The image of a precocious girl in a tutu danced in his memory. As he closed his eyes, the girl began to swirl faster and faster, and with each turn, her face became increasingly distorted. In the background, the mechanical carnival music exhorted the dancer on. When she finally stopped swirling, the dancer had been transformed into a rubber doll minus the blonde hair, and her head was now bald with small round holes through which her blonde hair had once been anchored. She stared at him. *Those blue eyes!* She mocked him in a low, jeering chuckle and stretched her left arm lazily at him as if she were summoning a naïve child. He stared down at his hands in revulsion and imagined his own hands around the girl's neck, squeezing desperately to snuff out her life. He felt himself putting all his weight and effort into the act and saw the blood vessels around the girl's eyes began tearing, and after that a red, barely translucent glaze began slowly tainting the whites of her eyes. Finally, a voice from inside his head cried out, *She won't die! She won't die!* When he next looked up, he saw a small clearing around a large oak, its massive gnarled branches sprawling outward and weighted down as if reaching for the ground below.

"I've been in this very spot before," Joaquín whispered. Settling down against the oak, he felt the rough texture of the bark on his fingers and sensed it strangely familiar. He backed up and leaned against the trunk of the huge tree and brought pressure to bear on his temples as he closed his eyes. Leaning on the oak, massaging the sides of his neck with his thumb and index finger, he hoped the touch would have a calming effect.

"Grandfather tree, Grandfather tree, why won't you share your secrets with me? Grandfather tree, Grandfather tree, please show me what I can't see."

As the jingle played out in his memory, Joaquín had the sensation of déjà vu. The rains had come that afternoon of the day before they left Decatur in 1967. He looked up and felt the cool drops of a September rain slap his face.

A hazy mist floated toward them, and silently enveloped the wood, snaking and wrapping its waves, like arms, around the tree trunks as it approached Joaquín and the blonde. The air around them noticeably chilled, albeit just slightly, and he felt its sensuous, moist embrace. Then came the barrage of thick droplets, clinging initially to the leaves and branches high atop the green canopy until their weight forced their release to the crisp bed over the aging peat and musty humus on the ground. Leaves and dead fall cracked and crackled as the raindrops crashed to the forest floor. And the moistened bark and the dark humus released delicious scents and aroused sensations previously unknown to Joaquín.

As he sat there against the oak, Joaquín breathed in deeply, the back of his head resting on the tree.

Joaquín and the girl—with the aid of a fifth of orange vodka—had lost themselves in the murky wood that day, shivering, walking aimlessly, seemingly for hours, occasionally holding their faces up toward the canopy, eagerly inviting the assail of the summer storm. He recalled it as at once discomforting, yet deliciously sensuous. Still, the forest seemed to want to keep its secret. Somewhere along the way, most of the pieces of Joaquín's memory had yellowed, withered, and faded. Now, there was no longer a face or a body attached to the memory—only that it was a blonde.

A dreadful frown took over Joaquín's face. He swallowed forcefully, and stared into his memory. "Are you still a virgin?" It was a girl's voice coming from behind the oak tree. As he turned, he saw himself as a teenager. In front of him stood the girl, her blonde hair in a ponytail strung around her neck over her left shoulder. In the next moment, he was facing her. She displayed an abnormal sultriness, over-affected somehow. *She's not real,* he told himself.

Joaquín felt the surge of hot blood rushing to his cheeks, where it

settled. He even felt his cheek with the back of his right hand to confirm it. Never in a hundred years would he have anticipated the inquiry. *How is a boy supposed to answer that question, particularly on a first
date? Well, it isn't a first date, is it? But it is, kinda . . . isn't it?* He would
have time later to mull over the range of responses that would have
been appropriate, he told himself. But, there and then, his ability to
process had gone completely dry, drier than a South Texas late July.
"What do you mean?" The whimper came out of his throat a full
octave higher than normal.

But Belínda was not in any mood to grant any quarter as she delighted in every second of her inquisition. The pretty smile Joaquín
had seen on her face that afternoon was replaced by a sardonic grin.

"Has anybody popped your cherry?" She shrilled mockingly and
looked away as she said it, as if either Joaquín's response was imma-
terial to her or as if she was absolutely certain of his answer and was
feigning disguising a sneer. In the next moment, she thrust the dag-
ger straight through without pity, staring into his eyes all the while,
a slight rising in her upper lip, as if daring Joaquín to lie. "You want
me to pop it for you?"

He was in way over his head. He knew it, and she knew it. His
mouth was parched. He thought of wetting his lips, but any mois-
ture left in his body seemed to have settled in the palms of his hands.
His tongue felt like felt and disproportionately large for his mouth.

As he began to sound a word, Belínda moved up to his face. She
craned her neck up toward his face and covered his mouth with hers.
She tugged him toward her with both arms. Joaquín remained
stunned and ambiguous. Without removing her mouth from Joaquín's, Belínda worked her head around his just like in the movies.
He eventually closed his eyes and went along. Joaquín's recollection
abruptly ended there as if cut off by a sharp blade. What had happened after that? His memory had blanks that needed to be filled in.

———⟶◆⟵———

As Joaquín regained consciousness, he realized he was laying on his
side, the prickly forest fall on the ground tearing into his flesh. He
knew that if he attempted to get up, he would become nauseous. Before, he had never been able to conjure up a face to go with his fleeting thoughts. Now, the blonde's face was vivid in his memory, and
he began to wonder what other memories were still lurking. He
closed his eyes.

"You finished all the vodka? Guess what, you also drank some of my magic." Belínda was back to her mocking.

"What magic?" Joaquín barely got the words out. "What . . . what are you talking about?"

"Oh, just some Quaaludes. You'll be in dreamland for a while."

Joaquín felt his eyes drooping, and while he sensed that the blonde had spiked the vodka with something that was beginning to numb him, he was powerless to react mentally or physically. He closed his eyes again.

It was the painful shrill that stirred him into a moment of lucidity, and he sensed he was face-down on the forest floor. Nothing like the feigned pain and black-veiled wails the women would put on at some-one's funeral back in the fifties, when he was a kid. This was hurt; unbearable pain, visual fear, a terrorized soul that was crying out. But he had neither the strength nor the will to lift his head, which was half-planted in leaves and dead fall on the forest floor. Joaquín was not entirely unconscious, but dazed like the kid somnambulized by inhaling cement glue or regaining consciousness after a thunder firecracker had exploded in his face and his brain was meticulously trying to connect the dots to figure out which decade of his life the explosion has shipped him to. He couldn't make out anything more but was aware that at least one other person was standing close to him. He then heard several powerful thuds that reminded him of the boxers' blows to the heavy bags over at Tino's boxing gym and a ter-rified voice that cried out, "She won't die! She won't die."

He sensed movement on the ground, as if the temporary loss of his other senses had dramatically heightened his sense of feeling. He sensed an object being dragged. With great effort, Joaquín opened his eyes and saw a man's hand pick up a black fedora and a metal rod. He then took a long last breath and closed his eyes.

EPILOGUE

FIRST WEEK IN SEPTEMBER, and then the second week in September 1967, the Newton, Indiana, *News Clip Weekly* carried the front-page story of the discovery of the body of a young girl at Clay Creek.

"She's between fifteen and eighteen," reported the coroner over at New Frankfort in his written press release.

"White female, blonde," said the *News Clip Weekly.*

As was custom, the editor of the newspaper would have used the victim's School Days black-and-white glossy on the front page. The editor of the newspaper wrote a poignant column about the young victim once he concluded that the identity of the girl would very likely never be determined:

"Mothers could always be relied on to purchase packages of the School Days multi-sized glossy portraits of their children. Sadly, in some unfortunate cases, the only place those pictures would ever be seen again would be in an obituaries column. But in this case, sadder still, there is not even a picture to remember the blonde girl by."

There was no picture of the blonde in the *News Clip Weekly* because no one knew who she was. Instead, it was John Gaines who got his mug on the front page, along with his Casey Jones cap and overalls. Everyone in Newton knew Gaines. Some joked that Gaines had probably been out hunting illegally when he'd come upon the body. Gaines had lowered the Casey Jones cap over his eyebrows and volunteered to Nathan Comeback of the *News Clip Weekly,* "I come upon the body 'cause I was chasing a fox out there. Trying to scare him away from the chickens, you know? I told that to Chief Clyde himself in Newton last night. Drove over there, the full lengtha road to Clyde's house. You ask him. He'll tell you."

Chief Clyde Davis had corroborated Gaines' story. The chief commended Gaines as a responsible citizen, of course, as was the chief's solemn duty, and he confirmed for the record that he had indeed been summoned by Gaines that night at about one in the morning to advise him of the find. Why Clyde said the next thing he said to Nathan Comeback, though, Clyde would regret until his dying days. After all, this was to be Clyde's first and only murder case investigation. But there it was on the front page on the first day the *News Clip Weekly* reported on the corpse: "Chief Promises Quick Results!" All Clyde had said to Nathan Comeback was that he figured it wouldn't take any more than a couple of days before someone would step forward — more than likely the missing teenager's parents — to identify the corpse. It was perfectly rational for him to feel that way, Clyde felt, and truthfully, he had anticipated that the girl's grieving parents would soon make their way down to the county morgue over at New Frankfort and identify the body. In Clyde's way of seeing things, this would lead to the identity of the person with whom the girl was last seen. And that would lead to the culprit. That would be the end of it, wouldn't it?